Grandmaster Arcanist

Frith Chronicles, the Final Book

Shami Stovall

Published by
CS BOOKS, LLC

Cover Design: Darko Paganus

Editors: Nia Quinn, Celestian Rince, Justin Barnett

IF YOU WANT TO BE NOTIFIED WHEN SHAMI STOVALL'S NEXT BOOK RELEASES, PLEASE VISIT HER WEBSITE OR CONTACT HER DIRECTLY AT

s.adelle.s@gmail.com

ISBN:

Contents

To John, my soulmate.
To Justin Barnett, who has helped me in so many ways.
To Beka, forever.
To Gail and Big John, my surrogate parents.
To Henry Copeland, for the beautiful leather map and book covers.
To Brian Wiggins, for giving a voice to the characters.
To Mary, Emily, Ryan, Scott, James & Dana, for all the jokes and input.
To my patrons over on Patreon, for all the support.
To my Facebook group, for all the memes.
And finally, to everyone unnamed, thank you for everything.

Chapter 1

To Find Luthair

Loyalty. Without it, we cannot know true friendship.
Luthair...

I stood at the edge of Regal Heights, watching the flicker of lanterns and torches as people moved throughout the city. The wind blew past, carrying the scent of sulfur as it tousled my black hair. A massive gorge split the city of Regal Heights in two parts. Metal bridges extended across the wide gap, leading from the fortified part of the city to the fancier side, though both were dominated by stone castles and wrought-iron fences.

The fur of magical canyon rabbits covered most of the walkways. I paced along the canyon edge, staring at the depths of Hydra's Gorge. Moonlight filtered into the canyon, causing the mists that filled the chasm to glow a dull silver.

Although it was night, people rushed between the large fortress buildings. Bells were ringing, and the guards went from home to home, informing everyone to stay where they were.

Because *Orwyn Tellia,* the sky titan arcanist, was here.

Normally, that would mean a fight, but these were unusual

circumstances. She had rushed to the city, begging for my help. Her protector, the ruthless assassin Akiva, was gravely injured. I had been the one to put him at death's door, but apparently, Orwyn couldn't stand the thought of his demise. And since she was so far from anyone else in the Second Ascension who could help or heal him, she had flown him to Regal Heights.

The Frith Guild had healers.

Atty would handle this. Her phoenix magic would mend his flesh.

In theory.

My god-arcanist magic was powerful, and it had been several hours since Akiva had been injured. Healing him would be difficult.

I stopped my pacing and headed for the nearest building. When I reached the window, I glanced through the thick glass. A single lantern was lit, keeping the room illuminated. I had moved Akiva to the fortress so he would have a comfortable place to rest. The man was stretched out across a bed, barely moving.

One arm, one leg, and his ribs all looked like raw meat that had been pushed through a grinder. Normally, Akiva was an intimidating individual. Muscled. Tall. Adorned in king basilisk armor. But now his armor was shredded—torn apart by my sword—and it obviously pained him to breathe. His copper hair was matted with sweat, and he kept his eyes tightly shut.

Nothing about his rest appeared peaceful.

Orwyn waited in the room with him. She held his hand, her own fingers delicate compared to his. Her strawberry-blonde hair hung around her heart-shaped face, framing her in a beautiful way. When she frowned, I almost felt sympathy for her. Almost.

Part of me still hated her for trying to kill us.

But Orwyn had provided us with useful information.

"Atty has arrived, Warlord."

The telepathic voice of my eldrin, Terrakona, startled me out of my thoughts. His regal tone was a comfort. Despite his youth, he sounded as powerful as he was.

While I watched through the window, Atty entered the room and rushed over to Akiva's side. Atty practically glowed in the lantern light. Her golden hair shimmered as she took a seat next to the bed and gently touched Akiva's injuries.

Unlike Orwyn, who had a vacant expression most of the time, Atty's gaze was focused. She pressed her hands down on Akiva, using her healing augmentation to stitch some of his flesh back together. She wore little—just sleeping robes—but they were tied tightly around her waist with a belt. Clearly, she had been sleeping when someone had pulled her from bed to help us.

Her phoenix rushed into the room shortly after. Titania glowed with an inner fire, her scarlet feathers sparkling with heat and magic. Her long, peacock-style tail, coupled with the neck of a heron, gave the phoenix a majestic appearance. She ran with her wings half-opened until she was at her arcanist's side.

"Do you need me to help heal him?" Titania asked.

I couldn't hear her through the window. I only knew what she had said because of my tremor sense. It had developed to the point that even the slightest of rumbles made their way to me.

"Yes," Atty replied. "Please, help. I don't know if he'll live."

Orwyn stood close to the bed, her eyes wide, her delicate hands clasped together.

"Warlord?"

I stiffened as I turned around. "Terrakona?" Although he wasn't nearby, he heard me nonetheless.

"Hexa and her hydra have prepared themselves for the trek. We have a map to Deadman's Bluff, and supplies gathered in a few bags."

"Thank you."

I wanted to run to the gates of the city and head out as soon as possible, but I knew I shouldn't go until I had told everyone what was happening. With my heart beating hard in my chest, I dashed farther into town, hoping Guildmaster Eventide had woken.

Deadman's Bluff...

It was a cliffside location where pirates were often hanged for their crimes. A tall cliff overlooking the ocean—the perfect spot to do away with criminals. Apparently, a small town and port had been built in that location as well.

And the Second Ascension had been using it for their dastardly plans.

Orwyn had paid for our help with secrets. The Second Ascension kept people and mystical creatures at Deadman's Bluff. Vethica, the khepera arcanist, was one such individual. Not only was she capable of curing the arcane plague, but she was Hexa's lover, and we couldn't rest until she was safe with us in the Frith Guild.

And while I definitely wanted to save Vethica, it wasn't her whom I thought of when I imagined tearing down the castle walls.

Luthair was also there.

Orwyn had said so. She had claimed that my first eldrin, Luthair, a true form knightmare, had been brought to the bluff to be shown to the Autarch.

I gritted my teeth just thinking about it. I barely even saw my surroundings as I charged through Regal Heights, my thoughts on distant places. Was Luthair okay? Was he hurt? I knew, deep in my soul, that his memories were gone. That was why he hadn't sought us out—and why the Second Ascension had gotten him so far away from us.

The Autarch could bond with multiple mystical creatures thanks to his gold kirin.

Would he... bond with Luthair?

I half-stumbled and almost collided with a post of the nearest bridge. I flailed a bit, but then I used my magical manipulation to shift the rocks under my feet, correcting my balance. After a short breath, I stopped running and glanced around. I had gone too far. My thoughts had been so all-consuming that I hadn't realized where I was.

"You seem angry, Warlord."

Terrakona could always sense my mood. It was bothersome sometimes.

"I'm worried about Luthair," I muttered as I ran a hand through my black hair. It had grown long—almost to my chin. "We need to leave soon, but I want to speak to Eventide first."

My eldrin didn't respond.

After a quick breath, I jogged over to a fortress-style building on the edge of the gorge. The front door was locked, but I shifted the stones around to create an opening into the foyer. Then I used my magic to close the entrance, recreating the wall perfectly so no one could tell I had gone through.

It impressed me how fine my control was. I took a moment to admire my own work.

"Volke?"

I would recognize my sister's voice anywhere. When I turned, I smiled, pleased to see Illia standing near one of the many doors. She, too, wore sleeping robes, though she had no belt. She kept them closed with her arms, her wavy hair tied back in a tight ponytail.

Illia wore an eyepatch, even while sleeping. It covered the fact that she was missing an eye, though her patch had the symbol of a rizzel stitched into it: a white ferret with silver stripes. It was playful and fun and made me smile wider when I spotted it.

"Illia, I'm leaving," I said, trying to think of a way to sum up the situation as quickly as possible. "I think I know where Luthair and Vethica are being kept."

Illia's one eye grew wide. "Is that why Zaxis ran off? He left in such a hurry, he didn't explain what was going on."

"Orwyn is here."

"*The sky titan arcanist?*" Illia tensed, her arms stiffly folded in front of her. "What're we doing about that?"

I hurried past Illia, heading for the deeper parts of the building. From what I could remember, Eventide had taken a room near the library. "Orwyn's not fighting us. I have to go. Ask Atty about it. She's healing Akiva."

"The assassin?" Illia balked, clearly out of the loop. "She's healing that madman?"

"Yeah. It'll all make sense." I waved as I ran deeper into the building.

My sister huffed, clearly irritated. She hated it whenever I kept information from her. I wasn't teasing her, though. There just wasn't enough time to explain everything. Using my tremor sense, I navigated the dark halls of the building. Why bother with lantern lights when my magic could guide me?

And I preferred the darkness.

It reminded me of Luthair's magic.

Fortunately, it didn't take me long to find Eventide's room. And to my great luck, she was already awake and standing in the doorframe, as though waiting for me. She wore a button-up shirt and long trousers. No belt or boots. This was probably the least amount of clothing I had ever seen her in. Even Eventide's silver hair, normally done in a tight braid, hung flowing over her shoulders like a waterfall of silver snow.

The laugh lines around her eyes and mouth betrayed her advanced age. Most arcanists didn't age like that, but for some reason, Eventide had lost her youthfulness.

"Volke," she said as I approached. "You could've had Adelgis contact me with his telepathy. You didn't need to run here."

"I wanted to speak to you in person," I said, not even winded. I had trained for years—this wasn't enough to take a toll on me.

"Adelgis informed me about Orwyn."

"That's not what I wanted to talk about." I stepped close, but the darkness obscured most details. I couldn't see her expression well, and the moonlight trickling in through a window only seemed to make the shadows darker.

"What is it?"

"I want to take a few people with me to Deadman's Bluff, but I don't want to abandon the city."

Eventide slowly nodded her head. "You don't trust Orwyn. She's a god-arcanist, and you think if you take everyone from here, she'll attack us."

"Yeah. Plus..." I wasn't entirely sure how to say it, but there was no getting around the fact that we had *another* god-arcanist I didn't trust in our midst. "Calisto just bonded with the typhon beast. I don't want to leave him unsupervised. I was hoping to take just a handful of individuals."

"Hexa, obviously." Eventide spoke with a smile in her voice. It always put me at ease.

"Hexa, yeah. And Illia. And you."

Eventide stilled for a moment. She didn't say anything, and I suspected I had caught her by surprise. "Me?"

"Your magic is weak here, since you're so far from your eldrin. If you come with us to Deadman's Bluff, you'll be much closer to Gentel. And your atlas turtle magic could really help us."

Eventide wasn't going to do much here besides be a voice of reason. I knew if she went with me, there was a chance her barriers and clear-headedness could come in handy.

"Very well," Eventide said with a chuckle. "It's been a while since I rushed off at the first sign of adventure. And I've been missing Gentel." She placed a hand on the doorframe. "But we should take Everett as well."

"Master Zelfree? Why?"

"His mimic magic can sense nearby mystical creatures. If he

senses a gold kirin, we'll at least have a moment to prepare before facing the Autarch."

I caught my breath, startled by her reasoning. I hadn't thought of that. Could the Autarch be waiting for us at Deadman's Bluff? I doubted he knew we were coming, but there was a chance we could *surprise him* by arriving.

"I figured Zelfree would be the one watching Calisto," I muttered.

"Zaxis is a god-arcanist. He can handle the assignment of watching Calisto. I think it's more imperative that Everett come with us."

Zaxis would be upset if I took Illia and not him, but there was probably no way around it.

"All right," I said. "Then I'll inform everyone that we need to leave as soon as possible."

Eventide grabbed her long hair and twisted the locks into a tight braid. "Very well. I'll make sure to get my good boots."

Chapter 2

Happy Travels

I waited by the gates of Regal Heights, the moon, stars, and my eldrin fine company.

After I had become a knightmare arcanist, the night had seemed so different to me. The stars, especially. Luthair's cape was lined with the shimmer of a thousand stars. Whenever I closed my eyes, I saw it clearly in my mind's eye.

It felt like forever since I had last seen him.

Terrakona circled closer, his emerald scales reflecting some of the stars' sparkles. His mane, pronounced like a lion's, was made of crystals with an inner darkness. When Terrakona lowered his snout to my eye level, I patted him gently.

"You seem anxious," Terrakona telepathically said. **"We will soon head to Deadman's Bluff."**

"I wish the others would hurry," I muttered.

As if answering my statement, I heard a tiny pop of air. When I whirled on my heel, I couldn't help but smile. My sister, Illia, and her rizzel eldrin, Nicholin, had appeared next to the gate in a puff of silvery glitter.

She wore a long coat and carried a small sack over her

shoulder. When I glanced at it, she patted the side. "I brought some supplies. Don't worry. Nothing too heavy."

"I'm sure Terrakona, my good friend, can handle it," Nicholin said with a slight squeak.

Illia wandered over to Terrakona and grazed her fingers along his side. "Are you ready?"

I nodded once.

A few moments later, Hexa came jogging up the path. Her hydra, Raisen, lumbered after her. Hexa's curly, cinnamon hair bounced as she moved. Lately, she had been keeping it in a ponytail, but it just occurred to me that she had cut it shorter than normal. Her hair defied gravity, though. It probably should've hung to her shoulders, but most of it puffed upward, too much energy to contain.

She had covered most of her body in scaled leather, but left her arms exposed. Scars lined her shoulders and forearms, evidence of her bonding with a hydra.

Raisen, with his six heads, stomped down the path and exited the gate with a rumble. He woke several citizens as he went, but they merely glanced out their windows and then shut the curtains afterward. I suspected they were all used to the sounds of a hydra thundering about.

"I'm here," Hexa said, waving a hand as she continued all the way to Terrakona's side. "Let's go!" Then she dragged herself up onto his back, not even stopping to catch her breath.

Raisen moved at a slower pace, but with the same kind of urgency. His scales practically glittered in the moonlight. I didn't consider them beautiful, though. Each scale was curled up at the end, like a small spike or prickle. Five of his heads flashed their fangs and glanced around as he ran, but his king head—the one with large horns and an intelligent gaze—kept his attention on Terrakona.

"I'm coming, my arcanist," Raisen called out between huffs.

Once he got to Terrakona's serpentine body, Raisen stopped.

All six of his heads exhaled and inhaled at different rates. Hydras were more like alligators—Raisen's short legs weren't really capable of hoisting his giant body up onto the world serpent.

Terrakona swung the tip of his tail around and slid it under Raisen's body. Then Terrakona lifted the hydra off the ground and dumped the beast on his back.

"Thank you," Raisen's king head said.

Terrakona replied with a single nod.

I paced around my eldrin as I waited for the last two of our group. When would they arrive? Hopefully before daybreak. I couldn't stand the thought of waiting, but I needed patience.

What did the Pillar say about that?

Patience. Without it, you cannot see a seed grow into a tree.

I tried to keep that in mind as I walked, but nothing seemed to quell my desire to just depart the city at full speed. Hexa obviously felt the same way. She practically bounced up and down on Terrakona's back, her eyes wide as she stared off into the distance.

Illia glanced over and frowned. "Did you tell Evianna about our departure?"

As I paced by her, I shrugged. "I told Adelgis to tell her. I'm sure she'll understand that she's needed here to watch over everything."

"You don't want to take her?"

"I want to take her everywhere with me," I said, a little confused by the question. "But she needs to get her rest as well. Plus, I'll be back shortly." I turned my attention to Illia. "Do you think we should take her?"

Illia shook her head. "I just... I'm surprised, that's all."

Nicholin scurried around her shoulders, ducking into her wavy hair and then out again. With a snicker, he said, "Everyone knows you two have started sharing the same bed."

My face grew hot in an instant. I wasn't embarrassed that Evianna and I were more of a couple—I was embarrassed that

Nicholin had shouted it out for everyone to hear. Did *everyone* need to know *everything* happening in my private life?

"That's a little soon, don't you think?" Illia asked.

"Haven't you and Zaxis been sharing the same room for over a year?" I snapped.

She caught her breath for a moment, her expression neutral.

Had I hurt her feelings? *I* wasn't the one who had started this conversation. Romance wouldn't even be my first choice for topics to discuss. Everyone else always wanted to make it a priority, though.

"Stop arguing," Hexa called down from the back of Terrakona. "Guildmaster Eventide and Master Zelfree are on their way!"

I stopped and turned to face the road. Sure enough, two individuals hurried down the main road of Regal Heights—the road built along one edge of the gorge. Once they made it past the gates, they headed straight for us.

Eventide wore her long jacket made of several different mystical creature parts. It was leather, but each patch was a slightly different shade of brown or gray. She also sported a tricorn cap that held back her hair. The glow of her arcanist mark was still visible, though. It shone brightly in the middle of the night.

Zelfree seemed... surprisingly energized.

Although we had just fought Orwyn and her sky titan, Zelfree rushed over to Terrakona and lifted himself onto the serpent's back. He landed rather gracefully, like the swashbuckler I always knew him to be in the legends.

He swept his dark hair back with one quick motion. Had he recently cut it again? The sides were short, and the top was longer, giving him a rough-and-tumble appearance. His long coat and worn trousers added to the image. He carried a sword at his side—one I had crafted with my god-arcanist magic—and he whistled to draw my attention.

"Let's get this show on the road," Zelfree called out.

With a smirk, I motioned for Terrakona to lower his head. My eldrin moved close and offered his mane. I stepped onto the crystals and then gestured for Eventide to join me.

My offer must've taken her by surprise, because her eyes widened a bit and then she tipped her cap in my direction. "Thank you, Warlord." She grabbed hold of the crystals and hefted herself up. Once we had our feet positioned so we wouldn't easily fall, I pointed Terrakona to the northern horizon.

"Take us to Deadman's Bluff," I commanded.

"As you wish, Warlord."

The world serpent lifted his head and then snaked his way forward. Normally, a creature his size would destroy everything in its path. Fortunately, Terrakona's world serpent magic rearranged the ground as he moved.

The dirt separated like the seam of a shirt. The very ground pulled away, shifting the trees, boulders, and vegetation. Terrakona slipped through the groove in the ground, slithering forward at surprising speed. Once he had passed, the ground stitched itself back together again. The landscape wasn't quite the same—some of the trees and boulders were slightly off, and there was still a noticeable groove in the ground, but it was much better than wrecking everything.

Terrakona picked up the pace. His concertina motions tended to make people riding on his back a little ill. And sure enough, barely a few minutes into the journey, I heard various curses and groans coming from behind me. None from Hexa, though. She gripped Terrakona's scales and pointed forward, as if willing him to go even faster.

Eventide and I had no problems, either.

I wasn't sure how long it would take us to reach Deadman's Bluff, but I knew it would be five days at the bare minimum.

Could Terrakona get us there sooner if he rushed? I wondered.

As the late afternoon sun shone over our heads, we stopped to take a break. I probably could've powered through, and Hexa wanted to, but everyone needed water and food—and a bit of time to stretch their legs.

We stopped at a river with a small waterfall. It was a peaceful place, probably untouched by anything but the nearby woodland creatures, and I only happened to see it because I was atop Terrakona's head. The angle was perfect to catch sight of the tiny rainbows cascading off the falls.

When Terrakona stopped, he lowered his head so Eventide and I could dismount. Then he rolled his serpentine body a bit to give the others an easier time getting off. That greatly helped Raisen, who had struggled to even maintain his grip on the massive world serpent.

"How long are we going to be here?" Zelfree asked as he walked over to the water.

"Just a few minutes," I replied.

"Perfect."

He knelt next to the river, but right before he plunged his hands beneath the surface, a pair of bracelets on his wrists shimmered and shifted. They flew off his arms and clinked together. A second later, they had formed into a gray cat with a short tail.

His mimic, Traces.

Zelfree smirked. "You don't want a bath?"

Traces arched her back. "You know I hate water!" She snorted and relaxed. With a purr, she said, "Just you wait. When you're sleeping, I'll have my revenge."

Zelfree slapped his face with some of the crystal-clear water.

The arcanist mark on his forehead was unique. It was just a seven-pointed star—no creature wrapped around the edges. That would change whenever his mimic transformed, though. The star would fill with whatever creature he decided to copy.

"You seem like you're in a good mood," Illia commented as she, too, walked over to the river. "Did you find some new type of rum at Regal Heights?"

"Heh. I *used* to try to drown my problems in rum." Zelfree stood and sighed. "But it turns out my problems are damn good swimmers. So now I handle my troubles the old-fashioned way."

Hexa frowned. "Oh, no... Did someone tell you about the mushrooms that grow around Regal Heights?"

"*No*," Zelfree snapped. He dried his hands on the side of his coat. "I'm just saying I have a new outlook on life."

"He's really grateful you didn't kill Lynus," Traces said. She walked over to my legs, rubbed her gray fur on her head along the side of my trousers, and even purred. "And he's extra thankful that Lynus isn't going to die anytime soon from something like *old age*."

Zelfree shot his eldrin a glare. "I told you that in private."

"I just wanted them to stop thinking you were eating strange fungus." Traces leapt up onto my shoulder, her grace incredible. I barely felt her land, and when she walked around behind my neck, I worried she might poke me with her claws, but the sting never came.

"I'm glad you're happy," Illia stated.

It was forced, though. I could tell by her tone.

I doubted anyone else noticed. I had just known Illia for so long, her emotions were never a mystery to me. She didn't hate Calisto anymore—Lynus, whatever—but she didn't like the man, that was for sure. Neither did I, if I was being honest.

I believed Calisto had repented, but repenting wasn't the same as absolution. He had spilled rivers of innocent blood and caused unimaginable amounts of pain.

He was a god-arcanist, however, and he had said he would help us, so here we were.

I was trying to picture Calisto as a different person. *Lynus* was the man who wanted to do right. *Calisto* was the dread pirate, the villain, the darkness of Lynus's past.

Illia opened her sack and handed out bits of jerky. Traces, Zelfree, Hexa, and Eventide all took their fair share and ate them in relative silence. Raisen, on the other hand, got more than the rest of us and proceeded to fight himself over the chunks of dehydrated meat. Each of his six heads snapped at each other. One even hissed.

I ignored them and chewed my own jerky, my body fidgetier than normal.

After we had all eaten, Eventide motioned to Terrakona. "We should head out." She pointed to the orange sky, the clouds shifting to a dark shade of red. "Once night falls, we can find a place to rest, but we should really keep moving until then."

Everyone nodded in response.

Hexa was the first to once again get on Terrakona. Even before Illia or Nicholin could teleport onto the serpent's back.

The moment we were all situated back on my eldrin, Terrakona headed for the northern horizon, his focus unbreaking.

It wouldn't be long now...

Luthair...

Chapter 3

The Folly Of Brigands

Time seemed to stretch out as we continued our journey, until minutes felt like hours. I kept checking the sun to gauge our progress, and at times it felt like the sun had decided to halt its journey just to spite me.

The trek was silent and tense, with everyone just waiting to spot Deadman's Bluff on the far horizon. Despite my unease, I forced myself to remain vigilant of my surroundings. I didn't know why, but some part of me was convinced we would be attacked by the Second Ascension at any moment, like they lurked in every dark shadow and crevice.

I knew I was just being paranoid. Our last few battles had weakened them. Slowly but surely, we were diminishing their forces. I shouldn't be afraid of them—they should be afraid of me. Because if I caught them out in the open like this, it would be their graves, not mine, that lined the side of the road.

Just as the sun disappeared beyond the horizon and I searched for a place to camp, my attention was stolen by a panicked shout.

Terrakona slowed and turned his head toward the noise. In the east, I spotted a thick woodland. It seemed a road led through it. Another shout echoed out of the trees, accompanied by a flock of birds.

It sounded as though someone was calling for help.

"Warlord?" Terrakona asked. **"Should I head in that direction?"**

My eldrin stopped, his scales flaring. It seemed to disturb the others. They glanced around and held on to the world serpent tighter than before.

Eventide clung to Terrakona's crystal mane, her attention on the woodland. "What're you waiting for?" she asked. "The Frith Guild doesn't hesitate when others are in danger."

Her words hit hard, and I realized as soon as she had said them, that no matter what, I wanted to help people. This would delay us a bit, but I couldn't ignore it. I pointed toward the woodland.

"C'mon, Terrakona."

"As you wish, Warlord."

My world serpent turned and headed for the trees, the ground parting in front of him. I held my sword close and buckled my shield on my left arm, just in case we ran into *real* trouble. Plague-ridden creatures could still be roaming the countryside, after all... And I didn't want them to harm anyone with me.

Another scream, this one soaked in panic.

The trees moved aside as Terrakona entered the woods. It didn't take us long to locate the road. Terrakona followed the path until we came upon a terrible scene.

A broken cart and two smashed carriages lay in the middle of the road. There were shattered boxes and barrels everywhere, the road littered with splinters and broken wood. Two individuals were dead on the side of the road, their blood pooling around their bodies. Well, I assumed they were dead from the injuries to their backs, and especially because I couldn't sense heartbeats. Someone had stabbed them more than once.

They wore blue robes and didn't seem to have any armor or weapons.

Not combatants.

Someone had stabbed these people in the back, despite the fact that they weren't fighters. Disgusting.

Three others stood by the destruction, their eyes wide as they took in Terrakona.

Two girls, one man.

One of the women wore the same type of blue robes as the dead men. She was the first to find her words.

"*Please, help me!*" she screamed.

Terrakona raised his head into the air and fixed his gaze on the group, giving off a growl that reverberated in both my ears and mind.

The other two—the man and woman—both wore thick pants and leather armor tunics. They stumbled in their haste to back away. They ran for their horses, and both jumped onto their saddles, carelessly rushing through everything. The woman almost tumbled off and fell to the ground as she kicked her steed into a gallop.

"These are mystic seekers." Eventide pointed to one of the ruined crates. "See that symbol there? It's the crest for the *North Winds Guild.* They specialize in gathering mystical creatures around the coasts."

The two running away on horses urged their mounts faster and faster.

While I wanted to give chase, I knew it wasn't urgent. I could easily catch up with them. My first priority was to see if we could help anyone here.

"Are you okay?" I called down to the woman in the blue robes. "Is anyone injured?"

Hexa, Raisen, and Zelfree leapt down from Terrakona. Hexa and Zelfree landed with a soft thud, but Raisen hit the ground like a meteor. Illia and Nicholin teleported down, both shaking their heads.

"I'm telling you, I can just port you all," Illia muttered.

"We have some skulls to bash," Hexa stated as she marched forward. She kicked at a piece of the broken carriages. "We don't have time to wait around for you to teleport when jumping can do the trick."

"We don't have any arcanists who specialize in healing," Eventide said as she glanced over at the bodies.

After a short sigh, I said, "I know. But maybe we can take the injured with us to town."

The woman in the blue robes hurried over to Terrakona. She stared up at him, her eyes widening. With shaky hands, she touched her heart and then offered me a quick bow of her head. "You must be... the world serpent arcanist."

"You're from the North Winds Guild?" I called down. "What happened?"

"Brigands attacked us." The woman pointed to the road—and the many bits of wood that littered the path. "Their arcanists came out of nowhere. They took the baby creatures, and Master Felvia. Please help them, Warlord. I... I don't know what to do."

Judging by the fresh blood and clear tracks, I assumed the brigands weren't far. "What kind of arcanist is Master Felvia?"

"She's a kelpie arcanist. She left her eldrin with the ship."

Kelpies were mystical water horses, often favored by the captains of small ships. They controlled the waters but had a harder time on land. I could understand why Master Felvia would opt to leave her eldrin behind.

"What kind of arcanists were with the brigands?" I asked.

"Orthrus arcanists."

Two-headed dogs. They were often smaller than cerberuses, but their bites were legendary. They weren't a match for me or

Terrakona, however. Not a match for anyone in the Frith Guild, frankly.

Were these brigands part of the Second Ascension? I doubted it, but I couldn't be certain.

Zelfree, Illia, and Hexa searched through the debris. They found a third body, but the man seemed to be breathing. There were probably others—mystic seekers typically traveled in large groups.

"Eventide," I whispered. "You and I will handle the brigands while the others search for more mystic seekers."

She nodded once, curt and ready. Then she gripped the edge of her tricorn cap. "I was wondering why you were taking so long."

With a smile, I patted the side of Terrakona's head. "Let's go. Follow the riders."

"Of course." There was some excitement in Terrakona's telepathic voice.

He moved around the wreckage and then rushed through the woods, the trees parting before him. It didn't take us long to find the riders. They had stuck to the path for most of the way, but when we caught up, one turned off while the other kept to the road, urging his horse faster and faster. I thought he would give his mount a heart attack.

The one who veered away went straight for a hole in the ground and entered it as fast as possible. The hole was an old mine tunnel, carved into stone and going down. It would've been hidden by bushes and trees, but I was so high up on Terrakona's head, it was easy to spot.

The hole was far too small for my world serpent. We could make it bigger, but I decided to dismount. Terrakona lowered his head, and I slid off. Eventide joined me. Then I pointed toward the second rider. "Catch him."

"At once."

Terrakona left us on the road. He dashed after the rider, his snake-like concertina movements intimidating. He moved like a deadly viper. Then again, with his size, anything would seem intimidating, even just rolling around.

I returned my attention to the old mine entrance. My tremor sense allowed me to detect on the vibrations traveling through the ground. These brigands had picked the worst possible hideaway.

I took a deep breath, closed my eyes, and then focused on the hole. There were definitely people in the mine shafts. Their footsteps and movements painted a picture in my mind's eye. Ten of them. And two dogs, likely the eldrin of the arcanists.

"Ten of them are down there," I muttered. "One of them is probably Master Felvia."

Eventide smiled. "Hardly seems like a fair fight—nine against two."

"These blackhearts don't deserve *fair*."

"That, we can agree on."

I pushed my way past the giant bushes and stood at the entrance of the abandoned mine. The voices of the brigands wafted up.

"It's the world serpent arcanist! *It is*!"

Laughter and shouts were the only answer. "Are you tryin' to trick us? Why would a god-arcanist be out here?"

"I saw it! I swear! *With my own two eyes*! It's a big snake—no—*a giant serpent!* As large as, well, *a castle*! He'll be here any minute!"

Her over-the-top panic was too genuine to be faked. The others must've sensed it, too, because the laughing stopped. With a steady hand, I pulled Retribution from its sheath. Powerful energy crackled along the blade.

The sword... I stared at it for a moment, admiring the emerald star constellation that ran down the center of the black blade. It was in Terrakona's image, but the blade had been forged from the bones of the apoch dragon and imbued with the magic of a knightmare, in addition to the magic of the world serpent.

Retribution cut through anything magical as though it didn't even exist.

"We should question them," Eventide said matter-of-factly. "From the looks of their setup, I suspect they're not affiliated with the Second Ascension, but they might be working with pirates."

"They killed those mystic seekers back there," I said, my tone dark. I tightened my grip on my blade. "We only need one of them for questioning."

"No one hates brigands, pirates, and thieves more than me," Eventide said, her smile never waning, her tone just as confident as ever. "But you should remember that most of them will be young. Most bandits are. Some of them might not have been involved in the killing. You won't know until you question them."

I forced myself to nod along with her words. She was right.

"If they fight..." I muttered.

"Oh, I'm hoping they fight. Just keep everything I said in mind if they don't. Letting your emotions dictate punishments is a surefire way to leave an ugly mark on the world."

I felt the bandits running around in their hideout, frantically stuffing supplies into bags. The baby mystical creatures—five in total—moved around in boxes, though they were almost too light for me to sense their movements. I didn't want the brigands to have time to prepare, so I held out a hand and manipulated the terrain.

The ground shook with my god-arcanist magic.

Eventide didn't react or even seem surprised. She just held the edge of her cap and watched as rocks jutted out of the ground, bursting from the dirt as though slammed upward. The mine tunnel twisted and closed, and the dirt sank in around the brigands and creatures.

They would be fine. I was just sealing up all their hiding spots.

Through the use of my manipulation—and the ability to sense every individual—I brought them to the surface, simultaneously destroying their lair and bringing them all out into the open. It was probably startling for them. Their hearts raced so fast and beat so hard, I felt that through the tremors as well.

The nine blackhearts, and Master Felvia, burst out of the dirt, like the dead rising from a grave. Each had wide eyes and shaky hands. They patted their own bodies, as if feeling to see if they each were still in one piece.

The two orthrus dogs glanced around with their dual heads. Both dogs were brown and short-furred, with long tails they kept tucked between their legs. They were large, though. The size of a horse. These were older arcanists.

The mortals, on the other hand, were just as Eventide had described them.

Young. Confused. Some of them held knives, but their grip was weak and their form terrible.

The five mystical creatures were all pegasi. The feathered foals were trapped in crates, their wings tied tightly against their bodies. Muzzles had been secured over their snouts to prevent them from calling out.

One of the orthrus arcanists—the star on his forehead covered by a black bandana—stood and immediately drew a short sword from his belt. Orthrus arcanists were stronger than normal people, and when he threw the blade at me, it whistled through the air.

I lifted my shield, hoping to block the sword before it struck me square in the chest, but it wasn't necessary. A magical barrier shimmered in the air in front of me. The sword bounced off the barrier and hit the dirt, harming nothing.

I glanced over at Eventide. She had her hand up—she had

evoked the barrier with her atlas turtle magic. Although she was far from Gentel, she still had the strength to evoke minor barriers. With a smirk, she motioned to the one who had attacked.

With a wave of my hand, the ground under the man opened and twisted. He fell, and then yelped as the dirt hardened to stone and crushed his arms. I could've twisted the ground further, killing him instantly, but I held back.

They were... so much weaker than I was.

The excitement and thrill of battle wasn't even present with these dastards. It was like punching an infant. No honor, no fight, no contest.

"Briggy!" the trapped arcanist shouted from his dirt prison. "*Kill him! Destroy that man!*"

One of the orthrus got to his four feet and then rushed forward, both heads barking and snapping their fangs.

The sight of the horse-sized beast running at me removed my hesitation. I clenched my hand into a fist—crushing the orthrus arcanist in a stone coffin—and then swung Retribution just as the dog came barreling down on me. My blade sliced right through the orthrus's body, clean and quick, like I hadn't even struck anything.

The creature's blood splattered across me as the body tumbled across the ground, the neatly bisected parts going in two different directions. The coppery, iron scent reminded me of the many battlefields I had seen. I hadn't wanted to kill them, but they clearly weren't thinking straight.

The orthrus twitched as the life left its massive body.

No one else moved.

They stared at me, and at the bodies, their mouths slightly open, their complexions pale. Retribution crackled as it consumed the orthrus's magic. Hunger and death radiated off the weapon so strongly, even the mortals seemed to sense it.

I took a deep breath and stood straight, my grip on my blade firm.

Eventide motioned to the nine remaining thieves with a tilt of her head. "Make your demands," she whispered. "Be assertive, but reasonable, and they will talk without further provocation."

After I wiped some of the blood from my chest and shoulder, I turned my attention to the dastards. "I'm Warlord Volke Savan, the World Serpent Arcanist. Those of you who don't want to meet a swift death will tell me what happened with the North Winds Guild."

"I-It was, i-it was, w-well..." one of the mortals stuttered so fiercely, he couldn't seem to get his words straight.

"The creatures are right there," another said, motioning to the trapped pegasi. "We're sorry. So sorry. We didn't know, that, uh—"

"That it was wrong to kill people and kidnap mystical creatures?" I interjected, my tone dark.

The brigand shook and stuttered, unable to cobble together an explanation.

A woman, covered in dirt from head to toe, swallowed hard and added, "It's hard. Living around here. Pirates attack. Other brigands steal. Why can't we? We... We didn't mean to kill those mystic seekers, but they fought back. If they had just given us what we had asked for..."

It occurred to me then that Master Felvia hadn't said anything. I glanced in her direction. Her blue robes were smudged with dirt, and she stared at me with the same kind of frightened, wide-eyed terror as the others.

"You're safe now," I said to her, hoping she'd relax. "Come. This is Guildmaster Eventide of the Frith Guild. We won't let them hurt you any longer."

Master Felvia got to her feet. Then she hurried over to Eventide's side. I probably looked a little grim, since I was still wearing the blood of the orthrus. I didn't blame her for not sticking close to my side.

"We'll make sure you and the rest of your guild members make it to town," Eventide said with a smile.

Master Felvia nodded, but said nothing.

I held out my hand, intending to evoke vines to bind everyone here.

But I couldn't.

I caught my breath as I remembered my last fight with a god-arcanist. In the heat of the battle, I had focused my evocation toward destruction. I had lost the ability to evoke plants and vegetation. Now all I could evoke was molten rock.

"Their hideaway probably had rope," Eventide said. "Drag it out of the ground, and we can tie them up and bring them with us."

That was probably for the best.

None of them were keen to attack after what I had done to the first arcanist. I didn't know if they'd be sentenced to death once we reached town, but I'd let the authorities deal with them then.

We still had to hurry to Deadman's Bluff.

Chapter 4

Deadman's Bluff

We needed to make a slight detour to bring the brigands and North Winds Guild members to a nearby town. I wasn't even sure what the name of the place was. I just stopped on the outskirts, waved to a group of children who were playing around the farm fields, and when the town watch rode out to greet me, I explained the situation and handed the bandits over to their custody.

The children, fascinated by Terrakona, pointed and whispered among themselves as the guards took our prisoners into town. One boy got close, but never within thirty feet of the world serpent. I could tell he wanted to touch Terrakona's emerald scales and feel them for himself. His dark eyes remained wide the entire time he stared.

A smile crept onto my face.

I gently patted Terrakona's head and then gestured to the child. As if knowing what I wanted, Terrakona brought his tail around. The boy gasped and turned to run, but Terrakona was much larger and faster. The tail wrapped around behind the kid, cutting off his path back to the fields.

Terrakona didn't coil around the child, though. He just

waited, his scales within inches of the boy's touch. Once the child realized he wasn't under attack, he reached out a hesitant hand and stroked Terrakona's tail. If I could, I would've offered him some sort of souvenir—a scale or bit of crystal mane—but they were powerful objects, not so easily given away, and not so easily removed, either.

But the memory would likely be enough. The boy would remember this for the rest of his life. Hopefully, it would inspire him to do his own great things—become an arcanist everyone adored and admired.

Once the watch had secured all the brigands, Terrakona headed toward Deadman's Bluff once again. Guildmaster Eventide rode with me on his mane while Hexa, Zelfree, and Illia held on to Terrakona's back. It was a comfortable configuration. Well, *comfortable* wasn't the right word. But it worked, and I could rest on occasion during the last stretch of our trek.

It was daybreak when I finally saw the ocean. The brilliant, orange light of a new dawn reflected off the distant waves, shimmering so brightly, it was almost difficult to look at.

The smell of brine filled my nose, and I smiled. Islanders had salt water in our veins, and while I had enjoyed my time in Regal Heights, it had also been the longest amount of time I had ever spent away from the ocean. I hadn't realized how much I'd been longing to hear the crash of the waves and feel the sea spray on my face.

Deadman's Bluff wasn't difficult to spot. The small port town had three distinct sections. There were the docks—tiny compared to places like Fortuna and New Norra—which included a market. Then there was the town, complete with a courthouse and jail, which were rare for small communities. But since Deadman's Bluff was the location for many hangings, it didn't really surprise me. And lastly, there was a tall cliff that faced the ocean, with gallows so prominent and numerous, I could see them from afar.

Apparently, in the past, they had hanged entire pirate crews all at the same time. The mass sentencing had been easier.

"We should've brought the brigands here," Hexa called up to me as she pointed to the gallows. "They're equipped to handle them!"

I nodded once. "Perhaps."

Eventide brushed back her long, gray hair. "I think it would be best if you left the world serpent here. We can travel into the town on foot."

"Why?" I asked. "Our presence here shouldn't be a surprise. Everyone in town saw us coming from miles away, no doubt. Terrakona is huge."

"The sky titan arcanist said people were brought here to meet with the Autarch, correct? So Second Ascension members are likely here, either as citizens or hidden forces lurking in the shadows. They likely saw Terrakona approaching, and that probably sent them into a panic. If we're aggressive in our approach, they might do something stupid, like take innocent people hostage."

I frowned. "But if we approach the town as diplomatically as possible, you think the Second Ascension won't attack?"

"I think they'll wait for an opportune moment if they believe it's safe to do so." She offered me a slight smile. "But since you're the world serpent arcanist, I think that won't go like they expect."

My head felt light.

I wanted to run into town and demand that everyone tell me as much as they could, but I couldn't cause a panic. That wouldn't help me.

"We could port in," Illia said.

Her rizzel eldrin poked his little head out of her hair. "Teleporting is so much easier."

"It'll be faster, too."

Hexa grabbed Illia's shoulder and nodded. "Yes. I agree!"

Her hydra nodded his many heads along with her statement.

I liked the option, but I didn't want to just appear in the middle of town. Startling the townsfolk wouldn't be helpful, and if some of them were enemy arcanists, they could catch us by surprise if we weren't careful.

"Let's teleport halfway," I called down.

"Sounds good." Illia disappeared and then popped into existence in front of Terrakona. She waited for everyone to join her, keeping her arms crossed.

"Warlord, be wary," Terrakona telepathically said to me. **"Corruption dwells in this hamlet. The Children of Balastar stink of fear."**

He lowered his head as he spoke to me, and I slid off his mane, dwelling on his words. Were there plague-ridden monsters nearby? Eventide and I would be safe from their tainted blood, but I always worried about the others.

I brushed myself off once I was on the ground. "I'll protect the others," I said. "Please stay ready, just in case I need you."

"I will remain vigilant until the end."

The way he had said the last part bothered me for a moment. Until the end? I really didn't want to think about the approaching disaster, but prompted by Terrakona's grim reminder, my thoughts drifted to the apoch dragon. Once all the god-creatures walked among us again, and once we handled the arcane plague, the wicked dragon would descend again to kill us all.

I clenched my jaw, my teeth hurting a bit as I walked over to Illia.

Part of me wondered if there was a way to avoid my fated demise at the claws of the apoch dragon. After all, once I found

Luthair, and once the Second Ascension and the Autarch were defeated, wouldn't I want to then build things? Shape the world into something grand?

Start a family?

Would I be able to do any of those things? Or would the dragon of ultimate death and destruction strike me down? Retribution weighed heavily on my hip. There was a dark irony to carrying a weapon made from the bones of a creature that would one day, in a reborn body, kill me.

"Volke?" Illia asked, jarring me from my thoughts.

She held out a hand. She already held Hexa and Raisen with the other hand, while Zelfree and his mimic had transformed so that they, too, had rizzel teleportation powers. Eventide stood with him, ready to enter the town.

I took Illia's hand. "Sorry."

She stared at me with her one eye. Her eyepatch was a little dirty at the moment, which was unusual. It was worn around the edges, clearly well used, and also well-cared for.

"Are you worried?" Illia whispered.

Hexa's fluffy hair bounced in the breeze. "What?" she balked. "Did you just ask Volke if he's *scared*? He's not afraid of anything. He fought Theasin Venrover, faced off against the sky titan, and even argued with the typhon beast." She stepped close, slapped my shoulder with a powerful *whack,* and then offered a smirk. "Volke has guts of steel and the spirit of thirty griffins."

That was an odd statement, but I knew what she meant by it, and I was touched.

"I'll be fine," I said to my sister. "Just take us close to town, okay? Not directly in the center of town square."

"All right."

Nicholin positioned himself comfortably on Illia's shoulder. Then he gave me a sarcastic salute. "Anything for you, Warlord. Hup-two!"

I narrowed my eyes, but I didn't have time to say anything.

Illia's teleportation felt like a sudden yank forward. I stumbled, my insides twisting, and then we were a few hundred feet from our destination. We stood just outside the town of Deadman's Bluff, on the dirt-and-cobblestone road.

The weather shifted, and I glanced toward the sky.

A chill rushed over us from the ocean, bringing with it dark clouds. The once glorious morning was now transforming into something gray and unpleasant. There would be a storm soon. The air smelled sour, as if soaked with salt. Clear signs it would rain within the hour.

Zelfree and Eventide popped into existence next to us, a shower of glitter their only herald. Both rubbed at their faces afterward, probably due to the porting around. Even Traces, who appeared to be a little rizzel riding around on Zelfree's shoulder, seemed a bit dazed.

I opened my shirt to show off my god-arcanist mark. The twelve-pointed star covered the left side of my chest, just over my heart, as well as my shoulder, ribs, and part of my arm. The serpent design woven through the twelve points told all the world that Terrakona and I were bonded.

Illia tugged my shirt open a bit more after I was done. "You really should show this off more." Then she pointed to the pendant I wore. "And don't forget to really show that off, too."

Most guild pendants came in various metals, but mine and Zaxis's were the only ones made of atlas turtle bone. I touched the pendant for a moment, remembering when Eventide had given it to me.

"Thank you," I said.

Then I turned my attention to the town.

It was a quiet seaside location built up the side of a hill. The road went from the docks, through town, and then all the way up the hill to the tippy-top of the cliffs. It only ended once it reached the ominous gallows.

The town itself was nothing more than one-story shacks,

hovels, and the occasional shop. The castle, courthouse, and jail were clearly the main attractions. All three were built from red and blackened stone. Not nullstone or anything magical, but harsh dark bricks that fit the gloomy demeanor of the town. The buildings matched the impending weather.

While the polite course of action would be to introduce myself to the mayor or captain of the guard, I headed straight for the jail.

That was Luthair and Vethica's most likely location.

Orwyn had said they were trapped here, and that would be the likely location to keep them. If they weren't there, I'd check the castle. It wasn't a large castle, though. A single surrounding wall and only two towers meant it was one of the smallest fortifications I had ever seen.

Luthair...

It would be easy to spot him, even in a dungeon. He was a tall suit of shadowy black plate armor, and his cape—which was long enough to touch the ground—was lined with the night sky, stars twinkling in the mythical fabric.

"Where you goin', lad?" Zelfree called out.

I stopped and turned. "To the jail."

Zelfree motioned to our surroundings. I took a few seconds to give everything a second glance. Upon reflection, I realized... there weren't any people around. None on the streets. None on the docks. Ghost towns were more welcoming than Deadman's Bluff.

After a deep breath, I paid attention to the vibrations in the ground with my tremor sense. It was easy to feel Illia, Nicholin, Hexa, Raisen, Zelfree, Traces, and Eventide. Even their heartbeats were normal, despite the tension growing in the group.

When I shifted my focus to the buildings, I felt people within. Children. A few adults. When I glanced at another home, I felt the same. But all the windows were shut, and the doors locked tight.

People were here, but clearly no one wanted to interact with us. Why? My tremor sense couldn't answer that question for me.

"Stay close," I said. "If someone is nearby, I'll sense it."

Everyone gathered around. What worried me the most, although I didn't voice my concerns, was the lack of mystical creatures I sensed. Terrakona had said there was corruption nearby, and he normally only said that when plague-ridden beasts lurked in the shadows. Where were they now? They couldn't hide from my senses.

Could they?

"You're certain this isn't a trap?" Illia whispered.

"No." I smirked. "But I'm pretty sure it's not a trap. I think we might've just surprised our enemies is all."

Eventide frowned. "I thought approaching casually would get our enemy to let their guard down, but clearly, I was mistaken. Someone knew we were coming. Look there."

Some of the nearby houses had windows boarded up from the inside. And if this town had horses, they weren't anywhere to be found.

The Second Ascension had done something like this before. When I had fought Rhys, he and his insane arcanists had hidden in such a way that I couldn't immediately detect them. And they had used the guise of a village to keep their numbers obfuscated. Maybe the people in the nearby houses weren't families—maybe they were just Second Ascension members pretending to be innocents until I let my guard down.

"I'll go ahead," Eventide said as she placed a hand on my shoulder.

I shook my head. "*I'm* the god-arcanist."

"My true form atlas turtle magic will protect me from the plague, and my barriers haven't ever failed me before." She had the easy smile of someone who had done this kind of thing hundreds of times before.

The glowing arcanist mark on her forehead did put me at ease.

"All right."

Hexa snapped her fingers. "Don't worry. Raisen and I are here to help."

With a nod, I held up a hand. "I think we should look into that house first. I suspect… the people inside aren't residents of Deadman's Bluff."

Even if I had to fight a hundred dastard arcanists all disguised as sweet, innocent little families, I would. Vethica and Luthair weren't going to disappear on me again. We'd fight our way to the jail if it came to it.

Eventide strode for the front door. "We'll soon find out who these people are, won't we?"

Chapter 5

Prisoner Experiments

Eventide knocked on the front door with three powerful bangs. In the utter silence, her knocking resounded like gunfire. Nothing happened. I felt the people inside flinch at the sharp bangs and sensed their pounding hearts. But none of them moved, and neither did we. We held our defensive positions as tension thickened in the air. Even the ocean wind seemed to still as we waited.

With a concerned glance, Eventide turned to face me. She narrowed her eyes, her expression questioning. I shook my head. While I could detect the movements of the people inside, I couldn't understand their motives. They were there, but for whatever reason, they refused to answer.

Eventide knocked three more times. "Hello?" she called out. "My name is Liet Eventide. I'm the guildmaster of the Frith Guild. Is anyone home?"

That caused the inhabitants to stir. One adult stood and slowly made their way to the front door, their steps hesitant.

They seemed... afraid. The more I dwelled on their movements, the more I figured they *weren't* part of the Second Ascension. The people in the house seemed timid. Most of the arcanists in the Second Ascension had infected themselves with the arcane plague and rarely had the rationality to feel fear. Besides, if they were here, wouldn't they be moving into an attack formation? Or at least executing whatever dastardly plans they had for me?

Hexa glared at the house and then the jail. "Let's just smash down the doors and search everything ourselves."

"We don't need to get violent," Illia whispered. "I can port us in. It wouldn't be difficult."

"Yeah. Okay."

I shook my head as I pointed to the house. "Wait. Someone is coming out. Let's hear what they have to say."

Illia and Hexa quieted and stared at the door.

It opened with a creak.

A man poked his head out slightly, his fingers tightly curled around the edge of the door. "Hello?" he asked, his voice soft. "I think you have the wrong house."

Eventide placed her boot between the door and the frame, preventing it from being shut quickly. "I apologize, but do you have a minute? Something strange is obviously happening here."

"I-I don't know nothin' about that."

The man attempted to shut the door, but Eventide refused to budge. She didn't force herself inside, but she didn't move her boot, either. The man tugged and then stopped, his shoulders shaking.

"Where is everyone?" Eventide asked slowly.

"They're... just waitin'."

"For what? Or *who*?"

The man shook his head. His home was so dark and shadowed that it was difficult to see inside. They had no candles or lanterns or glowstones? They were waiting in the dark? Were they *that* afraid of being spotted?

Zelfree turned to me. "These people have obviously been helping the Second Ascension. Probably against their will." He spoke quietly, but quickly, as though piecing everything together as he went along. "Perhaps our enemies just left. Or they're about to come back. Either way, this man clearly doesn't want to get in the thick of it."

Illia patted her eldrin's head. "Maybe the villains are close by. I can't teleport too far without needing to stop."

"I've seen them teleport great distances before," I muttered, thinking back to the time the Second Ascension had launched an assault on Thronehold. "They're likely far off."

While we discussed the situation, Zelfree glanced back and forth, following along with his eyes, but remaining silent.

Hexa clenched her hands into tight fists. "If our enemies aren't here, what're we waiting for? We can smash down the wall of the jail and get inside with no problems." She huffed. "We have *Terrakona* on our team! Not even the gates of the abyssal hells could stop *him*."

Although I was tempted, I waited for a moment. Eventide was still with the townsman, and she hadn't abandoned her line of questioning.

"What're you waiting for?" Eventide repeated.

The man hesitated. He tugged on the door, but when it wouldn't budge, he sighed. "I don't want any trouble. We just did as the arcanists a-asked. Everything is up in those buildings." He gestured to the jail and courthouse.

"What's there?" Eventide asked.

"All the experiments."

That was a cryptic response. I really didn't like what I was sensing here. There were so many people hiding in their homes. Were they all *that* afraid of the Second Ascension?

"Okay, that settles it," I said. "I'll be the first one into the jail. Something strange is going on here, and I don't want anyone else to get hurt. Whatever the Second Ascension is doing, nothing can affect my god-arcanist magic."

"Nothing can?" Illia asked, an eyebrow raised.

"Nothing *they* can do."

"Are you sure?" She crossed her arms. "Are you sure there isn't a trinket or artifact they could use that could get around your resistance?"

I turned to face her fully. "Do you know something I don't?"

"No. You're reminding me of... Well, you're reminding me of *me*." Illia glared with her one eye. "Don't you remember when I went to kill Calisto? I was so certain the king basilisk venom would end him in an instant. But then he had that artifact..." Illia sighed as she stared at the ground.

Nicholin nodded once and then wagged a paw at me. He didn't say anything, though. He took the posture and demeanor of someone disappointed and grumpy.

Zelfree chuckled.

Everyone glanced over, obviously confused. He cracked his knuckles and then offered me a shrug.

"You all grow up so quickly. Gone are the days of flying off the side of the ship the moment a problem arises." He smirked. "Taking things seriously? *Without* me demanding you think everything through? I never thought I'd see the day."

Hexa placed her fists on her hips. "Like you're one to talk. I saw how you've acted with Calisto. You jump to help him no matter the danger!"

"That's different. I'm older than you."

"What does *that* matter?"

"It means *my* mistakes are just lessons for you to learn from, and *your* mistakes are opportunities for me to lecture you," Zelfree quipped. "And it never goes in the opposite direction."

The door to the house closed, drawing my attention. Eventide walked away from the dwelling and slowly made her way back to the group. She grabbed the edge of her tricorn cap to keep it from blowing away in the stormy weather.

"I don't think the Second Ascension is here," she said as she approached. "This might be the perfect timing. Let's head to the jail."

"What about the townsfolk?" Illia asked.

"We should leave them be. I don't think they'll be a threat. They've been cowed."

With my heart pounding, I nodded. Together as a group, we headed to the brick jailhouse. The quiet roads were only filled with the howl of the weather. I turned my attention to the distance, checking in on Terrakona before heading the last little bit to the jail.

Terrakona waited patiently for us away from the streets and buildings. He must've known I was staring, because he turned his two-toned gaze in my direction. One eye was blue, the other a shade of red. Despite the distance between us, I sensed his concern and noticed the glint of intelligence in his mystic eyes.

It wasn't long before we reached the jail.

The stink of human waste lingered around the building, despite the breeze. For half a second, it reminded me of the excavation site—the area where I had found the bones of the first apoch dragon. The Second Ascension had dug up the corpse and used the bones for their many weapons.

Theasin Venrover had had tents and makeshift buildings all around. He had used them for his experimenting.

This place...

It felt similar.

"What's wrong?" Eventide asked.

"I wish we had brought Adelgis," I whispered.

"Why is that?"

"I have a feeling he would be one of the few people who would understand what we're about to find."

I held my breath. My heart refused to calm down. It slammed hard in my rib cage with each new thought that fluttered into my mind.

Theasin Venrover had done all sorts of unspeakable things to discover new magics and ways to create trinkets. His children were all part of the Second Ascension. Well, not *all* of them, but *most* of them. Adelgis would know his handiwork if we stumbled upon it. He might even be able to identify if any of his family were involved as well.

"Illia," I said.

My sister perked up. "Yes?"

"Can you search around the city? Don't bother the townspeople, but I want to know everything that's going on around here. Especially anything they have hidden."

Illia was stiff for a moment. Then she asked, "Is something wrong?"

"I just think there might be things hidden nearby. You're the only one—besides Zelfree—who can search quickly, and I want Zelfree to stay close, just in case I need to identify certain types of magic."

She nodded once, like it was a proper command she was proud to receive. "Right. I'll investigate the area."

Nicholin also straightened his posture. Then he saluted me—not sarcastically, but almost like he, too, was proud. "We're not going to let you down."

I smiled, thankful *this* group was with me. I didn't know why, but even in this dark moment, when I feared for Vethica's and Luthair's safety, the presence of Illia and her eldrin reassured me we would make it through this.

I returned my attention to the door of the jail. It was constructed from thick wood and held together with large iron fastenings. Words etched into the metal read: *Deadman's Bluff Jailhouse*. I shoved open the door and stepped inside, where I was met with a stench so foul I almost retched.

The front room was empty. A barred door blocked the main hallway, and a second barred door blocked the basement. There were no jailors to greet us. No signs or town guards. Glowstones were the only source of light, and they were built into the ceiling at least five feet apart from one another, creating pockets of gloom around the impressively sized building.

Eventide snorted and half-smirked. "The townsfolk seemed frightened of this place, and it wasn't because of the prisoners."

A cold chill lingered on the air.

It was something...

Worse than I had ever felt before.

Hexa pushed me aside as she stormed into the room. Raisen growled, as though he wanted to join us, but Zelfree held up a hand and then motioned to the street, commanding the hydra to wait for us. Raisen begrudgingly complied.

"Hello?" Hexa called out. "Is anyone here?"

Vethica and Luthair had to be here. They had to be.

"Why didn't we know things were happening here?" Hexa asked as she whirled around on her heel. "How come no one said anything?" Her hands were once again balled into fists. "If the Second Ascension was killing people here, we should've known!"

"It's a small town," Eventide stated as she stepped into the main room. The cold bricks of the floor were the same dark coloration as the walls. "And it's a town known for executions. Most people don't vacation here. There isn't much trading. People are *sent* here, and they never return. A perfect place for an organization like the Second Ascension to hide out in. At least... for a short time."

I hesitated at the threshold. Zelfree stood by my side, his gaze narrowed.

Illia's words had spooked me a bit. Was I being overconfident?

No. As a god-arcanist, I needed to leave that part of me behind. No matter what was here, I would face it. I'd deal with the consequences and the tribulations with confidence.

"Hello?" A faint voice echoed up from the basement. "Is someone there?"

"Hello?" Hexa shouted. She ran over to the barred door that blocked the staircase down. "Are you trapped?"

Zelfree stepped into the foul-smelling building. Traces, still a rizzel, puffed up her white and silver fur. Then Zelfree held a hand up. "Step aside."

Hexa leapt out of the way. Zelfree evoked white disintegration flames. They broke apart the metal bars—tiny bits of them disappearing and rearranging into particles all around. It left the door nothing more than iron flakes floating on the air.

Hexa charged forward. She ran down the stairs two at a time. With a sigh, Eventide followed after her.

I waited, still at the door, my body tense.

"Well?" Zelfree asked.

"Right," I muttered.

Then I headed for the basement.

The source of the disturbance and the cause of my unease.

Chapter 6

Dark Underground

The basement of the prison was draftier than I would've expected. A chill wind blew up from the underground rooms, carrying the foul smell with it.

The stairs were stone, the walls smooth brick, and the detail work all done in wrought iron. Images of justice, including books, scales, and the executioners themselves, were twisted from the iron and then mounted onto the walls. It made for an intimidating sight.

When I reached the bottom of the stairs, I found half a normal cell block. The front half of the room consisted of six cells, each made with bars from the same wrought iron. A single woman was held in the closest cell, her trembling form almost difficult to see in the dim lighting. Glowstones were mounted on the ceiling, but several had been removed, for some reason.

The back half of the room...

Looked as though it had been melted.

The other six cells—including the metal and stone—were twisted, waxy, and covered in a disgusting sheen that reminded me of mucus. Nothing about the room was right, even the walls were wrapped and twisted, practically collapsing in on each other.

A tunnel had been melted into the far wall. It led downward, like a maw into the very earth.

When I focused on my tremor sense, I realized something was there, but I could only faintly detect it. The ground in the tunnel was still in a fluid-like state. The fluid didn't translate the tremors well, but that didn't matter. I could still feel something, just as a man with one blind eye could still see, even if it wasn't as well.

Hexa stood by the jail cell with the woman. Her deep frown told me it wasn't Vethica.

Despite that, Zelfree held up his hand and used his disintegration to ruin the cell outright. He broke apart the iron, and the prisoner was free to go.

Part of me wondered if we should release prisoners, but then I reminded myself that whoever was here was probably just a captive of the Second Ascension and not an actual criminal. At least, I hoped that was the case.

The woman wore nothing but a tattered, woolen tunic and trousers. She hurried out of her cell but stopped when Hexa held out a hand.

"They took people to their cave," the woman whispered as she pointed to the windy tunnel. "They took them there, and they never came back."

Hexa nodded once. "Thank you."

As the woman hurried out of the room, Hexa touched the scars on her arms. She had a hardened expression, vacant and focused.

Eventide stood at the entrance of the tunnel, her stance stiff. The foul wind blew up and played with her gray hair. Her solemn expression reminded me we were already in a fight, even if our opponent had yet to show himself.

Being underground gave me the advantage, though. As long

as I didn't collapse the building, I was confident whoever was here didn't stand a chance.

"Careful," Eventide whispered. "It's coming."

"What is?" I asked.

Zelfree glanced over, his eyes wide. "A charybdis…" He waved his arms. "*Cover your ears!*"

The music wafted up into the room a mere second after Zelfree had given his command. Eventide had already pressed her hands on the sides of her head, blocking out the noise.

The melody was pleasant and soothing—it felt like a promise from a good friend that everything would be okay. The song chased away the irritation of the lingering smell, and when I breathed deeply, my chest untwisted, my anxiety drifting away.

Hexa hadn't covered her ears, either. She relaxed, her shoulders slumping, her frown blooming into a slight smile. The song had a powerful effect…

Rumbling shook the whole prison. Through my tremor sense, I knew a large creature was making its way up the tunnel, even if the fluid-like goo on the ground was hiding details from me.

A charybdis…

They were wyrms—dragon-like creatures with no legs, arms, or wings. They had lamprey-style mouths, large, circular, and filled with three rows of fangs. And while they had been hunted to extinction for the crime of being too dangerous, I had seen one in Thronehold the day the soul forge had used it abilities to resurrect dead mystical creatures.

The Second Ascension had wanted charybdis specifically…

The music prevented me from being anxious. The melodious tune eased all my worries and lulled me into a relaxed state. In my mind, I knew it was a type of mind-controlling magic, but my body fell into the trap, similar to a fatigue I just couldn't shake.

When *this* charybdis appeared at the edge of the tunnel, I

had been expecting something similar to what I had seen in Thronehold. Unfortunately, that wasn't the case.

The monster that slithered up from the depths of darkness was nothing like what I had seen. This beast was bloated, like a waterskin stuffed with too much liquid. Its scaled body was stretched and puffed outward, like it could rupture at any moment and spill its guts everywhere. Its mouth had fangs, but they had no rhyme or reason. They jutted out in every direction, some even *through* the creature's lips and heads. Teeth sprouted outward, lining its lips with sharp bits.

Charybdis typically had beady black eyes that shone with intelligence. This monstrosity had eyes that hung out of its head on thin scraps of flesh and nerves, dangling around like toys for cats, each dripping with blood.

I knew the arcane plague when I saw it, but this baffled me.

I had thought the charybdis were man-eaters, which meant they were immune to blood diseases, including the plague. Why was this monster twisted by its magic? It should have been impossible.

Or perhaps I had been mistaken about the charybdis?

The fat blob of a wyrm continued singing. Its mouth didn't move—the music came from deep within its bloated throat, as though the charybdis had a woman trapped inside its body, constantly singing from within.

Charybdis were known for being siren-like. They were creatures that lived out in the oceans, singing songs to lure individuals closer to them, only to then create whirlpools and destroy whole ships to curb their hunger.

This one was large, but not fully grown. It was ten feet in diameter, and big enough to eat a grown man whole, but not a ship. Still, it wasn't something to be taken lightly.

Eventide and Zelfree weren't enthralled by the music, though.

The charybdis vomited a mixture of saliva and blood. It

wasn't just a handful, either. Gallons of the foul-smelling liquid sprayed out of its giant mouth. Normally, I would've leapt out of the way, but because of the music, I barely took a few steps to the side, entranced by the scene before me.

Eventide held out her hand, uncovering one of her ears, and then evoked a powerful, shimmering shield. It hardened and blocked the splatter of saliva from hitting me or Hexa. Zelfree teleported out of the way with ease, reappearing on the staircase.

The saliva melted everything it managed to touch. The stone, the iron bars—nothing was immune to the acidic spit of the charybdis. And the music never stopped, even as the plague-infected charybdis vomited all over the room.

The whole room started to resemble a half-used candle.

Zelfree teleported to Hexa's side and used his white-fire evocation in a small amount, washing it over her and then also me. The fire broke apart some of my skin and clothing, and while it stung, and I shouted in surprise, it wasn't too damaging. I wasn't grievously wounded, more a cluster of scrapes across my back and shoulder.

The pain was enough to break me free of the intoxicating music. Same with Hexa. With a groggy stumble, I regained my ability to think straight.

"End this," Zelfree stated. His lip bled, and I suspected he had harmed himself to maintain his own self-control. "*Before the monster destroys the tunnel.*"

I wanted to evoke my magma, but that would only add to the problem—I'd destroy more of the structure as well. With a wave of my hand, I manipulated the stone of the underground to tighten around the charybdis, but also to reinforce the tunnel. Then I readied my sword and turned to face the monster. Retribution wouldn't be melted—I was certain of that fact.

The charybdis lunged forward. It collided with Eventide and managed to get one of her arms into its gigantic, circular mouth.

She hadn't defended—the music had gotten to her when she had shielded everyone.

The many rows of crooked teeth punctured her coat, and then her skin. She gritted her teeth as the monster lifted her from the ground.

"Liet!" Zelfree evoked a major blast of white flame. It broke apart some of the scales of the creature, but it didn't go deep. Charybdis had extremely resistant hides. They were dangerous creatures, and legends spoke of their ability to avoid death.

I rushed in and slashed at the monster's underbelly, my blade flowing through the flesh of the beast as though it weren't even there. Unfortunately, the beast practically burst. Blood, viscera, and clear mucus gushed out over me, exploding outward. I closed my eyes as I leapt away, but I wasn't fast enough to avoid the fluid.

It threatened to seep through my clothing, but before it got into my skin, or into my flesh, I evoked my magma and burned it away.

With a quick jerk of my hand, I manipulated the stone and created a wall. I was so fast, and so haphazard, that the stone slammed upward into the roof, rumbling the whole prison. Despite my worry, I clenched my jaw and stumbled backward, my thoughts on the building. I manipulated the stone again, shifting the bricks around until I *knew* everything would be structurally sound.

The charybdis thrashed its head to the side, attempting to rip Eventide's arm from its socket. Zelfree teleported to the creature. He evoked more white fire on its face, breaking apart its eyeballs and dangling eye stalks. The monster screamed and thrashed.

In order to help, I manipulated the stone to make sure Zelfree wouldn't be slammed into the ceiling.

The moment the charybdis released Eventide, Zelfree grabbed her and teleported away in a pop of glitter and air.

I didn't want to get close to slash the monster, so I threw my blade, aiming for the remaining eyes. Retribution slashed through the dangling eye stalks and then through the monster's bloated cheek. More vile liquid gushed out everywhere, but the beast was thoroughly shaken by the loss of its eyes.

It roared again, but this time, the sound seemed laced with laughter. The cackling never failed to disturb me. I hated it. This monster, the plague—*all of this.* Why was the Second Ascension *so* dedicated to their bleak corruption and empty destruction?

I manipulated the stone under Retribution to slide it toward me. Once the sword was at my feet, I ducked and retrieved it.

Near the stairway, Zelfree held Eventide close as she examined herself. Her arm wept blood.

"Stand back!" Hexa yelled.

She evoked a cloud of toxic gas. The deadly fog wafted through the room. There were no windows, and even though wind blew from the tunnel, the gas wanted to settle closer to the floor. Hexa waved her hand, and the gas washed over the charybdis. And when the monster took breaths, it did so in huge gulps. It swallowed her evocation like a man downed water in the desert.

In legend, charybdis were difficult to kill. They were physically sturdy, and magically resistant, but poison and venom were their only weakness. When the plague-ridden charybdis breathed in the gas, it choked.

I manipulated the stone under the creature, pushing it up toward the ceiling, slow enough to trap it, but not fast enough to crush the beast and spray its deadly insides. Hexa evoked more of her gas, funneling it toward the creature. The noxious fog, purple in tint, answered her nonverbal commands, swaying and moving with a mind of its own.

The charybdis coughed, hacked, wheezed, and laughed all in one bizarre noise. It never spoke, which I found odd. Most plague-ridden creatures spoke. They voiced words of obsession and power, and often seemed to know the thoughts of things nearby, like the corrupted magic was penetrating everything in the vicinity, trying to spread from one being to the next.

It took only a few moments for the charybdis to wheeze its last breath.

When it finally died, its guts sprayed out of its circular mouth, gushing forward in a halfhearted burst, as though it had finally lost the last of its muscle control. Acidic viscera splashed onto the stone floor and melted it enough to form a hole.

I manipulated the stone to keep it contained.

When the creature finally stilled, the liquid in the tunnel hardened, allowing my tremor sense to function perfectly.

There was a cave down the tunnel, and that cave opened to the coast. The water lapped across the rocks in the far distance—to the very edge of my senses. I understood now how the Second Ascension was getting away with all their experiments.

They were taking the prisoners out of the jails through their secret tunnel. If anyone "died" in prison, no one would question their disappearance. The Second Ascension could sail a boat up to this tunnel, and then take their experiments away.

This charybdis had no doubt been a test subject. Something for them to try their new powers on.

I didn't like any of that. And I didn't like that Vethica and Luthair had been taken here.

Hexa hurried around the lifeless corpse of the charybdis. "Let's go," she commanded. "We're not done yet."

I nodded to her, but then I glanced over my shoulder. Eventide had healed most of the damage to her arm. She offered me a tight smile.

"Go," she said. "Everett and I will be right behind you."

That was all I needed. If she could speak—if she was confident she was all right—then I didn't need to stay here. I turned and headed off with Hexa, making sure to follow her closely. She moved the deadly gas along the tunnel, away from us, as we made our way down to the mysterious cave.

It was darker—darker than ever before—but I whispered descriptions of the surroundings to Hexa as we went, giving her confidence in her footing. She would've charged forward regardless of my statements, but my words seemed to fuel her.

When we reached the seaside cave, the cool air of the ocean rushed to greet us. I breathed deep, enjoying the salty aroma. The scents of my home reinvigorated me.

That was when I spotted the nullstone cages.

And Vethica.

Chapter 7

The Seaside Retreat

I barely had time to glance around before Hexa shot forward.

The sand made it difficult to use my tremor sense. The grains shifted underfoot, causing a blur of motion, as though my terrain-sight were hindered by fog. Thankfully, the clear blue sky made it effortless to see in all directions beyond the cave—all the way to the ocean horizon.

The beach was covered in nullstone cages. And the cages were surprisingly large. At least six feet across. They were meant for large creatures and people, obviously.

Most were empty, but others weren't. The empty ones had their doors swung open or removed altogether. It seemed they had been torn open in a hurry—as though the Second Ascension had needed to quickly escape.

They were trying to get away, but when I turned my attention to the water, I saw nothing. Had they left hours ago? Or had they gone on foot?

The closed cages still had people and mystical creatures inside.

But none were Luthair.

He was the first person I checked for, and disappointment was my only reward.

"Vethica!"

Hexa slammed into the bars of Vethica's cage. She reached an arm through.

Vethica sat in the center, but turned and reached out a single hand to grab Hexa's. Vethica's lip quavered as she smiled, her words obviously choked up in her throat. They laced their fingers together as Hexa slid down the bars.

While I didn't know Vethica well, she had always come across as *tough* and *independent.* In the cage, she seemed more vulnerable than anything else. Afraid. But it only lasted a moment. The instant she held Hexa's hand, it was like her confidence had been zapped to life.

Vethica stood, her legs shakier than I had ever imagined she could be. The fire in her eyes never died, though.

"Hexa," she whispered. "You're here? But..."

"We're getting you out of here." Hexa pulled Vethica to the bars and hugged her with the metal between them.

Vethica returned the embrace. She was slightly taller than Hexa, but much thinner. Wasted away, practically. How long had it been since she had moved around? Vethica's reddish-blonde hair, practically orange, had grown longer. It almost reached her shoulders and was currently a mess of tangles.

Her clothing had also seen better days. The pants were torn at the bottom, her tunic frayed at the sleeves. She had a belt, and a simple pouch, but otherwise, she had nothing else.

"Hexa," Vethica muttered again, her voice raspy.

"I'm gonna get you *and* Akhet out of here."

Akhet...

He was Vethica's eldrin—a khepera. They were special creatures, rare and elusive, with the ability to rewind time in small, localized areas. It was with Vethica's magic that we had cured the arcane plague in a few select individuals.

The khepera weren't large creatures. The biggest I had seen had been the size of a human head. They were jeweled scarabs that shone with brilliant iridescent colors, much like oil on the surface of water.

But Vethica didn't have one with her in her cage.

Instead, Vethica reached into the pouch on her belt. She withdrew sand. Tannish sand and pinkish sand, mixed together in equal amounts. Although, most people wouldn't know what that was—I did.

It was Akhet.

Whenever a khepera "died" it turned into sand. Tan sand for the body, and pink sand for the soul. Had Akhet died at the hands of the Second Ascension?

"Don't worry," Hexa said as she grabbed Vethica's hand and curled her fingers around the small piles of sand. "We'll... We'll take this to New Norra."

The maze beneath the city of New Norra was the last known location that the khepera could reform. Instead of breeding, the khepera's sand slowly returned to the maze in order to reform. In theory, the khepera were immortal, but if the sand was ever used up—or consumed by others—the khepera suffered a final death.

Vethica tucked the sand away. "You need to be careful, Hexa. You don't know what—"

She never finished her statement.

The waters just beyond the shore roiled. The shadows of mystical creatures darkened the surface of the water. I ran beyond Vethica's cage with Retribution in hand. Now that we were outside, I didn't fear harming anyone with my powerful magic.

"Take care of Vethica," I stated.

Three more of the charybdis burst from the waters, each one more disgusting than the last. Normally, I would have been in awe of any wyrm. Even if they had no arms, legs, or wings, they were still a type of dragon, powerful and majestic. But these *monsters* were just putrid freaks.

The first didn't even have flesh on its head. The beast had a skeletal mouth and empty sockets where eyes should've been. The second looked as though it was wearing the extra flesh of the other. Extra scales covered its body, and two extra sets of teeth jutted from its circular jaws. The last reminded me of a bloated corpse found in the ocean. Fat, grotesque, its scales and hide barely keeping it together.

The three charybdis writhed toward the shore.

I evoked magma, the molten rock oozing from the lines in my palm. The heat coursed through me, mixing with my anger. I swear my rage made my evocation even hotter than it already was.

With a wide sweep of my hand, I evoked the magma in an arc in front of me. Some of it hit the monsters as they charged, but most of it hit the ocean waves. Hot steam immediately shot into the air, the sizzle of my molten rock a familiar music to my ears.

When my magma touched the charybdis, they melted beneath it. The globs of superheated magic carved their way through the creatures' sturdy defenses. They might have been wyrms, but they didn't stand a chance against my god-arcanist abilities.

Two of them suffered grievous injuries. My magma had struck them on the mouth and head, respectively. It drilled into them at such a fast rate, they gurgled and half-laughed.

But again, they never spoke.

The last one had only taken a small amount of my magic. It rushed onto the beach and charge straight for me. I held my sword, but I couldn't brace myself fast enough. The charybdis slammed the side of its head against me, sending me tumbling. I quickly recovered as the charybdis brought its gigantic, circular mouth down on my new position.

I leapt out of the way.

The charybdis smashed its mouth on the sand and then vomited blood. It poured onto the beach, staining the sand with its vile crimson.

"Are you plague-ridden?" I shouted, gripping my sword.

Normally, the twisted creatures would answer me, but this beast didn't even indicate it knew what it was doing. It was… acting more like an animal. A wild, crazy beast. No mind. No desires—other than eating flesh—and no plan other than mass destruction.

What was this?

The charybdis lifted its head. Bloody sand dripped from its fangs.

I had seen enough. I held my sword tightly and used my manipulation to change the sand to stone. Then I twisted it around the body of the charybdis, trapping it in place. The monster screamed, and I hesitated. Would it speak now?

No. It thrashed its body, acting no wiser than a deer caught in a trap. It squirmed so hard, it ripped apart pieces of its own body, harming itself in its desire to be free.

I didn't want to stab it. What if this *was* related to the arcane plague, just something even worse? Something mutated and disgusting? If I stabbed it, I feared the blood would touch me. And I didn't want that.

So I manipulated the ground and sucked it further into the stone beach. Then I crushed it, as fast and as painlessly as I could. It wasn't the charybdis's fault it had been driven mad.

Once I was certain all three were dead, I turned around. Hexa struggled with the door of the nullstone cage, trying her hardest to free Vethica.

I hurried over. Once by her side, I evoked a small amount of magma and melted away the hinges of the door.

"Thank you," Hexa said, breathless.

She pried the cell door open and then rushed inside to

Vethica. The two held each other for a brief moment before fleeing the cage and hugging a third time. I suspected, if given a choice, they'd stay in each other's arms all the way back to civilization.

The sight of it made me miss Evianna.

Then I felt awkward for staring, so I glanced away and examined the many cages. The closest one to me had a mystical creature inside. I went to it first and used my magma evocation to remove the door.

The mystical creature was a caladrius. It was a pure-white bird with a golden beak shaped similarly to a parrot. They were rarer creatures, capable of some of the most powerful healing. When I stepped into the nullstone cage, the bird remained in the cage, its eyes closed, her body shuddering.

"Are you okay?" I asked as I knelt beside it.

Upon closer inspection, I answered my own question. The caladrius was *not* okay. The poor bird... It was missing its legs. And I had thought its eyes were closed, but that wasn't the case. They had been removed.

I gently picked the mystical creature up.

The caladrius trembled harder.

"I have you," I whispered. "Don't worry."

The little mystical creature relaxed a bit, but it never stopped shaking. I held it close to my chest, hoping my warm body would comfort the bird.

"They were taking parts from it," Vethica said, drawing my attention.

Vethica stared at me, her gaze hard and icy. She released Hexa and turned her body fully in my direction. Then she motioned to the other cages with creatures.

"The arcanists who were torturing us... They had all kinds of mystical creatures. They were taking parts from them. To make items, or do experiments."

I returned my attention to the other nearby creatures.

Why would they want the parts of a caladrius? I understood why the Second Ascension would want Vethica. She could cure the plague. But a caladrius couldn't—we had already tried that.

One cage had a golden stag.

It was an ancient mystical creature with brilliant fur and metallic antlers. The beast had no hooves, and one of its antlers was missing. It couldn't walk, and it trembled just as much as the caladrius in my arms.

Golden stags...

Were creatures capable of healing ailments.

The pattern was clear. The Second Ascension had been experimenting with healing methods. Was it to cure their own plague? Or just to make sure *nothing* could cure the plague? I suspected it was the latter.

"I have you," I whispered to the caladrius.

The mystical creature nuzzled its head against my chest. Only after a few minutes of stroking its head did it finally stop shaking.

Had the Second Ascension done this to Luthair? Taken him apart? I knew Luthair was alive, but that didn't mean he had to be whole. People used the parts of mystical creatures all the time to make trinkets and artifacts. What if the Second Ascension had done that?

The mere thought caused my vision to tunnel with rage. I gripped the caladrius a little too hard, and it shivered again.

"I'm sorry," I said, patting its head. "Just a little bit longer. I know people who can help you." I didn't know anyone who could regrow body parts, but I knew of people who would care for an injured mystical creature.

"Thank you," she whispered, her voice graceful and feminine. "Thank you for coming for me."

"Of course."

I held the caladrius as I jogged over to Hexa and Vethica. My anger wouldn't leave me. I handed off the caladrius but I wanted to leap into the ocean with Terrakona. All my fantasies involved me swimming to the Second Ascension and making them sorry for everything they had done.

But I knew I couldn't just fly off. I had to have more of a plan.

Tranquility. Without it, we cannot control our rage.

I couldn't let myself become too angry. No matter what awful things the Autarch and his minions did. With a restraining breath, I forced myself to think about Liet. She was injured. She and Zelfree hadn't joined us on the beach. I needed to help her, and we needed to get Vethica to New Norra so Akhet could reform.

But we still hadn't found Luthair.

My anger…

It was like my shadow. Always there. At a moment's notice, rage could consume me once again. I would just have to keep it contained—learn to suppress it.

"We need to head back to the others," I said to Hexa, my voice stiff as I forced the words out one at a time. "You should help Vethica back to New Norra. And then I'm going after the Second Ascension."

Hexa lifted an eyebrow. Then she turned her attention to the ocean, her gaze landing on the bloodied corpses of the charybdis. "By yourself?" she murmured.

"If I have to," I replied.

Hexa didn't say anything after that.

Probably for the best. I wasn't about to be talked out of it.

Chapter 8

Qualities Of A Leader

We needed to take some of these charybdis with us, or at least samples of their flesh. I felt it was important, not because I was an expert on magic research, but because I knew other people who were. They would need to examine the flesh of the monsters and see what was wrong.

We released all the captured mystical creatures, but I gave instructions to have them quarantined.

I worked with Hexa, collecting everything we needed before heading back through the prison and up to the town of Deadman's Bluff. When I exited the building, Illia was there waiting for me, her eldrin on her shoulder.

Illia touched her eyepatch as she said, "Volke, I didn't find much in the town besides the citizens. I informed them of what was happening. A few of them told me the arcanists of the Second Ascension were here, but fled when they heard we were heading this way."

I nodded once. Then I placed a hand on her other shoulder. Her one eye widened.

"Thank you," I said.

She grabbed my wrist. "You didn't find Luthair."

Illia always knew what I was thinking, even if I never voiced my thoughts. With a sigh, I nodded again.

"Don't worry," Illia whispered, tightening her hold on me. "We'll find him. You'll see. We'll do it. Together."

I appreciated her support. Illia would always have my back—that I was certain of.

Nicholin slipped around the back of her neck and then placed both his front paws on top of Illia's hand holding my wrist. "Uh, if we're making a pact to find Luthair, you know *I* need to be involved, right? We and Luthair go *way* back. I'm the original friend."

Illia narrowed her eye at him.

With a wiggle of his nose, Nicholin snorted. "What? We lived through a shipwreck together. That makes us blood brothers." He rubbed his ears and then tilted his head. "Wait. Do knightmares have blood? I don't think they do..."

"They don't," I said, half smiling. "But you're right. Thank you. Both of you. I really appreciate the support."

A tremor of movement swept through Deadman's Bluff. I glanced over my shoulder and spotted Terrakona coiling himself just outside the boundary of the town.

"Warlord," Terrakona telepathically said. **"We have defeated bandits, saved this town from the Second Ascension's terror, and rescued Vethica from their clutches."**

"Is your eldrin speaking to you?" Nicholin pushed my hand off Illia and then stood on his hind legs, lifting his head high so he could get a better view of Terrakona. Then he waved. "Tell him I said I have everything handled here."

Illia placed a hand on Nicholin's face and forced him down into a sitting position. "I'm sorry about that. He's *excitable*."

"You have many great accomplishments. You should

revel in your good deeds." Terrakona shifted, and his black crystal mane caught the sunlight just right.

"I'll try," I whispered to myself.

Terrakona... He had better words than me. He was right. I couldn't dwell on what I *didn't* accomplish. I needed to focus on what I had done—and what I could do. If I had to chase the Second Ascension to the abyssal hells, I would. They wouldn't escape me.

And Luthair wouldn't want me to dwell. He was always so *pragmatic.* He valued my health and safety above all else. He wouldn't want me to worry—Luthair would recommend I focus on the bigger problems first.

The sky went black.

My thought abruptly ended. I whirled around and glanced upward, my heart hammering. Illia and Nicholin stared at the darkness as well, neither moving, neither saying a word.

The people of Deadman's Bluff emerged from their houses. They pointed and shouted, their confusion creating a white noise of panic. I wasn't afraid, but I understood what this meant. I kept my gaze on the sky, waiting for the pillar of light that indicated someone had bonded with a god-creature.

But I didn't see any.

The sky was black for at least thirty seconds, and then the inky void disappeared. The sun shone bright again, washing over the town like it had never disappeared.

"Did you see that?" Nicholin twitched the tip of his ferret-like tail. "Oh, man. I didn't think *another* person would bond with a god-creature so quickly! You god-arcanists are worse than weeds. Springin' up everywhere."

I wanted to agree with him, but...

The Autarch could bond with multiple god-creatures. What if that was him?

Since I hadn't seen a pillar of light, I wondered if it was

because the god-creature's lair was far from here. *Very* far from here.

"If that *wasn't* the Autarch, we need to find them," I said.

"Warlord, I suspect that is the endless undead. The Frith Guild does not have the runestone for that god-creature."

"That's true... But the *endless undead* was supposed to be the last god-creature to show up." It just didn't make sense to me. Or were all the creatures already here and waiting?

Illia stepped back. "I'll go get the others. We should hurry—if we need to deal with god-creatures, you and Zaxis should be ready."

She was right. We needed to get back to Regal Heights. While it was sad that we didn't have Luthair, we now had many tasks at hand, and the most important was the god-creatures. Vethica and her eldrin needed to get back to New Norra as well.

I'll come get you afterward, Luthair.

"I'll meet you at Terrakona," I said to my sister. With a forced smile, I added, "Don't take too long."

Illia chuckled right before she teleported with her eldrin, disappearing in a pop of silvery glitter.

Together as a group, we traveled south, away from Deadman's Bluff.

The first night we stopped, we did so because of foul weather. Terrakona reshaped the terrain around us, and made a cave-like structure for us to rest in and to shield us from the icy rains. The floor of the cave was smooth, benches jutted out of the ground, formed by rocks, and the walls protected us from the weather.

We needed all the protection we could get.

Liet wasn't feeling well.

We holed up in our temporary home, with Terrakona and Raisen just beyond the entrance. No one would bother us with a world serpent and a hydra guarding our door.

I had created a fire for us, so we could stay warm through the night, but I expected we'd leave first thing in the morning. A small chimney-style hole allowed the smoke to escape without allowing any weather to get in.

We couldn't press on in the cold darkness. But once the morning came, we would leave, regardless of the wind and rain.

"Do you need anything?" Hexa asked Vethica.

She didn't have an *indoor voice*. She spoke with boisterous energy no matter the situation, and even now, while Hexa sat with Vethica nearly thirty feet away, I heard everything.

Hexa pulled off her coat and offered it to Vethica. Then she motioned to the fire near the center of our cave. "Are you cold?"

"No," Vethica replied.

"Too warm? Should we move away from the fire?"

"I'm fine."

Hexa scooted closer, until they were hip to hip. She patted down her own curly hair, saying nothing else. With my tremor sense, I felt her heart hammering. I wondered if she was still anxious from worry, or if now it was something different. Vethica held her pouch of sand close, clearly worried about her eldrin.

Vethica had lost an eldrin before. She had once been a thunderbird arcanist, but now...

I understood why she would find it difficult to be cheerful.

Illia stood closer to me. She glanced over at Hexa and Vethica, occasionally frowning, but not saying anything. Although she didn't say anything to me, I knew she was worried about Hexa. They were close friends, and Illia always frowned like that whenever she was doubtful.

Zelfree and Liet sat on one of the benches near the wall. They spoke in tones that were neither frightened nor excited—

completely neutral and controlled. But something was wrong. Liet sweated more than normal, and her heart skipped a few beats from time to time.

I suspected she didn't want anyone to know she was feeling off. Liet always radiated confidence, and now I knew how skilled she was at maintaining that façade. Even if her body was weakening, she didn't falter.

And Liet didn't do it for herself—she did it for everyone else. To keep their spirits high.

We *could* be discussing the Second Ascension, or the new god-arcanists, or the arcane plague. But everyone here knew what needed to be done. Discussing it further would only lead to anxiousness and uncertainty about the future.

I wanted to be more like Liet. I wanted to instill a sense of security and normalcy with my mere presence.

In all the legends I admired as a child, I enjoyed the tales where a swashbuckling arcanist swooped in, and everyone immediately felt a sense of relief. *Master Arcanist Gravenwell will handle this!* It was as if everyone considered themselves already saved as soon as the arcanist showed up, even if the problems hadn't been resolved yet.

With a smile I didn't feel, but desperately wanted to, I turned around. The others glanced over, the silence of our cave meant everyone heard every tiny movement.

"Have any of you played *vanguard* before?" I asked. "I haven't played in years, but I really loved it."

"That requires a game board and pieces." Illia motioned to the cave. "Not to be a bummer, but we don't have any of that."

With my manipulation, I formed a long table from the stone. It lifted straight out of the rock, as though it had always been there, it had just been hidden. Then I created chairs—enough for each of the arcanists.

A game board...

That was so small, and the pieces were even tinier. Was my

skill with my magic good enough to create a *vanguard* playing set?

I wandered over to the table and focused on the stone. The minerals here were hard. Dense. I placed my hand on top of the table and concentrated on rearranging everything. Changing the rock, changing the shape.

A small rectangular board formed. One with little rails, to keep marbles in the game area. I tried to create marbles, but the little stone balls that formed on the board were lumpy, and one cracked.

Hexa, Vethica, and Illia all walked over to the table and took a seat. When I glanced over to Zelfree and Liet, they smiled, never hinting at any distress. They were slower getting to the table, though. And Liet took a seat farther away from everyone, at the end of the table.

"How do you play?" Hexa asked, poking at the game board. "There are holes in this?"

The board was flat except for a few divots. Everyone picked a little hole they wanted, and then players would take turns rolling their marble. The point of the game was to successfully roll your marble into each of the holes before any other player could. It was harder than it sounded, only because people often rolled their marble into the same hole over and over again.

It wasn't a complicated game, but I remembered laughing a lot when I was younger.

Vethica picked up a stone marble. "These look frail."

I grabbed one of my impromptu marbles and held it in the palm of my hand. Then I closed my fingers around it as tight as I could, focusing my magic in on the center. For a short moment, I tried to harden the rock, but then I imagined glass. Something lighter. Something transparent.

When I opened my hand, I caught my breath.

A clear crystal orb rolled along the lines of my palm. It

wasn't a perfect sphere, or even that smooth, but it was far prettier than I had imagined.

"Since when can you do that?" Illia asked, her one eye squinting at my creation.

"I haven't really made anything like this before."

Zelfree's mimic leapt onto the table. She purred as she walked over to the board game, her gray fur catching the light of our fire. "Oh, vanguard is that game where you roll little objects? I like this one. Whenever I see tiny sparkly things, I can't help myself. I just want to pounce on them. Can I play?"

"Please do," Zelfree muttered. "Play for me. I hate this game."

Hexa snorted and half-smiled. "Why? Is it difficult?"

"No. It's the opposite. It's simplistic. I like games that involve strategy. This is for children."

Liet gave him a sidelong glance. "I tend to remember you losing this one a lot."

Zelfree matched her gaze with a glower. "It's luck based. Of course I would lose. *Everyone* loses. As an old wise man once said: if you play, you're a loser."

"The words of someone with a bitter chip on their shoulder."

"I'm *not* bitter." Zelfree turned to face her, one hand balled into a fist. "I just know a terrible game when I see one."

"I've never played," Hexa interjected. She pulled the board closer to her, the stone scraping along the surface of the stone table. She cringed and kept it still afterward. "I wanna try it. C'mon. Show us how, Volke."

Vethica tucked her pouch away and sat closer to Hexa. "It's a simple game, really. We played a few times on the airship, when the treks were long and we had nothing else to do."

Nicholin teleported from Illia's shoulder and appeared on the table. Then he scurried over to the board and touched everything—the sides, the little divot holes, the marbles—and after his "inspection" he nodded to me and everyone at the table.

"This is up to regulation standards," Nicholin declared. "I approve."

Illia dragged a hand down her face. "It's a children's game..."

While they all argued over the game, I grabbed each of the marbles and used my magic to alter them into the shiny, beautiful crystals like I had before. They weren't like star shards—they were more like geodes. Beautiful, multicolored. The more marbles I made, the better they became.

They were smoother, more spherical, and captured my attention.

For my manipulation, I could alter land—the creation route—or I could manipulate water—the destruction route. I hadn't much manipulated water, even though I was born on an island and lived my life on the waves. Manipulating the earth and the soil and the terrain spoke to me.

If I kept heightening my understanding of it, I would lose the ability to manipulate the water. I'd master the creation aspect of my god-arcanist ability.

It was probably for the best.

Illia sat down on the other side of Hexa, still smiling. "I actually hated this game when I was younger."

"Why?" Hexa asked.

"I never got my marble into the right hole." Illia pointed at her eyepatch. "Lack of depth perception made it difficult. All the other kids would make fun of me."

"Jerks."

Vethica huffed a laugh. "Sounds just like kids, honestly."

"Volke would always chase them off." Illia's gaze fell to the table. After a short pause, she added, "He never let them make fun of me for long. But just to get back at them, I threw all their marbles into the ocean."

Nicholin brought both his paws to his mouth, his eyes wide. "That's so... *devious.*" He coyly smiled. "I love it."

I placed our new marbles on the table and rolled one to each player—including one for Zelfree. He took the small orb and rolled it between his fingers, showing off a bit of his impressive dexterity and sleight-of-hand. He stopped just as quickly as he had started when he glanced over at Liet.

She held her marble and examined the inner sparkle before smiling at him. "I bet you I win."

"It's a game of random chance," Zelfree barked. "There's no point in betting."

"There's skill involved. You need to aim the marble, and shoot it just right."

"The board is too small, and the holes are placed at random. There's no real skill here. No strategy. You just aim and shoot."

"So, you're too afraid to make a wager with me?"

Zelfree opened his mouth, and then closed it. When he opened it a second time, it was with a smirk. "Very well. I'll bet that you'll lose."

"You have a special talent for turning things negative," Liet said with a laugh—so easy and effortless. No one seemed to sense her struggle except for perhaps Zelfree. Everyone else smiled and chuckled at her challenges.

Vethica even murmured, "*She seems a lot better now—you were worried for nothing.*"

I kept my concerns hidden, but when I met Liet's gaze, there was a hardness there. We needed to get her back to Regal Heights, and then perhaps New Norra. She went quiet and rubbed at her arms, shivering more than the others whenever no one was looking.

Illia showed everyone how to play while I stood by the table. They were laughing and pointing, and part of me was proud for turning the situation around—for lifting their spirits.

"Volke, it's your turn," my sister said.

Just to spite Zelfree, I barely aimed and missed my hole. I really wanted Liet to win.

And it seemed everyone else wanted that as well, but everyone giggled and stifled laughs whenever they missed. Marble after marble went into the wrong divot.

Except for Liet's. She leaned onto the table and made a perfect shot. It wasn't that impressive—it was a small board and everyone was correct, it was a game designed for children. As adults, we should've had more success. But everyone was too busy having a good time.

"I guess that means I win." Liet lifted an eyebrow and turned to Zelfree. "We didn't put anything down as a wager."

Zelfree crossed his arms, his expression the very definition of *grumpy*.

"What's my prize?" Liet asked.

"This piece of string in my pocket." Zelfree pulled it out and tossed it onto the stone table.

"That's not very valuable."

"Yeah, well, play stupid games, win stupid prizes."

Nicholin snickered. Then he jumped around the game board before curling up in the center, like a cat that had found a tiny container to cram itself into. "This is my bed now." He poked his nose over the side of the board. "You all sleep elsewhere."

"We should rest," Illia said as she stood. "We have a lot to do tomorrow."

Everyone else stood and complied, their moods infinitely better. Illia was right, though. I returned to dwelling on my problems. I doubted I would find much sleep at all.

Chapter 9

God-Arcanists Of Regal Heights

When dawn arrived, we continued toward Regal Heights even through the downpour. We traveled for days, stopping only to relieve ourselves and get a little rest. The constant travel gave me little to do but wrestle with my thoughts.

It seemed as though the god-creatures were appearing much faster than I had been told. Why? Had they been born years ago and just been waiting in their lairs? The arcane plague had been around for a while.

Perhaps that was it.

No matter the reason, I would need to speak with Zaxis. As the fenris wolf god-arcanist, he would be my greatest ally.

But there were two others in Regal Heights that I would *also* need to discuss things with. First was Calisto. Well, *Lynus*. He was bonded with the typhon beast—a powerful monster capable of great devastation. Lynus had agreed to help us defeat the Second Ascension, but that didn't mean I trusted him.

We would need to come to an understanding. *I* was in charge. *He* wouldn't act without my permission. I would accept nothing less. Lynus had been a dread pirate, after all. He couldn't be allowed to operate at his own discretion. Ever.

The other person I would need to speak with was Orwyn. If she was still in Regal Heights.

I suspected Atty had finished healing the assassin, Akiva, which would mean there was no reason for Orwyn to stay in town. But she was the sky titan arcanist, which meant one way or another, she would be involved in this grand conflict. What if I could convince her to use her magic to help us? She hadn't been willing the last time we had spoken.

And just like Lynus, I didn't trust her judgment. Orwyn had worked with the Autarch, after all. Her decision making was poor at best.

She would either answer to my commands or...

"Warlord?"

My eldrin's telepathic voice brought me back to the present. "Yes?"

"We have arrived."

The afternoon light shone across Hydra's Gorge, the massive canyon where Regal Heights was built. The vast crack in the earth stretched on for miles, some points narrow, others wide. The bridges that crisscrossed back and forth from one side to the other were a pleasant sight. The citizens of the city were busy going about their daily activities.

Which meant no one was hurt or panicking.

They were still rebuilding from the typhon beast's rampage, but they weren't *actively* in danger. That meant Orwyn hadn't attacked while I was away. If she was still around, I'd be able to speak to her a bit more.

Terrakona slowed just outside the gates of the major city. He turned his attention to a grove of trees not far outside Regal Heights.

It was a strange grove. The trees were set in a perfect circle, and the vegetation was a brilliant shade of emerald, whereas the other trees in the area were orange, red, and dried out from the heat. Not much grass grew around Regal Heights, but the patch of grass in the grove was lush and bright, unlike anything I had seen before.

"Are you worried about your dryads?" I whispered as I patted Terrakona's head.

The gargantuan world serpent flickered out his tongue and then exhaled. **"I worried someone would harass the dryads while I was away."**

"You can check on them." I motioned to the ground. "Just let everyone off here. Then go see them."

Terrakona lowered his head, allowing me, Illia, and Nicholin to get off without much effort. My eldrin kept his gaze on the mystical grove. It was his pride and joy. He had created it after we arrived in Regal Heights—as a place to keep all the dryads that had been appearing in the nearby area.

No one knew why the dryads were here. They had never formed in these parts before. Which was why Terrakona wanted to protect them.

And it was likely that his presence caused them to form in the first place. Terrakona—and the dryads—seemed to believe more magic was being seeded into the world, and that was causing new mystical creatures to appear.

It made me wonder...

How many more would show up? And if dryads formed around Terrakona, what kind of creatures would form around the typhon beast and fenris wolf?

Or the sky titan?

Hexa slid off Terrakona's back, and then helped Vethica get down. Her hydra, Raisen, confidently leapt off, slamming to the ground with a solid *stomp*. Raisen's many heads bickered as the creature lumbered around Hexa.

Zelfree dismounted Terrakona next. He waited for Liet, offering his hand to help her, but she said nothing. She got off Terrakona, her gaze distant.

Liet hadn't spoken much during the trek, and she shivered as though cold. I said nothing, because I didn't want to draw attention to it. Even her hair, once silver, had faded to a sickly white. But perhaps I was seeing things.

I *hoped* I was seeing things.

"Volke?"

I flinched and turned to Illia. She stood closer to me than I had been expecting.

"Yeah?" I whispered.

Illia ran a hand through her wavy hair. Then she pursed her lips. "You haven't been sleeping."

"Well, I—"

"You also grind your teeth when you're agitated," Nicholin added. He held up a paw. "Don't deny it. We heard."

Illia stared into my gaze as best she could. "Just remember to rest, okay? I'll help. We'll find a way to get Vethica to New Norra, and then we'll ask Adelgis to help us find where the next god-creature is. We have this under control."

She wanted me to be confident. I appreciated that.

With a reluctant smile, I nodded. "All right. I'll relax and get some rest."

"You better," Nicholin said with a glare.

It sounded more like a threat than I figured he intended. It almost made me laugh. His cute little squeaky voice wasn't suited for intimidation.

Terrakona slithered his whole body around me and Illia. The ground moved and twisted to accommodate his motions. Then it stitched itself back together again. Never quite the same, but good enough.

"Warlord, will you visit the grove once you have a

moment?" Terrakona lowered his snout until it was directly above my head. My black hair fluttered up and down when he inhaled and exhaled. **"I'd like you to see all the dryads when you get a chance. They would benefit from human interaction, I think."**

It seemed like a silly waste of time to play with some dryads when I had so much to do, but I knew that wasn't fair to Terrakona. He seemed extremely attached to his dryads. I needed to be there for him.

"All right," I said.

"Thank you."

"I won't stay too long, though."

"Such is the way of life."

His statement shook me for a moment. What did he mean by that? Before I could ask, Terrakona lifted his head and headed for his grove, his movements controlled and precise. He clearly didn't want to disturb his quaint little creation.

Illia and her rizzel eldrin disappeared in a puff of glitter and a pop of air. She teleported into the city, no doubt to help me with all my tasks. Illia was my steadfast confidant, and I knew she would help in all the best ways possible.

A rumble beneath my feet caused me to tense. I turned my attention to the gorge. At first, I thought hydras were moving in the caves throughout the canyon, but then I realized what had caused the minor quake.

Vjorn, the second fenris wolf, stood in an empty field just beyond Regal Heights. He was near the gorge, but not so close to the edge that I feared he would fall in.

He was massive. His black fur, coated in white rime, gave him the appearance of perpetual winter. When Vjorn lifted his head, and his wolf-ears stood erect, he had all the presence of a vicious hunter.

Chains hung on his body parts, each engraved with runes. I

couldn't read the symbology, but all the god-creatures seemed to have similar markings somewhere on their body. Terrakona had them on his tongue.

Vjorn was a mighty wolf with rippling muscles beneath his dark fur.

Next to him stood the typhon beast.

That surprised me. Vjorn and the typhon beast hadn't been "friends" when I left the town. Now they were standing around in a field together? What for?

Xor, the typhon beast, was a terrifying monster. He had one hundred heads—ninety-nine of them snake-like in appearance. They were a mane of snakes around a singular dragon head. The necks of the creature—even the dragon head—were considerable. And the snakes moved around on their own, each writhing, glancing, and hissing in all directions.

There was no rhyme or reason to it all. It was as if each little head had its own mind.

The typhon beast also had plenty of rune markings. Each snake had a glowing mark on their forehead, each one stranger than the last.

Xor's scales were dark green and black, and shiny enough to catch the light. The beast also had six legs, much like the king basilisks. They were stout and powerful, each muscled enough to be noticeable. Nothing about the typhon beast was sleek or agile—it was a mass of power and destruction.

The beast's tail was longer than the rest of the body and ended in spines, each point deadly sharp.

I had expected the typhon beast to be raging or out of control. Nothing could be further from the truth. Xor stood next to the mighty Vjorn, his dragon head still, even if the ninety-nine snakes were tossing and turning. The beast watched *something* with rapt fascination.

I panned my gaze over the area. Although I couldn't see any details out in the field—it was just too far away—my tremor sense provided me with ample amounts of information. Two people were there. They were fighting. Each step and strike they took was with power and purpose.

It seemed serious.

And I knew who they were, even if I couldn't see them properly.

Zaxis and Lynus.

Were they fighting? Zaxis had a hot temper, and Lynus was a damned pirate who never worked well with authority. Of course they were fighting! Why had I left them alone?

"Terrakona!" I shouted, panic in my voice. "To me!"

There was no hesitation in my eldrin's actions. He snapped his attention away from his peaceful grove and dashed to my side, the terrain twisting to accommodate his passing. He lowered his head, and I grabbed his crystal mane. Then I pointed to the other god-creatures.

We didn't need any more words. Terrakona knew exactly what I wanted.

In a flash, he lunged for the field. We created more rumbling and quaking than Vjorn and Xor—Terrakona was the largest among them, and when he moved quickly, everyone knew about it. Even without their own tremor sense.

We were there in a matter of moments. As soon as Terrakona reached the field, he lowered his head and I leapt off, my sword in my hands.

Sure enough, Zaxis and Lynus were in the middle of the field. Ice coated everything. The grass was dead, blood had been splattered to the dirt, and scorch marks were visible on nearby boulders that jutted from the dirt.

"What's going on?" I demanded, more authority in my voice than I had expected.

Terrakona roared, shaking the houses of Regal Heights and causing the other god-creatures to tense.

Zaxis and Lynus stopped fighting and turned to face me.

Zaxis wore his salamander scale armor—a fine outfit that had been tailored to fit him perfectly. It was a magical item, a trinket, and sleek. While it wouldn't stop the heaviest of attacks, it was immune to all forms of heat.

It matched his blazing red hair.

With a dramatic sweep of his hand, where he removed sweat from his face and then slicked back his fiery locks, Zaxis glared at me. His green eyes were always so expressive—especially when he was angry.

"What do you mean, *what's going on?*" Zaxis barked. He sarcastically motioned to himself, and then Lynus. "What does it look like we're doing?"

Lynus wasn't wearing armor. He wore a pair of ratty trousers—and that was it. His "outfit" probably made him look more intimidating than Zaxis's did, though. Lynus was a large man, and he had enough muscles for three warriors. His copper hair had a metallic sheen, and the stubble on his chin was unkempt, giving him a wild demeanor.

Nothing about Lynus looked civilized. I would sooner expect him to mug me than speak civilly.

But it was easy to see his new god-arcanist mark. Each god-arcanist had one over their heart. The twelve-pointed star was so large it encompassed their shoulder and even their left arm. Lynus's typhon beast, and its many heads, were etched into his flesh, prominent and awe-inspiring.

"You're not... trying to kill each other?" I asked as I lowered my weapon.

Lynus sneered. "If I wanted to kill the lad, I would've done it."

"*Hey*." Zaxis turned all his rage on the man in front of him. "Which one of us *just* bonded with our god-creature, huh? I'm *the Hunter*, the fenris wolf arcanist. If I wanted, I'd—"

"Yeah, yeah," Lynus growled, keeping his attention on me.

"Just tell your world serpent chum we're training so we can get back to doing what we're doing."

Zaxis garbled out some more words, like he was choking back a tirade, but he managed to calm himself just long enough to say, "You heard him. *We're training.*"

"*Just* training?" I asked as I slowly made my way over.

Nothing about Lynus's presence put me at ease. I didn't like the man—not now, not ever. But I did appreciate the fact he crossed his arms and relaxed as I approached. Nothing about him seemed aggressive or ready to fight.

Unlike Zaxis.

"What's wrong now?" Zaxis asked. "Did you not find Vethica? Do we have to go somewhere?" He glowered at me. "You just *took off* to go rescue her without telling me, ya know. I had to pick up the pieces and guard this place. By myself."

I glanced around, my gaze lingering on the city. "Seems you did a good job."

For a short moment, Zaxis didn't have anything to say to that. Finally, he muttered, "Thank you. I did do a pretty good job." His tense stance waned, and he finally took a deep breath. "I just want to go next time you do something heroic, all right? I can help. Vjorn and I are ready."

Lynus huffed out a single laugh, but he said nothing.

"You have something to say, pirate?" Zaxis snapped.

"Of course not." Lynus forced a smile. "You're clearly a grandmaster arcanist. Peerless. Composed. Without weakness."

I couldn't help it. I half-laughed, but I caught myself when Zaxis shot me a glower. With a shrug, I just shook my head. "Okay, seriously, enough of this. If you were training—I'm sorry. I thought you two were trying to kill each other."

"I wish," Lynus muttered.

Zaxis waved away the comment. "No. This lunatic just... He was helping me."

"You bonded before Lynus did," I muttered. "Don't you mean *you* were helping him?"

But Zaxis didn't reply. His gaze fell to his boots, and he grumbled something to himself.

His reaction surprised me a bit, but only for a moment. Lynus had once been a manticore arcanist—and a damn good one. He was one of the few people who had managed to achieve a true form with their eldrin, and he had always seemed *in tune* with his previous eldrin whenever I had seen them.

Lynus just had a talent for magic, that much I was sure of. And he was ruthless—the type of person who would do anything to master their power. Sometimes that was a boon, even if it often made people into villains.

"You already know what you can evoke?" I asked Lynus.

The man had an intense gaze. He held up a hand, his fingers flared. For a short moment, nothing happened, but then he tensed, and a torrent of white-hot flames rushed from his palm. The blaze washed over the nearby area, melting any leftover ice and blackening the dirt. Embers floated on the air, and were then caught by the wind.

Before a wildfire could break out, Zaxis waved his hand. A flurry of ice snuffed out all the embers.

"Fire is your destruction evocation," I muttered. "I think it's the easiest to manifest of the two."

Zaxis sighed. "Lynus already knows his creation evocation, too."

That surprised me. Taken aback, I was a little at a loss for words. When I faced Lynus again, he just huffed.

"I also evoke *hallucinations*," Lynus said.

"Really?" That sounded useful. "I… I'm impressed."

"You shouldn't be, lad. Learning the basics of your magic should be a *day one* experience. It's almost pathetic that it has taken the both of you so long to get your act together."

His condescending attitude probably would've bothered most individuals, but I had long gotten over it. Bonding with Terrakona hadn't just brought me power, it had also brought me a mountain of responsibilities. I had a million things to do, people to protect, and things to accomplish. My mind was pulled in many directions, and I knew that hindered my growth in magic. I had come to terms with it. Now wasn't the time for regret.

"So, you're helping Zaxis with his magic, then?" I asked.

Lynus clicked his tongue. "*Tsk*. I didn't want to, trust me. But here we are."

"Well... thank you."

Zaxis's face grew pink. "I, uh, actually managed to use my creation evocation because of Calisto—I mean, *Lynus's* help. I evoked illusions, all by myself, with no help from Vjorn."

Lynus didn't react to my thanks or to Zaxis's sheepish statement. He just turned away, his expression so neutral I couldn't read it. For some reason, it seemed as though he didn't want to acknowledge anything he had done.

That was fine by me.

Lynus didn't really deserve any praise. Not after the atrocities he had commited.

"So, now that you're back, what're we going to do about the sky titan arcanist?" Zaxis crossed his arms. "I mean, Atty healed her little friend, and they've been waiting for you to return ever since."

"They *waited* for me?" I asked, pointing to myself.

Zaxis nodded once. "Yeah. She said she wanted to speak to the Warlord. She wouldn't talk to me—I'm not important enough, apparently." He couldn't hide any of the bitterness in his words.

This was my chance. I needed to speak with her, that way I could convince her to help us in our quest to dismantle the Second Ascension.

"You should come with me," I said to Zaxis. Then I turned to Lynus. "And I'd appreciate it if you came with us as well."

Lynus just huffed in response. He never even glanced over—he just stared out at the horizon. Again, that was fine. We didn't need to make small talk. He just needed to follow orders.

"I'm ready," Zaxis said, rotating his shoulders. "Let's do this."

Chapter 10

Orwyn The Kirin Arcanist

I motioned to the city of Regal Heights, but before we went anywhere, the ground quaked and rumbled. Xor stepped forward, the mighty beast's colossal weight causing the earth to shake with every step. The monster worried me, only because of the amount of destruction he was capable of in a short amount of time.

"I am... worried," Xor said, his voice echoing down his long throat before reaching the air. His tone remained confused and distant, as though he were perpetually lost in a fog, and asking directions in a non-native language. **"Death awaits you. Stay."**

Lynus turned to face his eldrin. "Death?"

"The king basilisk arcanist... Kill him, before he kills you."

Xor's voice became louder with each word, clearly emboldened by anger. The typhon beast stomped forward, his large head flashing his draconic fangs. When his mane of snake heads screeched, it sounded similar to chittering. It hurt my ears and rattled my thoughts.

"Calm down," Lynus said. He walked to his eldrin, and the

beast stopped his screaming. Then Lynus placed a hand on Xor's foreclaw. "I'm not afraid of death—but even then, you don't need to worry. Akiva doesn't scare me."

The fenris wolf got to his feet and ambled to Zaxis's side. A chill wind rushed by as the large wolf approached. The god-creature was much larger than his arcanist—nearly fifteen feet at the shoulder—and his cunning expression, mixed with his claws and fangs, made for a frightening appearance.

"I agree with Xor," the fenris wolf said, his breath coming out as a fine mist. **"You shouldn't take unnecessary risks."**

Zaxis scoffed and forced a laugh. "You're worried, too? I think you're overreacting. Akiva couldn't handle a single strike of Volke's magic. And besides..." He shrugged as he walked around his wolf eldrin. "We know Akiva's weakness now."

"Which is?"

"The woman—Orwyn—of course." Zaxis smirked as he passed me. "I mean, didn't you see what happened in the fight? Volke was about to drown Orwyn in magma, and Akiva *jumped in the way*. Even if he's a mighty assassin with a gruesome list of kills, we know exactly how to get him."

"That's a little dark," I muttered.

"But it's true."

I turned to Terrakona and nodded. He acknowledged my gesture and then returned to his homemade grove. For whatever reason, Terrakona was much gentler than his appearance led people to believe. I wondered if it was because of our bond—my soul influencing him—or if he was just naturally that way.

Lynus patted the leg of the typhon beast, occasionally murmuring reassuring words.

He, too, was gentler, whenever he thought no one was watching. But I shook away the thought and followed Zaxis.

Vjorn didn't accompany us. He tracked Zaxis with his eyes, and then trotted off toward the distant trees. Most of the vegetation was smaller than the fenris wolf, but a few trees had a canopy that would shade him from the afternoon sun. If I had to guess, Vjorn would rest until night—then he would be active again.

"How did Lynus help you develop your magic?" I asked.

Zaxis rubbed his scaled armor. After a long minute of silence, he replied, "I don't know. He just *gets it*. We talked about how I was upset with Vjorn—and about losing Forsythe—and how it might affect the way I see my new eldrin. It's... hard to describe."

"I see."

"Don't tell Illia," Zaxis quickly added.

Lynus had been the one to cut out my sister's eye. She hadn't forgiven him, but she no longer demanded his death, either. Still, I suspected she didn't want to hear about how Zaxis was becoming friends with the man.

"I won't say anything," I said. I wouldn't hide information from her, though. If Illia asked me directly, I'd give her a direct answer.

When we got closer to the city, I glanced over my shoulder. Lynus headed in our direction, his eldrin patiently waiting in the field. All one hundred heads watched us, their eyes glittering in the sunlight.

I...

Didn't like the typhon beast.

While Xor appeared to be a massive hydra, something about him was too unsettling for me. Like he was plague-ridden and twisted. Or something.

I glanced away and slowed my pace until Lynus joined us.

The man said nothing. He slipped his hands into his pockets as the three of us passed through the southern gate.

His outfit—or lack thereof—gave him the appearance of a homeless man. Well, a homeless warrior with enough muscles to spare. But still. He was a god-arcanist. I doubted anyone would chide him for his lack of etiquette.

Regal Heights had an industrial side and a luxurious side. The industrial side was characterized by the many shops, practical houses, and city guard stations up throughout. The stonework was simple, but skilled, and the roads along the side of the canyon were wide enough for carts. Railings were set up in most places to prevent individuals from falling to their death by accident.

The luxurious side of Regal Heights had tall fortress-like mansions. The wrought iron was shaped to resemble hydras and canyon shrimp, and the windows were large and sometimes colorful.

Zaxis, Lynus, and I walked along the industrial side. The smell of fresh bread and jerky wafted throughout the city. Merchants called out their wares or food, trying to sell to each individual who passed by.

When I walked down the roads, people waved and giggled. A few individuals offered me free food, one even held out a blanket. I politely waved away their gifts, trying to stay focused on the task at hand.

Zaxis took a small loaf of bread. "Thank you, thank you." He ate it far faster than any person should, and coughed down a mouthful of food. Then he patted his chest and dismissively waved to the citizens offering me wine and water. "I'm fine," he managed to rasp.

A woman with a giant basket of apples approached Lynus. She held out the fruit and smiled wide. "Thank you so much for saving the city from the typhon beast! Please, take one."

Lynus said nothing.

He walked by the woman without even acknowledging her existence.

The woman's smile slowly faded as Lynus continued forward. He didn't glance back or hesitate—he just kept going, as though nothing had happened. When the woman turned to me, I shrugged.

"I apologize. He's new to being a god-arcanist, and just nervous."

The slight joke had her smiling again. A few others nearby also joined in, some talking about the day Lynus had bonded with Xor.

The citizens of Regal Heights told the tale as though it were an epic to rival all tales. They all claimed that Xor was out of control, and that he had slammed his way into the city and would only stop his destruction once Lynus arrived.

That wasn't really how it had happened, but I didn't correct anyone. It was a fine tale, and I'd rather people think Lynus was a hero, even if he wasn't.

Zaxis pointed to a bridge, and we crossed.

The metal bridge was covered in the fur of canyon rabbits, which made the walk quite enjoyable. Fog swirled in the canyon beneath us. Heights didn't bother me, but there was nothing to see down there, so I didn't bother looking over. Once on the other side of Hydra's Gorge, Zaxis pointed us to the building where Orwyn and Akiva had been staying.

"She never really left," Zaxis said, obviously awkward about the fact. "I mean, I thought she would leave the moment you were gone, but she didn't."

With a frown, I walked to the door of the giant home. The door was made of thick wood and iron—sturdy enough to withstand a ballista bolt. "Has her sky titan stayed near the city as well?" I announced my presence using the home's large brass knocker.

"I don't know," Zaxis muttered. "The sky titan is invisible, but I kept trying to feel the winds around here..."

"You didn't sense it?"

He shrugged. "I don't know what I'm looking for. Vjorn seems to think it's close, though."

"It's definitely close." Lynus narrowed his eyes as he glanced toward the sky.

The sky titan was a creature almost entirely made of air. It was a difficult beast to fight against, as it was both impossible to see and basically immune to physical weapons. How did you defeat a breeze? Or in this case, a hurricane? There wasn't much someone *could* do.

The door to the home opened. A tall man had answered—someone who worked for the city, given his black robes and proper posture. I suspected he had been sent to watch over Orwyn and report if she left.

Without a word, the man motioned to the large waiting room just off the foyer. "This way." He led all three of us straight to the colossal couches positioned near the fireplace. The stone floors were covered in lush red rugs, and the curtains were closed on all the windows. The home had all the welcoming presence of a cave.

Then the man left.

Lynus walked over to the fireplace. A small flame burned on a couple logs. He stared at the embers, never bothering to remove his hands from his pockets.

Zaxis took a seat on the nearest couch. "I'm so hungry. All the time. I don't understand why."

"You use a lot of your magic needlessly," Lynus growled. He glared at the burning wood in the fireplace. "Whenever you do *anything*—create ice, illusions—you put all your effort into it."

"That's a good thing, right? I don't hold back."

"Heh. Would you congratulate the butcher if he cleaved an animal in half with every slice? Or an artist if they threw *all* their paints on the canvas at once?" Lynus shot Zaxis a cold glare. "You need some control. It's the one skill you're actively lacking."

Zaxis stood from the couch. "Don't talk like you know me." He spoke much louder than necessary.

I stepped between them. "The two of you, repeat after me: *I'm an adult, and I like acting like one.*"

"Oh, *ha ha*." Zaxis sardonically rolled his eyes. Thankfully, though, he sat back down on the couch. "And don't lump me in with *him*. I'm fine. I'm in control. You'll see."

"Am I interrupting something?"

The whispered question almost escaped without being heard. I turned and found myself facing Orwyn Tellia.

She was beautiful in a mystical sort of way. For some reason, Orwyn had a stare that seemed to see past the physical—like she saw the world differently than everyone else. She was short—at least a foot smaller than me—and as thin as a willow branch. Her short strawberry blonde hair fell to her chin, framing her heart-shaped face in a pleasing way.

Orwyn's green eyes were paler than Zaxis's—everything about her was paler than Zaxis—but they were still striking.

"Hello," I said, failing to think of another way to start the conversation. "Zaxis told me that you wanted to speak?"

Orwyn brushed back a few locks of her fine hair. She tucked them behind an ear and half-smiled. "Yes. I did." She glanced over to Lynus. "I... wanted to speak to you alone. Away from the others."

She wore white robes, with the front open to expose some of her body. Cloth wrappings kept Orwyn decent, covering most of her chest, but it didn't hide her god-arcanist mark. The gigantic twelve-pointed star, and the depiction of her eldrin, started over her heart and went to her shoulder and arm, just like Lynus's, Zaxis's, and mine.

The sky titan marking...

The picture etched into her flesh made it look like the sky titan was a two-headed bird with four wings, but everything about it was abstract. Its extremities half-floated away from its body, like a toy with its limbs held to the torso with string.

And since it was invisible to the naked eye, I could neither confirm nor deny what it *really* looked like.

"Be cautious, lad," Lynus growled, his eyes set on the fire. "Her assassin is skulking around here, I guarantee it."

My tremor sense alerted me to everyone moving around the fortress-style mansion. Zaxis, Lynus, the house workers, the man who had opened the door, Orwyn—I felt every footfall and heartbeat. Although there were hundreds of little movements, I didn't have problems following them in my mind's eye, but I did need to focus to find specific individuals.

Like Akiva.

Lynus was correct—the assassin was just around the corner, outside the room. How did I know it was him?

He was so... still. Even his heartbeat was quieter than the others, like the man was imitating a shadow. If I didn't have my tremor sense, I doubted I would've ever known he was nearby.

There was also something else in the mansion that caught my attention. A four-legged creature trotted around a bedroom. A horse? No. It was too delicate. It had to be Orwyn's kirin. They were horse-like in appearance, and rather elegant and sleek.

"You want to speak to me alone?" I asked as Orwyn ambled over to me.

She nodded once, her big eyes practically circles. "Just for a moment."

Zaxis scoffed. "Whatever you need to say, you can do it in front of us." He motioned to himself and—hesitantly—over to Lynus.

But I ignored him. There was something I wanted to ask Orwyn, and I wanted to do so in private. Her request to speak aligned nicely with my own desires.

"If you need to say something to me in private, that's fine, but there's something we should discuss as a group afterward." I pointed to the far door. "There's a greenhouse over this way. We can talk uninterrupted there."

"Seriously?" Zaxis stood from the couch. "You're just going to do whatever she wants?"

"I was hoping you and Lynus could speak to Akiva," I said, turning to him.

"Why?"

"Because Lynus has worked with him, and you aren't easily intimidated. You're the perfect duo."

That mild compliment seemed to turn Zaxis's opinion about the whole thing around. Once again, he relaxed, and then offered me a smile. "Fine. But don't take too long. If you're gone more than ten minutes, I'm going to assume she did something and I'll cover this whole city in winter."

With a chuckle, I nodded. "Fair enough."

Chapter 11

The Autarch's Plan

The greenhouses in Regal Heights weren't the most impressive I had ever seen, but it was the were most exotic. Small trees with giant fern-like leaves grew in wide pots. Fruit with spines hung from bushes that grew near the gargantuan windows. Vines crept up the walls, snaking around metal posts and pillars.

I couldn't identify most of the vegetation in the room.

Orwyn didn't seem interested in any of it.

The two of us walked into the greenhouse, the heat washing over us like a warm fog. Three of the four walls were windows, along with the ceiling. This mansion was perched higher up on the canyon, which allowed for a pleasant view of the metal bridges across Hydra's Gorge.

I stopped near the far window, my gaze on a few citizens as they went about their day.

So peaceful, even though there had been fighting all throughout here mere weeks ago.

"You wanted to speak with me?" I asked, never looking away from the sights of the city.

Orwyn stepped to my side, her movements gentle and

practically silent. She fidgeted with her short hair, tugging on the ends.

"I think you should reconsider serving the Autarch," Orwyn whispered.

I shot her a glare. "Is *that* why you wanted the privacy? I already told you that I won't serve him. Not now, not ever."

"He's very powerful, and—"

"He's *insane*," I interjected. "And he started the arcane plague. I just... I can't forgive him for that."

Orwyn turned to me, her pale green eyes alight with curiosity. "Why?"

"*Why?*" I balked. Was she serious? I almost laughed. "Where do I begin? His plague infected Gregory Ruma—my ideal as a child. It twisted innocent griffins living peaceful lives on nearby islands. *I* was affected by the plague, *and* it took Forsythe from Zaxis." With a dark laugh, I concluded, "And that's just a few reasons off the top of my head. If you gave me a pen and paper, I could write you a whole tome on why the man should never be forgiven for this *one* heinous act."

"He couldn't begin the turning of an age without it," Orwyn stated, no emotion in her tone. "Helvetti told us his plans. He needed a catalyst. Something to make the world's magic grow."

I stared into her eyes, wondering if she even knew what she was saying. Her expression was so neutral and blank—I had no idea what she was thinking.

"I don't care what his intentions were," I stated. "His wanton disregard for life is enough to know I would never trust him."

"But the gold kirin trusted him." Orwyn had said that more enthusiastically than anything else. She stepped closer to me, and her eyebrows slowly knitted. "You don't understand. Gold kirin are rare. *Beyond rare*. When they arrive, they're destined to bond with the greatest people. *Only the greatest.*"

Her excitement over this one fact barely fazed me.

"I don't care." I stepped away from her, tense and frustrated. "He could be bonded with a hundred of the rarest of all mystical creatures, and it wouldn't change what he's done."

"I'm trying to tell you that... Helvetti will win if you fight him." Orwyn looked away. She placed a hand on the nearest window and sighed. "He has the most powerful of magic on his side. And if he's bonded with more than one god-creature, you won't have the might to best him."

Orwyn had another arcanist mark—one on her forehead, just like normal arcanists. She touched the seven-pointed star, her fingers grazing the outline of the kirin.

It was true—kirin arcanists could bond with another creature. And according to everything I knew, the kirin's magic empowered the other creature. That was all it did. Kirins didn't have much magic themselves. They acted as an amplifier that empowered others.

So, if the Autarch's gold kirin was the most powerful of all kirin, his god-creatures would be far greater than anything we had faced before.

But I still didn't care.

I glared at Orwyn, knowing in my heart that she might return to the Autarch and fight against us. If that happened...

"Tell me," I said, trying to pick my words carefully. "Do you follow the Autarch because you believe he's the right man for the job? Or because you're afraid of him?"

The question seemed to startle Orwyn. She hesitated, her eyes searching the distant horizon as though she might find the answer. When she finally turned to me, it was with a puzzled expression. "In my village, I was taught that kirins only bonded with great people. Not good people. Not bad people. Just... great people who were meant to rule."

I waited, my heartrate increasing.

If she said she'd always serve the Autarch—and the Second

Ascension—I would have to kill her before she left Regal Heights. I didn't want that, but I couldn't allow her to add her strength to our enemy.

What arguments could I make to change her mind? A great leader would find the right words.

Wouldn't they?

"I suppose I'm afraid," Orwyn whispered. She removed her hand from the window and faced me. "Because what if everything I was taught is wrong? What if you defeat him? What if Helvetti *wasn't* meant to rule, and my place by his side was incorrect from the beginning?"

"You're not afraid of him killing you?" I asked.

Orwyn shook her head. "No. I... don't usually think much of myself. I'm more afraid for other people." She placed her hand over her god-arcanist mark. "All my life, I was told I would have great power. That's what my kirin says—what she whispers to me. I've had a lifetime to think about what I would use it for."

"What did you decide?"

"I'd use it to make the world better." She met my gaze with such confidence and earnest enthusiasm, I knew she wasn't lying. Something about her demeanor—the way she spoke. "That's what I wanted. Helvetti said he would make that happen. He would seed the world with more magic than ever before."

I said nothing.

"The Autarch has a glorious plan. He will become the most powerful god-arcanist, and then use his magic to improve everything."

"Except for those infected with the plague," I quipped.

Orwyn shook her head. "No. He said they would get cured once he developed his salvation aura. Helvetti thought of that, too. He thought of everything. Even the death of the apoch dragon."

I almost wanted to admire the man's ambition.

Almost.

"You already told me this," I said. "This whole conversation is nothing new. Why rehash it? What made you even *think* that I would change my mind?"

Orwyn hesitantly took in a breath. Then she clasped her fingers and gripped so hard, her knuckles turned white. "I thought I would best you in a fight. With my kirin magic, my god-creature should've been more powerful. But that wasn't the case. You and the fenris wolf arcanist won. But you didn't kill me."

"No," I said with a sigh. "Because if we're going to fix the arcane plague, we need all the help we can get. I wanted *you* to join *us*."

Orwyn frowned. She never loosened her grip on her own hands. "Me?" she whispered.

"Yes. You're a god-arcanist, just like us, and your magic is more powerful than anything else I've ever seen."

"If we fight against the Autarch, we'll die."

"You thought you would defeat me, didn't you?"

She nodded.

With a half-smile that made me feel like Zaxis, I confidently said, "Then you're clearly terrible at judging who will win in a fight."

Although I thought I came across as arrogant and rude, Orwyn finally relaxed her fingers. She turned her pale green eyes to my chest, examining my god-arcanist mark. "Hm. I suppose that *is* logical. Most of my training wasn't in the art of death."

She had taken that much better than I had thought she would.

"But even if we can defeat the Autarch, it won't come easy. It won't come without a price."

"I know." I had known for a while. But any price was better than letting that tyrant have his way with the world.

Orwyn wrung her hands. "I'm not concerned about whether

I live or die, but I am concerned about... about the people under my care."

"Akiva?"

"Yes." She glanced down at the greenhouse floor. "And the Keeper of Corpses arcanist. They are both my retainers. They're important to me."

While I knew Akiva—the assassin who had disrupted the whole Argo Empire—I didn't know much about the *Keeper of Corpses arcanist*. We had fought him when we fought Orwyn, and she had pulled him from the battlefield before he could be killed, but I knew nothing about him as a person.

"Who is he?" I asked. "The one who bonded with the Keeper of Corpses."

"Ezril Rivers," Orwyn replied, her voice singsong.

But she didn't elaborate.

I stared at her for a long moment, hoping she would enlighten me, but all she did was move her attention around to the plants in the room. For some reason, Orwyn seemed to dislike focusing on one thing for too long.

I forced a cough and then asked, "Why do you care about them more than your own life? That seems... odd. Even if you want to be selfless, you shouldn't disregard your feelings."

Orwyn shook her head. "I apologize. I just never feel the same way about myself as I do with others. As a child, my mother thought I was touched in the head. Once I bonded to a kirin, she never mentioned it again, but I knew she thought of me as strange. I'm just... I find it hard to think of my wellbeing."

While I didn't understand her situation, I understood it caused her some concern. She wanted to protect Akiva and Ezril Rivers, whoever he was.

"If you help us against the Autarch, I can probably have Akiva's and Ezril's previous crimes forgiven."

I wasn't *certain* I could, but the Argo Empire had technically sworn to me. The new queen answered to my summons, as did many other nations. If I wanted to forgive someone for a war crime, I probably could—but the more I did it, the less respect I'd have when interacting with powerful arcanists.

If everyone thought I was corrupt or abusing my position of power, how would I be any different than the Autarch? It was important to maintain my word and my reputation.

But we needed Orwyn's might. If guaranteeing her retainers' safety was the price, I was willing to pay it.

"Will you protect them?" Orwyn asked, her voice strained. She furrowed her brow.

"They're *your* retainers. Why would I need to protect them?"

"In case I fell in battle. You would... protect them in my stead?"

Her concern for them went far beyond what I had originally envisioned. I crossed my arms and dwelled on her request. Would I want to protect Akiva the Assassin? It sounded silly, even in my head.

But if that was what it would cost...

"If I agree to protect them, will you help us?" I asked.

The warm afternoon sun sparkled through the many windows, illuminating the beautiful greenhouse. Orwyn had the appearance of a flower when she turned to me. Strawberry blonde hair, green eyes—gentleness in her demeanor.

"I'm afraid I'm making a terrible mistake," she whispered. "Helvetti is a gold kirin arcanist, and you aren't. My home village would be aghast if they found out..." Orwyn tepidly smiled. "But the Autarch will not forgive my failings, and I fear he'll kill Akiva if we return without having done what we were supposed to. I can't... I can't live with that."

"So you'll help us?"

"Yes, Warlord. I will."

I rubbed at the back of my neck. "What did the Autarch want you to do, specifically? Just kill me?"

"He wanted several things, including acquiring your runestones." Orwyn tilted her head to the side. "But the worst was the spread of his arcane plague. He wanted you to become infected."

"I'm immune," I stated. "All god-arcanists are. I thought he knew that?"

"Oh." Orwyn narrowed her eyes in concern. "I thought you went to Deadman's Bluff? Surely you saw... Theasin Venrover's son used his abyssal leech magic to alter the arcane plague. The vile disease will now infect those with god-creatures—and even those who are true form."

Chapter 12

The Abyssal Leech's Purpose

"What?" I asked, my breath trapped in my lungs. I couldn't breathe. There was no way that was possible. No way.

Absolutely no way.

"Theasin Venrover desperately wanted a way to manipulate magic and bend it to his whims," Orwyn replied, her tone just as emotionless as it had been. "There aren't many mystical creatures with that ability. None as powerful as the *abyssal leech*, a creature once thought extinct."

"Adelgis—Theasin's son—had the abyssal leech in his body."

I remembered the day it had been extracted. Adelgis had almost died. His father had been *so* obsessed with obtaining the creature, he hadn't cared who he harmed to get it. And it harmed Adelgis. His magic worked in bizarre ways, sometimes out of his control. The abyssal leech *was* powerful.

Orwyn shifted her weight from one foot to the other. With an unfocused gaze, she muttered, "I think Theasin envied kirin arcanists. When Helvetti spoke about his gold kirin's ability to empower his other eldrin, Theasin would remind him that whoever controlled magic would be the true victor in any conflict. Theasin was a saint to my people, but upon reflection, I think his words were steeped in jealousy."

"I don't doubt it."

"His mind worked in long-term plans."

Oh, I knew all about Theasin's unrivaled ability to plan elaborate schemes. It didn't surprise me at all that his disgusting fingers were still pulling the strings of our enemies, even from the grave. His ambitions had such a life of their own, they continued without him.

But if Theasin *had* created a version of the arcane plague that affected anyone and everyone, that meant...

I turned on my heel, my thoughts narrowing into a single concern.

"Thank you," I murmured, purely out of politeness as I headed for the door.

Orwyn said something, but I didn't hear any of it.

All I could think about was Liet. She had been hurt at Deadman's Bluff. She never really recovered, even though arcanists healed remarkably well. And she hadn't been herself, even though she tried to hide that fact.

Now I knew why.

In my panic, I scoured all of Regal Heights searching for Liet Eventide without really telling anyone else where I was or what I was doing. I hadn't even bothered to speak to Zaxis or Lynus before leaving. I hoped they would forgive me, but this was too important to ignore for even a second.

I found Liet in one of the city's many inns. The sign outside said it was the *Rocky Shrimp*, a place to eat and find a bed. It was built into the canyon face, with balconies that overlooked the gorge. Perhaps if I hadn't been so anxious, I would've appreciated the aesthetics, but as it stood, I barely saw anything as I made my way inside.

"Oh, Warlord!" someone gasped as I passed them.

I didn't reply.

The interior of the *Rocky Shrimp* was neatly circular. There was a chimney in the center of the room, with tables all around, to take advantage of the heat. The place wasn't busy. There were four patrons, at the most.

Two of which were Liet and the minister of Regal Heights, Vinder Akiona.

They were the only two arcanists in the room with glowing marks. The slight illumination from their seven-pointed stars was an indication that they had achieved a true form with their eldrin. It granted them powerful magics, and allowed their eldrin to transcend—and it should've granted them immunity to magical corruption.

Not anymore.

A bartender called out to me as I made my way over to Liet's table. I didn't really hear their words, and I didn't care.

When I reached their table, Vinder was the first to turn to me.

He was a gargoyle arcanist. The picture of a winged beast was wrapped around the star in his mark. And strangely, just like Liet—and unlike almost every other arcanist—the man had gray hair. He appeared older, though not decrepit.

His hair was thinning, but his beard was thriving. Vinder tugged on it as he narrowed his eyes and gave me the once over.

"Warlord? You're pale. Is there trouble afoot?"

"Liet," I whispered, ignoring the man. "I need to speak with you right away."

When she turned to me, our eyes met, and I saw dread there. Somehow, she, too, knew something was terribly wrong. But like always, her smile hid any fear or doubt Liet actually had. She glanced over at Vinder.

"I'm sorry, old friend. I'll have to catch you up on everything later."

Vinder lifted an eyebrow. For some reason, the man was dressed in fine clothing. A nice black tunic—open down his chest, as though he were proud of the hair there, too—held in place with a leather belt that had clearly never been worn before today. His trousers were crisp, and his boots shiny.

"You said once you got back, we'd have the whole day," Vinder grumbled.

He didn't seem to sense her fear. I decided not to say anything—Liet would know how to handle the man. They were good friends, after all.

"It'll just be a moment." Liet stood from the table, her posture straight, her demeanor cheery. "Now, let me show you the room they gave me, Volke. I'm sure you'll appreciate the decorations."

She motioned me to a door near the back of the circular room. I nodded, and then followed her away from the warm fire. The door led to a hallway, and then to a set of stairs that brought us to all the cliffside rooms.

Liet led me into her room—a spacious sleeping area with a balcony large enough for ten people. It was a beautiful sight, especially on such a nice day.

I barely gave it a glance.

Once the door was shut, I faced her. "You're infected with the arcane plague."

I didn't have any way to soften the information. She just needed to hear it. Liet would know what to do. She was the leader of the Frith Guild, after all. She always had a plan, a method, a way to move forward.

"You're certain?" Liet asked, far calmer than I had thought she would be.

"Theasin used the abyssal leech he grew in Adelgis to alter

the plague so it could infect people with true form magic. And god-arcanists."

Liet's eyes darkened as she turned her attention to the stone floor. Despite the dreadful news, she maintained her breathing and her heart rate. Panic didn't overtake her. It seemed to give her clarity. A trait I wished I shared.

"I see," Liet whispered.

A few minutes passed between us in silence. I didn't have an answer for this, but I knew Liet would find one.

"Then it seems I should remove myself from the city," Liet eventually stated. When she glanced back up at me, it was with a weary smile. "I was considering heading to New Norra anyway. Now I have a real reason."

"The khepera can't reverse the plague if too much time has passed." I knew all the limitations. I had once been infected, after all. Achieving true form with Luthair had saved me, but that option wasn't available to Liet.

"Perhaps," Liet said, her voice growing a bit bolder. "But there are other avenues for me. Obviously, I have yet to go insane… Though, something is off. I feel it in my bones. This version of the plague might be far worse than before. It will probably take me faster than it took others in the past."

Hearing her say that drove a spike through my chest. I couldn't speak.

But Liet must've sensed it. She offered me a reassuring smile —always bright, even when things seemed so dark.

"You needn't fret! If the khepera can't help me, there are other ways to handle the situation."

"Like what?" I managed to choke out.

What did we have? There had been no cure for the plague before the khepera, and if that didn't work…

"You," Liet said, no doubt in her voice. "You and the other god-arcanists are going to solve the problem, aren't you?"

"W-Well, yes, but that requires us to develop our auras, and that can take time, and what if we can't—"

"You'll find a way," Liet interjected, cutting me short. "Perhaps I don't have much time, but there are ways around that. The khepera can't cure me, but they can delay my fall. Or perhaps I can find a skilled relickeeper arcanist. They have magics that can put people into a stasis."

I held my breath. That was true. Theasin had once used his relickeeper magic to hold me hostage. Would that work? Would it keep Liet from becoming twisted by the arcane plague?

I ran an unsteady hand down my face, trying not to think about Gentel. What if the atlas turtle became a monster? What if she destroyed the Frith Guild?

What if I had to be the one to fight her?

The thought hurt worse than most injuries I had experienced.

Liet placed a gentle hand on my shoulder, pulling me from my quicksand of negative thoughts. She kept her distance, her arm fully stretched out, as though she didn't want to even risk infecting me, not even with a stray breath.

"I will find a way to delay this," Liet stated. "Because I know you will eventually solve the problem."

"So you're just going to New Norra? What about everyone here and—"

"You're the one in charge, Volke. You have been for a while. You've been doing a good job."

My throat tightened. "But..."

"You don't need my guidance." She chuckled to herself. "It's not like I can give you any. You're a god-arcanist. You're walking a path few have traveled. Everyone is counting on you. *I'm* counting on you."

The weight of her words stuck with me. She wasn't afraid I would fail. It was the opposite. Liet was certain I would succeed. That was why she was willing to go to New Norra and delay the corruption of the plague. That wasn't a solution—it was just her knowing in her heart of hearts that I would eventually solve everything.

I was amazed by her confidence, but at the same time, it was an honor.

Liet Eventide, a legendary arcanist, was depending on me. She trusted me with her life—with her eldrin's life—with her guild. No title or celebration could equal such a recognition.

"I won't let you down," I said.

Liet stepped away. Then she brushed back her gray bangs. "Tomorrow morning, an airship will arrive in Regal Heights. I will board it, along with Vethica and Hexa, and a few others, and we'll head to the Amber Dunes—to the city of New Norra."

I nodded once.

"After that, everything will be up to you, Volke."

"I understand." I formally bowed my head. "May the good winds keep you safe."

CHAPTER 13

YEVIN VENROVER

There were a lot of pressing issues on my plate.

I hadn't forgotten about them, but sometimes they didn't come to my mind when I was busy dealing with an emergency, like with Vethica and Liet and Luthair.

Technically, we still had Rhys in our custody. He was the right-hand man to the Autarch, and a strange individual with magics I didn't understand. I had defeated him when I fought Orwyn, and we had him trapped in nullstone. Soon, I would question him, but I needed to rest first.

It was difficult to sleep, though.

Night had descended over Regal Heights, and I never managed to return to my temporary home. The people of Regal Heights had given me a beautiful fortress-style mansion, but I was too filled with anxious energy to head there.

Instead, I went to Terrakona's grove.

My massive eldrin had wrapped his serpentine body around the perimeter of the trees, protecting them from the chill winds. I sat with my back against a trunk, one leg out, the other up. A small dryad clung to my knee. She was child-like—human in shape, but nothing else. Her green skin had the waxy sheen of milkweed, and she kept herself wrapped in an outfit of leaves and vines.

The dryads that Terrakona protected didn't have normal eyes. They had open flowers where eyes would normally be. The pink petals were beautiful, if a bit disturbing. The dryads had vines for hair, which swished back and forth whenever they moved. The sounds they made reminded me of crinkling leaves.

I patted the dryad's head.

She giggled and continued to cling to my leg as though something exciting would happen at any moment.

Terrakona hadn't allowed anyone in Regal Heights to take any of the dryads' Trials of Worth. When I had asked, he had said he was afraid of being left alone. Yet when I glanced around the grove, I counted a grand total of twenty-five little child-like dryads.

That was an excessive amount.

And when I had asked them where they had come from, none of them had a suitable answer. They had all just *spawned* in the nearby area, clawing their way out of the dirt like people born from seeds.

It was Terrakona's presence that caused them to form. That much I was now certain of.

God-creatures were magical unlike any other creature. They didn't need to eat—magic sustained their lives. And they created magic whenever they went. The more god-creatures came into the world, the more they would alter it.

I wondered...

Could the world have *too* much magic? Normally mystical creatures were rare. What if they one day outnumbered human beings?

The thought captured my imagination.

"If the world had too much water, everyone would drown," Terrakona telepathically said.

"You think it's a problem, then? Your magic?" I hated the idea that his presence was somehow harmful to the world.

"Magic—just like water—brings all forms of life. Too little, and you dehydrate. Too much, and you sink beneath the waves. As it is with all things."

"*Moderation*," I whispered. "*Without it, our vices destroy all else*." With a smile, I glanced up at Terrakona's body. "That's the thirty-fourth step of the Pillar."

"It is a wise Pillar."

The shadows in the grove shifted. The dryads gasped and scurried away. Most plunged into the dirt, practically melting into the earth. Some hid behind trees, their flower eyes shaking.

From the darkness rose a person. While the sight might scare others, I knew the properties of knightmare magic well.

And I knew Evianna.

The moment she lifted from the shadows, her white hair glittered in the moonlight. She wore black leather armor tailored for her and her alone, her sleek elegance a welcome sight. She kept her hair tied back, so the long locks wouldn't get in her eyes. She looked beautiful no matter what she did, but the style suited her more than others.

At least, in my humble opinion.

"Volke?" she said once she was fully out of the darkness. Evianna strode over to me, her bluish-purple eyes unlike anyone else I knew. "Here you are. Is everything okay?"

Evianna stood next to me, her brow furrowed.

I hadn't spoken with her since I returned to Regal Heights. Guilt flooded me.

"I'm sorry," I immediately said. "I've just been... busy. And that's not an excuse, just an explanation. I should've let you know what was going on once I returned, but I jumped from one task to the other, barely thinking."

"You're not hurt?"

I glanced up at her, one eyebrow raised. "No. Why?"

Evianna glared as she placed her hands on her hips. Gone was all her concern. "I was worried about you! Everyone said you ran off to Deadman's Bluff to find Luthair and Vethica, and I didn't even hear that from you! Illia told me. And you get back and you say nothing? *I heard rumors that Guildmaster Eventide is sick!* Do you know how much that made me worry about you?"

Her volume increased with every word until she was shouting. The remaining dryads in the grove hurried into the dirt, vanishing from sight, some even crying.

I stood and rubbed at the back of my neck. "Uh... Right. I'm really sorry."

To my surprise, Evianna threw her arms around me. She squeezed so tight, and so suddenly, that I lost some of my breath. She was much shorter than me, and smaller, but she always managed to pack some hidden strength away somewhere in her petite frame.

"Evianna?" I asked.

She held me even tighter, her cheek pressed firmly against my chest. "What's wrong with you?" she angrily whispered. After a short breath, and steadying her voice, she continued. "I was worried."

"Didn't everyone tell you I was okay?" I gently wrapped my arms around her. "I spoke with several of them."

"I shouldn't have to hear it from them." Evianna nuzzled against me, her grip loosening. "And you keep things hidden sometimes, you know? What if you were hiding from me because you didn't want to tell me some horrible truth?"

"That's what you thought I was doing?"

"I. Was. Worried." She gripped my shirt tight. "My mind played tricks on me... All I could think of was the worst scenarios. Like, what if you were slowly dying and you just didn't tell anyone, and you left before anyone could stop you—like when you had the plague?"

I chuckled. "I would've told you if something like that had happened."

Evianna huffed and just refused to let me go. "Well, my mind wouldn't believe anything other than the darkest scenarios." After gritting her teeth in blatant anger, she managed to calmly say, "And look what you're doing. Just sitting out here in the middle of nowhere."

She glowered up at me, her eyes squinted.

Evianna was adorable. I couldn't stop myself from smiling.

That upset her.

She released me with a shove and then crossed her arms. "Don't *laugh*. I was really worried."

"I'm sorry," I said, unable to stop my grinning. "I promise I'll tell you more about my activities in the future."

"Really? You really promise?"

"Yes. You have my word."

"You'll go straight to the abyssal hells if you break it," Evianna said with a hint of finality.

I nodded once. "Deal."

Her irritation vanished in that instant. When she grabbed my hand, it was much gentler than before. Evianna pulled me closer, and I noticed the shadows around her feet moving around us as I stepped close.

"Hexa is really excited that Vethica is back," Evianna stated.

"I figured." I leaned down and kissed Evianna on her forehead, the etchings of her arcanist mark rough on my lips.

"Vethica was telling us what they did to her eldrin." Evianna went still. Her shadow still danced around our feet, but she was as stiff as a statue. "They wanted her to use her magic, so they could test their magical corruption—to see if she could undo it."

"Is she okay?" I whispered.

The darkness of the grove seemed more menacing as I envisioned the fear Vethica had to have been drowning in. Then again, she had always seemed resilient to me. Sturdy and unbreakable, even when shaken.

"Vethica said there was someone there—a young man by the name of Yevin—who was convinced her magic wouldn't work. He made her a deal. He wouldn't kill her or her eldrin if she tested his theory."

"Yevin?" I felt as though I had heard that name before.

"She said her khepera magic *didn't* work." Evianna sighed. "And then they destroyed Akhet, but Yevin gave her Akhet's sand. He said her eldrin wasn't really dead, he just didn't want her using it." Evianna frowned. "Isn't that despicable?"

The name *Yevin* lingered in my thoughts. And it disturbed me to learn that khepera magic couldn't cure this new plague at all. That meant Liet was in real danger. I supposed, perhaps she could prolong her existence with a relickeeper or some other means, but there would be no cure until the others and I developed our auras.

"Was she infected?" I asked.

Evianna shook her head. "Apparently, Yevin was true to his word."

Who was Yevin?

"*My brother,*" Adelgis telepathically said to me, his voice familiar and comforting, but ultimately startling. "*Yevin Venrover was my father's favorite. He did everything my father ever wanted.*"

I glanced around, though it was foolish. Obviously, Adelgis wasn't here. He was somewhere in Regal Heights, far from the grove. His telepathy seemed to reach great distances, though. It was both a boon and a sadness. Had he just been listening to me and Evianna this entire time? What if...

"*I try not to intrude,*" Adelgis said, answering my inner thoughts. "*But please—let's not focus on that. I'm becoming better at controlling everything, and filtering through the noise of everyone's disorganized minds.*"

"Do you know what's going on, Adelgis?" I asked.

Evianna let go of my hand and backed away. Her shadow actually rose from the ground to reveal her eldrin—Layshl. The knightmare was beautiful and sleek, almost as much as Evianna. She was as black as midnight, with an empty cowl and dragon-wing cape. Her scaled leather armor body was hollow, and moved on its own, graceful and silent. When she "looked" at me, it was without a face to display an emotion.

"What's Adelgis saying?" Evianna asked.

Her knightmare stepped close to her.

"He said that Yevin is his brother." Of course he was. The whole Venrover family seemed involved in everything, even if unwittingly, like Adelgis.

"*I didn't want to be,*" Adelgis said, once again answering my thoughts.

"Sorry," I muttered. "I didn't mean it like that."

"*It's fine. I understand. But what I wanted to say was... You should come back to the city. Everyone is gathered here. Vethica told us everything, but despite the torture and abuse, she has a cheerful disposition and wants to celebrate.*"

"Celebrate?" I asked aloud.

Evianna's eyes lit up. "Oh, right. *Yes!* Everyone was looking for you. We want to celebrate Vethica's return. Well, mostly Hexa, but since her whole family is in Regal Heights, they're all happy for her. They're the ones preparing everything."

"That's kind of them."

Evianna crossed her arms and leaned her weight back on one foot. "Is it? I feel like that's what families should be doing. Hexa's lover has been rescued! *Everyone* should be happy."

I didn't reply. Part of me still thought about Luthair. If they had been testing out corrupted magic on Vethica and her eldrin...

Had they used it on Luthair?

"*You shouldn't worry,*" Adelgis said, his telepathic voice

reassuring, even though I couldn't hear it. "*Please, come spend time with the other arcanists. They're looking to you for guidance.*"

Although it was difficult, I pushed away the dark thoughts. Then I walked beyond the trees of the grove and placed a hand on the scaled body of my eldrin. Terrakona's muscles rippled with movement as he uncoiled himself to allow me an easy exit.

"Stay here and protect the dryads, okay?" I asked.

"They will remain protected as long as I am here, Warlord."

He almost sounded happy to do so.

Chapter 14

The Arcanists Of The Frith Guild

Light radiated from every corner of Regal Heights. Torches, glowstones, lamps, and lanterns were scattered around the streets, and some hung from the bridges, giving the canyon an ethereal glow. Most of Regal Heights was constructed without wood. The buildings were stone, the bridges were iron—the only fire risks were the numerous rabbit pelts, and even then, they were minor.

It allowed some of the citizens to be reckless with their flames. A few drunken lads walked up and down the streets with beer mugs in one hand, and blazing torches in the others. I thought it was a terrible idea, but no one stopped them.

The celebrations were too important, apparently.

Evianna and I strode into the city. My shirt remained half-opened, mostly because Evianna said it was proper, but I think most everyone would've recognized me regardless of my god-arcanist mark. Whenever someone cheered for me, I smiled and waved. Unfortunately, a few people thought it necessary to grab me for a hug.

Even a few hydras grabbed me.

It made it difficult to get anywhere in a timely manner.

And there were *so many* hydras. The mystical creatures lived here in the canyon, and the people of Regal Heights kept them safe in their home caves. Hatchling hydras were brought up for the celebrations, their giant eyes and cute scales reminding me of Raisen when I had first met him. He had once been so adorable...

Now Raisen was a massive beast with multiple heads.

Time had a way of changing things.

"Oh, Volke, look at that!" Evianna grabbed my arm and pointed.

Paper hydras were placed over some of the lanterns in town. The colorful paper, which had been dyed with woad plants, changed the lanterns from a bright yellow and orange color to a vibrant purple. The city slowly transformed into an indigo sea of creative paper crafts.

"Isn't it pretty?" Evianna's voice was soaked in wonder.

I shared her enthusiasm. When we walked by a lantern, I gently grazed my fingers over the hydra. The little heads were held on the body with string, and yellow eyes had been painted onto each head. Someone had even drawn the fangs onto the mouths. It must've taken hours—maybe days—to craft them all.

"Thank you, Warlord!" someone shouted. They added a *woo* to the end of their sentence as they stumbled by me.

A man nearly crashed into me. He smiled, his hair wild, his arms covered in scars. An arcanist mark on his forehead told me everything I needed to know about his injuries.

"Warlord," the man said with a hint of surprise as he straightened his posture. He held a mug of beer close. "Oh, it's so great you're here." He hiccupped and tried to swallow it, resulting in an odd noise. Then he narrowed his eyes. "I'm Angus. And, uh, I'm so happy you helped, uh..."

"Hexa?" I asked.

"*Yes.* Hexa. That's the one." He saluted me with his beer, which resulted in half of it sloshing onto the ground. Angus either didn't care, or didn't notice—he just moved around me and continued through the city. "I'll be at the celebration! I have to, uh, get some supplies, though!"

Before I could ask *which* celebration, the man hurried away.

"What was he talking about?" I whispered to Evianna.

"Hexa's family's fortress is hosting the main celebration," she replied matter-of-factly. "They're all there. Probably drunk. I think most people have been drinking since this afternoon."

"That long?"

Evianna shrugged. "I suspect none of them thought it strange."

Regal Heights was... different. That was for certain. I liked it here, just because it seemed the walls between people were more dismantled than in other locations. Nothing was taboo or disgraceful. Well, except for maybe *whining* or *quitting*. But I could understand that, at least.

"The d'Tenni fortress is this way." Evianna guided me through the throngs of people. They parted once they noticed us, but the few who didn't only acted as stumbling obstacles. "Have you ever wondered why her name has that *D* in it?"

"A long time ago, in areas to the south and west, families that founded towns and rest points were given that *D* in front of their last name to denote their status as caretakers or lords." I had learned about it in books I had read, though I couldn't remember which.

"My family name doesn't have that," Evianna muttered.

"It's an old custom. And I think the Argo Empire got rid of it long ago. Probably around the time they dictated that sovereign dragon arcanists were the only ones capable of being rulers."

Evianna wrapped her arms around one of mine. With a tiny smile, she said, "That's one of the reasons I like you so much. You're really fascinated by how things came to be."

I ran a hand through my hair. The celebrations and purple

lights were everywhere, threatening to steal my attention. "I really like tales of people who went from something average to something extraordinary. Legendary arcanists, and great empires… Who *doesn't* find that fascinating?"

She held me tighter, her smile growing. "You'd be surprised."

It didn't take us long to reach the d'Tenni fortress. It wasn't much bigger than the rest, but it did have a few decorations that made it stand out. Most notable were the statues of hydras and gargoyles. Every perch on the roof, and the beginning of every railing or fence, had a stone statue built into it.

The fortress house—which was at least three stories built into the canyon itself—was already packed full of people. Most of them seemed to be citizens of Regal Heights. They had tanned skin, cinnamon and pale brown hair, and several of them had scars that they prominently displayed. Some of them weren't even hydra arcanists. People in Regal Heights just loved to show off their battle injuries or childhood mishaps.

Evianna and I made our way inside. No one stopped us. It was the exact opposite, actually. As soon as people saw who I was, they practically shoved me inside.

The foyer and the front sitting room had been converted into bars. Kegs and rum barrels were stacked against the wall. Tin mugs were passed around, each frothing with alcohol. I declined the drinks, and so did Evianna.

When we reached the main hall, I spotted Hexa with her family. Vethica was with her as well, but Vethica didn't have a boisterous demeanor—not like everyone else. She was easily lost in the crowd.

Except for her bright white dress. It was pristine, and went to her ankles. It flowed like water when she moved. Even I took a moment to admire the craftsmanship. Normally Vethica didn't seem to care what she wore, so long as it was practical, but tonight, she was a stunning beauty.

Even Hexa seemed dressed for a celebration. She wore a long

shirt, and a tight fitted top with no sleeves. Her outfit was black—a nice complement to Vethica. The two looked like they had come up with the outfits together.

"*Volke!*" Hexa waved me over. "C'mon! Join us."

Evianna and I made our way into the small group of relatives. We were handed a wooden board of meat, and someone shouted at me to try it. The conversations grew so loud, it was as though everyone was in a competition to be heard. Their booming voices echoed around the room, bouncing off the stone walls.

Evianna and I ate the meat, but it was difficult to taste.

Music played from somewhere in the fortress. I would've loved to hear it, but it was impossible while I waited in the main hall.

Once we were close to Vethica and Hexa, the couple waved us over to a couple chairs. They were gigantic—but somehow too small to fit two people comfortably. They were an awkward medium, or perhaps sized for someone over three hundred pounds.

Hexa sat down, and then Vethica curled up on a single chair next to her.

When I took a seat, Evianna decided to just sit on my lap, which I hadn't been prepared for. She wrapped her arms around my neck before anyone could see my face heating. No one seemed to pay attention to us, not when the party was about Hexa.

Her family came over, and passed around mugs.

"I bet I can drink more than you!" Hexa shouted to me.

I chuckled as I set my mug on the floor next to the chair. I was thankful no one was paying attention. If they were, they would realize this wasn't my kind of party. Like a duck swimming with fish, I was the odd man out.

"Drinking to excess is tacky," Evianna replied, but her voice was drowned out by all the shouting.

Hexa held a hand to her ear. "What?"

"I said—"

"*What?*"

A few of Hexa's relatives shoved their way over and thanked me. They slapped my shoulder, and a couple playfully whacked the side of my head. They all spoke at once, though, so any semblance of a normal conversation flew right out the window.

I just nodded and dodged whenever they went for my head a second time.

That seemed to work. After a few minutes, where someone sloshed some of their drink onto me, they eventually wandered away to find more to eat.

I wanted to speak with Hexa, but she and Vethica devolved into their own personal conversation. They were their own island in a sea of noise, their conversation kept private by the sheer amount of disturbance all around us.

It was probably best to leave them alone.

Vethica didn't seem as cheery as the rest. And I understood. She had been through a lot—and she wasn't very social. Sitting next to Hexa, she appeared confident, but I suspected she didn't want to interact with anyone else.

Evianna leaned onto me and whispered into my ear, "Can we get some air?"

My face heated again as I nodded. She was so soft and warm. I almost wanted to snuggle with her for the rest of the evening like Hexa was with Vethica.

As the shouting and celebration grew louder and louder, I guided Evianna out of the main hall into a large hallway. Once we shut the door behind us, I could finally hear myself think once again.

I leaned against the metal door and sighed. "Have you ever gone somewhere and immediately regretted the decision to go?"

Evianna held a hand over her mouth and giggled. "You weren't enjoying that?" She held up a small slice of meat she had taken from the room. It was brown and red, with a few markings of white marbling. "Do you even know what this is?"

"No. What is it?"

Evianna popped it into her mouth and slowly chewed. Then she swallowed and shrugged. "I have no idea. But it was flavorful. Like deer, really. But it's definitely not deer."

"Well, there's another ancient custom where wealthy families will snatch children off the streets and serve them to guests," I said.

Evianna reflexively gagged, her expression one of horror.

I just chortled and shook my head. "I'm messing with you."

Her disgust shifted to playful anger. With a huff, she crossed her arms. "You can't do that! You're the honest and truthful one. It's unfair to use that kind of reputation to trick me!"

"The look on your face was priceless, though."

Evianna frowned and pouted at the same time. It was adorable. I wanted to grab her and hug her close, but before I could do any of that, a group of individuals strode down the hallway. I waved to them, and then they nodded and offered thanks. Then they continued on their way.

"This place is huge," Evianna said with a sigh. "The other Frith Guild arcanists should be here, but where do we even start?"

"I can locate them."

She lifted an eyebrow. "Oh? Well, then, lead the way."

My tremor sense was a useful tool, but it was much more difficult to use when there were so many people around. And loud people. They stomped and toppled things over at an alarming rate. I tried to locate people who were in smaller groups, so they would be easier to identify.

Some people had distinct eldrin, after all.

Fain, for instance, always had his wendigo nearby, though Wraith was typically invisible. The wolf-like creature was familiar to me, and I searched the fortress through the tremors, looking for the soft padded steps of the wendigo.

And I found him.

Wraith was in a room not far from us. Two other people were there, and if one of them was Fain, the other had to be Adelgis. And Adelgis's ethereal whelk was made of light. It was one of the few creatures I *couldn't* sense. So, with a half-smile, I led Evianna down the hall and straight to their location.

We reached a large iron door. I knocked, even though it was difficult to do so. When no one answered, I pushed the door open and allowed Evianna in first.

It was a library.

Well, it was a *sad* library.

There were several bookshelves, and a couple desks, but almost everything was empty. A couple tomes were on each shelf, each one collecting dust. I wandered inside, glancing around, wondering why everything was so barren.

Two people were speaking, their voices the only sounds in the whole room.

I spotted Adelgis and Fain. The pair were on a long lounging couch. Wraith wasn't visible, even though I felt his paws every time they touched the stone floors.

"I just don't think it makes sense," Fain growled, already in the middle of a conversation, his attention squarely on Adelgis. "You don't have to go. You don't have to do any of this."

"Yevin is *my* brother," Adelgis said, no anger in his voice. He sat next to Fain on the couch, his hands on his lap, his long black hair tied in a ponytail.

"Volke can handle it."

"I feel responsible. I think Yevin might be bonded to the abyssal leech that grew—"

"*I don't care.*" Fain sat straight. He wore black trousers and a black tunic, but for some reason had a red cap with a circular brim. It reminded me of merchants who wanted to keep the sun out of their eyes. A small white feather was tucked into the leathery folds on the side of the cap, giving it a distinct look.

"I'll be okay," Adelgis said.

Fain threw an arm up in frustration. "You just said it would be dangerous. Leave it to the god-arcanists."

I wanted to interject, but the two seemed too wrapped up in their conversation to interrupt. Adelgis must've known we were here, however. He smiled at Fain, and the other man calmed a little.

"I really appreciate that you're always concerned about my safety," Adelgis whispered. He leaned forward, and Fain's face grew as bright as his red cap. When Adelgis pressed his lips to Fain's, the whole room was quiet.

I was even holding my breath, even though that wasn't a conscious decision. I suspected Evianna was in the same boat.

With a forceful cough, I declared my presence.

Fain whirled around, his face brightening to the shade of a tomato. With an aggressively neutral expression, he stood. "I thought people around here knocked before entering."

"I did that," I said. Then I awkwardly gestured to the door. "Should we go?"

Adelgis also stood. He was thinner than ever, his white robes practically a tent over his body. Despite that, his smile was bright, and his eyes alight with interest. "No. I think you should stay. I can contact everyone else to meet us here. It's one of the quieter places in the fortress."

Still pink in the cheeks, Fain lifted his cap and brushed his dark hair back with his fingers. They were black, almost frostbitten, but I knew they worked just fine. His bizarre digits matched his dark clothing. I wondered if he had made that decision on purpose, to avoid people asking about it.

Evianna glanced around, her eyes narrowing. The shadows moved with each subtle gesture. "So, why did you two come to this room? It's dead. Don't you want to see Hexa?"

"We saw Hexa," Fain said, no more anger in his voice. He was cool and collected as he sat back down on the couch. "She's in the main room with her family. Their celebrations... They remind me of parties we used to have on the *Third Abyss*. Her cousins drink more than pirates."

"I think she wanted to drink me under the table," I muttered.

The door to the sad library burst open.

I turned, but my shock vanished the instant I spotted Zaxis. He had kicked his way inside, and practically sauntered over to us. He, too, wore his shirt mostly open to display the fenris wolf marking etched across his chest and shoulder.

Illia walked in behind him, her attention on Nicholin. Her eldrin was arguing with her.

"It'll only be a sip," Nicholin said.

Illia narrowed her eye. "No. Absolutely not. The stuff here is too potent."

He held up a paw and squished two of his fingers together. "Just a teensy-weensy bit! Please?"

Illia shook her head. "Nope. Not this time." She motioned to Zaxis. "I already have *one* person to watch after, I can't do two."

"I'm fine," Zaxis said with a dismissive wave of his hand. He threw himself onto the couch next to Fain. Then he glanced around. "So is this it? Only us?" He glared at Fain. "Why are you wearing that red cap?"

Fain touched the brim with his black fingers. "It looks good."

The two men stared at each other for a long moment.

"Yeah, I guess so," Zaxis replied, much to my surprise. "It reminds me of phoenix colors, ya know? Those are good colors."

Fain nodded once. "Moonbeam said I should be more... vibrant." His tone was as flat as a board. It almost made me laugh.

When Illia took a seat, it was on the other side of Zaxis. She glanced over at Fain, and without much prompting, said, "I think it looks good, too."

Which was huge, because she basically never spoke to Fain. I wanted to comment, but I held it to myself. Only Adelgis would know my relief, and he gave me a smile to acknowledge it.

Evianna moved and took a seat on another couch near an empty bookshelf. I went to join her, but Adelgis held up a hand.

"Volke, can you gather everyone else?" he asked.

"I thought you spoke to them telepathically?"

"I did, but some of them don't want to join. I think it would be best if *you* spoke to them. They'll open up to you."

Adelgis said things in such cryptic terms that I sometimes thought he spoke in nothing but riddles. I didn't want to argue with him, though. I trusted his judgment. I gave Evianna a quick nod, and kiss, before heading for the door.

"*Down the hall and out the front door,*" Adelgis said through telepathy. "*Most are outside, and Atty is just down the way in the nearest inn.*"

I exited without saying anything. The noise within the fortress house bombarded me the moment I entered the hall. While rubbing my ears, I went outside, beyond the foyer and the entrance hall.

Once I made it through the front door, I allowed the evening winds to wash over me. The purple lanterns were still a glorious sight. Dozens of individuals funneled their way into the d'Tenni home, most bringing gifts with them.

They were mostly knives and booze, but I suspected Hexa's family would appreciate that.

I shoved my hands into my trouser pockets and headed for the path, but I stopped once I spotted someone standing next to the railing that prevented people from falling into Hydra's Gorge. It was a wrought-iron fence that came up to my waist—

tall enough to protect people from stumbling over, but not tall enough to prevent someone from jumping over.

Lynus leaned on the railing, his muscular form hard to miss.

He wore a coat, hiding his mark. Because of that, most people walked right by him without a second glance. His coppery hair fluttered in the night air, and his gaze was on the mists far below, deep in the canyon.

Was he one of the people I had been sent to gather?

After a long sigh, I ambled my way over to his position by the railing. "Lynus?" I said as I approached. "Did you hear Adelgis's telepathy? The celebrations are inside."

He placed his elbows on the railing and leaned forward. If he wanted, he could easily leap over the barrier, but I knew he wouldn't. Lynus was against killing himself—he had made that clear.

He didn't answer me.

"Calisto?" I said instead.

"*Tsk.*" Lynus shot me a cold glare. "What do you want? Make it quick."

I motioned to our surroundings. The pathway to the fortress home was packed full of people, and Lynus was just twenty feet off to the side, alone and staring at the void of mist in Hydra's Gorge.

"What're you doing?" I asked, trying not to be sarcastic. "Why aren't you celebrating with everyone?"

He forced a smirk and then turned away. Still glaring—this time at the mists—he said, "Because I don't deserve to celebrate. I was one of the arcanists who enabled your chum to get snatched in the first place, or don't you remember?"

Well...

That logic was airtight. I didn't really have any counter for it. I completely agreed, actually. It *was* partially his fault that Vethica had gotten abducted.

With an awkward chuckle, I nodded once. "Okay. Enjoy the outside, then."

And Lynus didn't argue. He continued to stare off into nothing, his thoughts clearly distant and all-consuming. We needed him, because he was one of the god-arcanists, but that didn't mean I had to be best buddies with the guy.

I stepped a few feet away from him. Then I turned back around. "Lynus," I muttered.

He glanced over, his eyes narrowed.

"You're really talented when it comes to learning magic." It was a statement, not a question.

He just stared at me.

"Can you help everyone learn their god-arcanist aura? We need to do it as quickly as possible." Liet needed us.

With one eyebrow lifted, Lynus replied, "Me? You're the one who created an eclipse aura while still a journeyman knightmare arcanist. If anyone here is going to teach auras, *it's gonna be you, lad.*"

His statement caught me off-guard.

I had forgotten I had used my eclipse aura in front of him. That had been a long time ago, when I helped fight off another pirate ship—the night he had defeated Redbeard. Lynus remembered that? And he thought I was talented at creating auras?

He returned his attention to the gorge. "I'll focus on learning it, but many arcanists find it's the most difficult form of magic to manifest."

That was true. But we had to do it. We just had to.

Without anything else to say, I left Lynus to his contemplations. I headed to the main pathway, with the gorge to my left, and all the massive stone buildings to my right. It didn't take long to reach the nearest inn. I knew it because of the many paper hydras hanging from the awning and sign.

The Hydra's Den.

My favorite name for an inn yet.

I entered through the swinging front door and found myself drowning in a sea of bodies. There was *another* celebration going on here, and I had to wade my way through people to reach the back area with tables and a bar counter.

I apologized as I went to the back, but stopped once I spotted my brother, Ryker.

He was seated in the darkest corner, his table lit with a single candle. I almost didn't recognize him, but we shared a lot of the same features. Tall. Black hair. Tanned. Ryker was gaunt, though. Not muscular. And he held himself with a timid disposition.

Tonight, he wore the fanciest outfit I had ever seen him in. A fitted coat, a vest, a frilled and puffy shirt. The collar was so big, and went up to his chin, that I suspected he might be suffocating.

And his hair had been slicked back and held in place.

As I walked over to the table, I noticed he was alone.

Except for the mouse that sat on the table next to him. It was his eldrin—the Mother of Shapeshifters—or MOS for short. She was a bizarre mystical creature born of god-creatures. She had strange properties that didn't seem to conform to the standard. She could shapeshift into almost anything, which was unique to her.

Tonight, she was a white mouse with glowing red eyes.

I would've said it was ominous, but the way she twitched her nose and squeaked as I approached made me relax a bit.

"Ryker?" I asked as I approached.

My brother glanced up, his forehead dappled in sweat, his dark eyes wide. Then he sighed, wiped his brow, and frowned. "Oh, Volke. It's just you. Welcome."

The crowds in the inn weren't as loud as Hexa's family's home. In here—the *Hydra's Den*—it was easy enough to hear my brother when he spoke. I even heard the slight irritation and trepidation, though I didn't know why.

"Why are you here?" I asked. "The arcanists of the Frith Guild should be celebrating with Hexa."

"Ah. Yes. About that." Ryker tugged at his collar and forced a smile. "You see, tomorrow a lot of people will be leaving for New Norra. Hexa will be one of them. And, uh, I think I'll be accompanying her."

That was a surprise. "Why?"

"MOS doesn't like the Keeper of Corpses." Ryker patted the little mouse on the table. Then he touched the mark on his forehead. It was a nine-pointed star, unlike other arcanists who had seven points. "MOS and Keeper are siblings, it seems. She said that long ago, they used to travel the world together, but they had a falling out, and went their separate ways."

"Okay." I hadn't spoken with the Keeper of Corpses or the arcanist who had bonded with it. At least, not yet. I would soon. "And MOS wants to stay away from him?"

"At least for now. So, uh, I'll have plenty of time to speak with Hexa and Vethica as we travel."

My brother tapped his fingers across the top of the table. He stared at me expectantly.

I just stared back.

Did he want me to do something?

"I'm busy tonight," Ryker finally stated. He motioned me away from the table. "And I'm waiting for someone." He genuinely grinned. "A special someone. So, I'd rather this be private."

A special someone?

My brother was already with someone? It intrigued me—because he was younger. And didn't like confrontation. Who was he courting?

"Is it Karna?" I asked, even though I knew it was rude.

Ryker placed a finger to his lips and hushed me. Then he

glanced around before leaning forward on the table. MOS hopped onto his shoulder, her red eyes never leaving me.

"Yes, it's Karna. Keep your voice down."

"Is that why you're here?"

"Yes, obviously. I thought this place would be romantic. I didn't realize it was another place for celebrations."

I half-laughed as I turned my attention to our surroundings. Even if everyone was gone, this was a standard inn built into the stone of the gorge. Why would Ryker think it was special? They had several hydra decorations. That was something.

With a sigh, Ryker sat back in his seat.

"Why do I need to keep quiet about this?" I asked.

"I'm afraid everyone will get jealous." Ryker lowered his voice to add, "She's so beautiful and talented. Who wouldn't be jealous?"

That was... a reason. I supposed.

"Well, as long as you're happy," I said.

Ryker vigorously nodded. "Oh, yes. She's wonderful. She reminds me of our mother."

That had me raising both my eyebrows.

"*Not like that*," he quickly said. He gripped the edge of the table. "I mean, our mother was, uh, a lot like Karna." Ryker's face reddened more than Fain's. He ran a hand from his hair to his chin, clearly flustered. "They don't look alike. It's just... personality. They're confident. And I like that."

"You like women like our mother?" I asked, messing with him, since he clearly couldn't get his words out.

"N-No! I mean, *yes*. Basically." Ryker shook his head. He hid his face in his hands. "You're ruining the moment," he mumbled into his palms.

With a snort, I stepped away from the table. I had already known about my brother and Karna, but I supposed it wasn't formalized yet. Would Karna stay with him? She was so much older. Not that it was bad—they were both arcanists now—but it made me wonder what she liked about Ryker.

"I'll leave you two alone." I stepped away from the table, confused by Karna's absence. "Stay safe on your travels to New Norra."

Ryker mumbled something else, but I didn't hear it. Instead, I headed straight for the rooms. An odd thought crossed my mind.

Several arcanists in the guild, especially those my age, were finding partners in life. But now I was heading to find Atty, and out of everyone in the Frith Guild who I had trained with, she was definitely not with anyone.

I used my tremor sense to locate all the rooms, and then find one occupied by a single person and a bird.

It wasn't difficult.

There she was. Not far from my location.

All alone, as usual. Trying to achieve a true form with her phoenix.

If anyone needed to be celebrating with everyone, it was Atty.

Chapter 15

A True Form Phoenix

I approached her room, far from the citizens of Regal Heights—far from the arcanists of the Frith Guild. I knocked, knowing full well she was inside. The boom of my knuckles echoed in the hallway louder than I had anticipated.

"O-One moment, please."

Atty rarely sounded flustered. She moved around the room in a panic, stepping quietly from one corner to the next. What was she doing? Her heart rate had increased, and she moved around several objects.

"Who's there?" she called out, still rearranging the contents of the room. "I'm quite busy."

"It's me," I said. "Volke."

"Oh!"

Her speed increased. She grabbed things and threw them all around. Her phoenix, Titania, hopped toward the door. She stood on the other side, the light of her body shining through under the door and into the hall.

"One moment, please," Atty said again, breathless. She

hurried to the door and placed her hand on the handle. "Um. Titania will entertain you until I'm ready."

The door opened just a crack, and Titania hopped out of the room, her talons scratching across the stone floor. Then the door shut, leaving the phoenix in the hallway with me. We were alone, but I was fine with that. If Atty needed a little time, I could give it to her.

The night was still young.

Titania stood in front of me, seemingly bigger than even just a week ago. She had a long tail, with a few feathers that reminded me of a peacock. Her scarlet coloration, as beautiful as the day we first met, practically glistened when she moved.

Soot also fell from her feathers, dirtying the floor.

Titania lifted her head. She had a long heron neck, both graceful and delicate. Her golden eyes locked onto me.

"Volke, how are you?" she asked, her tone formal.

"Good."

"What brings you to these parts? Shouldn't you be at Hexa's side? You helped save Vethica, after all."

"I'm here to bring Atty to the party," I stated.

Titania lowered her head. Then she fluffed her feathers out, practically doubling in size. She resembled a beautiful turkey when she was so round. I didn't voice that, though.

In a whispered voice, Titania said, "Atty is busy."

I knelt next to Titania. "Doing what?"

"That's a secret."

We stared at each other for a moment. Titania never blinked. She met my gaze with unflinching determination. When I said nothing, she puffed out her chest and tucked her wings tight to her side. Embers flared underneath her feathers, as though her inner body was nothing but flames.

"Volke," Titania said, just as soft as before. "May I ask you a question?"

I nodded.

"You don't think... it's *my* fault Atty hasn't managed to achieve true form, do you?"

That was an interesting question, but one I ultimately knew the answer to. I shook my head. "It's not your fault. It's never the eldrin's fault. Mystical creatures bond with people to grow—to develop their magic."

"But my arcanist is trying so hard." Titania wilted, her wings drooping a bit. "I fear I am somehow the obstacle."

With a gentle pat on her warm feathers, I said, "No. It's just not true. But if you want to help her, maybe you should encourage her to—"

The door opened.

I stood and glanced over at Atty.

She was...

Dressed in unusual gear.

Atty wore thick traveling trousers, a vest with many pockets, a long coat that went to her knees, and a brown shirt with a collar that shielded her neck from the weather. Her long blonde hair was tied back in a ponytail, and she wore a tricorn cap that half obscured her phoenix arcanist mark. When she stared up at me, it was from under the brim of the cap, but through her long eyelashes.

"Volke?" She took a step back. "Did you want to come in?"

With a nod, I stepped into her room. Normally, I wouldn't want anyone getting the wrong idea about our relationship, but I doubted anyone was paying attention—or sober—and I needed to be frank with her, which was best done in private.

Atty closed the door once Titania and I were inside her room.

There wasn't much here. A bed. A dresser.

And a large backpack stuffed to capacity. It sat at the end of the bed, ready to be picked up and moved at a moment's notice.

"Atty?" I asked, one eyebrow raised.

She stood between me and the pack. "You came to see me?" She tucked her hands behind her back and forced a smile.

"Uh, yes." I crossed my arms and faced her fully. "Why aren't you celebrating with the others? Everyone is waiting for you."

Atty had the bluest eyes. When she met my gaze this time, the blue had darkened. She was stiffer than before, less open. With her hands still behind her back, she hesitated.

"We had this conversation before," I said, trying not to sound exasperated. "You shouldn't separate yourself like this. I know you're doing great things with magic, but I don't think it's really healthy."

Atty was one of the few people who had mastered her evocation and augmentation to such an extent, she could use them at the same time. Her flames—golden flames—could heal people. She didn't need to physically touch the person, her fire could do it for her.

That was an incredible feat, one she had achieved just by practicing over and over again in her bedroom. But that hadn't gotten her a true form phoenix. Now it seemed as though she had abandoned that advancement of magic to focus on something else.

"Well, I hadn't planned on telling you this just yet, but I have something to say," Atty muttered.

Reluctantly, I nodded. "Okay?"

She tugged at the collar of her shirt and then lifted up her guild pendant, tugging it over her head and removing it. Then Atty held it with both hands, cradling the object as though it could creak if she breathed too hard on it.

"Well then, you know that a few arcanists are heading to New Norra, yes?"

Again, I nodded, though I didn't like where this was going.

"I told Guildmaster Eventide that I would secure supplies and then join them once a second airship arrived in Regal Heights." Frowning, Atty waited a moment. Then she said, "But

I don't intend to do that. I intend to send them the supplies, and then head out on my own."

Titania perked her head up. She hopped over to her arcanist, her wings half-spread. "I thought you weren't going to tell anyone!"

Atty shook her head, her blonde ponytail swishing back and forth. "It's fine. Volke needs to know. He's... he's the one in charge, and I should make this more formal. I just... didn't want to tell the others."

"What?" I asked. "What're you talking about? You shouldn't go out on your own. Why would you do that?"

Atty snapped her eyes to mine. "W-Well, because *you* did that. When Thronehold was under attack, you just... you just flew off in an airship and left everyone behind."

"I was infected with the arcane plague. I didn't want to risk any of you getting it."

"Yes, but when you returned to us..."

I had a true form knightmare.

Was that why Atty was leaving? Was she trying to replicate my journey so she could achieve a true form with Titania? I ran a hand down my face. This was the third time tonight I felt like people were acting bizarre. What had gotten into everyone?

"It's not like that." Atty brought her hands in front of her and laced her fingers together. "I know you think I'm just trying to mimic what you did with Luthair, but that couldn't be further from the truth."

"Then why?" I asked.

"I need to be away from the Frith Guild because..." Atty clenched her jaw. She trembled slightly as she said, "Because Calisto the Dread Pirate is correct. Phoenixes are creatures of rebirth. They forge themselves from fire. They... they rise from the ashes when everything seems darkest and bleak."

"Okay?" I wasn't sure where she was going with this.

"And if I stay in the Frith Guild, I'll never have a chance to embody the truest qualities of a phoenix!"

After her statement, we were both quiet. Titania made a slight whistle sound as she ducked her head.

"Why is that?" I finally asked, my voice tense.

Atty motioned to me. "Because *you're* here. Because Guildmaster Eventide is here. Because I'll never know the fires of life when I have defenders like you two at my side. I've been *hiding* away from the world, trying to study, but I need to risk everything, and I can't have *Volke the Warlord* there to help if something goes wrong."

I said nothing.

Did she want me to abandon her? Was that what she was saying?

No. That was silly. Atty wasn't like that.

"You want to forge your own might," I said in realization.

She nodded twice. "Yes. I do. I want the opportunity to grow. To experience a rebirth." She grabbed the backpack on the floor and hefted it onto her back. It was a little heavy, and she swayed on her feet for a moment. "And… and I don't need anyone's permission to leave the Frith Guild, you know. I can go at any time."

Atty handed me the pendant. She was leaving the guild.

Which was selfish, given the circumstances. We were in the middle of a war against the Second Ascension. I gave serious thought to rejecting her pendant. Then again, she obviously thought she was weak. Forcing her to fight wouldn't help us.

"Where do you plan to go?" I asked.

"West of the Amber Dunes, over the Locke Mountains, to the Sunset Desert."

I shook my head. "*The Sunset Desert?* They say that place is uninhabitable. It's filled with pyroclastic dragons and syrocko drakes. The heat could cause diamonds to melt." That was an exaggeration, but it was a common phrase used by anyone who lived in the area.

"I'm immune to fire," Atty stated matter-of-factly. She pushed her pendant toward me again. "I've made up my mind."

I took her guild pendant, her name carved on one side with the words *phoenix arcanist*.

"Atty..."

She fidgeted with the straps of her backpack. "You can't stop me from leaving anymore. B-But I will be back. Once I'm strong. Once I can do things. You'll see."

Why did Atty always want to do things alone? *Always*. Perhaps I never noticed it when I was younger, because she was so set apart, but this was *her*. Alone. Contemplative. Doing amazing things but never giving herself enough credit.

Somehow, it was always never enough.

I slowly stepped aside. "Atty," I whispered. "I hope you find what you're looking for."

"R-Really?" The shock in her voice was amusing.

Even Titania glanced up at me, her gold eyes wide. "You aren't upset?"

"Well, forcing you to fight won't do us any good." I shook my head. "And if you think you can make yourself stronger, fine. But keep in mind we need you. And I don't think this is necessary, though. I don't think you *need* to fly away from everyone to experience the fires of life. But it might be easier. You're right. Liet and I would always try to save you if we could."

My statements seemed to shake Atty. She just waited in silence, as though my speech would be much longer. I didn't have much else to say, but I figured I would try to articulate my closing thoughts.

"Atty..." After a deep breath, I settled on what needed to be said. "I know why you want a true form phoenix. I know your mother thinks it's important—that she wants you to bring your dead family members back to life. *But she isn't you.* If you experience anything out there by yourself, maybe just experience life free from your mother's shackles."

I suspected my words struck a chord. Atty said nothing.

"Please," I said in a low voice. "For me. Just let that all go. It's not worth basing your whole life around."

Atty's eyes glazed over.

Then she rubbed at her face and turned away from me, her backpack rattling as she moved. Her phoenix hopped around her feet, dropping soot all across the floor.

"My arcanist?" Titania whispered. "Are you okay?"

"I'm fine." Atty stopped her rubbing. Then she gulped down a breath. "Volke. Thank you for your time."

Was she upset?

Atty had always done what her mother wanted. Perhaps my statements had crossed a line.

"If you need anything, just let me know," I said as I turned for the door.

"Thank you."

With slow and heavy steps, I made my way out of the simple inn room. I opened and closed the door, no more words between us. What else was I supposed to say? I pocketed her guild pendant.

Hopefully, Atty would find whatever it was she was looking for.

Chapter 16

Gathering A Team

After everything I had been through, I left Atty's room feeling exhausted.

Thankfully, this was a calm evening. Well, aside from the wild number of celebrations. It was calm in the sense that no enemies were nearby, the Second Ascension wasn't here, and besides Liet, I wasn't aware of anyone potentially having the plague.

I could rest, gather my strength, and then head out in the morning.

But I would need to determine who was traveling with me. So many arcanists were heading to New Norra. Or in Atty's case, beyond the desert surrounding New Norra. Who would I ask to join me? Who would I have accompany Liet?

I left the *Hydra's Den* with the intent of sneaking back into Hexa's party and informing the others of my decisions. Unfortunately, something strange caught my attention. My tremor sense picked up on all kinds of movement, but I had become accustomed to most of it. Footfalls were distinctly different compared to someone falling, or a horse galloping across a road.

Now I felt...

The *click-clack* of hard objects being tapped across stone.

I stopped dead in my tracks, trying to picture what kind of creature would be doing such a thing. Nothing was moving. The clacking came from a single position on the roof of a nearby building. It felt like someone was impatient and bored, and they were tapping their fingernails on a table in boredom.

Just much bigger.

Whatever was tapping had to be about the size of Vjorn, but I knew the fenris wolf wasn't near me. So who was it? No other god-creatures were here.

Anger overtook my actions. I headed straight for the creature's location, intent on finding answers. I wouldn't let anyone—or anything—ruin this evening. If this was some sort of attack, they would regret facing off against the Warlord.

With a wave of my hand, I manipulated the stone around me and created a staircase up to the roofs. My sword, Retribution, was always by my side. I was too paranoid to leave it anywhere, considering how dangerous it was.

When I reached the flat rooftop of the fortress mansion, I reached for my weapon, but stopped with my hand on the grip. There was a monster here, just lying down, relaxing. It was a terrible, disgusting monster straight from a child's nightmare.

The beast was at least eight feet at the shoulder. It had the shape of a wolf—like Vjorn—but unlike the fenris wolf, this beast was made entirely of corpses. Dogs, cats, humans, unicorns, drakes—their rotting bodies were fitted together like a patchwork quilt, pieces sewn into random places.

Minotaur horns protruded from the monster's shoulder. The talons of hurricane hawks made up the beast's paws. Broken iron bones from syrocko drake skulls—sharpened to a deadly point—constituted its fangs.

This monstrosity was an amalgamation of corpses. His glowing red eyes fixed on me, his gaze cold and serious.

He smelled like a graveyard.

This was the Keeper of Corpses. I had met the beast only briefly, while on the battlefield against Orwyn. He was just as disgusting as the day I had met him.

Sitting in the corpse-dog's "lap" was none other than his arcanist.

Ezril Rivers.

Again, I had only seen him briefly, but I now knew he was one of Orwyn's trusted knights. She wanted me to protect this man if anything were to happen to her. The last I had seen Ezril had been when Orwyn took him and escaped from our fight. Orwyn must have gone and got him as soon as our agreement was finalized.

"Are you lost?" Ezril drawled.

He was an odd person. Most would call him *deformed*. He wore a silk shirt, and fine trousers, but they couldn't hide his shriveled leg and sunken chest. The man's arms were nearly strings, and when he took in breath, I heard the strain of his lungs. He sounded as though he had just run ten miles, but it was obvious he hadn't moved in quite some time.

Ezril remained curled up in the flesh folds of his eldrin.

As I stared, Ezril's neutral expression shifted into slight disgust. "Hm? What's that? You've never seen a man like me before?" With his string bean arm, he motioned to himself. "Go ahead. Say it. I look like a dehydrated grape."

"I wasn't going to comment," I replied.

I stood a good twenty feet away from Ezril and his monster eldrin. I was on one side of the roof, and the Keeper of Corpses was on the other. The tapping I had heard *was* him. With his talon claws, he tapped the roof, creating a soft *click-clack* that I felt more than I heard.

"If you didn't come here to gaze upon my majesty, why are you here?" Ezril slowly swished back his dark hair, his hand shaky. "The Warlord should be the center of attention, receiving all the glory."

"Believe it or not, I'm out running errands."

Ezril lifted an eyebrow.

The Keeper of Corpses was just like the Mother of Shapeshifters. A unique creature, unlike any others. A child of the *progenitor behemoth*. Their magic was primal and vast, far different from normal mystical creatures.

"What're *you* doing here?" I asked, my tone more accusing than I wanted. "This is no place for an arcanist of your power."

Ezril batted his eyes in comical confusion. "Whatever do you mean? I'm just *the sick kid*. No one wants me at their party."

Kid?

"You look like you're in your twenties," I said as I took a few steps closer to get a better look. "You're definitely not a kid. You must be older than me at the bare minimum."

The Keeper of Corpses chuckled, his dark laugh strangely familiar.

"I just say I'm the *sick kid* because that's what everyone always says when they want to exclude me from events." Ezril crossed his thin arms and then took a ragged breath. "If I'm just a kid, then I don't need to be invited. You understand."

"Everyone says that?"

"Well, mostly the fools in my old hometown." Ezril leaned onto the fleshy corpse of his eldrin. "Ever since I met Orwyn, things have been different. She... sees me as a man. Which I appreciate."

"I don't know much about you or Orwyn, but she's asked me to protect you. And while I'm uncertain of her allegiance, I think highly of Orwyn's character."

Ezril leaned forward and wheezed. "Why is that?"

"Because anyone with such loyalty to her friends and peers must value righteous virtues." I thought back to the steps of the Pillar, and how the teachings had shaped me. "Anyone who strives to keep their friends safe is probably not all bad—even if she once served the Autarch."

"Heh."

"Is something wrong?"

"The people of my village said I would never know greatness because I was born deformed. They treated me poorly because of it. But Orwyn was different. She said greatness could come from anywhere." Ezril glanced up at his corpse eldrin. The massive beast stared down at him. "And I knew then that she was different than others."

Their bond was more than something cultivated by the Second Ascension.

"Did you serve the Autarch?" I asked.

Ezril shook his head. "Me? No. The man never spoke with me. All I knew was that I wanted to follow Orwyn."

My thoughts circled back to my future plans.

The Frith Guild was going in two different directions. One group was heading to New Norra. Hexa, Vethica, Liet, Karna, Ryker—perhaps others. And the other half, I would be leading on a search for the Autarch.

If I sent Ezril and Akiva to New Norra, they would be protected, just as Orwyn wanted. I doubted the Autarch would venture into that city, and if he did, it was well defended. But I would need allies. Powerful allies.

I would need to take Orwyn. She was a god-arcanist, and she needed to develop her aura.

Lynus would come with us for the same reason, even if I didn't much care for the man.

Zaxis, too. Which meant Illia would likely go with us. Zelfree as well, if I was using the same logic.

And Adelgis, since his brother, Yevin, was one of the individuals we would be facing. Fain would likely refuse to leave his side.

What if I brought Ezril and the Keeper of Corpses? I needed

to protect them, but did I trust them? While I didn't know them well, they valued the same things I did. And I had seen their might in combat. If they brought that same fervor to our mission, they would be potent allies.

I stepped close, the stench of rot hanging heavy around us. "You fought alongside Orwyn."

Ezril patted the Keeper of Corpses. "I'm a powerful arcanist, despite what some might think when they look at me. Of course I fought by her side."

"Will you remain at her side if we hunt down the Second Ascension? I could use someone of your caliber."

Ezril lifted an eyebrow. His sunken chest lifted and fell, his breathing still audible and ragged. "You need *my* help? Or are you planning to just use me as a meat shield?" He chuckled to himself, his tone dark and sardonic. "*We'll throw the sick kid at our enemies! That'll slow them down while we make our escape.*"

"Wow—what an *optimistic* worldview." I just shook my head. "I would never throw anyone to the Second Ascension. I went out of my way to make sure no one died in our fight. And I didn't use *anyone* as a meat shield, even when it looked as though Orwyn might win."

Ezril mulled over my comments. Was he thinking everything over? After a long minute, he met my gaze. "You were rather straightforward, weren't you?"

I wasn't sure what he meant by that.

Before I could say anything, Ezril continued. "And when Orwyn was frightened because she thought Akiva might die, she *immediately* thought to ask you for help." He laced his thin fingers together. "Your actions speak louder than words, Warlord. I will fight with you. But I should warn you. I remember everyone who insults me."

My immediate concern was Zaxis and Lynus. Both those men were jagged when it came to human interactions.

"I'll keep that in mind," I said.

I returned to Hexa's family's home without convincing anyone to join in the celebrations. I hoped Adelgis wouldn't be disappointed. And Hexa. Or Vethica.

But everyone I spoke to wanted to be left alone, or had no intentions of joining a celebration. When I returned to the sad little library with a grand total of three tomes, I was met by a gathering of Frith arcanists.

Zaxis, Illia, Fain, Evianna, and Adelgis were all where I had left them.

Hexa and Vethica had apparently snuck away from the main visitor hall and were now with us. I preferred having them here, simply because it was quieter.

The moment I stepped into the library, and everyone noticed me, Zaxis shot up from the couch. Illia's one eye went wide, and I saw the worry form in her expression.

"Is it true?" Zaxis demanded.

He didn't *sound* drunk. I hoped he hadn't been drinking. He sometimes got incoherent when he had a little too much liquor.

"Is *what* true?" I asked.

"That you're in charge? That Guildmaster Eventide is leaving us? That you're running everything?"

The accusation silenced everyone in the room. Illia stared at me, Nicholin on her shoulder, his little blue eyes wide and twinkling.

Hexa and Vethica didn't seem surprised. If I had to guess, Hexa told them all about the trip to Deadman's Bluff, and Vethica had likely explained Liet's situation, since she was one of the few people who understood.

And Adelgis knew everything all the time, anyway.

"It's true," I said. "I'm in charge. And I'm going to lead a hunting party to track down the Autarch. After this party, I'm going to get information out of the Autarch's right-hand man, Rhys, and then—"

"When were you going to tell me?" Zaxis barked.

"Well... Tomorrow. Obviously."

Despite the logic of my conclusion, Zaxis huffed and threw his arms up in the air. He paced around one of the couches, Nicholin watching his every step. When Zaxis finally stopped stomping, he asked, "Who are you taking?"

"You. As long as that's okay."

"And?" Zaxis snapped, clearly irritated at the thought of traveling with certain people.

"Lynus, too."

"But not Orwyn, right?"

At that, I said nothing.

"*Right?*" Zaxis demanded. "She tried to kill us!"

I held up a finger. "To be fair, Lynus tried to kill us, too."

"And he took my eye," Illia whispered. She touched her eyepatch, her finger lingering on the leather.

I grimaced at the comment, hating the way she said it. Part of me wanted to remind her that she'd had her chance to kill the man, but she had allowed him to live. And if I had gotten my way, he would've been publicly executed a long time ago.

Everyone was tense after Illia's comment.

She snorted a laugh and waved it away. "It's fine, everyone. I was making a joke."

"A dark joke," Hexa muttered.

Adelgis nodded once. "I thought it was funny."

"You weren't laughing." Fain narrowed his eyes.

"Actually, human beings can express their appreciation of humor in several ways. Laughter is the most common, but some individuals become quiet or even tense. As a matter of fact, some nations used a *giggle test* to see if people were possessed by abyssal creatures. According to ancient—and unfounded—text abyssal creatures can't laugh, so any human who didn't laugh when tickled was assumed to be a spawn from the ocean depths, and needed to be executed."

The entire story, from start to finish, was told in such a monotone and matter-of-fact way that it might as well have been read straight from a book. Adelgis had expressed no emotion recalling all the gruesome details, he just quickly vomited the words out, explaining himself without interruption.

Hexa fluffed her puffy cinnamon hair, the curls of her ponytail so small and bouncy, they practically jiggled. "Wow. You sure do know a lot about, uh, random things."

Adelgis shrugged. "I like to read whatever catches my fancy."

"Do you ever listen to yourselves?" Zaxis barked. "This whole conversation is insane." He returned his glare to me. "Can we really trust Orwyn? What if she tries to kill us again?"

"Then we'll handle her again," I replied, my voice calm, my posture relaxed. "But we need her. All of us need her. Our main goal while traveling will be to develop our auras, okay? And we're going to do it together."

"Like a family," Nicholin chimed in. He clapped his paws together several times, the soft *pat-pat-pat* rather adorable. "A beautiful *god family.*" Nicholin frowned. "Is that the right word?"

"A pantheon." Vethica sighed. "The word you want is *pantheon*."

"Oh, sure. You all will be a *found pantheon.* Created from strong friendships. Forged through adversity." Nicholin's voice notched up in drama. "*Made sharp by success!*"

Illia placed a hand on her eldrin's face. Nicholin yelled a few things, his words muffled by her palm.

"I'm so sorry about him," she whispered. But a small smile crept onto her face. It made me wonder if she liked Nicholin's shenanigans.

Zaxis stepped around the couch and stood in the middle of our little group. With a frown, he gestured to Adelgis. "Why are we waiting to interrogate Rhys? I thought Adelgis could just *read minds?* Why isn't Adelgis handling this? Why aren't we chasing the Second Ascension as we speak?"

"Because Deadman's Bluff was stressful and costly," Hexa said, no anger in her voice, just irritation. She held Vethica close, hugging her like a child might hug a doll. "Vethica and I need a break."

"Our enemies don't need a break. We shouldn't stop until we catch them." Zaxis pointed at Adelgis and directed his speech toward the man. "Right? Rhys was the right hand of the Autarch. He knows things! He knows all the man's plans. We should question him *right now.*"

Adelgis lifted both his eyebrows. "I have tried to read some of Rhys's thoughts, but it's been difficult. He's mostly kept in a nullstone prison, and when he sleeps—and I can see his dreams—everything is jumbled. The man is absolutely insane, trying to navigate his psyche is like wandering a shifting labyrinth that screams madness at you. It would be better if someone questioned him while I listened to his inner musings."

Zaxis stormed over to the door, passing me with a glower as he went. "Then, what're we waiting for? Let's go!"

Chapter 17

Interrogating Rhys

Zaxis, Illia, Evianna, Adelgis, Fain, and I headed down the pathways of Regal Heights.

Nullstone wasn't natural to these parts. It was mostly in the Argo Empire, specifically around the capital city, Thronehold. But before Orwyn had attacked Hydra's Gorge, we had some nullstone flown into the city. The trap I had constructed allowed us to capture Rhys with ease.

However, we couldn't take Rhys *out* of the nullstone. If we did, the man would somehow vanish. I thought he was a rizzel arcanist—I had seen him with a rizzel eldrin! Or at least, I thought I had. But no matter what his source of teleportation was, I knew he had it, and we couldn't allow him to flee.

So, we could interrogate him the old-fashioned way, or we would need to come up with a plan to question him in an area where Adelgis could still use his magic and not be hindered by the nullstone.

We arrived at the makeshift prison with little trouble. No one was celebrating in this area of Regal Heights. The courthouse, jail, and city carpenter's buildings weren't fun areas to congregate, and there weren't any inns or bars to serve alcohol.

Two guards stood outside, each one so bored, they looked like a corpse someone had propped up with a broom. Horns hung from their belts, which told me their primary function as a guard was to call for help. If something happened—in theory—they would blow their horns and alert the whole city.

It wasn't a bad idea.

The arcanists held in the nullstone prison couldn't be allowed out for any reason.

"I can't believe you didn't tell me the plan," Zaxis said as we approached the door.

He exhaled, and a puff of mist filled the air. The night was chilly, but not as much as Zaxis's blood. The winter of the fenris wolf ran through his veins.

The two guards gave us a quick glance and then both did a double take. They stumbled as they hastily moved out of our way.

"Good evening, god-arcanists," one muttered.

I nodded to him and opened the door. "I figured I would tell you while we were relaxing at the celebration." I held the door open so the others could enter. "Why do you always assume the worst?"

"I don't do that," Zaxis snapped.

Illia patted his shoulder as the two of them walked by. "Yes, you do, my love."

"*What?* Since when?"

Nicholin twitched his ferret-like nose. "This morning, the servants didn't bring you any breakfast, and you thought they were disrespecting you." He held up a paw. "Turns out, you yelled at them not to enter your quarters until noon, and had completely forgotten that. So, it was really all your fault, yet somehow you were angry for four hours."

As Zaxis and Illia continued into the building, Zaxis softened his tone. "Everyone always treats Volke a certain way. I just... worry they'll treat me differently. Like I'm his *junior* or something."

Illia kissed his cheek. "For me, just let it go for a day."

He said nothing as he headed down the long stone hallway of the jailhouse.

Adelgis, Fain, and Evianna slowly entered afterward. While Adelgis and Fain walked forward, whispering to themselves, Evianna hung back to take my arm.

"We don't argue like that," she stated.

"I don't think they were arguing." We entered, and I shut the door.

The lights in the jailhouse weren't as festive outside. There weren't any paper hydras or beautiful purple lights. Everything was harsh and flat and cold. No decorations, barely any windows—and all had bars—and the glowstones were a harsh yellow. I would've rather been wandering a crypt than this place, but I kept the comment to myself.

"We don't ever *play argue*," Evianna said, correcting herself. She squeezed my arm. "I think it's improper. The nobles of Thronehold would all sneer if they saw me acting like Illia and Zaxis."

"Good thing the nobility isn't here."

She tightened her fingers. "You don't think... it's a bad sign, do you? That we don't fight."

"Of course not." I gave her a sideways glance. "Why would it be?"

"Maybe we're not passionate enough." Evianna met my gaze with a serious expression. "Do we need more heat between us?"

I held back a laugh. "Uh, I don't think that's what the arguing indicates." My face heated as I hurried us toward our destination. I really didn't want to delve deeper into this conversation in the middle of a jailhouse.

A single jailor ushered us into the main portion of the building.

We entered an area of suffocating pressure. It was the aura of nullstone rocks. When I was a normal arcanist, it would've shut down my magic, but that wasn't the case any longer.

There were four hastily constructed "nullstone cells." The jail had originally been crafted from normal rock, and the nullstone was brought in afterward and pressed up against the walls like bricks, or a bizarre wallpaper. Metal bars—they went from the floor to the ceiling—made up the last wall of the cell, so that anyone walking down the hall could see everything inside the cells.

Nullstone were bluish-black. Each cell looked like they had been carved from the night sky.

The jail was empty except for one cell.

Rhys sat in the far corner, his back to the nullstone wall, his eyes unfocused. He kept his knees close to his chest, and he slightly rocked back and forth with all the energy of the insane.

He was a full-grown man, but in that moment, I almost felt sad for him.

Rhys was thin, damn near emaciated, and wore the standard tunic and trousers given to all prisoners. His bugged-out eyes caused me to shiver. Was *he* infected with the arcane plague? Probably not, but we would need to be careful. Rhys's long, black hair was matted and out of control. Some of it was stuck to his oily face, and some of it was tangled into an impromptu bun on top of his head.

Before we reached his cell, Adelgis stepped in front of us and held up a hand.

Everyone stopped. Zaxis crossed his arms, his irritable energy obvious from the way he tapped his fingers on his biceps.

"Please, wait," Adelgis whispered. "I can't use my magic here."

"*I* can." Zaxis motioned to me. "And so can Volke. We're god-arcanists. We're not affected by nullstone."

That was how we caught Rhys in the first place. We tricked

him into a pit of nullstone, and then with our magic, we defeated him.

Adelgis tilted his head left and then right. "It's fine that *you* can access your abilities. What I'm trying to say is... I can't hear his thoughts while he's awake in the nullstone. When he sleeps, however, we can move him. Then I can hear the whispers of his dreams. So, I recommend we just ask our questions and leave."

"Why?" Evianna asked. She narrowed her eyes. "Is this just a waste of time, then?"

"If you ask Rhys the questions in a way that'll make him dwell on them, I can likely hear his answers in his dreams. If you ask the questions in a forgettable or weak way, the man won't think of them later."

Illia lifted an eyebrow.

"Is *that* how dreams work?" Nicholin asked. He glanced around at everyone. "That's a serious question, by the way. I really don't know."

"Imagine dreams as a gateway to a person's mind." Adelgis held his hands together to make a tunnel. "It's a pathway to their soul. You see, dreams are not only connected to your mind, but your life as well. When you're asleep, you're the closest to death you've ever been. You take in less air, your heart slows—everything about you is vulnerable. Even your thoughts."

"Oh." Nicholin smiled and then rubbed his forepaws together. "Okay. I'll make all the questions memorable. I just need you guys to hold him down while I get into his trousers."

Fain groaned. Even Wraith, his wendigo, invisible and stalking around us, joined his arcanist in the guttural sound of disgust.

I turned to Nicholin and frowned. "Can't you teleport? Why would we need to hold him down?"

The little rizzel stuck out his tongue. "I just want the process to be as dramatic as possible. Very memorable!"

Zaxis pointed to Nicholin. "No. We're not touching anyone's trousers. We're going to do this *my* way."

"With lots of fire and yelling?"

"No fire, just winter," Zaxis replied, his tone icy. Then he pushed Adelgis out of the way. He headed over to Rhys's cell, no words for any of us. "C'mon."

Nicholin ducked down on Illia's shoulder. He probably realized he shouldn't have brought up Forsythe, Zaxis's late phoenix. Everyone hesitated for a moment as we exchanged glances. Illia seemed worried, and I shared her sentiment.

Hopefully Zaxis didn't accidentally kill this guy.

I hurried to reach his side.

Zaxis approached the bars of Rhys's cell. The thin man inside continued to rock back and forth, mumbling the entire time. Zaxis slammed his palm on the bars, the resulting *bang* echoing throughout the jailhouse.

Rhys stopped moving.

He glanced up with his bug eyes only—he didn't move the rest of his body.

"Had a good rest?" Zaxis growled. "Because you won't be getting any more rest for the rest of your short life."

Rhys said nothing.

As I approached, my attention went straight to his forehead. He had an arcanist mark. There were seven points to the star, but the image of a creature was... distorted. It wasn't a mystical creature I recognized. It had multiple legs—five or six?—and it had a tube-like body. No head? Was it a misshapen rizzel? Or was it something else?

Evianna, Illia, Adelgis, and Fain hung back. They lingered by the bars of the nearby cell, each of them blending into the shadows in their own way. None of them could use their magic. Even Evianna's knightmare didn't shift around the darkness like she usually did.

Without warning, ice washed over the jailhouse. A thin layer of rime and frost ran down the bars of the cells, covered the floor, and coated the nullstone walls. The snowy white cold dropped the temperature in a matter of moments. The once bluish-black walls were ivory and welcoming.

My breath came out in visible mist.

Rhys shivered.

"I'm the Hunter," Zaxis stated, his words filled with more heat than all of Regal Heights. "And this is the Warlord. We're here to ask you a few questions, and you're going to answer them."

We didn't need that, but I understood why Zaxis said it. He was pulling off *intimidating* really well. I was impressed, because the last time we attempted to question someone, he wasn't nearly as confident.

Despite all that, Rhys didn't reply.

"Where is the Autarch?" Zaxis asked.

"I don't know," Rhys replied, his voice rusty, his words laced with a chuckle. He shivered back the cold, and even wrapped his arms around his knees, pulling them tight against his sunken chest.

Zaxis slammed his hand on the bars again. "Don't mess with me, ya stooge. You're the Autarch's dog. *I saw you during the attack of Thronehold.* You took the corpse of the soul forge! You *know* where the Autarch is."

"I do not."

Rhys's quick answers irritated me. He was trying to mess with us.

"If you don't know, maybe we don't need you."

Zaxis waved his hand and—to my shock—three simple steel longswords appeared hovering around him. They darted straight through the air, heading for Rhys like javelins.

With wide eyes, Rhys flinched back to the wall. The longsword shot at him, but stopped abruptly a few inches from his neck and face. The blade twirled in the air, seemingly under Zaxis's control.

"Y-You evoke *swords*?" Rhys managed to stutter.

"*He can evoke swords?*" Fain mouthed to Adelgis, never actually voicing his words.

Adelgis slowly shook his head.

Again, Zaxis slammed his hand on the bars of the cell. When Rhys jumped, I felt a hint of satisfaction. I probably shouldn't have delighted in Rhys's terror, but he deserved it.

After a long moment of confusion, I finally remembered what Zaxis had told me. He wasn't evoking *swords*—that was preposterous—he was creating illusions. He was trying to scare Rhys into answering by creating fake weaponry to attack him with.

I was impressed. The swords weren't extremely detailed, but Zaxis had created three of them, and he seemed in control, even if his focus was totally consumed by his magic.

"Well?" Zaxis barked. "Where is the Autarch? *Answer us or else.*"

Rhys blubbered something incoherent. After a few gulps of air, he managed to say, "I d-don't know. He no longer s-stays in a single location!"

"Then where is he going?"

"I would never tell you, *worm*. And it won't matter! Soon, the Autarch shall come find *you*."

When Rhys said the last bit, he swung his hand at the blades. Was he trying to knock them away in dramatic fashion? Probably. Instead, his arm went right through the longsword. They were just illusions, and now Rhys knew for himself.

With a sneer that transformed into a half-smile, he pressed himself up on the bluish-black nullstone. "You *frauds*. You're nothing like my lord. The one true ruler! The king of magic! The Autarch will strike you all down."

Oh, this conversation was turning out to be quite

memorable. If the guy didn't dream about screaming his lungs out about his *lord*, then I didn't know what else would be on his mind.

"Do you know what was happening at Deadman's Bluff?" I asked.

My question startled Zaxis. He whirled on his heel and stared at me with a glower. Was he upset that I interrupted? What did it matter? Rhys clearly wasn't going to tell us anything of his own volition.

"Deadman's Bluff was our secret testing grounds," Rhys said as gleeful as a plague-ridden monster.

I hadn't expected that answer. It was rather truthful and forthcoming.

"You made an improved version of the arcane plague with the help of the abyssal leech arcanist," I muttered. "We know all about it."

Rhys's expression shifted from happiness to hate in an instant. Glaring at me like a deranged cat, he practically hissed, "*You know nothing.*"

"A true form knightmare was taken to Deadman's Bluff. Do you know what happened to him?"

"The knightmare..." Rhys's voice faded away. He licked his lips and thought for a long while, as though recalling a whole lot of information that caused his brain to physically slow down. "He was yours," Rhys eventually concluded.

But I didn't reply. I didn't want him to know that, but I supposed it would be obvious. Luthair's mark was still on my forehead, after all. It was a faint etching in my skin, but it was still there—the seven-pointed star with a cape and a sword.

With a dark snicker, Rhys slowly rose to his feet. "You should despair, *Warlord*. Your eldrin is no more!"

"You're a liar," I immediately snapped.

I knew Luthair was alive.

I knew.

My blood now matched the cold temperature in the room. Rhys was always a disgusting crony to the Autarch, and now he wanted to taunt me about Luthair? He had a death wish.

"It's true," Rhys said, smiling wide. His yellowing teeth sent a shiver down my spine from pure revulsion. "The knightmare is nothing like it was before. We needed true form creatures to test our plague, you see! How would we know if it worked or not... unless we had subjects?"

Evianna gasped.

My vision tunneled. I practically saw red as I stepped closer to the cell, my heart hammering. I could destroy this whole building. With a small flex of my power, I could crush Rhys into nullstone until he was nothing more than a crimson puddle.

"Hey, hey," Zaxis said.

I didn't even realize he was standing in front of me.

He had both his hands on my chest, his gaze focused on mine. With a furrowed brow—he was clearly concerned—Zaxis whispered, "Calm down. What's gotten into you?"

"I'm calm," I forced myself to say, both words coming out in a precise manner.

"You're wrecking this whole jailhouse. Get a grip. You could hurt someone with your powers."

"I didn't do anything..."

But when I glanced around, I realized that some of the walls were cracked and warped. A portion of the ceiling had lowered in one of the other cells, and the floor was jagged around the walls. In my frustration, my manipulation had twisted the building.

"He's lying," Zaxis whispered. "Don't let it get to you."

I thought it deeply ironic that *Zaxis* was the one telling me to calm down.

But then Evianna placed a hand on my shoulder from behind. Before I could turn around, she placed her forehead on my spine. In a soft voice, she said, "Volke, it's okay. Don't listen to this monster. We'll find Luthair. And even if something is wrong, we'll help him."

Evianna was so much gentler than anything before.

She almost sounded scared.

When I glanced over my shoulder, I noticed that Fain and Adelgis were stiff and paying attention to me. Only Illia was calm enough to shake her head. Obviously, my mild outburst had worried everyone.

"Your knightmare is a beast! A monster! A piece of corrupted magic!"

Rhys's shouts filled the jailhouse. And while each felt like a bullet straight to the chest, I didn't allow his words to affect me. I took a deep breath and repeated Evianna's reassurances. We *would* help him when the time came.

With a laugh, Rhys concluded, "You're a fool, Warlord. You, too, *Hunter*. You will both know defeat at the hands of my lord! He will show no mercy. Your blundering has caused him enough trouble!"

"We don't need to be here anymore," Adelgis said. "Tomorrow—in the morning—we can reconvene and discuss everything."

"That's a good plan." Evianna wrapped her arms around me.

I nodded once. "All right. Tomorrow then." With a sigh, I pulled Evianna close, and then we all left the jailhouse, Rhys shouting the entire time. I ignored him. He was just trying to get under my skin.

Nothing more.

Chapter 18

Four Runestones

Evianna and I walked the pathways of Regal Heights. While the celebrations were calming, and most of the lanterns had been snuffed, there was still a pleasant purple hue over the city. I didn't feel tired, but I knew we didn't have much night left before the dawn. If I wanted to be well rested for tomorrow, I would need to get some sleep.

"Evianna," I said as we headed for a bridge that went across the gorge.

"Hm?" She held onto my arm for most of the trek. Both for warmth, and for the closeness. She shivered from time to time, especially whenever the wind whipped by.

"Do you mind if we go to Terrakona's grove?"

Evianna pushed back some of her white hair. "Out in the wilderness?"

"Well, I can make us a fire. It won't be too bad, I promise."

"But why?"

"I just..." We walked across the bridge, the groan of metal echoing down into the canyon. When we reached the other side, I exhaled. "Terrakona is always alone. He never gets to be indoors, like other eldrin, and no one goes to see him."

Terrakona frightened most people, even if they didn't want to admit it. While I understood—he was gigantic—I realized it must be so lonely for him. Of course he would want to spend time with his dryads. They never ran from him.

"All right," Evianna said, surprising me.

She didn't like to camp out in the wilderness.

When I glanced over, her beautiful eyes locked onto mine. "It's obviously important to you," she whispered. "So now it's important to me."

With a half-smile, I nodded. "Thank you."

"Well, I have one stipulation."

I lifted an eyebrow.

"I get to grab us a blanket." She said it very matter-of-factly.

I chuckled and then nodded. "That would be appreciated."

"Good. Then I'll meet you there."

Before I could reply one way or another, Evianna sank into the darkness. She shifted with the ease of a shadow across the stony surfaces of Regal Heights, vanishing from my perceptions. Her shadow-stepping didn't trigger my tremor sense. She might as well be invisible.

Determined to see Terrakona, and spend time with him, I hurried through the city. For the most part, everyone was too busy to stop me, or try to engage in small talk, which I was thankful for.

When I reached the edge of Regal Heights, I smiled.

Terrakona was easy to spot.

He slept in a coil position, his body still wrapped around his tiny grove. He would protect his dryads whether he was awake or sleeping, and I thought it an admirable trait. Still smiling, I headed over to him, energy in my step.

As I drew near, Terrakona must've sensed my presence. His gigantic eyes snapped open—one blue, one red. He lifted his head, his crystal mane glittering in the ivory moonlight.

"Warlord?" Even his telepathic voice was groggy. He

lowered his snout until it was next to me. **"Such odd hours you keep."**

I placed my palm on the tip of his nose. When he exhaled, the warmth of his breath washed over me. "Sorry. I've been busy. But I'm not anymore. I figured I could come keep you company."

"You haven't business to conduct?"

"Well, probably." I always had *something* to do. "But I also need to rest."

Terrakona lifted his head, and then uncoiled a portion of his body to allow me in the grove. **"True."** He waited until I walked into the grove before coiling his serpentine body back into place. **"The Children of Balastar are known for their recklessness. But you are different. I like this."**

With a chuckle, I found my favorite tree in the grove and took a seat. I was about to ask Terrakona some questions, when the shadows shifted and swirled. Evianna stepped out of the darkness a moment later, a large blanket held firmly in both her arms.

It was made of gray rabbit fur, some of the warmest and softest material I had ever experienced.

She hurried to my side, took a seat next to me, our hips touching, and then threw the blanket over us. Snuggled close, Evianna rested her head on my shoulder.

Terrakona shifted so that his head rested on top of his body and faced the center of the grove. His tongue flicked in and out of his mouth, tasting the air of his small forest.

His dryads were sleeping. None of them popped up from the ground to play with us.

Crickets sang us songs as the minutes crept by. Evianna was the first to fall asleep. She held me close, her breathing even. Layshl, Evianna's knightmare, lifted from the darkness and stood watch over us—an ever-faithful guardian who I appreciated.

I gently brushed Evianna's hair from her face.

Terrakona was the next to sleep. He closed his massive eyes and practically became still as rock.

When I finally found sleep, it was a welcome break from reality.

"Curse the abyssal hells and all the ships at sea."

Someone had spoken?

When I awoke, I thought I was still dreaming. I opened my eyes and found Evianna lying against my chest. The morning light dappled down through the tree canopy, speckling her face with soft illumination. She was so... mystical.

It had been her striking white hair that had surprised me when we had first met. Even now, I found it beautiful beyond words.

But I shook away the thought.

Someone had woken me.

Who?

When I glanced around, I realized Terrakona was still asleep and Layshl was nowhere to be found. Before I stood—and woke up Evianna—the shadows around the grove shifted away from the morning light. I held my breath, waiting for someone to show themselves.

To my surprise, Zelfree stepped out of the darkness. His mimic arcanist mark—now a knightmare's mark—explained how he could shift through the shadows. But that didn't explain why he was here.

I lifted an eyebrow, hesitant to speak, simply because I could wake Evianna. She seemed so peaceful.

Zelfree rubbed at the dark bags under his bloodshot eyes. The man hadn't slept all night. Had he been drinking? It was a celebration, after all, but I had hoped he wouldn't have indulged. After a long stretch, where he lifted both arms, a loud *crack* sounded through the grove. Zelfree groaned as he rubbed at his spine.

He wore a long black coat, a white shirt, and black pants that looked as though they didn't fit. Had he assembled his outfit from multiple places? Where had he even found all of it? So many unanswered questions...

"Damn," Zelfree said aloud. "I can't believe it's morning."

He stared at the sky through the small holes in the tree canopy.

"Are you okay?" I whispered.

Zelfree slowly brought his attention down to me. "I'm great." He patted himself off. "Fantastic even." Then he stepped close and spotted Evianna. For a long moment, he said nothing, but then he also lowered his voice. "Liet will be leaving soon."

I nodded. "To New Norra."

"That's right."

Hexa, Vethica, Ryker, Karna, and a few others were joining her. I wasn't sure about the rest, so I glanced up at Zelfree and asked, "Where is Captain Devlin?" I had left him in Thronehold long before I traveled to Regal Heights. He was supposed to help the king basilisks relocate, but I didn't know if he had finished and rejoined us yet.

"Captain Devlin arrived in the city a week or so ago. Now he's with Liet. I'm sure she caught him up on everything."

"And my father? Where is he?"

"Who? Gravekeeper William or Jozé?"

That always became confusing, especially when I considered both of them to be my father. With an awkward shrug, I whispered, "Both."

"They're both with Liet."

"Can you get William to stay? I want to take him with us."

Zelfree nodded. "That's fine. But why?"

"I want to hunt down the Second Ascension, but we also

need to find the other god-creatures. I have reason to believe the endless undead is bonded, which means all the others should be somewhere in the world, hiding in their lairs."

That information didn't seem to shock Zelfree, even though I thought it was rather important. As if he had been waiting for me to say it, Zelfree reached into his pockets and withdrew four runestones.

They were rectangular slabs of rock, each a different color, and each with a picture of a god-creature etched upon it. Zelfree handed them to me, all four at once, and then took a step back. "Liet wanted me to give these to you. She said you would know what to do with them."

I said nothing.

With shaky hands, I examined each.

The first was the lapis lazuli runestone, pale blue and wondrous. On one side was the picture of a fish creature—like a mermaid, only reptilian and frightening. It was the runestone for the *scylla waters.*

The second was the opal runestone, and the white had an iridescent sparkle when brought to the light. The picture on the front was a snake with four wings and a feather mane. Its body almost resembled lightning. It was the runestone for the *tempest coatl.*

The third was the sandstone runestone, almost plain with how tan it was. The creature on it... was disgusting. Snakes—or eels?—sprouted from its back, and it ran on six stumpy legs, no wings or anything like that to speak of. It had horns, like a ram or a bull, but a face that was an amalgamation of several beasts.

This was the *progenitor behemoth.*

The last runestone was the most beautiful.

It was the bauxite runestone.

The reddish stone was laced with veins of gold and blue. Unlike the other runestones, it had a beautiful sheen. And the creature on the back was none other than the *corona phoenix*. It was a bird, but its chest was a hole. Or perhaps a black spot? It was hard to tell. The picture was so small.

The other runestones were with the Second Ascension. From my understanding, they had managed to bond with the soul forge, the sky titan, the garuda bird, the abyssal kraken, and the endless undead.

The soul forge was dead.

And the sky titan was on our side.

That only left them with three. If we could find individuals to bond with the four god-creatures we still had, we'd be far ahead of the Second Ascension. Which got me hopeful. Perhaps it wouldn't matter that the Autarch had a gold kirin. How much more powerful could it really make him?

"Zelfree," I muttered as I stared at the runestones.

"Hm?" He rubbed at his eyes. "What is it? I need to get some sleep before we head out for the Second Ascension."

"Who do you think should bond with the remaining god-creatures? Besides William—if he can pass the Trial of Worth."

The question sat between us for a long and painful moment. Technically, anyone could bond with the god-creatures if they passed the test. William should've bonded with the typhon beast, but that monster only wanted someone as conflicted as it was.

And what if someone already had an eldrin? In order to become a god-arcanist, they would have to kill their eldrin first. Not many arcanists were willing to do that.

"I'm not sure," Zelfree said. "You're the *Warlord*, though. Aren't *you* supposed to determine this?"

I fidgeted with the runestones. "I don't know. Should I be picking everyone who gets a chance to bond? I mean... I can. It just doesn't seem right."

"Have you considered Captain Devlin?"

"He loves his roc, Mesos. I'm not sure if he would kill her to become a god-arcanist, even if we needed that."

Zelfree nodded once. Then he rubbed his stubble-covered chin. "What about his cabin girl? Biyu is a nice girl. She would follow orders—and she'd never betray."

"She's really young. Too young. We couldn't rely on her."

"You could just let random people bond with the creatures. If you want to take the chance."

"N-No." What if someone worked with the Second Ascension? I couldn't take that risk. After a long exhale, I said, "Fine. Ask Captain Devlin to join us. Okay? And... perhaps my father, too. My other father. Jozé."

"Your father loves his phoenix," Zelfree muttered.

"I know. But... just in case. He can say no if he definitely doesn't want to go. That's fine."

"All right."

We didn't have many options.

Chapter 19

Wounded

I couldn't get back to sleep. I kept the four runestones close, trying to think of who would make a competent god-arcanist. Perhaps it would be best if I just let nature take its course... Maybe there was someone out in the world who would make for a great god-arcanist, but I just hadn't met them yet.

"*Volke?*"

Adelgis's telepathy wasn't like Terrakona's. His was softer, more akin to a whisper. I rubbed at my ear as I said, "Yes?"

"*I explored the realm of Rhys's dreams. He thought of the interrogation. He also dreamt of the Autarch, and his role in the Second Ascension.*"

"And?"

Evianna stirred. She moved around in my arms, and eventually her eyes fluttered open. I offered her a smile but then pointed to my head. She awkwardly stared at me, her grogginess plain to see in her narrowed gaze.

"*Rhys believes that the Autarch is far north. His eldrin allows him to move quickly. But that his servants—like Rhys—are hurrying to catch up.*"

"What else?" I asked.

Evianna must've realized what was happening, because the irritation drained from her face. She stretched and then manipulated the shadows around us to fix the blanket so she was tucked in again.

"*He wasn't lying about testing the plague on true form creatures.*"

Although I hadn't wanted that to be true, I had known he probably wasn't lying. That sounded like something Theasin would've wanted.

And while my chest knotted, and breathing hurt, I wouldn't let the news bring me down. If I could develop a salvation aura, I could save both Liet *and* Luthair. No one would have to suffer from any of this ever again.

That was what this was all about, after all. This accursed plague.

Everyone I cared for was in danger, and I had to do something about it.

Despair had no place in my heart.

"Thank you, Adelgis," I whispered, my chest hurting from the anxiety that had built up in my veins. "I'll keep all this in mind."

"*Rhys believes the Autarch went beyond the islands. Far to the north, where it's cold. We will need to travel hundreds of miles across the ocean. Perhaps more.*"

"I understand."

Adelgis didn't say anything else. I exhaled, allowing some of my frustrations to leave me along with my breath. Evianna was close, and it reassured me. Not *everyone* I knew was in mortal peril. I still had people I could rely on.

We could do this.

Together.

Once I fully woke up, and washed away the dirt and chill from sleeping outside, I realized we had a problem.

Terrakona couldn't fit as many people as I wanted to take with us on the hunt for the Second Ascension. And Regal Heights was a landlocked city. There were no ports for boats, only towers for the occasional airship. Most people left the city via caravans pulled by horses or donkeys or goats.

And that was a slow way to travel.

That wouldn't do. We needed to move—and we had to do it quickly.

I paced around the conference room in city hall. The smooth stone floors, large granite desk, and gigantic stained-glass windows were a marvel to gaze upon, but I just didn't see it. My thoughts consumed me. The only airship in town was taking Liet and the others to New Norra. I couldn't take that from them—Liet *needed* to get to master arcanists as soon as possible.

The next airship wouldn't be in Regal Heights for another few weeks.

Illia could teleport—and she could teleport groups of people —but only a short distance each time. While it would be quick, we couldn't cross the ocean or even carry many supplies. It was a foolish mode of transportation for anything other than a quick trip or emergency.

The conference room was empty.

Everyone else was either gathering supplies or packing their things. What was I supposed to tell them? To just wait a few weeks?

Perhaps we could head to another town...

One with more airships...

As the world serpent arcanist, and as the Warlord with several nations sworn to me, I could request an airship and manpower to help accomplish my task of defeating the Second Ascension. All I had to do was get somewhere to speak to someone.

Terrakona and I could get to another city in a few days' time. Then we could fly back and pick everyone up.

A knock sounded on the door.

I stopped in my tracks.

"Yes?" I called out.

"May I enter, Warlord?"

The soft, feminine voice bordered on singsong. The only person I knew who constantly spoke in a dreamy manner was Orwyn. Well, perhaps Adelgis as well... But definitely Orwyn.

"You can come in," I said.

The door opened as I took a seat at the polished granite table. When I glanced up, I almost pulled my sword out. My heart hammered as a scarred, disgusting man entered the conference room. I jumped from the seat, but calmed once I realized who it was.

Akiva.

His face was half-melted, like a used candle. The red flesh, fresh and waxy, almost matched his coppery hair. Except, some of his hair was missing from the right side of his head. He walked with a limp as he made his way over to the table, his posture straight, despite his obvious pain.

The man wore his favorite gray-scale armor, which had once been perfectly fitted to his body. Now it was in shambles. It was nothing more than a patchwork of its former glory, with most of the pieces sewn together.

Orwyn walked in behind Akiva, her green eyes watching his every step. When he reached for the nearest chair, Orwyn grabbed it for him.

"What happened?" I blurted out.

I hadn't interacted with Akiva since he was "healed." But no one had told me he was still this bad. What had happened? Atty had seemed confident he was fine.

"Your god-arcanist magic nearly killed him," Orwyn said matter-of-factly. When she attempted to help Akiva push in his chair, he grimaced away from her and growled. "I'm sorry," she whispered to him. "Please, just let me help."

Akiva said nothing.

But he also didn't protest when she finished helping him sit at the table.

With a smile and a single clap of her hands, Orwyn took a seat next to the former assassin.

I sat at the table a second time, still baffled. "Atty wasn't able to heal him fully?" I asked.

Orwyn shook her head. Then she placed a hand gently on top of Akiva's forearm. Except for his face, and the obvious limp, he wasn't actively bleeding or dying. It seemed he would be okay.

"I know a healer in Fortuna," I said, thinking of Gillie. "We can take Akiva there."

"Traveling is what I came here to talk to you about, Warlord." Orwyn brushed back some of her strawberry-blonde bangs. When she glanced at me, it was with a neutral expression, as though her smiles were for Akiva alone. "I can fly us to a city, if that's needed."

Fly? Of course!

"Really?" I asked.

"Yes. I'm the sky titan arcanist. My title is *the Falcon*. And for good reason. I control the winds and air."

I knew Orwyn could fly. I had seen her do it. I had even seen her fly off the battlefield with both Akiva and the Keeper of Corpses. But could she fly dozens of people? And their supplies?

"I can take everyone," Orwyn firmly stated. "If it's just to a nearby city—one on a river, so we can take a boat to Fortuna or Thronehold—then I'm more than capable of getting us all there."

"And you won't drop anyone?" I asked. I was used to newer arcanists messing up their abilities when they weren't confident with them.

"I'm also a kirin arcanist, Warlord. My magic is far stronger than normal, even though I've only just bonded to my god-creature."

She sure did like to remind me of that fact.

"When can we go?" I asked as I stood from my chair. "Everyone is almost ready."

Orwyn's eyebrows lifted. She held on to Akiva's arm. "W-Wait, please. You must promise me nothing will happen to Akiva. A-And I was hoping for a small request."

Her concerns about Akiva were valid. He was a wanted criminal who had killed the last queen of the Argo Empire. If we flew him into a town, there was a semi decent chance someone would recognize him, and then he would be dragged away.

Same with Lynus.

We would need to invest in cloaks. At least until the Second Ascension was dealt with. Then I could go about pardoning them for helping in the war effort. But only after we were done.

"What's your favor?" I asked.

"May we stop to see the king basilisks?" Orwyn asked in a whisper.

Akiva tensed, but he added nothing to the conversation.

The arcanist mark on his forehead—which was half-destroyed by his injuries—was the classic seven-pointed star with a six-legged beast wrapped around the design. It was a king basilisk. Not too long ago, he had been the last of his kind, but after so many creatures came back to life in Thronehold, there were new king basilisks—and king basilisk arcanists—around.

"Akiva and his eldrin used to know those king basilisks," Orwyn added.

"They don't have any of their memories," I said.

"I... I'm aware. But it would mean a lot to Akiva to see them."

He shook his head. Then he grimaced and grabbed at the melted part of his face. "It's a waste," he managed to say through gritted teeth. "Forget it."

"But—"

"*It's not important*. I've told you. Stop worrying about me."

Orwyn hesitated. Her gentle grip on his arm only tightened, and when she glanced up at him, all I saw was concern. And when he looked at her...

I almost felt like I should glance away. As though this was a moment too intimate for outsiders to view. Akiva's harsh gaze was so much softer. He didn't even say anything. And despite the fact that his face was wrecked, he communicated so much through his expression.

"But I thought it would make you feel better," Orwyn whispered. "To see all the king basilisks, I mean."

"My wellbeing isn't important right now," he replied, his voice almost too soft to hear.

"You never think about yourself."

I cleared my throat. Akiva returned to his tense and emotionless self. As if defeated, Orwyn's shoulders fell. She turned to me and then shook her head. "Disregard my request to see Thronehold. It seems it's unnecessary." She gave Akiva a small side smile. "Perhaps afterward. When everything is finished."

But he didn't reply.

I wondered if he thought he wouldn't make it.

"I promise no one will take Akiva from my custody," I said as I walked around the table to stand closer to them. "So if you can fly us to a port city, or someplace where we could recruit an airship, I would be most grateful."

Orwyn stood from her chair. She was so short, but she held herself with such dignity, it was hard to tell. "Thank you, Warlord. We can leave at once."

"No, thank *you*, Falcon. I appreciate you coming to me to offer your magics. I think this will turn the tide of our chase."

"Let's hope."

Chapter 20

One-Way Flight

Everyone scheduled to join me on the hunt met outside Regal Heights.

There was a large open field near Hydra's Gorge where we had fought Orwyn. It was the perfect place for everyone to gather, especially since so many of us had creatures that were legendary in size.

And we had the appearance of an army. Everyone wore their best armor and weaponry. Whatever personal supplies they needed were carried in a pack on their back. We had a few crates with dried food and some star shards, just in case, but otherwise, we weren't taking much.

Once we arrived at Fortuna, we would gather the last of what we needed, including the last of the arcanists. Gillie, and the Ace of Cutlasses should be waiting there. According to Liet, they were at that port.

When I glanced around, I counted up the number of people here.

Terrakona, my eldrin, the mighty world serpent.

Evianna and her knightmare, Layshl.

Adelgis and his ethereal whelk, Felicity.

Fain and his wendigo, Wraith.

Illia and her rizzel, Nicholin.

Zaxis and his fenris wolf, Vjorn.

Lynus and his typhon beast, Xor.

Zelfree and his mimic, Traces.

Captain Devlin and his roc, Mesos.

Akiva, *without* his king basilisk, Nyre.

Ezril and his Keeper of Corpses.

William, my adoptive father.

Biyu, the little cabin girl.

And lastly, Orwyn...

She had two eldrin. Her sky titan, Sytherias, was wind itself. And just like the wind, Sytherias couldn't be seen, only felt. When the sky titan moved, a breeze swirled around us, kicking up dirt and creating a pressure that felt like water.

Orwyn's second eldrin was her mystical kirin.

It was a horse in shape, but tiny scales covered its body instead of hair. The beast shimmered and moved with the fluidity of a fish, elegant in all regards. Its cloven hooves were practically stolen from a deer, and its tail reminded me of a lion's.

All kirin had a horn on their head, similar to unicorns, but distinctly different.

This kirin had a horn that was twisted into the shape of an antler. It was made of semi-transparent crystal and glittered with inner power.

The kirin's black eyes reminded me of a starry night—and of Luthair's mystical true form cape.

I didn't know the name of her kirin. It didn't speak with anyone other than Orwyn, and I wondered if that meant it didn't even speak to Sytherias the sky titan.

Most everyone was quiet. It was the middle of the day, the sun overhead, but no one wanted to speak. The clear blue sky and gentle breeze indicated our trek would be smooth. There was no need to worry.

Yet I felt the tension as I stepped into the center of our little gathering.

Orwyn had been our enemy only a few weeks ago. Now everyone had to entrust her with their lives? Of course there would be doubts. It was my job, as the leader, to ease everyone's worries. It was my decision to trust her. My choice to use her sky titan to fly to Fortuna. My plan to chase the Autarch.

If I couldn't convince the others this was sound, their determination would crumble.

What would Liet Eventide say?

Or better yet, what could I do to get people to understand Orwyn more?

"Orwyn," I said, motioning her to come to me.

Her emerald eyes went wide. With a slight tilt of her head, she wandered closer to me. "Yes?"

"When was the last time you visited Fortuna?"

She brushed back some of her chin-length hair. "Never, Warlord."

"*Never?*" Zaxis asked with a huff. "It's a gigantic trading hub. Everyone eventually stops at Fortuna if they do any travel in the northern islands."

"I didn't leave my kirin village for most of my life," Orwyn said, her voice distant. "Traveling away for any length of time was forbidden."

Illia crossed her arms. Nicholin shifted around her shoulders, and even perked up his tiny ears. "Forbidden? So... you haven't traveled much?"

Orwyn shook her head.

"What do you think of Regal Heights?" Illia asked.

"It's so loud." Orwyn turned her attention to Hydra's Gorge, and then the city built on either side of the canyon. "The people, the activities... But I like it. So full of life." Then she glanced over at the massive typhon beast. "I can understand why this god-creature had his lair here."

Xor, the one-hundred-headed beast, opened his largest mouth and roared. His booming voice shook the nearby trees, sending dozens of birds into the sky. Then he stomped his feet, and the ninety-nine snakes of his mane hissed.

"This city is a grave," Xor shouted. **"I died here once... To Luvi."** The typhon beast stepped forward.

Lynus jumped in front of his monster. "Down! We're not hurtin' the lass."

Xor shook his massive dragon head. **"But she... she is a Child of Luvi. Her blood... smells of him. Tainted."**

Akiva limped to Orwyn's side, like he would do whatever he could to protect her. It was both touching and sad. Akiva couldn't handle a poorly made sandwich in his condition. How did he think he was going to protect Orwyn from the typhon beast?

"Everything is fine," Lynus stated. "That was a past life. The *first* typhon beast died here. Not you." He reached out and touched the snout of the dragon head. "I'm here. Remember that."

His eldrin sniffed deeply and calmed himself.

I was impressed. It seemed Lynus already knew how to control his typhon beast, even though it had once been a mindless force of destruction. He truly had a talent with creatures. It was a shame he had led such a long life of wanton murder.

With a sigh, I glanced over at Orwyn and muttered, "I apologize. I just wanted the others to get to know you before we went anywhere."

"Oh, I see." Orwyn forced a smile. "But you don't need to concern yourself, Warlord. I know I'm an oddity. Like I said to you in private, I'm not... Well, I don't think like the others. Being an outcast is commonplace for me."

"I just want them to trust you. So they know you won't drop them into a ravine while we're traveling."

Orwyn pointed over to Adelgis. "You have an arcanist who always knows my intentions. You won't be surprised by any sudden betrayals. No one needs to fear me."

I hadn't thought of it like that.

Still, it made me a little sad that Orwyn had just accepted her fate as the lonely kid on the side of the field—the one no one would pick to play with. But there wasn't much I could do about that at the moment. We had villains to chase down, and wrongs to right. Perhaps when this was over, people would come to see Orwyn as someone they could depend on.

"Okay," I said, loud enough for everyone to hear. "Orwyn and her sky titan, Sytherias, will be taking us to Fortuna." Then I generally motioned to the air. "Uh, Sytherias? Are you ready to transport us?"

It felt weird talking to nothing.

Could the sky titan even hear things?

It was just... air. Completely invisible.

As if to mock my inner musing, the wind around us rushed and howled. In the airstream was a voice, and it spoke to all of us all at once, without being too loud or blaring.

"I am ready," the wind howled. ***"Do not fight my powers. Relax, and the sky will be your transport."***

I stood still.

Terrakona tilted his head, his scales flaring as though he was worried. I offered him a reassuring smile, and the massive world serpent seemed to calm. I wondered why he was so agitated, but then it became apparent.

The wind under us rose at a frightening speed. I practically lost my breath as I was scooped up into the sky, whisked away by unseen forces. With a shout, I tumbled upward—like gravity had lost its tether—and I tried to correct myself.

"Relax!" Orwyn called out.

The others shot into the sky as well. Illia, Zaxis, Zelfree...

I spun, and lost sight of them. To keep my lunch inside my stomach, I closed my eyes and focused on just breathing. When I opened my eyes again, I was floating high above the field, the wind rushing through my hair. It was colder than I had imagined, and I heated my body with my magic, relying on the magma.

Then the larger creatures took to the winds.

First Vjorn, who was the smallest of the god-creatures by far. He leapt into the winds, and flew upward in a controlled fashion, a mist of ice floating around him as he traveled. Then went Terrakona, who snaked his body as though swimming through the waves.

Then Xor, who moved in such an awkward and clumsy fashion, I wondered if he even knew how to swim. The monster shook his legs and flailed his snake heads. Some of them even screamed and chittered, as if terrified.

Traces transformed herself into a blue phoenix.

It only reminded me that my father, Jozé, had refused to join us. His blue phoenix was nearby, probably in town, with Liet and the airship.

As a blue phoenix, Traces could control herself in the air. A trail of soot dusted away from her each time she flapped her wings.

Zelfree tumbled into the sky, but with all the expertise of a bird, corrected himself once he was at my height. He moved like a fighter, ready for whatever came next, his coat billowing behind him like a cape.

"Volke!"

I twirled around in the air until I spotted Captain Devlin, Biyu, and my father, William.

Captain Devlin, being a roc arcanist, had control over the winds himself. He seemed to add his magic to the sky titan's, creating a steady stream of wind that lifted William and Biyu with perfect precision. Biyu giggled and flapped her arms like she was a bird.

His roc, Mesos, spread her golden wings and took to the air with expert skill.

My father pointed to himself, and then to the air around him. It was as if he couldn't believe this was happening.

"Having fun?" I called back.

"This is amazing," he said, breathless.

Orwyn's kirin flew through the air. It galloped on the wind, moving with such grace, I was entranced. The silvery scales of its body shimmered in the afternoon light. Orwyn climbed onto the back of her kirin and rode it like a wingless, flying mount.

"Please don't get sick," Orwyn said. "We will be traveling to Fortuna shortly." She half-laughed as she added, "But since I don't know where I'm going, I would appreciate it if someone called out directions, or let me know whenever I get off track."

"It's northeast," Zaxis said, trying to point in the correct direction, but tumbling through the air as he did so.

"Thank you, Hunter. I will attempt to head that way."

Attempt to?

"We're all heading straight to the abyssal hells," Fain said. He was stiff—practically a statue and awkward, trying not to move, despite being caught on the winds. "We're all going to plummet to our doom," he muttered, his face paler than ever.

Illia just laughed, like Fain was making a joke. Little tears were being tugged from Fain's eyes, which told me he probably wasn't joking.

His wendigo was in the same boat. While Wraith was normally invisible, the shock of flying must've jolted him out of it. He was visible—his black fur and skull face mask as clear as day—and his legs were held stiff and straight, like he was a nightstand or end table. Maybe a stuffed hunting trophy.

Even Wraith's bright red eyes were wide and filled with worry.

Nicholin "swam" through the air, moving like an eel, his ferret body reminding me of a serpent. His white fur, mixed with his elegant movements, most resembled a luck dragon from ancient tales. They were extinct, but I had heard they were adorable.

When Nicholin made it to Fain's side, he grabbed Fain's arm. Rizzels could manipulate gravity, and he somehow righted Fain, giving him more stability in the air.

"Your tiny savior is here," Nicholin said as he air-swam around Fain. "You have nothing to fear!"

Illia teleported to Wraith and nodded. "Even if the sky titan drops us, I'll be here." She gently patted his fur.

Their combined statements of reassurance seemed to help Fain and Wraith. The two loosened a bit.

Then the winds carried us forward. Slow at first, but then faster and faster. It was difficult to breathe, what with all the air rushing by, but I managed to take one deep inhale before we really started moving.

We flew over Regal Heights.

It came and went within a matter of seconds, the citizens beneath us pointing and staring. I saw several hydra arcanists, and even the leaders of the city, Vinder and Brom, and I tried to wave to them, but I doubt they saw.

Zelfree laughed loud enough that his voice echoed into Hydra's Gorge.

It was good to know *one* of us was having the time of their life.

"Faster, Sytherias," Orwyn commanded. "Please."

The wind rushed and howled again, the mighty sky titan complying with its arcanist's wishes. The wind pressure became so strong, it was difficult to keep my eyes open.

As the most bizarre group of birds ever, we shot through the sky, heading straight for the wonderful and familiar Fortuna.

Chapter 21

Flying Home

For some reason, I thought Orwyn's flight would've been faster. In my mind, we moved as quickly as light, shooting through the sky and arriving in Fortuna in a matter of seconds.

Instead, we spent several hours in the air, going higher and faster, practically becoming one with the weather. We entered a cluster of clouds, and I thought they would've tickled my face like a fine mist, but I felt nothing.

Orwyn's wind whipped around us, protecting us from the elements. We were encased in a bubble—a shield of air—which explained why we hadn't been pelted by a million insects.

Then we flew up out of the clouds, sailing straight into the fading sunlight. The sunset set the world ablaze. The blue sky shifted to scarlet and orange, tinting the clouds with its vibrance, dazzling everyone in our group.

And for a brief moment, as the sky titan broke through the clouds, it was visible. The nimbus mists tangled around the sky titan's body, giving it visible shape. The massive creature had four wings, and the body of a bird.

Its wings...

They weren't really attached to its body. They were separate, as if tethered to the body with strings.

The sky titan was a strange creature.

"So wondrous," Adelgis said.

Illia laughed aloud, almost giddy.

"We'll be fine, we'll be fine, we'll be fine," Fain chanted to himself.

Everyone's voice was clear in my ears. The winds that shielded us also swirled our words around, trapping them in our group.

Several hours in, Biyu flew closer to Captain Devlin. She whispered something to him, and he turned to her with a glower. "You can't hold it?" he asked.

Biyu shook her head.

Devlin sighed loud enough that I heard. Then he waved his arm around and pointed at Orwyn. "We need to stop for a moment. The girl needs—"

"Don't tell them!" Biyu interjected. She grabbed his arm and hung on tight, her frown and wide eyes adorable. "It's embarrassing."

"Fine." Devlin rolled his eyes. "We need to stop for an unspecified reason."

At first, I thought Orwyn hadn't heard him. She didn't reply, nor did she alter her behavior. She stayed at the front of the ground, riding her kirin as though lost in deep thought. A second before I called out to her, she pointed to a field of grass and rocks far below us.

"Sytherias," Orwyn said, her tone commanding. "Right there, please."

The winds answered her command.

Our large group of individuals—gigantic eldrin, several arcanists—descended from the sky and headed straight for the flatlands. Terrakona moved closer to me. I wondered if it was because he was frightened, or because he wanted to protect me.

Either way, I appreciated his presence.

I reached out, grabbed his crystal mane, and held on tightly.

When we reached the ground, most people landed on their feet, but they came in slowly, one at a time. Fain collapsed to his knees and grabbed the grass, practically strangling it. Adelgis stood by his side and patted his back.

"You did remarkably well," Adelgis muttered.

"*Don't*," Fain hissed. When he stood, he brushed himself off with his frostbitten fingers. "I'm fine, Moonbeam."

"Fear of falling is very common."

"I've been on airships before. I'm not *that* afraid."

"I have a theory that falling from a great height, and subsequently dying, results in a rare fable birth of a mystical creature."

Fain slowly turned to face Adelgis, blinking twice in confusion. Then he sighed and shook his head. "Fine. If I die, make sure to take care of the mystical creature that springs out of my corpse."

Wraith whined, his tail drooping. "I can't eat it?"

"No."

Adelgis chuckled to himself as he watched Fain and his eldrin argue. Adelgis's ethereal whelk—a sea snail that floated through the air all on its own, and was basically made of light—sparkled around the area as it drifted between us all.

Captain Devlin grabbed Biyu once they landed and pointed to a set of far-off bushes. "We'll be back," he said with a groan.

"I can go by myself!" Biyu huffed and hurried away before the captain could retort.

Zaxis walked over to me, his fenris wolf close behind. A chill overcame the field, and he crossed his arms over his chest and just glared. "Why did we bring a little girl?" He shot the distant bushes a glare. "This is ridiculous. We should never allow a child to get anywhere near these god-creatures."

"Devlin refuses to go anywhere without her," I muttered.

With a frown, I added, "Are you going to tell the little girl she has to stay home while the only family she's ever known goes off on a dangerous mission and may never return?"

Xor touched down on the field and everything rumbled. The massive typhon beast was anything but graceful.

Once everything settled, I shook my head. "We'll make sure Biyu stays close to us at all times. Everything will be fine."

"That's the only requirement to join us? *Stay close?*" Zaxis scoffed. "What if she gets killed, huh? What do you think Devlin will do then? And what if he's a god-arcanist? What if he finds out after he's bonded with the corona phoenix?"

I stepped closer to Zaxis and lowered my voice. "Do you have a better idea? Because if you do, I'm all ears."

He met my gaze and held it. But he ultimately said nothing.

Why were we arguing? There was no reason for this. And it wasn't productive. We were supposed to be a team united against the enemy. We weren't very team-like when we couldn't agree on simple matters.

Lynus walked over to us, his hands in his pockets, his expression bordering on melancholy. He wore a long cloak with a hood—as did Akiva—specifically to hide his identity. "Well?" Lynus asked, ice in his words. "Why have you two gathered over here?"

"We're discussing Biyu." Zaxis motioned him close. "You should weigh in on this as well." Then he pointed to Orwyn and gestured her over.

She was helping Akiva stay on his feet. When she noticed Zaxis pointing, she whispered something to Akiva and then slowly made her way to us.

"Yes?" she asked, almost absentmindedly.

Zaxis kept his voice low as he said, "You're both god-arcanists. I think you should weigh in on Biyu's presence. She's a hindrance. A liability."

"Devlin wants her," Lynus immediately said.

Orwyn nodded. "Yes. And if we're considering Devlin as one of the god-arcanists, I think we should make it as easy as possible for him. He doesn't have a kirin, which means his roc will have to die. Do we really want him alone at that time?"

She liked to bring up the fact that we didn't have kirins, for some reason. It seemed odd to mention it so many times.

"What if she gets killed?" Zaxis asked.

Lynus shrugged.

I shot him a glare. He rolled his eyes.

"Oh, you want me to pretend I have feelings for the lass?" he growled. "All that matters is whether the man Devlin will be wrecked by her passing. But it's clear he cares for her. Let this one go."

Zaxis glanced between Lynus and Orwyn. "Really? You both don't care that she's here?"

"I don't think it's good or bad," Orwyn stated. "It's a decision made for the comfort of one of our own. As god-arcanists, we can protect one single girl, can't we?"

Lynus crossed his arms but said nothing.

Orwyn tilted her head to get a better look at Biyu. The little girl hurried away from the bushes, smiling wide.

"Why is she missing an eye?" Orwyn asked.

"Dread Pirate Redbeard cut it out of her skull," Lynus replied, no emotion.

"Unfortunate. Perhaps that's why Devlin is so protective of her. He seemed concerned with her emotional state more than most men in his position." Orwyn turned on her heel, her back to the group. "I'm going to speak with Akiva, and then we'll leave. I suggest you use the bushes now, if you need to."

Zaxis frowned as she walked away. "Hmpf."

"Why are you upset?" Lynus narrowed his eyes. "Nothing has come to pass. You're barking at shadows like an untrained dog."

"I just don't want to have to worry about a child."

"Heh. Don't let your woman hear that."

Zaxis grew red in the face. "Leave Illia and me out of this. I'll make a great father. Just... not right now."

"Sure."

Terrakona lowered his head. His hot breath cascaded around us. With a smile, I held up a hand and touched his snout. Although he hadn't participated in the conversation, I could tell he thought highly of Biyu. Terrakona seemed to have a soft spot for those with gentle natures.

"Unless you have a better suggestion, I say we don't have this conversation again." I hefted myself up onto Terrakona's mane. "We have four god-creatures that need an arcanist, and currently, we only have two candidates. Let's not give Devlin a reason to leave, all right?"

"You won't hear me complain," Lynus stated. Then he headed off toward Xor.

Zaxis didn't bother saying anything. He waited for Vjorn, and then climbed up onto the fenris wolf's back.

Then we all took to the air once again.

The flight to Fortuna lasted all the way to the following dawn.

We had to stop a few more times, but each instance was brief. Everyone was exhausted once we reached the city, and I promised the others they could rest while all the god-arcanists went to speak with Fortuna's city council.

Which turned out to be easier than I had thought.

The moment our group touched down outside the walls of Fortuna, the city guard came to meet us. We were escorted to my estate—itself a gift from the city—and told that the council would see us at my convenience.

My estate...

I had forgotten I owned land in Fortuna. It was convenient,

though. Everyone could rest and relax without having to worry about finding an inn room.

Fortuna was a glorious city. No matter how many times I visited, I always enjoyed it.

As the morning sun crept up over the horizon, the city glittered. Sunlight bounced off the many windows, and sparkled across the clock tower, a massive building settled on top of the highest hill in the middle of the city. Buildings lined the flatlands around the baseline of Fortuna, and roads led up to the step-like terraces of the massive hill.

The clock tower—named *the Astral Tower*—was unique to the city. It was adorned with bells and a representation of the stars in the night sky etched on a steel dais—a gigantic machine to keep track of the celestial changes throughout the year.

Our god-creatures waited in the gardens of my estate. They were too gigantic to walk the narrow roads of Fortuna. Well, except for the sky titan. It flew over the city, staying close by, even though no one could see it.

I felt it, though. The pressure of its dense wind-filled body occasionally washed over me.

The city guard led us through the main street, clearing the road of carts and people. One of the guards was a troll arcanist, and with his enhanced strength from his troll magic, he managed to move barrels from the road, as if we were a parade that needed all the space we could get.

Zaxis, Orwyn, and I wore our clothing mostly open to reveal our god-arcanist marks. Lynus remained swaddled in his cloak. He lurked behind us, like a personal honor guard, never saying a word. He was as intimidating as he was large and muscled.

The city guard brought us straight to the Astral Tower.

The fence surrounding the Astral Tower stood fifteen feet tall. The main gate was a few feet taller than that, and the metal bars were twisted into designs—owls, stars, and ships. When I first saw it, I had thought it impressive, but the charm had worn off. Terrakona was so much bigger than this fence.

The Astral Tower was quiet. There were no visitors or attending diplomats. I doubted anyone knew we would be visiting today.

It was improper etiquette to arrive unannounced, but I didn't have the luxury of being formal.

The guards opened the gate and bowed as we passed.

"Thank you, gentlemen," Zaxis said.

Orwyn and Lynus were quiet. Both of them tilted their heads back, taking in the sights.

The inside of the Astral Tower was much more impressive than the outside. Exposed gears and cogs covered the ceiling, each turning at a steady pace. The clang of operation echoed in the long, central hallway. I led the way, showing everyone else where to go. I had only been here once before, but I remembered it clearly. The brilliant shine of the brass, copper, and steel machinery reminded me how well this place was cared for.

Lynus shivered. With a sneer, he muttered, "I should've brought Everett."

"Why?" Zaxis asked.

"He's a better talker than I am."

"You don't have to say a thing. Volke and I have this handled."

Lynus narrowed his eyes. "Heh. Everett's a better talker than *you two*. I'd trust him more in this situation."

"Pfft. Master Zelfree may be good, but we're super talented, isn't that right, Volke?"

Part of me hoped Zaxis said nothing during this entire interaction. The ruling council of Fortuna was old and set in their ways, from what I could remember. Yelling at them would do little good.

"I'm sure it'll be fine," I muttered.

Orwyn tapped the tips of her fingers together. "Such machinery... My village had nothing like this."

Images of owls and feathers were etched into the thick glass of the windows.

The place had a theme, even if it was mostly barren.

We came to a large door with a silver cog overhead. This door was bluish-black—nullstone infused and resistant to all magic. I went for the handle, but Lynus grabbed my wrist, startling me.

"What're you doing?" he growled. "This is a trap."

"The... door?" I asked.

"It's made with nullstone." He yanked me away, concern in his voice. "We shouldn't flippantly enter there, lad."

Zaxis chuckled. "Have you already forgotten we're immune to the suffocating effects of nullstone? The door is no obstacle for us."

The information seemed to calm Lynus. He grumbled something and then rolled his eyes. With a scoff, he released my wrist and stepped back. I rubbed at my arm, surprised by his strength, but also by his actions. Was he truly worried about me? Or had he acted on instinct alone?

"You should still be mindful, lad. Doors like this are only found in places where people suspect there might be trouble."

I hadn't thought of it like that.

After mulling over the comment, I opened the nullstone door.

Inside, there was a U-shaped table large enough to seat more than thirty people. But that was it. The room was empty. No people. No food. No arcanists. This was just the banquet hall—the place I had met the ruling council before.

"Why is no one here?" Orwyn asked as she poked her head into the room.

"Because Volke led us to the wrong place." Zaxis exhaled.

"Oh. I see." She smiled to herself. "This is fun. I didn't imagine this being entertaining."

"How is it *fun*?"

Orwyn leaned out of the room and shrugged. "This building is unique, and I've never gotten lost before."

"Never."

"No. I've always had someone to guide me. Someone to watch over me." Orwyn glanced around. "I like that we might need to find the way ourselves."

Zaxis shook his head. Then he shot me a sideways glance and mouthed, *What's with this lady?*

I shrugged. But before I shut the door, I noticed a small note on the floor. I knelt and picked it up, confused. The only words written on it were: *We are in the council room. Straight down the hall. Last door. We await your arrival, Warlord.*

The arcanists who ruled Fortuna had mild amounts of divination. They could see things without leaving their tower, and they saw small glimpses of potential futures. Had they seen me coming? And seen that I might get lost? I set the note down and then shut the door. I motioned the others to the long hallway.

The four of us wandered down until we came to another door with a silver cog. I assumed, given the knowledge on the note, this was the council room.

I grabbed the handle and took note of the nullstone-infused wood. Everything in the Astral Tower was protected. Which was interesting, but I pushed the thought aside.

And then I entered the room.

Chapter 22

Results Or Excuses

Two mongwu arcanists were the only ones in the council room.

Mongwu were owls in form, but majestic in all other ways. Giant "horned" feathers grew from the sides of their head, as if they wore the helmets of warriors. Their black talons, gold eyes, and red-tipped wings were iconic, and spoken of in most tales that involved them.

Mongwu were mystical creatures of wisdom and death, and they supposedly had powerful clairvoyance.

The arcanists themselves were somewhat familiar to me. I had met them both exactly one time.

The first was a man with slumped shoulders and bags under his eyes. Like Eventide, he had graying hair. His name was Walter Gonni, and he was the Master of Coin for the city of Fortuna.

The second arcanist was the city's mayor, Halladay Lanes. He, too, had graying hair. He sat in his chair with a slight hunch, his robes covering him from his neck to his ankles, but it was still apparent how very thin he was.

The two of them wore gold sashes and shirts so ruffled, I saw the trim poking up from under their robes. Mayor Lanes had medals pinned to his shoulders, no doubt showcasing his many accomplishments, though I wasn't aware of the details.

And they both sat behind a large desk. They had five chairs on their side, no doubt for all the council members, but three were empty.

"Ah, there you are," Mayor Lanes said. He waved us forward. "We were wondering when you would come to us next, Warlord."

I entered the room. Zaxis, Orwyn, and Lynus entered after me, each remaining a few feet behind. They said nothing, and instead turned to me.

"Hello," I said as I approached the desk. "Master of Coin. Mayor. It's a pleasure to see you again."

They both offered a slight tilt of their head. So did their mongwu owls.

"The council of Fortuna swore fealty to me." I took in a breath, trying to picture how I would word this. "I need your cooperation now. The Second Ascension is on the move, and they have several god-creatures."

"What can we do to help?" Mayor Lanes asked. His tone seemed skeptical—bordering on irritation.

"I need an airship."

The two arcanists exchanged glances. The Master of Coin quickly nodded to me. "Fortuna can provide an airship and crew."

"And I need you to send word to the many nations who swore to me," I continued. "I need to mobilize soldiers."

"Under what banner?"

At first, I wasn't sure what he meant. But then I remembered the many tales of war I had read in Gravekeeper William's tiny library. "Under *my* banner," I stated. "The soldiers will answer to me. This is a war against the Second Ascension, and I know they have plague-ridden arcanists in their ranks."

Once again, the arcanists exchanged glances, this time more irritated than before.

"We swore to you because we wanted you to protect us," Mayor Lanes said. "So, surely, *you* should be the one to fight the Second Ascension."

The owls on their chairs shifted their weight from one taloned foot to the other. Their horned feathers fluttered, and one even hooted.

The mongwu behind the mayor nodded his head. "I agree with my arcanist. What kind of *Warlord of Magic* are you if you need common soldiers to fight your battles?"

"Let me speak, Watson," Mayor Lanes said as she lifted a hand.

The reason I wanted to mobilize soldiers was because I couldn't be everywhere at once. And what if it came to a war? The Second Ascension had attacked Thronehold with hundreds of arcanists—and tactics to take advantage of their magics. While Terrakona and I could've defeated each individually, we couldn't do so all at once. We were just two individuals. If we wanted to mitigate damage, and protect as many people as possible, we needed to have soldiers dedicated to keeping things safe.

And most likely fighting the plague-ridden arcanists when the time came.

"Mobilizing soldiers will take time," I said. "If we send the others now, then in a few months, they can work to protect us—or perhaps hold off the soldiers of the Second Ascension while I deal with the Autarch."

Zaxis forced a loud cough.

"While *we* handle the Autarch," I muttered, correcting myself.

The Master of Coin leaned onto his desk. With a frown, he stared at me. "Warlord, Fortuna is a trading port. We have long disassociated ourselves from politics and war. Mustering soldiers would require us to hire master arcanists skilled in combat to train fresh recruits. And that's if anyone volunteers."

Watson, the mongwu, nodded along with the explanation, though he remained quiet. His gold eyes were narrowed in scrutiny.

"But your port makes this the perfect place to gather soldiers," I said. "Ships can easily get here, and so can supplies."

"Supplies are costly, and what if the nations who have sworn to you ignore our messages?" The Master of Coin deepened his frown. "What you're asking… It's too much."

My chest tightened as I absorbed all his words. What good was having their fealty if they couldn't do anything? Sure, they were providing me with an airship, but if they couldn't even muster a few troops in my name, why have the backing of nations at all?

Of course, Fortuna wasn't a nation. It was a single city in the Isle Nation Perphestoni, but they often acted on their own. And I knew they had the coin to hire arcanists and train some soldiers. So why were they hesitating?

"Give me a moment," I said to the mongwu arcanists.

Before they could even answer, I turned my back to them and stepped closer to the other god-arcanists. Anger roiled beneath my skin, but I held it in check, just in case I was being unreasonable. I didn't know the logistics of forming an army, but it seemed within their capability.

Whispering, I asked, "What do you all think?"

Orwyn remained quiet. Zaxis scoffed and seemed just as upset as I was. He was about to open his mouth, and give me a tirade, no doubt, but Lynus just smiled, cutting him off with that simple gesture.

"You can have results or excuses, not both," Lynus growled. "It's up to you to decide what you're going to accept from these weak-spined layabouts."

That sounded more like the Dread Pirate Calisto than

Lynus, the reformed man, but this time, I agreed with his sentiment. The mongwu arcanists hadn't even *tried* to do anything I had asked. Their first response was to say it was too difficult. Was protecting the world from magical corruption and disaster just too much of an inconvenience for them?

I turned back to face Mayor Lanes and the Master of Coin. The two arcanists were staring at me with interest, the golden eyes of their owls unblinking.

I stepped forward. "It's my duty to protect Fortuna," I stated. "And sometimes that requires bolstering our defenses. If you can't muster forces, I'll need to build natural barriers around the bay. Terrakona and I will rearrange the terrain so the Second Ascension can't attack this location with any amount of ease."

"Well, but surely you won't do anything to disrupt the trade coming through the city?" Mayor Lanes asked.

"It'll likely disrupt the trade, but I'll make a new bay in a city capable of building an army. That way, the citizens will be defended, even if I'm away—even if the Second Ascension sails ships into their ports."

The Master of Coin held a hand up to the ruffled collar of his shirt. "Are you threatening us?" he whispered.

I half-smiled. "No. I'm telling you the Second Ascension is dangerous. And I fear they might attack while I'm off dealing with the Autarch. When I asked you to gather soldiers—and to simply send messages to other nations to send their own troops—you told me that was too difficult. So I'll make sure you're safe before heading off to another nation who can honor my requests."

The two city council members acted as though I had slapped them across the face. They hastily whispered among themselves, arguing for a moment—even with their eldrin—before returning their focus to me.

"Perhaps we had misjudged the situation," Mayor Lanes said, smiling the fakest smile I had seen in a long time. "We didn't realize how dangerous you considered the Second Ascension. If things are this grim, of course we can muster some soldiers."

"And send my message to neighboring nations?" I asked.

He nodded several times. "Of course. Yes. It would be our pleasure."

"It will happen at once," the Master of Coin added. "Now that we know the gravity of the situation, we will endeavor to make everything happen as you desire."

I held back a chuckle. They seemed more than willing to bend over backward and get this done now. But I shook the thought from my head. It didn't matter that I had to pressure them—all that mattered was they would get it done.

"Thank you," I said. "Then as soon as the airship is ready, I'll be leaving. Until then, I'll be at my estate. If there's any word of the Second Ascension here in the city, please let me know."

The two mongwu arcanists gave me formal bows of their heads. Then I turned on my heel and strode out of the council room. Zaxis was at my side, smiling the entire time. Orwyn and Lynus followed as well, both quiet, but they, too, seemed content with the outcome.

That night, I walked the long halls of my estate. I was a stranger in my own home. The furniture and grounds all belonged to me, but they were foreign and unfamiliar. Sometimes, when I entered a room, I was surprised to learn its purpose. Of course, this estate had been given to me a little over seven months ago, so it was natural I didn't know my way around, but it still felt strange.

Thankfully, I had Evianna at my side. When I glanced over, and she smiled at me, the whole estate seemed warmer and brighter.

The two of us walked the halls together, bathed in the moonlight that streamed through the windows. Nothing was more tranquil or relaxing. Nothing felt as right.

The others were in their own rooms—the estate had around twenty-five or so—or in sitting rooms, waiting until we got word from the city council that our airship was ready.

This quiet time before the storm was needed. My thoughts dwelled on Luthair and the Second Ascension, but occasionally, with Evianna here, my musings drifted to pleasant things. Like what kind of future we could have once this was all over.

Our soft footfalls on the hallway rugs eased my tension and brought me to the present. The moonlight caught on Evianna's white hair, practically giving it a glow. It was ethereal and magical. I enjoyed it more than I should've.

"Why do you keep looking at me with that grin?" Evianna asked with a laugh. Then she took my hand and held it as we strolled the hall.

"Is it bothering you?" I asked. "My looking?"

Evianna brushed back some of her beautiful hair. For a moment, her face grew pink. "Well, no, but you keep making the same expression over and over. It makes me think you're having thoughts."

"I'm always having *thoughts*," I playfully said.

"Y-You know what I mean."

"All right. If you don't want me to look, I won't."

Evianna frowned. "I didn't say that. I just... want to know what you're thinking."

"I'm thinking you're gorgeous," I said, no hesitation. "And that I wouldn't trade this moment with you for anything."

Without warning, Evianna stopped and tugged at my hand.

I stopped and turned to face her. "Is something wrong?"

Her cheeks darkened to a bright red, and even her ears shifted color. Evianna refused to meet my gaze. She kept her eyes on the floorboards, and her hand seemed sweaty. That had never happened before.

Then, with a frown and seemingly fueled by anger, Evianna snapped her bluish-purple eyes up to meet mine.

"Volke Savan," she said, her tone bordering on accusatory. "Why haven't you asked me to marry you?"

"W-What?" I stammered. Then I glanced up and down the hall, wondering if anyone had heard that. It was empty. We were still alone.

Marriage was common for individuals our age, no matter which nation they hailed from. Typically, marriage among nobles was arranged. I wasn't a noble, and Evianna had left most of the Argo Empire behind, so it likely wasn't an issue, but I wasn't certain.

And in most nations, presenting a *token of affection* was common when asking someone to become their betrothed. The token was different within certain cultures, but it was most common to gift something wearable.

Although, I had heard of some island nations where the individuals marked themselves with tattoos—to mimic the bonding of mystical creatures to people. The marriage was a new "bond," and so a special mark was tattooed on their shoulders.

I hadn't yet decided what I wanted to do, and with all the fighting, and worry about the Second Ascension, I hadn't had time to dedicate to planning anything elaborate.

"We should officially be betrothed to one another," Evianna said matter-of-factly. She grabbed my other hand with her own, so we were fully facing one another. "I've known we should be together for years now. All this waiting is ridiculous and uncalled for. We both l-love each other." Evianna's voice became strangled with emotion. She pursed her lips, her face still bright red.

"Love each other?" I repeated.

We had never actually said that to one another.

"Of course." Evianna took a deep breath. "Of course we love

each other. I mean... *I love you.*" She spoke everything as though it was both fact but also uncertain. "And you love me. R-Right?"

This time, when she met my gaze, her eyes were glassy.

The moment felt fragile and beautiful, like holding a thin vase made of crystal. If I wasn't careful, it would fall and shatter.

"I love you," I said.

My words were firm and confident—I didn't want to risk even cracking a moment so wonderful.

Tears streamed down Evianna's face. She quickly let go of my hands and rubbed the tears away, smiling the entire time.

"Are you okay?" I asked as I stepped closer.

"O-Of course," she stammered. She swallowed hard, stiffened her lip and then stared me straight in the eyes. "Volke... I... I don't want to wait any longer."

Evianna reached into the pocket of her inner coat. She withdrew a small box made of wood and gold. It had the seal of the Argo Empire on it—a rose and dragon. Then she held it in both hands and presented it to me.

"We m-met in a river," Evianna said, struggling through her words, more silent tears rolling down her face. She smiled the entire time, as though she couldn't stop. "I was l-looking for glitter crabs. You remember?"

"I do," I said, my own throat tight.

"I wanted to give one to my s-sister, because they're good luck. And I know I gave one to you for your birthday a while back, but I thought... the shells of the glitter crabs are important to us. And they must be good luck. Because they brought us together."

Evianna opened the box and held it out. Inside was a charm —something to hang on a necklace or other piece of jewelry. It was a glittery sliver of a shell, crafted to be both beautiful and small. It had all the shimmer of a star shard, even though I knew it wasn't anywhere near as powerful.

"It's a symbol," Evianna said as she rubbed at her eyes. "Of my love for you." She gently placed the box in my hand. "Take it. And... and we'll be officially betrothed."

"You're asking me to marry you?" I asked.

"Well, you were taking too long." Her statement was a mix of playfully grumpy and happy. "But... do you accept?"

I gathered her in my arms for a tight embrace, so overwhelmed with joy, I almost joined her in crying. When I smiled, it was bordering on painful, it was so wide. I just couldn't stop myself. Things had been hectic and demanding for so long that I hadn't thought to set things aside and advance my relationship with Evianna.

"Of course I accept," I said as I brought my lips to hers.

We embraced for...

Several minutes, at least.

Honestly, I lost track of time.

Chapter 23

Knightmare Duel

The next morning, I was awoken by banging on my bedroom door.

I lifted my head off the pillow and groaned. Evianna slept next to me, bundled in several blankets, her long, white hair tangled over everything. After a yawn, I glanced over.

Layshl, Evianna's knightmare, lifted out of the shadows, her cape fluttering behind her as she walked over to the door. The hollow suit of armor opened it up and spoke with the person outside. Then Layshl shut the door and stepped into the darkness.

She emerged out of the shadows near the bed, her empty cowl "staring" at me. "Volke," she said, feminine and regal. "There is an arcanist at the door who wishes to speak with you."

"Who is it?" I asked, my voice rusty.

"Apparently, he calls himself *Lucian Nellit.*"

Lucian?

I knew him.

With my heart pounding, I threw off my blankets and quickly dressed. While I normally wore a necklace with the atlas turtle shell fragment that Liet had given me, today I made sure it was definitely around my neck. The glitter crab shell fragment was right next to the guild pendant, and I touched them both before proceeding.

Once I had my sword on my belt, and my shield on my back, I patted down my messy hair and exited the room. Layshl stayed with her sleeping arcanist, no doubt to guard her while I was away.

I had met Lucian in Thronehold a few years ago during the Sovereign Dragon Tournament. Lucian had been apprenticed to the Grandmaster Inquisitor—and he was also a knightmare arcanist. He was about my age, and while he was someone to be admired, he had always been difficult. For some reason, Lucian didn't particularly care for me.

It didn't take me long to reach the front door. Before I opened it, I took a moment to make sure my shirt was slightly open, to expose my god-arcanist mark. After a deep breath, I pulled open one of the double doors.

Lucian.

He hadn't changed at all. It was like he was frozen in time.

He wore a fierce expression just as much as he wore a tight-fitting black tunic and long, puffy white pants. His dark hair was cut short, and the shadows around his feet swirled with excess energy.

Lucian's knightmare, Azir, was here and messing with the darkness, but the creature didn't reveal himself before me.

I stepped outside and shut the door behind me. The morning sun brightened the sky and made everything warm. The song of the ocean tide crashing on the beach was a pleasant sound to hear after so long in Regal Heights.

"Lucian?" I asked.

The man bowed deeply. "Warlord," he said as he straightened his posture.

Which was odd. The man never really liked me before. Then

again, I had helped him to interrogate a pirate once. Perhaps he thought fondly of me now.

"Lucian," I said again, a little more relaxed. "Why are you here? At my estate?"

"When I heard you had returned to Fortuna, I figured I could offer my assistance." He held both his hands behind his back, his demeanor very *military*. "I own my boat, the *Midnight Thorn*, and I'm a skilled knightmare arcanist."

I mulled over his statement for a long moment. "You want to help?"

"You *are* going to fight the Second Ascension, correct? That's the gossip flying through the city streets. Flyers have been posted that say you're forming an army to fight against them."

"I... Well, *yeah*, actually. That's exactly what I'm doing."

Lucian lifted an eyebrow. "Then, I'm here, answering your call to arms. I want to fight alongside you."

"Wait, didn't you once say you would never swear fealty to me?" I rubbed at the back of my neck. "I could've sworn you said that."

"I did. But do I need to swear myself to you? Or can I just swear myself to the cause? No one wants the Second Ascension defeated more than I do."

He had such a rough edge to his voice, like everything was about to devolve into a fight. I crossed my arms, debating with myself on whether or not he would make a good ally. On the one hand, he was a talented fighter—and he was devoted to defeating our enemies.

On the other hand, he was difficult. Prickly. Didn't work well with others.

But...

He was also a knightmare arcanist. And I did have a special spot in my heart for those creatures. And the *Midnight Thorn* was a large boat. If we were heading across the ocean, the *Midnight Thorn* could sail the waves, and the airship could fly through the clouds—we would be defended top to bottom, and be able to carry more supplies. It was a good idea.

If only Lucian was more cooperative. I already had both Zaxis and Lynus with me, and those men were barely keeping it civil most of the time.

"Come inside," I said, pulling the door so it was more open. "Perhaps you should speak with the other god-arcanists first." If they all got along, it would be good to have Lucian and his knightmare, Azir.

I stepped aside and allowed Lucian in.

Since we were the same age, roughly, it was easy to compare us. Lucian was shorter, but he seemed just as muscled and trained and sure on his feet. It put me on edge. I didn't think he would attack me, but knowing he was a warrior—and that he wasn't necessarily my friend—left me a little uneasy.

Evianna stood in the middle of the entrance hall, her armor on, her hands clasped together. Her knightmare stood by her side, and Lucian's eyes went wide.

"Princess Evianna?" he asked. Then he bowed deeply at the waist. "It's a pleasure to see you're well, Your Highness."

Evianna threw some of her white hair over her shoulder as she strode over to me. Then she wrapped her arm around mine and held me close. "Good morning, Lucian. I'm glad to see you continue the good fight. Have you come to join us?"

"That's the plan." He straightened his posture.

"*Volke.*"

Adelgis's telepathy caused me to flinch. I had been focused on the events unfolding before me. Why was Adelgis reaching out now? Why not talk to me in person? He was in the same house.

"*The thoughts of Lucian... He's excited to join our cause.*"

"That's good," I mumbled aloud.

Both Evianna and Lucian glanced over at me. I forced an awkward smile and then motioned for them to wait here in the entrance hall. "I'll be right back." Before they could protest, I turned and walked off. "What's wrong, Adelgis?"

"*Lucian is excited because he wants to slay Akiva. It's his highest priority, because Akiva killed the Grandmaster Inquisitor. That's all Lucian can think about, even right now. If the man finds out Akiva, wounded, is here in the city, and that you plan to get him healing from the Grand Apothecary, he won't take it well.*"

I entered a random room and almost stumbled over a set of brooms and a bucket. I'd had no idea this was a closet. With a nervous chuckle, I untangled myself from the supplies and then entered the *next* door. "Okay, that might be a problem, but if we don't tell Lucian about Akiva, I think it'll be fine. We can just leave Akiva here with Gillie and sail off on his ship."

"*You're putting a lot of faith in everyone's ability to stay silent on the matter.*"

I had entered a study of some kind. The empty desk and shelves made me think the last person who owned the estate had long since died, and their possessions had been sold off.

Technically, Akiva was still here. Gillie wouldn't return to her home until this evening, and Orwyn refused to be separated from him.

"No one ever talks about Akiva," I said with a shrug. "We'll be fine."

"*I have bad news.*"

I stopped in the middle of the study and crossed my arms. "Worse news than Lucian wanting to kill Akiva?" If he did, Orwyn would turn against us. This entire trek would suddenly become a lot more complicated, and I didn't need any of that.

"*Volke, you need to return to the entrance hall immediately.*"

"Hm?"

"*Evianna just told Lucian all about Akiva and his presence on the estate.*"

"What?" I practically barked.

I didn't even hear what Adelgis said next. I leapt from the study and dashed back to the entrance hall, my head practically spinning. Why would she mention anything like that? In my heart, I knew why. Lucian had probably asked. Since Evianna wouldn't think he would immediately lose his control, she would have told him all about our encounters.

The moment I spotted Evianna and Lucian, I was surprised.

They were standing stiff and straight, but not yelling or fighting. When I made it back to Evianna's side, Lucian's shadow swirled around his feet.

Azir rose from the depths of the darkness and then coalesced to form a suit of black armor.

Azir was thin metal and leather armor with an empty hood where a head should be. Dozens of shadow daggers hung from a bandolier across his chest, each as sharp and pointed as a stiletto. When I had last seen Azir, he was young and missing parts to his armor. Now he was more a fully grown knightmare, with empty gloves, boots, and a shoulder guard.

He looked like a master assassin.

"Is it true?" Lucian demanded, drawing my attention back to him. "You're harboring the king basilisk arcanist? *You have Akiva?*"

I held up a hand. "Wait a minute."

"*Is it true?*"

"Yes," I barked back. "But *listen.* Akiva has been dealt with. The man is in no condition to fight."

Lucian pulled a hidden dagger from the tight folds of his shirt. The blade had been so thoroughly concealed, I hadn't noticed it at all. The black weapon was small, but I recognized the material it was made of.

Nullstone.

A weapon to hurt arcanists specifically. A blade made of nullstone would cut through most magical defenses.

"Akiva is the assassin who killed Queen Velleta! The monster who stole the life of the Grandmaster Inquisitor! If Akiva is here—if he still draws breath—there's no reason you shouldn't end him."

"*Akiva is a dog*," I shouted. I placed a hand on Retribution. "He answered the commands of his master, the Autarch. Now he serves another master, *and* he's been crippled. If you really want revenge for the Grandmaster, you'll redirect your vengeance."

Lucian held his dagger firmly in his hand. He narrowed his dark eyes, his expression stony and cold. "You were a knightmare arcanist, just like me. How can you allow this to happen?"

"I'm being pragmatic."

"You're being *pathetic.*"

This wasn't the right time for this. Last night had been magical, and now I would have to deal with *this?* Sometimes the world felt like it was tossing me jokes.

To my surprise, Evianna stepped in front of me. She waved her hand over the darkness, and her own knightmare formed from the shadows. Layshl's wing-like cape and scaled armor were distinct—like her empty suit of armor had been crafted from the hide of a dead dragon.

Then Layshl knelt and pulled a thin—but long—blade from the shadows.

"How dare you step foot on this property and speak to my betrothed that way," Evianna stated, her voice loud and carrying throughout the manse. "You disgrace yourself. Volke Savan is the Warlord of Magic, and one of the few people to hold back the evils of the Second Ascension. Who are you to call him *pathetic?* You have a death wish."

Azir melted into the darkness and then lifted up again around Lucian. The once empty assassin armor formed over Lucian's body, fitting him perfectly from head to toe. He grabbed one of the daggers from the bandolier, so that he had two, and then leapt away into a defensive stance.

Were we about to have a fight? The entrance hall was only twenty feet from one wall to the other, and small decorative tables with vases were positioned near the front windows. This wasn't really the place for combat.

"Weakness," Lucian and Azir said together, their voices fused into one haunting tone. "That's what this is. The Grandmaster Inquisitor gave his life to save others. I trained under him for years. If you, too, are a knightmare arcanist, you should understand the lust for vengeance."

Layshl melted away and then also formed again, this time around Evianna. Her scaled armor hugged every portion of Evianna's body, creating a sleek and agile suit of armor.

"Lashing out at Volke won't get you the vengeance you seek," Evianna and Layshl replied, their voices equally as haunting, though not as uniform as Lucian and his eldrin's. "This course of action will only net you enemies."

When I attempted to step forward, Evianna held out an arm.

"I'm defending your honor," she and Layshl said.

A part of me wanted to tell her that wasn't necessary—I could handle Lucian—but another part of me understood that Evianna wanted to be there for me. She was defending me from slander because these were threats that she *could* handle, and not world-ending dragons or magic-corrupting diseases that were outside of her control.

So I said nothing.

"I'll show you what it means to be a knightmare arcanist," Evianna and Layshl stated.

Lucian smirked. He held up his daggers. "You're a fool if you think you can best me," he and Azir muttered. "But I can't wait to see you try."

Chapter 24

Lucian

Evianna manipulated the darkness to create long tendrils. The tentacle-like shadows coalesced into a physical form. When they thrashed around the entrance hall, they knocked over the tables and vases, shattering them across the floor.

All the tendrils then went for Lucian.

The man wasn't lying, though—he was an accomplished knightmare arcanist.

When Lucian waved his hand, the shadowy tentacles froze mid-swing. Then he redirected their attack toward Evianna, his control over the darkness clearly superior.

Evianna slipped into the void and then emerged closer to Lucian. She stabbed with her thin blade, her skill and confidence on full display. Lucian parried her blade away from his body using the nullstone dagger. It sliced through the shadows of Evianna's weapon, cutting it in half.

She leapt backward with her broken sword.

Fortunately, the weapon was made using her knightmare magic. It wasn't a permanent weapon constructed with star shards—it was manipulated darkness made physical. Evianna dipped the broken blade into her shadow and then slowly pulled it back out, everything completely repaired.

She held her blade high over her head.

Lucian threw his other dagger. Evianna dodged, but then he threw another—and another, and another. The bandolier on his chest had dozens, and Lucian ripped up the wall behind Evianna with his many strikes.

Then he waved his other hand, and the shadows answered his call.

Technically, knightmares could evoke terrors, but Evianna and Lucian would both be immune to the fear effects. There was no point in using that.

The darkness spread across the floor, covering the rugs and tile like a flood of black liquid. Everything Lucian managed to touch with the shadows was held in place. His tar-like alteration of the darkness made it a sticky trap.

Evianna stepped on some of the shadows, and her boot stuck. Then the darkness spiderwebbed up her leg, clinging to her knightmare armor.

With clenched teeth, Evianna slashed at the shadows. She manipulated the void at the same time, freeing herself and then backing further away. Which was exactly what Lucian wanted. He threw more daggers—one even slashed Evianna across the upper part of her left armor. At range, he had the advantage, and if he could catch her in any trap, he could potentially win their little duel.

I would step in if I thought Evianna's life was in danger, but until then, I just watched, my whole body tense.

The shadows on the floor spread to my feet, but never actually touched me. Was Lucian excluding me? That was wise of him. If he attacked me, it would be the perfect excuse to intervene without upsetting Evianna too much.

Bleeding from her arm injury, Evianna moved away again, almost reaching one of the doors to the kitchen. She held her injury and cursed under her breath. At first, I thought she would run, but then she dove head-first into the darkness.

Lucian readied his nullstone weapon.

Evianna shadow-stepped up the wall and onto the ceiling. Both Lucian and I watched her movement, but Lucian was much more surprised than I was. It was clear from his sneer that he hadn't expected this.

Evianna flew out of her shadow on the ceiling and plunged straight for Lucian.

The smart move would've been for Lucian to duck into the darkness himself, but for whatever reason—I suspected *pride*—Lucian held his ground.

In one quick, and brutal, stab, Lucian thrust his nullstone dagger up as Evianna came down on him. He stabbed her just below her left collarbone, but that didn't stop *her* attack. She thrust her long sword through his leg, practically piercing his right femur, pinning him to the floor.

Then Evianna released her sword and swung her hand at Lucian's face. To my shock, Layshl's gloves formed claws made of hardened darkness. They were dragon claws—and Evianna slashed them across Lucian's face, ripping up part of Azir's hood in the process.

Her surprise attack had obviously caught him off guard.

I held my breath, my attention completely consumed by the fight.

But then the wind howled throughout my home. A gale-force blast ripped through the entrance hall, disturbing everything. It was so powerful, some of the wallpaper was torn from the walls.

Lucian was blasted backward into one wall while Evianna was thrown into the opposite. They both hit hard enough that they shouted. Then they crumpled to the floor.

"*Orwyn*," I yelled. "Enough!"

Orwyn walked down the far staircase, her expression neutral, her emerald eyes on Lucian. When she finally made it halfway into the entrance hall, she said, "You're the one here for my Akiva?"

With a deep breath, and blood trickling down his leg, Lucian forced himself to stand. He held his daggers close.

"Who are you?" Lucian and Azir asked as one being.

"I am the sky titan arcanist—the Falcon—and the one responsible for Akiva's actions." She stepped forward, wind blowing in circles around her feet. Lucian's control of the shadows had ended when he slammed into the wall, but it was clear from the way they crept across the floor a second time that he was attempting to set up his trap once again.

Lucian huffed. "Akiva works for the Second Ascension."

"He *used* to work with the Second Ascension. Now he is my ward. If you have qualms, I'm the one you should be dealing with."

"You harbor a known murderer and call him your *ward*?" Lucian grabbed at his injured leg. Shadows sprang to life. He removed Evianna's blade, and then the darkness wrapped around the wound, preventing most of the blood loss. "What kind of insanity is this?"

Orwyn faced him, her expression never changing. "Akiva is a soldier in war. All soldiers kill—that doesn't make them murderers."

"Akiva killed Queen Velleta! He murdered the Grandmaster Inquisitor! He *slaughtered* hundreds of innocent people in Thronehold just to fuel his *requiem aura!* He's no soldier—he's a force of evil."

"Hm." Orwyn glanced at the shadows on the floor, her gaze unfocused. "I see..."

Then she went quiet.

Perhaps she hadn't known? No. She likely had. But Orwyn had been working under the assumption that the Autarch's actions were just and rightful. Now that she was straying away from him to protect the people she cared about, what would she think about Akiva's own fanatical behavior?

Evianna rubbed at her head as she, too, got to her feet. Her injury wasn't as terrible as Lucian's, but she was still bleeding. She shadow-stepped to my side and manipulated the darkness to create a new sword.

"Akiva had a grudge against the late queen," Orwyn finally said. She met Lucian's gaze. "She murdered his family and deserved to die."

"Not the Grandmaster Inquisitor." Lucian brandished his nullstone dagger.

"Orwyn..."

Someone came hobbling down the staircase. At first, the cloak made me think it was Lynus, but the limping told me it was Akiva. He held on to the railing of the stairs until he reached the bottom, then he awkwardly, and painfully, made his way toward Orwyn.

"You shouldn't be walking around," she said as she hurried to be with him.

Akiva took a ragged breath as Orwyn gently grabbed his arm and helped him stay on his feet. "I told you," he muttered, his voice strained. "People will come for me."

Orwyn tugged at his cloak and stared up into his eyes. "I won't let them take you."

The moment between them almost pained me. Why was he so important to her?

Lucian glanced over at me. After a few deep breaths, he asked, "Is this how god-arcanists will conduct themselves? Above the law? Above all consequence? Because they can't be defeated by average arcanists, they will do whatever they please?"

I had been afraid of this. The people of several nations trusted me. They trusted I *wasn't* a tyrant, like the Autarch, and that I would put their well-being before my own. If I pardoned my friends—or anyone I liked—and punished those I didn't, I was probably no better than the Second Ascension.

Perhaps Orwyn thought this, too, because when she turned back to face Lucian, she said, "During times of war, extreme measures must be taken."

Lucian said nothing. He and his knightmare remained merged—ready for combat at a moment's notice.

"After this war is over..." Orwyn stared Lucian dead in the eyes. "*I* will answer for Akiva's sins. But until then, my sky titan and I are needed to win the battle."

Akiva grabbed her shoulder and held tight. "Are you insane?" he growled. "*I won't allow you to answer for me.*"

"Wait." Lucian stood straight, dropping his daggers to his sides. "Is that... Is that frail old man Akiva?"

Frail old man were words I never would've associated with a legendary assassin, but strangely, they were apt. No one replied to Lucian's question, though. Not even Akiva himself. Orwyn just held his cloak tighter, her eyes focused on a singular spot.

The front door slammed open, and a burst of icy wind rushed through the hall. Everyone turned, most with wide eyes. I shielded my face and just sighed.

Zaxis stood in the doorway, his eldrin standing out in the front garden. Everything was either dead or coated in ice and dying. Zaxis strode into the building wearing only a pair of trousers. His red hair, tipped in frost, was wild and went in all directions.

"What's going on?" he barked, his breath coming out as frost. "I heard fighting."

Vjorn growled loud enough to drown out all other sounds.

"I have this handled," Orwyn said.

"Handled?"

Zaxis took a moment to slowly pan his gaze over everyone. He was probably confused. No one here was an enemy, yet the house was a war zone. When his gaze found nothing to destroy, Zaxis pulled up his trousers and then thumbed his nose.

"You all need to keep it down in here." He whirled on his heel and headed back out for the garden. "Training outside is what civil people do."

I appreciated that Zaxis was willing to jump into a fight at literally any moment, but sometimes he was just aggressive for no reason.

Orwyn returned her attention to Lucian. "Knightmare arcanist—once this war is over, you will have your pound of flesh for the injustices against you. Either from me, or from Akiva himself. But for now, as a god-arcanist focused on ridding the world of the arcane plague, you may not exact your revenge. I forbid it."

Lucian tucked his knives away. Then his knightmare, Azir, melted off his body, pooling as an inky blob around his feet. Lucian's white pants were stained crimson, and the shadowy binding over his wound was still in place.

"Akiva..." Lucian glared at the man. Then he glanced over at me. "*You* did that to him?"

I nodded once. "I told you. I fought and crippled him."

"And he works for you?"

"For *us*. We're fighting the Second Ascension, and he's here to help, once he's healed by the Grand Apothecary."

Our group didn't really have any healers at the moment. Zaxis's phoenix had died, Atty had left us, Vethica and her time-reversing khepera were in New Norra... Who was here who could mend wounds? No one. Gillie was our only hope at the moment, and both Evianna and Lucian could use her aid as well.

Lucian took a deep breath and then exhaled. After a long moment, where I suspected he was debating the merits of killing Akiva in his sleep, he eventually relaxed. Evianna must've noticed as well, because Layshl melted off her body and returned to her shadows.

"Very well," Lucian said, stiff. "I will accept these terms. As long as—after the war—Akiva's crimes have been settled, I will still offer you all my assistance."

Akiva growled something to Orwyn. She gently patted his chest and smiled. "It's fine," she whispered.

"As long as you don't harm anyone here—anyone under *my* protection—then we'll welcome you."

Lucian ran his hand over his shaved-short head. "Thank you, Warlord. And please forgive my rudeness. I never should've said the things I did. I was acting on emotion, and that's unbecoming of an inquisitor."

"Are the Steel Thorn Inquisitors still around?" I asked.

He nodded as he walked over to me. "They are. Just not many of them. And once the Second Ascension is dead, I will rejoin their ranks and one day become the guildmaster—to follow in the Grandmaster's steps."

That made sense. It was a role that suited Lucian well.

"In the meantime," I muttered, "you should prep your ship for departure. We need supplies, and room for a god-creature or two, before we leave Fortuna."

With a bow, Lucian said, "By your command, Warlord."

Chapter 25

Heading North

The council of Fortuna paid for us to travel with the *Diamond of Dawn*, an airship known for transporting a large amount of people and merchandise. The crew was small, but talented, and the captain of the airship was a griffin arcanist, which I appreciated.

Captain Chase Wiley, was his name, though I only met him briefly before we packed our supplies onto the airship. I oversaw everything while Orwyn, Evianna, and Zaxis took Akiva to the Grand Apothecary for healing.

Once we were packed, and everyone was healed, we still couldn't leave, though. Adelgis and Fain requested time to handle "things." Although they didn't elaborate, I knew what Adelgis wanted to do. His sister, Cinna, was living on my estate. Adelgis and Cinna had always been close.

The *Midnight Thorn* was also packed, and we decided Terrakona would swim in the waters, where he was comfortable. Xor and Vjorn would ride on either the ship or the airship, depending on what the captains wanted. The sky titan didn't need any special accommodations, which made things easier. Having three gigantic creatures already complicated things.

What would happen once we acquired the others?

I stood on the docks, and the people of Fortuna went out of their way to give me space. They also bowed deep and muttered well wishes. I waved to most, but focused on my duties.

"Warlord," Terrakona telepathically said. **"I know you wish to pursue the Autarch, but one of the god-creature lairs may be closer."**

"You can sense it?" I asked. The winds from the bay rushed over the docks, bringing with them a salty mist. I smiled, enjoying every moment.

"Your companion has explained the dreams to me. The lair of the corona phoenix may be across the ocean."

Across the ocean was *close?* Well, it might be closer than the Autarch, but still. From my understanding, it would take us a few months to cross over the waves and tides. Could we afford a few months?

Perhaps we didn't have a choice.

"What do you think we should do?" I whispered. I kept my attention on the horizon, wondering what the best path was.

"The corona phoenix will lend us its strength. We may need it."

I hated getting distracted from my main purpose, but Terrakona wasn't wrong. We needed to gather the god-arcanists. The more we had, the more strength we had over the Autarch. But it wasn't like the god-creatures were going anywhere. They sat in their lairs, waiting for a worthy individual.

And since we had the runestones, no one else was going to gain entrance to the lairs.

We *could* take our time in gathering them. We could defeat the Autarch first, and then find individuals to bond with the creatures. If we weren't under such pressure, we wouldn't need to thrust everyone we knew at passing god-creatures.

I was only pushing for Devlin because of the pressure to beat the Autarch.

"Terrakona," I whispered.

My eldrin swam through the bay, his serpentine body reminding me of leviathans. I liked it. It made me think of times long past.

"Yes, Warlord?"

"Do you think the corona phoenix can revive people?"

That was the only reason Atty wanted to achieve a true form with her phoenix. She wanted the ability to raise the dead. Would the corona phoenix have that power?

"I do not know."

That was a shame. Resurrection sounded useful. Then again, it also seemed... macabre. I tried not to think too hard about the details.

"*Volke.*"

Adelgis's telepathy practically clashed with Terrakona's. It seemed strange to me that I was having multiple conversations with people while standing all alone on the dock, but that was the reality of it.

"Yes?" I asked.

"*May I bring my sister, Cinna, with us on this trek?*"

"Why?"

But I knew the answer. He wanted to know if she could be brought into the lair of the god-creatures. If she bonded, perhaps she wouldn't be so sickly.

"*Exactly,*" Adelgis telepathically said, answering my inner thoughts. "*If Cinna bonds with a god-creature, she'll become strong—certainly strong enough to live. And the god-creatures sometimes have interesting requirements for bonding, as seen with the typhon beast.*"

"She can come."

"Thank you," he said aloud—and from behind me.

I slowly turned around to find Adelgis standing a good twenty feet down the pier. His sister was by his side, her silky black hair tied back in a braid. She refused to put any weight on her left leg, and instead walked with a cane. Her thin and shriveled body told a sad tale of someone bedridden for most of their life.

"You already brought your sister to the docks?" I asked, glancing around.

Adelgis nodded once. "I figured you would say yes. I apologize if I was too presumptive."

"It's fine."

Although I didn't know Cinna well, I knew Adelgis cared for her greatly. And when she glanced around, she smiled, her eyes alight with happiness and life, even if it was marred by her suddenly coughing up a storm.

We could use all the potential god-arcanists we could get.

"She should ride on the *Midnight Thorn*," I said, pointing to Lucian's boat.

The brig-style ship had two masts, but was one of the faster and more maneuverable vessels. It was smaller than most of the larger galley-style ships, but still had room for plenty of cannons. I liked it. The *Midnight Thorn* would likely keep up with an airship just fine, as long as we didn't run into many storms.

Adelgis motioned to the gangplank with a slow sweep of his arm. "Come, Cinna. This way. I'm sure there will be a space for you to relax on the vessel."

"Thank you, Adel." She happily took hold of his shoulder and limped along with him. "And you're sure no one will mind?" she whispered as they headed down the pier. "I don't want to be a burden..."

"I'll watch over you. And so will Fain. You need not worry."

"I saw a young man who walked with a limp as well... Is he like me?"

They headed to the *Midnight Thorn,* but I couldn't help but pay attention to their conversation.

"I think he was born with shriveled and unusable limbs,"

Adelgis replied. "He has no dreams where he received the injuries."

"Oh." Cinna held her brother's arm even tighter. "Perhaps it's better that way. He might be happier, never having known what he's missing."

From what I knew, Cinna's "injuries" had come from her father. He used his children as experiments. Well, he used *everyone* as his experiments, but his children had often been subjected to the worst of it.

I hoped Cinna would be okay.

When the darkness around my feet swirled, I knew Evianna was nearby. Sure enough, she stepped from the shadows, wearing her knightmare, and stood by my side.

The ocean winds picked up. Evianna's wing-like cape fluttered.

"No one congratulated me," she said, her voice mixed with her eldrin's.

"On what?" I asked.

"Our betrothal."

My eyebrows lifted. Then I nervously chuckled. "Oh. Yes. Well… I haven't told anyone."

"Why not?" Evianna was so taken aback, her knightmare melted from her body. Her shocked expression, mixed with her knitted eyebrows, honestly hurt my heart. "You… you're not *ashamed*… Are you?"

"Of course not." I grabbed her hand and pulled her close. "But you've seen what we've had to do to get ready for this trek. I've just had a lot on my mind. I'll tell everyone as we travel. I promise."

Evianna stared into my eyes. When it seemed as though she finally believed me, she leaned onto my chest and nodded. "Good. I was worried when the others said nothing to me. I thought they might be bitter. Or jealous."

"I doubt it."

She narrowed her eyes. "Well, once you announce it, I will write to my relatives in the Argo Empire. Since I never bonded with a sovereign dragon—and thus, can't rule—I doubt they will have any problems."

"I'm a god-arcanist," I said, almost baffled. "Why would they ever have problems?" I was one of the most powerful arcanists *ever*.

"Oh. You don't know nobility." She sighed. "They can find a problem with *everything*." She wrapped her arms around my torso. "Just promise me that you won't let anything come between us."

I leaned down and kissed her forehead. "I promise."

Until my death, I would do everything in my power to make sure we stayed together.

As soon as the *Diamond of Dawn* and the *Midnight Thorn* were packed with supplies, I had everyone board and prepare to set sail. Orwyn and Akiva still hadn't joined us. According to Adelgis, who kept in touch with everyone here in Fortuna, the Grand Apothecary was still trying to repair all the damage that had been dealt to Akiva's body.

It didn't make sense to me, and as I paced the deck of the *Midnight Thorn,* Zaxis was there to talk me through it. He sat next to Vjorn, who was curled up and sleeping on top of the quarterdeck. Vjorn's massive wolf body practically covered half that deck, causing the sailors a bit of trouble. They didn't dare yell at the fenris wolf, though. They apologized and always went the long way around.

Zaxis leaned his weight onto the ship's railing. "You're *worried* about Akiva now? Since when?"

"I just don't understand why the healing is taking so long," I said. "Gillie is the best healer we've ever known. Shouldn't it have happened instantly?"

"Magical healing is more complicated than that." Zaxis dismissively waved his hand. "If Akiva naturally healed any injuries, or if Atty's magic healed him only partway, permanent damage could've set in. Arcanist magic doesn't heal *scars*. It heals active wounds."

I didn't argue with him. Zaxis had been a master at healing when he had been a phoenix arcanist. If he said that was how it worked, then I believed it.

The sun set in the distance. The water of the bay reflected the orange and red of the sky. Everything blazed with inner life. Even the sails of other ships coming into port. Despite the beauty, I paced the ship even faster.

Terrakona swam around the hull of the *Midnight Thorn*. When he lifted his head out of the water and then dove back into the waves, he created massive swells and surges. The ship rocked slightly with each passing he made.

After a deep breath, I glanced over at Zaxis. "I'm betrothed, by the way."

"Oh, yeah?" He scoffed and smiled at the same time. "Took ya long enough."

I stopped pacing. "What's that supposed to mean?"

"Illia and I have been betrothed forever."

With my breath held, I ground my teeth. Since *when*? I didn't remember this. They had never told me! Then I chuckled to myself—I instantly realized why Evianna was so upset I hadn't mentioned anything to our friends and family.

With a smile, I returned to my pacing. "Congratulations."

Zaxis half-smiled as he tucked his hands behind his head. "Yeah. It's pretty amazing. She's the best woman I've ever known."

"I think you were supposed to say *congratulations* back to

me," I quipped. "At least, that's how normal conversation works."

"Well, it's awkward, because what am I supposed to say?" Zaxis huffed a single laugh. "*Congrats on getting the second-best girl?* I mean, I didn't want to make you feel bad."

Once again, I had to stop my pacing and just glare at him.

He met my gaze and actually laughed aloud. "I'm just messin' with you." He sat straight and placed his hands in his lap. "Seriously. Congratulations. You're a god-arcanist, practically a king, a ruler—you've now done it all. There's nowhere left for you to go."

"Except the grave," I muttered before I could even think of what I was saying.

The statement completely ended our conversation. Zaxis was silent. I didn't know what else to say. The threat of the Autarch, his plague, or the apoch dragon made it seem as though there was no returning from this war.

Once we engaged in the final combat, we would probably never return.

I *wanted* to return, but part of me was prepared to never see any of this ever again.

Without warning, Zaxis stood. Vjorn twitched his wolf ears and then lifted his massive head. **"Hunter?"**

"I think... I need to speak with Illia." Zaxis leapt over the quarterdeck railing and then landed on the central deck of the ship. He brushed himself off as he headed to the gangplank. "I think we've been betrothed long enough."

With earnest curiosity, I watched him disembark from the ship and hurry down the pier. Was he really going to marry Illia sometime soon?

The thought hadn't occurred to me until now...

Perhaps we wouldn't get a chance in the future.

I crossed my arms and returned to my pacing, my thoughts on the present. What if I never got to do a great many things? I shook my head. It was a price I was willing to pay, I just... I just wanted to make it willingly.

"*Volke*," Adelgis telepathically said.

"Yes?"

"*Orwyn and Akiva are heading your way. Also...*"

I lifted an eyebrow. "Is something wrong?"

"*The corona phoenix. It stirs. If you want someone to bond with it... I vote we head to it right now. It'll take us a month or two to even reach it.*"

I clicked my tongue in disappointment. "All right. I'll tell the captains where we're heading. You know, right? You can still sense the god-creatures?"

"*This one, yes.*"

That was a cryptic reply, but I didn't care.

As long as Adelgis knew where to take us, we would be fine.

Chapter 26

Ocean Training

When Orwyn rode through Fortuna, everyone parted for her as well, but none of the citizens waved or called out. I didn't know why, but I suspected it was because Orwyn was so... odd.

Her kirin mount trotted down the middle of the street, practically disrupting the normal flow of carriages and carts. Orwyn's gaze never strayed to the denizens of Fortuna. She kept her attention on the path forward. The wind blew around her, carefully fluttering her hair and gracefully playing with her clothes. Her white robes rippled behind her, open and exposing her god-arcanist mark.

Akiva walked alongside her kirin, his cloak up, his whole body covered from head to toe. He didn't limp, but he wasn't as agile or confident as he had been before. My tremor sense told me as much. He took his steps carefully, and his body was tense.

Gillie the Grand Apothecary had healed him, but Zaxis was correct. She couldn't solve everything because some injuries had already settled.

And then there was the Keeper of Corpses.

The gigantic beast was made up of nothing but corpses—all

intertwined to resemble a large dog. Shattered bones made up its legs, flesh and discarded skin were stitched together to make its hide, and bizarre pieces of corpses were melted together to create the semblance of a spine.

Everyone pointed, but whenever the Keeper of Corpses turned its canine-looking head to stare, the people of Fortuna hurried along.

Ezril rode on top of his eldrin, seated on the dead bodies that made up the Keeper of Corpses. He didn't seem to care. He kept his eldrin close to Orwyn, as though he would do whatever he could to defend her.

It occurred to me then that Orwyn was making herself as noticeable as possible, just as Ezril was. Were they trying to distract everyone? Were they taking everyone's attention away so the people of Fortuna wouldn't examine Akiva too hard before we left? He was a known criminal.

Orwyn rode her kirin straight down my pier, slow enough that Akiva never had to struggle, Ezril following close behind. When they reached my location, Orwyn stopped her kirin and slid off its back.

"Warlord," she whispered. "Thank you for waiting."

I pointed to the *Midnight Thorn* and then to the *Diamond of Dawn*. "We're set to head out." Then I glanced over at Akiva. The man didn't say anything. He didn't even look at me.

"Is something wrong?" Orwyn placed a hand on Akiva's shoulder.

"Just make sure he doesn't harm anyone. His king basilisk magic is deadly." The poison he created could kill most arcanists in an instant.

"You have my word," Orwyn said, her tone almost singsong. "Nothing will happen on this trip."

"Then it's almost time to go. I suggest you board."

With everyone on our ships, including Lucian and now Cinna, we had more people than I had ever imagined heading toward the corona phoenix's lair.

The morning sun greeted us first on our journey. Then a pod of dolphins swam in front of the *Midnight Thorn* as it made its way through the waves.

I stood on the deck of the ship, with my anxiety high, but my focus tight on the rocks in my hands. While out on the ocean waves, sailing away from Fortuna and far to the north, I knew I wouldn't have land available to me to train my manipulation.

In theory, I could manipulate the water, but that was the way of *destruction*. I wanted to master the *creation* side of my manipulation, so I had brought several small rocks with me on the ship. Whenever I had a moment to myself, I squeezed the rocks in my palms and focused on rearranging them.

I turned one to sand.

Another into quartz.

A few into one giant clump.

I kept altering and shaping them, mixing everything around until I finally understood every small fleck. It was the only way I could train my magic.

I had already picked *destruction* for my evocation. I created magma, and my body hardened from the inside out whenever I did it for any length of time. It was a useful trick, but now I needed to pick my other magic.

So did all the other god-arcanists.

I shoved my "training rocks" into my pockets and then turned around. Zaxis was on the other side of the boat, practicing his magic with his fenris wolf.

While he had been fast to pick up his icy evocation, Zaxis seemed obsessed with his new illusions. He did everything in his power to create them, and while I observed him, Zaxis managed to make an illusion of a bird, a barrel, and even a sailor.

They were brief, but distinct. It was as if the illusions were shaped from the icy winds. They swirled through the air and then coalesced to form an image. The illusions couldn't move or touch anything, however, which meant they were limited in use, but it was still interesting.

I glanced up at the *Diamond of Dawn*. The airship sailed through the clear skies right above us. Normally, airships were much faster than seafaring vessel since they didn't rely on the winds to fill their sails. Airships were powered by magic alone, and moved at a constant rate, regardless of the weather.

Fortunately, we had Orwyn with us. Her sky titan made sure the *Midnight Thorn's* sails were always filled, giving us an advantage.

And it was interesting to see Orwyn dancing through the sky. Her invisible eldrin swirled around her, playing with her short hair and messing with the mane of her kirin.

She evoked wind constantly.

And nothing else.

I suspected she had decided on her evocation—though I didn't know if *wind* was creation or destruction. Likely destruction, since wind had the power to erode, but I wasn't confident.

The only person who *wasn't* training was Lynus. He was on the deck of the *Diamond of Dawn*, outside my view—even outside my tremor sense—but I knew he wasn't training.

The typhon beast was loud and powerful. He often chittered or screeched whenever he used his magic, and since Xor could evoke fire, I suspected Lynus didn't want to risk damaging the airship.

"Volke?"

The question startled me. I whirled around and found my sister standing close.

She wore her wavy hair tied back in a tight ponytail. She wore a tricorn cap, but had cut a slit through the back, to allow her hair to poke through it, rather than being tied underneath it.

Part of me was impressed, but another part of me wanted to laugh, because I had never seen it that way.

Illia pulled her coat closed and then frowned. "The cap kept flying off," she said with a sigh. "So I made it so it can't escape now."

"Ah. I see."

Then Illia crossed her arms and stared at me with her one eye. She had a sort of playfulness about her, like this trek was already something grand.

"Yes?" I asked. Then I glanced around the ship. I didn't spot Nicholin. It was just me and my sister. "Is everything okay?"

"Did you want to go up to the airship now?" she asked. She pointed to the *Diamond of Dawn.* "You keep looking up there." Illia placed a hand on her chest. "I'm the *transport officer* for our convoy, so if you need any porting, either up or down, you need to speak to me or Nicholin."

Ah. Her eldrin was on the airship. That was rather ingenious.

"Who appointed you the transport officer?"

"I did," Illia said with a coy smile. "And unless you correct me, everyone has been going along with it."

"I like it. The title suits you."

She brushed off her shoulders and held her head a little higher. "I was made for this position." Then my sister relaxed and pointed to the airship a second time. "Well? Do you need to go up?"

"Uh, no. Thank you, though." When it seemed as though she might leave, I held up my hand. "Actually, I have something to tell you."

"You're betrothed," Illia flatly stated. "I know."

"How do you know?"

"Zaxis told me."

Ah. Of course. He had probably run straight to her in order to divulge the whole story.

"Everyone knows," Illia continued with a shrug.

"Really? *Everyone*?" I ran a hand down my face. There went my plan to tell people individually.

"Zaxis couldn't stay quiet. He had to tell everyone." Illia leaned forward. "He's addicted to having people pay attention to him. I've told him that before, but he always denies it."

"Are you and Zaxis going to get married?" I asked.

That question seemed to catch her off guard. Illia held onto her coat, her one eye searching my gaze. After a long moment of silence, she half-smiled. "We are." Then she narrowed her eye. "You don't have any objections, do you?"

I shook my head, though it was slow. "As long as he makes you happy."

Illia's cheeks went pink. She rubbed at her face, trying to hide the change in coloration, her attention on the deck below her feet. "He said he already lost one soulmate, he didn't want to lose another."

I held my breath and then slowly released it, my thoughts on Forsythe.

Zaxis...

"I'm happy for both of you," I said.

"And I'm happy for you." Illia poked my chest with a single finger. "But we need to make a promise right now. Whichever of us has a son first, we need to name him *William*, all right?"

That got me smiling more than anything else the whole trip. "Did you tell our adopted father we would do that?"

"No. It's supposed to be a surprise." Illia held out her hand. "Promise?"

Although I needed to speak with Evianna about the matter, I had a strong suspicion she wouldn't mind. And if she did, I could always explain the situation to Illia. Both of them were reasonable people.

I placed my hand in Illia's. "It's a promise."

Five weeks of sailing, and we hadn't found much.

Sailing across the ocean, far from land, was one of the loneliest ways to travel. The ocean went on in every direction. The sun reflected off the waves, often hurting my eyes. The sky was typically clear, meaning the blue above mixed with the blue water below, creating a monotone landscape of sapphire.

That was why sailors had so many games.

Cards. Dice. Marbles.

They played with anything and everything.

And now they were taking bets on our training.

Orwyn sailed through the sky over the *Midnight Thorn*, swirling through the air with the grace of an eagle. Lynus leaned against the railing of the airship and held out his hand. He blasted *waves* of fire through the sky, practically creating a second sun's worth of light. Orwyn nimbly dodged each blast.

"I bet she gets hit," one sailor on the *Midnight Thorn* mumbled as he swabbed the deck with a dirty mop.

Another sailor—one lazily tying down empty barrels—just chuckled. "Two leaf says she gets through this unharmed."

"I say the lass at least gets singed. And two leaf is too high. I say thirty copper. That's *thirty copper if she gets singed.*"

"I'll take that bet. But nothin' will happen. Mark my words."

I watched from the deck of the sailing ship as Orwyn controlled the winds around herself and her kirin. She never went flying without her odd horse-dragon—the beast was practically her flying steed. It kept its long legs tucked close to its body whenever the flames rushed by, and its crystal horn glittered in the afternoon sun.

Then Lynus moved. He lunged down to another area along the railing of the airship. He blasted more fire, larger and hotter than ever before. Orwyn must've been caught by surprise, because instead of dodging, she commanded the wind to protect her.

A gale-force blast of air shielded her from the flames, but then she sent it everywhere. The fire *exploded* toward the ocean waves—and some of it went straight for our ship.

The sailors shouted.

I lunged over to one and hefted my shield, Forfend, onto my arm. The embers that reached us were absorbed by my black shield, harmlessly disappearing.

The shaken sailor stared at me for a moment before bowing his head over and over again.

He wasn't in much danger. He might've been wounded a bit, but not much.

I stared up at Orwyn and Lynus, who both waved down at me. Perhaps my irritation wasn't justified—where else were they supposed to train?—but I didn't like the thought of harming our sailors.

"Is this always how it goes?" Lucian called out.

I glanced over. He stood near the helm of the ship, his posture so stiff and straight, he could've doubled as a fence post.

"God-arcanist magic is powerful," I said as I stepped away from the sailors. "But I'm here. I won't let anything happen to your men."

"Good. I would expect no less."

I didn't know how to reply to that, so I didn't. After a deep breath, I took up my position on the far side of the deck.

"Your friend is leading us to the Rocky Coast," Lucian called out again.

"Where?"

"The Rocky Coast. Not many ships venture there. The volcanos have known to be active and then inactive at random times. And the sharp rocks threaten to pierce even the sturdiest of hulls."

Why was he telling me this?

"If Adelgis wants us to go to the Rocky Coast, it's because the corona phoenix is there. We aren't going to stop pursuing the creature just because the trek is dangerous."

Lucian nodded once and then returned his attention to the horizon. Apparently, he just wanted some sort of reassurance.

Hopefully, his ship wouldn't sink. That would cause more problems than I cared to admit.

That night, I had a dream. Not a normal dream created from forgotten memories, anxieties, and imagination run rampant—this was a story. Adelgis, with his ethereal whelk magic, was weaving me a dream, like he had done many times in the past.

I thought it would be something pleasant, since it started with a beautiful emerald meadow bathed in the light of a clear afternoon. But then fire swept over the grass, turning everything to ash in a matter of seconds.

The once glorious meadow had turned into a battlefield. Men with spears and long shields linked together to fight off soldiers wearing square hats and metal plate armor. Some rode horses, and a few charged forward with war elephants.

This wasn't a war I had learned about during my youth.

This was a battle during the first god-arcanist's war. This took place long before anything I knew had been created or built.

Before I voiced a question, the sky above the war-torn meadow filled with flame. The blaze was beautiful, shifting the blue into crimson and gold.

Then I saw it. The fire was actually a creature—a gargantuan phoenix. The chest of the beast was a hole filled with darkness. A literal void that seemed to pulse with power. The fire was bird-shaped, but somehow malleable. It shifted and moved, always tethered to the sphere of black at the center of the corona phoenix.

And its legs and talons...

They were darkness given form, just as knightmares could make shadows tangible.

The corona phoenix was a creature of both light and darkness, it seemed. A beast that held sway over shadows, just the same as fire. It was a beautiful mix of opposites that seemed to speak to the duality of life.

A woman in a long robe stood under the corona phoenix. Her hair was a striking brown, and long enough to reach her knees. She held a hand up, and the phoenix of flame and darkness landed on the meadow next to her, its eyes pools of ink that matched its void heart.

"I am Tamrin the Solstice, keeper of these lands," she said, her voice loud, though she never had to shout. "You shall not advance any farther."

With a wave of her hand, the corona phoenix screeched. Its flame body dove into the meadow and rushed forward, the flames becoming a wall that moved across the battlefield. Darkness sprung up around the soldiers with spears, shielding them from the fire. The shadows didn't protect the soldiers on war elephants, or the ones with tall hats. They were burned—all of them—taken away from the battle in the glory of a pyre.

The Solstice...

A solstice happened twice a year. It was both the longest and the shortest day. Just as the phoenix was both light and darkness. A creature that sees both ends of the spectrum.

The dream, with dream-like quality, melted away, taking me to a new location. I stood on the edge of a cliff that overlooked the ocean. It reminded me of Deadman's Bluff. I was at least a hundred feet from the waves below.

And the Solstice stood with her phoenix at the edge, overlooking the vast body of water.

The world serpent and his arcanist wasn't too far behind.

I held my breath when I spotted them. Terrakona was large, but not as large as Jörmungandr, the first world serpent. I knew why. Jörmungandr was much older. He was a vast beast—a serpent with no equal. His mane of crystals wasn't black, like Terrakona's, it was red, like the fire blazing off the wings of the corona phoenix.

Jörmungandr could be his own island. His scales were thick and powerful, and his fangs so large they couldn't be contained by his mouth. He exuded power.

But the first world serpent arcanist was blurry in this dream.

I had met Luvi before, as an illusion. He was a tough man... Why couldn't I see him now?

He held out a hand, as if offering the corona phoenix arcanist to join him. But Tamrin the Solstice kept her back to the world serpent and his arcanist. She never took his hand.

"Leave me," she said. "I will protect this place and I will help you end the *blight of the sky*, but I won't fight the others."

"We're just in our convictions," Luvi replied.

"Killing the others won't prove you're right. It'll just prove you were stronger."

Then Luvi, the world serpent arcanist, dropped his hand. He and his eldrin turned and left the Solstice to her cliff gazing. For a brief moment, it almost reminded me of Atty. Were all phoenix arcanists this way? I shook my head. No, Zaxis was the opposite. Nothing like this.

I hoped Atty was okay, wherever she was.

The dream melted again, and I thought it was over.

But I was wrong.

Days passed. The moon and the sun shot across the sky, speeding up with each passing minute until years had flown by. When time slowed and flowed normally again, the corona phoenix and its arcanist had returned to the cliff.

In the distance, just at the horizon, where the water met the sky, there was a black spot. Not the moon, or an eclipse, or something I had seen before. My heart raced when I stared at the strange object. It grew larger and larger, until I realized it was a dragon heading this way.

The apoch dragon.

That was when I awoke. I sat up, my breathing labored, sweat dappling my whole body. My muscles were so tense, I felt strained.

Where was I? I glanced around and found myself in a small cabin within the *Midnight Thorn*. The cot wasn't comfortable, and was now soaked in my cold sweat. I forced myself to take a few deep breaths. The gentle moonlight that streamed in through the porthole was comforting.

The previous corona phoenix arcanist...

Had died to the apoch dragon. That was her fate. She hadn't fought with the others, but she had ended the blight of the sky with them.

I ran a hand over my chest, feeling my heart until it calmed.

"Everything is fine," I muttered to myself.

No one in the cabin answered.

Although my cot was awful, I was too tired to do anything about it. I rested back and stared at the ceiling of the tiny cabin. "Everything *will* be fine." Then I closed my eyes.

Chapter 27

The Lair Of The Corona Phoenix

Six weeks of sailing, and the rocks in my pockets were practically gemstones.

When I had first thought of manipulating the terrain, all I had pictured were mountains, lakes, rivers, and valleys, and the ability to shift them around. That was obviously useful, but I hadn't thought about the small manipulations—the changing of material.

Sand.

Rock.

Clay.

Most minerals seemed to be made of the same basic components, just... rearranged differently. When I held basic sandstone in my hand, I could change it with heat and pressure into something else. My world serpent magic was just that powerful.

I wanted to make the sandstone into a diamond—but for some reason unknown to me, I just couldn't. The rocks became granite, obsidian—even pumice—just not diamonds. Quartz was fascinating, and that seemed to be the peak of my ability to change things.

It made me wonder, though...

If I somehow got Terrakona to his true form, could I make diamonds then? Or was my limitation due to my lack of knowledge? Perhaps diamonds weren't a form of rock. I wasn't sure.

The deck of the ship creaked as it bobbed on the waves.

Night had descended, covering the ocean in an inky darkness. The crew of the *Midnight Thorn* didn't seem to mind the night. They hung lanterns on the two masts and continued on without a complaint.

The footfalls of boots drew my attention.

I turned around to find my adopted father, William, idly pacing the deck. I hadn't spoken to him much during this trip. I had been too busy.

That was my excuse for everything, lately. Nothing made me feel more like an adult than my complete lack of free time.

But seeing him was like sitting in front of a fire on a cold day. Everything felt safer—and better—when he was around. That was probably the childish part of me. In my memories, William was so much bigger than me. On the deck of the *Midnight Thorn*, he was just a normal man. Still, his presence was welcome, and I walked over with a smile.

"It's cold out," I said. "Shouldn't you be down below, with the others?"

William glanced up. He was a man with a broad set of shoulders and muscled arms. His face was clean—as always, ever since his time in the navy—and when he smiled, I saw the laugh lines. It reminded me he was older. So did the white hair speckling his dark hair.

He tugged on his dark coat and patted his thick trousers. "I'll do fine," he muttered.

But that was all.

"Everything okay?" I asked as I walked up to his side.

William brushed some of his hair back. "Aye." He offered me

a forced smile. "But you shouldn't worry about me, my boy. Your problems are much greater than mine."

The cold night wind interjected into our conversation, howling across the deck and sending a shiver down William's spine. My ability to evoke magma seemed to keep me warm no matter what. The weather didn't bother me.

"What problems do you have?" I asked. "I thought you were happy? Who or what is bothering you?"

William shook his head. "I told ya it's not worth worrying over." He placed a hand on my shoulder. "Pretend I didn't even mention it. A parent should never burden their child with silly concerns."

"Silly?" With a laugh, I added, "You know, you're one of the few people we're hoping to bond with a god-creature. That makes you more my peer than just my parent. And as a peer, I think I should be able to help with *any* concerns."

William stopped his pacing and clenched his jaw. I also stopped, confused by his standoffishness. As a gravekeeper, William had always been so forthcoming with information. Why was he so secretive now?

"Not everyone is an arcanist," William finally said. He turned to me, and then touched his own chest. "I told you once that I failed a Trial of Worth, didn't I?"

"Yeah. But that was a while ago."

"But then I went to the lair of the typhon beast."

I hesitated for a moment, wondering where this was going.

"And I'm still not an arcanist," William said, his voice growing quieter.

"Well, yes, but, the typhon beast knew who it wanted to bond with." I shrugged and shook my head, dispelling the thought. "It's not like you failed the typhon beast's Trial of Worth. It was just not meant to be."

William crossed his large arms and turned his eyes to the

stars in the night sky. "Aye. That's what I'm worried about," he whispered. "What if it's just not meant to be?"

"We're heading to the lair of the corona phoenix." I forced a bit of cheer into my voice. "The Isle of Ruma is known for its phoenixes. I'm certain this bird is destined for you."

"But what if I head in there, and it bonds with someone else, hm?" He kept his gaze on the stars, his tone distant. "How many chances are you all gonna give an old man like me before you realize you've made a mistake?"

I didn't answer that.

I hadn't thought about it.

"I'm just sayin'," William muttered. He lowered his eyes to meet mine. "These are the silly concerns of an old man. I already accepted my place as a mortal—as someone who would never become an arcanist. Perhaps I shouldn't have gotten my hopes up again."

But I hated when he said that.

It was never too late to chase dreams. To change oneself.

To grow.

"You'll do fine," I said. I slapped him on the back, and he shot me a sideways glance. "You're tough, and knowledgeable, and wise—and have you spoken to any of these god-creatures? For *babies* they sure do talk like old folks themselves. It's like... they all lived a lifetime before, and they struggle to remember everything."

"Well, your Terrakona is like that, sure."

"It's the same with the others. Like I said, you'll be fine. And doubt is a killer more than swords. You have no need for it."

It felt odd encouraging William like this. Wasn't *he* supposed to be comforting *me?* But life was full of surprises, I had learned. And life had a way of circling around.

William genuinely smiled, which made me happy. "Well, look who went off and became a proper man." He chuckled. "I'll keep your advice close to heart, my boy. Whenever we reach the lair of the corona phoenix, I'll give it my damnedest."

"Good," I said. "That's all I've ever wanted."

Then William hardened his expression and pointed to me. "Oh. And you owe me an apology."

"I-I do?" I stammered. Then I rubbed the back of my neck. "For what?"

"I had to hear of your betrothal from *Zaxis* of all people? And that boy just talked and talked. I couldn't believe it. I was the last to know. Heh."

I almost laughed aloud. After I rolled my eyes, I said, "I'm sorry. I didn't mean for it to happen that way. I am engaged."

"To the lovely princess?"

"Y-Yes. But she's not going to rule anything in the Argo Empire. Not with her eldrin."

"What does that matter?" William chortled. "I'm just glad the two of you are happy, and that you found someone you want to spend your life with. That's a rare and special event. Don't take it for granted."

"I won't," I said.

William held up a finger. "*Love. Without it, we lose our empathy and compassion.*" Then he smiled wide. "And without it, we never know family."

That last part wasn't on the Pillar, but I appreciated the sentiment regardless.

"That's right. Thank you."

After that, we both turned our attention to the sky. It was a beautiful night. The stars twinkled like diamonds.

Seven weeks into our trek, we reached the Rocky Coast.

It wasn't an imaginative name—more descriptive, and *very* accurate. The rocks that jutted out of the waves were sharp and jagged. They were in clusters of five to six, all along a rock-covered shore. And they were all the same dark reddish color, though the tallest of the rocks were green with algae and dried-up seaweed.

The *Midnight Thorn* would've been in danger if the sky titan hadn't been with us. The massive invisible beast had control of the winds, and prevented our ship from ever hitting the jagged rocks.

Fortunately, we didn't have to search the perilous coast for long. The lair of the corona phoenix was plain to see—so obvious that I didn't even need to tell Lucian where to sail.

I didn't need Adelgis to tell me it was our destination, either. *Everyone* could tell the moment we laid eyes on the distant mountain. The afternoon sky made that easy.

A pillar of flame actively raged out of control, covering the mountain peak in a blaze that rivaled the afternoon sun. The column of fire wasn't too tall—perhaps forty feet—but it was big enough to be noticeable from a mile away. It reminded me of a lighthouse.

I shuddered when I remembered the plague-ridden phoenix that had been hiding in a lighthouse...

But I shook the memory away. This was a different phoenix. A different time. We were almost there. We would have another god-arcanist soon.

I withdrew the bauxite runestone from my pocket. The image of the god-creature phoenix was so intriguing. Hopefully, William would have no trouble bonding with it.

The air practically vibrated as the sky titan grew restless. Sytherias screeched, and the wind guided our ship through the maze of rocks jutting out of the water. The helmsman didn't even have to man our vessel—the god-creature had everything under control.

The airship sailed over the dangers and went straight to the base of the mountain.

Mountain was possibly too strong a word. The *hill with ambitions* went a few hundred feet in the air, and was mostly made of red rocks and dirt, but there were a few brave trees growing from patches of dirt. They were pines, still green, despite the chilly temperature.

The large hill was just beyond the rocky shore, and all by its lonesome in a field of charred trees and blackened ground. A forest fire must've swept through the area a year or two ago.

Perhaps that was when the lair of the corona phoenix had appeared.

I waited until the *Midnight Thorn* drew close to the shore before heading to the railing. Terrakona swam next to the ship, his scales shimmering beneath the surface of the waves. When he lifted his head, water cascaded from his crystal mane like waterfalls. Then he turned to me, his blue and red eyes vibrant with life.

"It has been a long journey," Terrakona telepathically said. **"The waters are dull, and the fire of the mountain excites me."**

"You took the words right out of my mouth," I replied with a chuckle. Then I leapt over the railing. I had no fear I would hit the water. Terrakona leaned over, and I effortlessly slid onto his back, his scales slippery.

My eldrin went right for the shore. Once he was on land, the rocks rearranged themselves to better allow him passage. Terrakona glanced back at the ship, his eyes wide, his pupils nothing but thin lines.

Vjorn the mighty fenris wolf swam onto shore, Zaxis on his back. The ocean waters were already cold, but when Vjorn stepped out of the waves, he left solid ice floating across the water in his wake. His chains rattled, his fur frosted over in an instant, and Zaxis shook out his hair to clear away the salt water.

"Volke," Zaxis shouted.

His eldrin ran over to Terrakona.

"What is it?" I called back.

"I have this." Zaxis pointed to himself, then to the fire at the top of the tall hill. "*I'll* lead the team through this lair. You should watch the boat and the airship."

"Why?" I barked.

"Because this is clearly a lair with fire, and I'm a master of winter. I can protect everyone."

I narrowed my eyes into a sarcastic glower. "Are you serious? I'm immune to heat in all forms."

"But you can't make *others* immune." Zaxis snapped his fingers, and a puff of icy mist wafted from his fingertips. "I can quell the flames. Which is why I should lead the way."

"We can go together."

Zaxis hardened his expression and stared at me. In a softer tone, raw with emotion, he said, "I'm the expert on phoenixes. And I just... I want to be the god-arcanist who runs this. Please."

When Zaxis demanded things, my first reaction was always to fight back. But he rarely asked for anything in a pleasant or agreeable manner, and the moment he said *please*, my desire to fight him on this issue vanished. I didn't care who went into the corona phoenix's lair—all I cared about was that it was bonded with someone *not* in the Second Ascension.

"All right," I said. "But are you sure you'll be okay?"

Zaxis smiled wide. "Yeah. Of course." Then he motioned back to the airship. "I was also thinking about asking Lynus to join me. I mean, he's immune to fire, too, and after training with him in Regal Heights... I just thought we would make a good team."

His statement frosted me a little. We had known each other our whole lives, but *Lynus* was the one he wanted to take.

I shook away the petty jealousy. It was good to incorporate Lynus into our planning. And Zaxis seemed to have a lot in common with the man on an emotional level.

"Who else will you take?" I asked.

"Illia, of course. Master Zelfree." Zaxis patted his eldrin's black-and-frost fur. "And your father, William. Cinna, Adelgis's sister. And I guess the little girl..."

I motioned Terrakona to lower his head. Once he did, I climbed into his crystal mane. "Just be careful," I called out to Zaxis. Then I pulled the runestone from my pocket and gently tossed it his way. "We don't want anyone to disappear on us, okay?"

Zaxis caught the bright red and gold runestone with a confident grip. "Nothing will stand between us and the corona phoenix."

I appreciated his certainty. Vjorn must've felt the same way. The fenris wolf threw back his head and howled, his fierce roar practically shaking the sails of the *Midnight Thorn*. Then the wolf headed up the rocky hill, agile and powerful, leaping from one rock to the next.

"I trust him to get the job done," Terrakona telepathically stated.

Although I felt the same way, anxiety still gripped me. What if someone got injured in the lair? I didn't want to lose anyone else. But I buried the thought deep in my heart, knowing it wouldn't help me to worry.

"Adelgis?" I asked aloud.

"*I spoke with Zaxis,*" Adelgis replied in my thoughts. "*And I told the others what will be happening. Everyone is gathering their supplies now, even your father.*"

"Thank you," I whispered.

I appreciated how competent and prepared everyone was. Which reminded me...

Terrakona turned to face the ocean, and I held out my right hand. With a wave of my arm, I rearranged the Rocky Coast—well, just our small area. I stamped down the rocks, smoothed out the shore, and then lifted stones from the bed of the ocean to create a single pier for the *Midnight Thorn*.

My manipulation was becoming easier and easier.

I felt it. Deep in my body. Soon, it would become my permanent—and only—manipulation. Which was just what I wanted.

While I constructed a place to tie down the ship, Illia and Zelfree teleported to the shore. Biyu, Devlin, William, and Lynus were with them, but Lynus waited on the rocks for the typhon beast to disembark from the ship. Unlike all the other god-creatures, the typhon beast was less mobile. It was *powerful*, but I understood why the first typhon beast had died in a canyon. Xor wasn't particularly nimble.

Biyu...

I wondered why she was down with the others, but I didn't voice my concerns. Devlin would know best. Or perhaps he was giving her time away from the boat before returning her to the care of the crew.

Once Xor was on the rocks, Lynus led the creature closer to the mountain. Biyu, Devlin, and William followed, all talking merrily.

Again, I almost wanted to stop them, but I didn't.

Devlin's roc soared overhead. Then it dove and join them on the boulders, her golden feathers bright. Would she die soon? Or would William bond? I hoped it all worked out.

I had never seen anything like the pillar of fire on top of the mountain before, but all the lairs had difficulties to overcome.

I was more surprised by the lack of the Second Ascension. Every other lair had been guarded by them. And in the world serpent's case, several individuals had been attempting to break into the lair. Without the runestone, however, it wouldn't matter if they got in through trickery. The runestone was required for the last door—the one to the creature itself—and without it, Liet believed the creature wasn't capable of bonding.

Evianna stepped out of the darkness around the rocks on the

base of the hill. She turned to me, her white hair fluttering. Then she pointed to another patch of shadows.

Lucian stepped out, already wearing his knightmare. He was a stealthy little assassin who waited in the darkness. When he noticed me staring, he crept backward into the shadows, hiding himself from sight, but not my tremor sense.

Orwyn, riding her silver kirin, flew through the air and landed on the smoothed rocks of the shore. Her kirin's cloven hooves clacked as it carried her over to us.

"Warlord," she said with a chipper tone. "It looks as though we have located one of the four remaining god-creatures."

"Zaxis is handling it," I muttered. "We'll wait here and guard the ships."

"From what?" Orwyn glanced around, her eyes wide.

"From... Well, anything that might show up. The Second Ascension. Plague-ridden mystical creatures. Anything."

"Hm." When she returned her attention to me, she smiled. "I have no doubt you'll be able to handle any monsters that lurk around here. And if there is a problem, our combined magic will put an end to almost anything."

"I agree."

I liked Orwyn's optimism. It was what we needed in this trying time.

Evianna leapt through the shadows and emerged next to Orwyn and her majestic kirin. After pushing some of her white hair over her shoulder, Evianna stood straight. "Ah, Lady Orwyn—the Falcon—perhaps you haven't heard the good news? Volke and I are to be wed."

Orwyn lifted her eyebrows. "Oh. How fascinating. In my small village, most marriages were arranged. Unless someone bonded with a kirin—then they were allowed to wed whoever they wished."

Evianna stepped closer to Terrakona. She placed her hands on the world serpent's scales. "Volke and I have known each other for a long time. He saved me from the Second Ascension, actually. He was so heroic and knightly."

I remembered that night. I also remembered how much Evianna hated me, and how she had blamed me for her sister's death. It wasn't my fault, but Evianna had been wrecked by grief. I *had* saved her from the Second Ascension, but she hadn't made the process easy.

"Akiva saved me," Orwyn whispered, her gaze losing focus. "I thought it heroic. But perhaps..."

She didn't get to finish her statement.

The small mountain of rocks rumbled. Terrakona and I immediately snapped our attention to the peak. Something moved up there—and it was much larger than I had suspected.

And then the mountain moved. It practically *opened up*, like a maw of the earth, and swallowed Zaxis's whole team. The fenris wolf, the typhon beast—even Devlin, Biyu, William, and the mighty roc. They were pulled into the ground, swallowed by the terrain.

And then the pillar of fire...

It blazed hotter than ever.

I was tempted to open the ground and pull Zaxis out, but I figured this was all part of the phoenix's lair. I'd let him handle everything, because the flames...

They were moving.

"Warlord," Terrakona said with an audible hiss. **"There is a creature here. It stirs."**

He was right. I slid off his mane and landed on the rocks, my heart beating fast. The flames on the top of this mini-mountain moved and swirled. At first, I thought it would reveal itself to be the phoenix, but then I realized the flames were *growing out of the back of a creature*. Not something person-sized or even horse-sized—it was a giant.

A fire giant.

They were rare mystical creatures—all giants were—because

their fable birth was so difficult to achieve. And most giants had difficult Trials of Worth, though their physical capabilities were said to rival dragons.

What was a fire giant doing here?

Normally, giants had the shape of a human, and depending on the type of giant, they had characteristics of certain primal elements. Wind. Fire. Water. But this giant wasn't like the ones I had read about.

This giant was a monstrosity. It was as if someone had pieced together three giants and stacked them on top of each other, one by one, and then fused their flesh. The giant had two thick legs, but six human-shaped arms. They jutted from its bizarre torso at odd places, most with claws that wept blood. The giant had two heads, one growing from the side of its neck, and one on top.

The head on top was on fire, as was its entire back. It wasn't a small flame, but a giant pyre—an inferno that raged out of control.

The second, smaller head, had fangs and bloodshot eyes that bulged from its head.

When the head spotted us, it laughed.

A sick, twisted cackle that echoed throughout the area.

This wasn't a normal fire giant. It was plague-ridden.

Chapter 28

The Fire Giant

"What is this?" Evianna whispered.

The fire giant was at least thirty feet tall. It was something older—it had to have been bonded to someone for a long time in order to reach such a size.

"A giant," Orwyn said, her voice singsong. "He's been touched by the arcane plague."

"Why is it here?"

The giant chuckled and giggled as it headed down the small mountain, its giant feet cracking stones with each step. The ground rumbled. No one needed my tremor sense to know it was approaching.

"Adelgis," I said, startling Orwyn and Evianna. "Tell the others this beast is plague-ridden. Orwyn and I will handle it. Everyone else should stay on the boat or the airship."

"*Of course*," Adelgis telepathically replied.

This creature wasn't infected with the advanced version of the plague like the monsters at Deadman's Bluff. Those creatures hadn't been capable of speaking. They didn't laugh or ponder or ask for things. They had no desires.

They were just monsters. No better than animals infected with madness.

And as the fire giant lumbered toward us, shaking the earth with each step, it chuckled.

"You won't... *you won't*... Get away... *ever*..."

The two heads attempted to construct sentences, but they were discordant and awkward. One practically choked out its words, and the other hissed them.

"I'll fight with you," Evianna said.

I motioned her to the boat. "Get back. Orwyn and I can handle this." I turned to Orwyn, and the woman nodded to me once. She had no fear in her expression. She had *nothing* in her expression, actually. She just blankly examined our opponent, as though the giant were a mildly interesting puzzle to overcome.

Evianna reluctantly slid into the shadows. I hoped Lucian did the same.

"*The others entered the lair of the phoenix,*" Adelgis said. "*Now I can't reach them. Just be careful for when they emerge.*"

The fire giant leapt down the last portion of the mountain. I held my breath as Terrakona braced for the monster. In mid-leap, the giant clenched two of its fists together and then slammed them down on the ground as it landed, blasting a wave of flames in all directions.

I had Forfend on my arm and Retribution in my hand before I even thought about the situation. The giant's fire washed over everything. When it hit the shore and then the water, the flames sizzled and died out, turning into clouds of steam.

My shield absorbed some of the magic from the attack, and I shook off the heat. It wouldn't affect me. Terrakona's scales flared, but he also felt none of the attack.

Orwyn had taken to the sky to avoid the wave of fire. She rode her kirin around, practically prancing on the air. Her sky titan swirled around the fire giant, stealing the air, and attempting to choke the beast and its fire by taking away its ability to breathe.

The giant swung with its massive hands, all six of them clawing at the wind. The sky titan wasn't corporeal, though. No physical objects could harm the god-creature.

Then the flames on the giant's back flared. The inferno exploded from the giant's back, blasting the mountain with the fury of an active volcano.

Again, I held up my shield, but it was more on instinct. When the fire giant's magic hit me and Terrakona, it didn't harm us. Instead, it scorched the rocks and once again sizzled off into the water. The *Midnight Thorn* was almost hit, and the sailors rushed to untie the ship and move it away from land.

The sky titan, Sytherias, screeched and avoided the fire giant. She probably wasn't hurt too bad—god-creatures were tough and healed quickly—but *magic* was the key to harming the sky titan. She had no physical body, just magic holding her together. And the fire giant was corrupted... Its attacks likely harmed Sytherias at a basic level.

"Terrakona," I shouted and then pointed with my sword.

Terrakona roared. He lashed his tail around and swept the giant's legs out from under it. The fire giant hit the ground, shattering stones with its massive weight. Its two heads laughed and gleefully giggled, as though the attack was nothing but a joke.

We couldn't evoke magma to win. Fire giants were immune to the heat.

"Bite it," I commanded.

Terrakona lunged. In one swift and brutal strike, Terrakona bit down on the giant's shoulder. The fire giant laughed and tried to roll away, but Terrakona hung on, his powerful jaws locked onto the giant's flesh.

I was tossed about on Terrakona's mane, and instead of holding on for dear life, I leapt off and rolled across the ground.

With a wave of my hand, I manipulated the terrain. Sand formed under the giant, making it difficult for the monster to get to its feet.

"*What playful...* things. Your blood and bones will tasty... *like all the others.*"

The giant's taunts came from both heads. Why wasn't it dead yet? Terrakona had potent venom. Most creatures seemed to die only a few seconds after being bitten.

This fight wouldn't last long, even if the giant was immune to Terrakona's venom. My world serpent eldrin wrapped his serpentine body around the giant's massive and disgusting torso. Terrakona could squeeze this thing to death.

And the sky titan screeched and returned to the fray, obviously trying to steal the giant's breath once again. The fire giant would asphyxiate.

But before that could happen, the whole area went dark. At first, I thought someone had bonded with the corona phoenix. All the god-creatures seemed to change the sky whenever they bonded with their arcanists.

That wasn't the case.

I glanced up and spotted the source of the darkness. It was an eclipse. Not something natural, like a celestial body moving in front of the sun—this was magic. I had seen it several times before.

It was an *eclipse aura*. Knightmare arcanists were capable of creating an artificial eclipse to block out the sun, casting everything in darkness. It empowered their magic and made it difficult for anyone else to see.

Which was exactly what happened. The eclipse formed over the sun, and everything was blanketed in darkness as thick as midnight. Although it limited my vision, my tremor sense allowed me to retain my "sight."

Lucian emerged from the thick shadows and struck at the neck of the fire giant. The massive beast was held immobile by

Terrakona, so Lucian's strike was true. He sliced open the giant's jugular, and blood gushed out onto the rocks.

"*He's plague-ridden*," I shouted.

With my terrain manipulation, I altered the ground and created cracks. The mini fissures drained the blood away, keeping it from spreading to the ocean waters.

Lucian leapt away from the giant as Terrakona held it on the ground.

"You're taking too long to kill it," Lucian yelled back. "Allow me to assist."

I almost changed the terrain around his feet to trap him in place, but I knew knightmare arcanists could shadow-step out of those kinds of traps. Why was he here on the battlefield? He was a liability. I couldn't allow him to become infected.

"*You won't...* kill me, maggots!" the two heads of the giant shouted. "*I am all powerful!*"

To my surprise, the giant's injury healed up much faster than most other mystical creatures. Was the beast empowered by the plague? Was it a *dread form fire giant?* Perhaps its arcanist had died after it achieved the "peak" of its corruption.

The fire giant grabbed Terrakona with its six hands, trying to rip the serpent from its body.

But it wasn't strong enough. Terrakona was one massive muscle, and the more he squeezed, the less the giant could do.

The eclipse...

Then Terrakona spoke to me through our telepathic link. **"Warlord—your aura is just as potent. Try it now."**

"*Now?*" I asked aloud.

"I have the monster held down. Sytherias has weakened it. The others have protected the boat and the airship. There is no danger we cannot handle. Create your aura. Use it on this giant, just as the knightmare arcanist has used his to shroud the sunlight."

Terrakona's suggestion caused me to hold my breath. I

hadn't thought about using my aura without the help of the others. But what would happen if just *one* god-arcanist created their aura? Would it do anything? Did I need all the god-arcanists to help? Or would my aura be localized?

What if…

What if my personal salvation aura could cure the plague? Or would my personal armageddon aura destroy the plague?

But creating an aura was difficult. In order to make one, I would have to force my magic out of my body in all directions. Most arcanists struggled, but clearly, that wasn't the case with Lucian. His eclipse aura was perfect. The sun didn't shine for us —everything was darkness.

"Orwyn," I yelled. "Tell your sky titan not to kill the giant!"

"For what reason?" she asked, her voice above me. She was the only one I couldn't see with my tremor sense since she floated through the air.

"I'm going to attempt to create my aura."

She didn't reply, but I assumed she wasn't objecting to my proposal.

So, while we had the fire giant restrained, I took a deep breath and then closed my eyes. When I had been a knightmare arcanist, I had *halfway* formed the eclipse aura. It had been in anger, and born from a desire to see my enemies defeated.

When Lucian moved around the battlefield, his shadow-stepping making him difficult to track, I clenched my jaw. I'd had one very simple instruction, and for some reason, he had ignored it. That was fine. I would just have to deal with the giant before Lucian accidentally harmed himself or others with his meddling.

After a long exhale, I focused on my body. Evoking magma hardened my bones and made me difficult to kill. Manipulating the terrain gave me advantages like no others. My aura… I tried to push these powers out of my body. I tried to imagine them entering the world.

And for some reason, the dryads in Terrakona's grove came to mind.

They had just *appeared* because of the world serpent's presence.

My magic flared. I grabbed at my chest, my insides twisting.

I hated the thought of the dryads getting infected with the arcane plague. Or Lucian. Or anyone else, for that matter. I wanted it to go away. I wanted my aura to *work*.

"Don't force it, Warlord."

"I have to," I said through gritted teeth.

"We have time to practice."

"No. We don't."

Everyone was depending on us. *Liet* was depending on *me*. What if I could make this aura and cure the giant of the arcane plague? I could head straight to New Norra and help her!

I had to do this. And I knew I could. There was no reason to wait. No reason to take it easy. This aura was everything we were building up toward.

So I pushed. Even when the magic hurt my body—I pushed it outward, forcing the aura to manifest. It felt like plunging into the water—an icy shock that rippled through my whole body. The eclipse aura overhead flickered for a moment as my world serpent aura washed over the battlefield.

But...

A spike of pain flared through my head. I grabbed at my temples, my heart pounding.

The fire giant screamed.

Something was wrong. I shook my head, trying to concentrate. For some reason, magma flared from the lines in my palms. My bones hurt. The ground shook, as though rocked by an earthquake.

I dropped my sword and my shield, and shook my head, trying to dispel the magic.

"Volke?" Orwyn shouted in concern. "What're you doing?"

I couldn't answer her.

"Warlord—you've created the armageddon aura. I thought you wanted salvation?"

But I couldn't answer him either. My heart just kept hammering. Why couldn't I make it go away?

"Warlord!"

But it wasn't working. I couldn't make it stop.

Chapter 29

The Corona Phoenix Arcanist

The rocks cracked beneath my feet.

The air sizzled as the temperature escalated.

Everything felt wrong. My chest hurt. My thoughts were a blur. Why couldn't I end this aura? My magic gushed from my body, emptying from me as though I had an injury that wouldn't stop spilling blood.

"Volke!"

Someone grabbed me. They wrapped their arms around my body and held me tight. It was Evianna, I could tell by her grip and the familiar way she held me. And then panic set in. Was she in danger? My magic, the heat—why was she so close?

"Volke, it's okay. I'm here."

In that instant, the aura ended. My magic shut tight as it reacted with me. I couldn't hurt Evianna, even by accident. I would never forgive myself. When I turned around, there she was, her knightmare over her body, shielding her from the worst of the harsh conditions.

Evianna stepped away from me. Smoke wafted from her armor. Touching me had almost harmed her, yet she had done it regardless.

But without my aura, everything calmed. The mountain stopped its rumbling, and the heat in the air faded. Even the eclipse vanished, though I had nothing to do with that. Lucian must've realized there was no reason to maintain his eclipse aura.

Hot magma dripped from my hands, and I had to wait a moment until it fell onto the stones around my feet. The molten rock sizzled and burned everything it touched, but fortunately, there wasn't much.

"Volke," Evianna and her eldrin said, their voices intertwined. "What's wrong? What happened?"

"I... I don't know," I muttered. With my hands now clean, I ran a hand down my face. "Evianna..."

"What can I do to help you?" She walked over and held my elbow.

It was good to see that she wasn't hurt. The relief that flooded me was wonderful. "You shouldn't have gotten so close. It was dangerous." I motioned to the cracks in the red rocks, and the destruction I had caused.

"I'm always going to be there for you," Evianna said, defiant. Her grip tightened on me. "Especially if you need me."

Her voice had brought me right back to the present, that was true. With a long exhale, I stood closer to her, but I didn't hug or kiss her, for fear I would somehow injure her.

When Terrakona uncoiled himself, the mountain rumbled again. Evianna and I both turned to see what was going on. Why would Terrakona release the fire giant? It wasn't time. But to my surprise, there was nothing for him to release.

The fire giant...

Its whole body had *melted*.

I held my breath as I examined the "body."

There were no bones, no flesh, no creature left. Terrakona was soaked in the blood of the beast, because crimson liquid was all that remained of the fire giant. My armageddon aura had destroyed the monster completely. There was nothing left to save, just a puddle of vital fluid.

Terrakona stared at it with his reptilian eyes. His tongue darted from his mouth, and then he turned his attention to me. **"Warlord... Is this what you wanted?"**

I shook my head. "No. I just... I don't know what happened."

"Your aura eliminated all corrupted magic in the nearby area."

With a shaky hand, I combed back my hair. "My armageddon aura can do that?"

"Of course. You are a god-arcanist. It's your duty to judge this plague and either eliminate it or make it something new."

I knew that. Terrakona had told me before. And I saw it now. The armageddon aura was powerful. My magic had warped the whole area, purging the corruption. But I must have created it incorrectly because my magic had run amuck. I couldn't end it. I couldn't even control it.

Orwyn flew down with her kirin. Her beautiful scaled horse glistened in the afternoon light, her strawberry-blonde hair practically shimmering. When she met my gaze, she wore a slight frown.

"That was your aura?" she whispered.

I nodded once.

"If I created my aura at the same time, I suspect our magics would amplify each other. That's how we're going to cover the world... To affect everyone all at once."

"You're probably right," I said.

But when I glanced back at the puddle of blood, all I could think about was Liet Eventide. If she had been standing next to me when I activated my armageddon aura, she would've died. Just like the fire giant.

"I need to practice my aura creation abilities a little longer," I said with a huff and a laugh.

Orwyn nodded along with my words. "You were rather sloppy about it."

Evianna stood a little closer to me. "Volke did the best he could."

"I hope it wasn't actually his best, because we'll need a better performance than that if we're going to eliminate the arcane plague."

While her words were harsh, Orwyn was correct. I needed to do better. And I definitely couldn't activate my armageddon aura again. That had been a mistake. What if I accidentally sealed away the salvation aura? What would we do?

Lucian—still wrapped in his knightmare—emerged from the darkness. He stepped straight out of the shadows, smooth and confident.

I wanted to yell at the man for his bumbling during the fight, but Lucian held up a hand and forestalled my tirade.

"I apologize," he said with a sigh. "I didn't realize you had things so..." He glanced over to the lake of blood left by the melted fire giant. "So *handled*."

I nodded once. "God-arcanists have powers beyond what a normal arcanist can achieve. And our magic is specifically tailored to handle this corruption. You shouldn't get involved if we tell you to step aside."

Lucian said nothing. He just stared at the blood, his attention focused.

After an hour of waiting, I grew nervous.

Orwyn, Evianna, and I stood on the rocky shore, waiting for Zaxis and the others to return. The sun continued its downward trek. Soon it would be twilight. During the wait, I manipulated the terrain to put it back to normal. I removed the cracks, improved the structure of the mountain and even created a small staircase up the side.

"Volke," Evianna whispered.

I stopped my practice to give her my full attention. In the dying sunlight, ablaze with reds and oranges, Evianna's white hair shimmered with cloud-like elegance. I found myself momentarily distracted.

"Yes?" I finally asked.

"Do you think they're okay? Zaxis and everyone else, I mean."

"Definitely."

Evianna frowned. "What about Biyu? I don't even think she was supposed to go with them. What if she's scared? Or what if… something happened to her?"

"Devlin is with them. So is his roc. Mesos would never allow anything to happen to Biyu."

Orwyn nodded along with my words.

While I wasn't entirely confident, I figured everyone around Biyu would keep her safe. While Zaxis had been grumpy about her presence, the man was always grumpy. And Lynus was a pirate at heart, but he wouldn't do anything to let Zelfree down. Biyu would be fine.

But I had to admit, I *was* worried that something could have happened to *all* of them. If they all failed the tests of the lair, Biyu would be in just as much trouble as the others.

"I don't think we should barge our way in," Orwyn said. She glanced between me and Evianna. "The god-creature would've made its anger known if something had gone terribly wrong. I think they're just going through the Trial of Worth."

"I think, with Volke's powers, we could get into the lair if we wanted," Evianna stated.

I shook my head. "Let's just wait a little longer, okay? If the sun goes down, and we haven't heard anything, we'll go into the lair."

I thought Orwyn was about to accept my proposal, but something strange happened. The sky went dark. Evianna caught her breath and glanced upward, her brow furrowed. "It's happening," she whispered.

Orwyn and Terrakona turned their attention to the sky.

Sure enough, the pillar appeared. A red-and-gold light shot up from behind our small mountain. It pierced the heavens—a pillar of solid light—as someone bonded with the corona phoenix. I couldn't see who, nor could I see the creature, but it was happening, much to my delight.

Finally.

Although Biyu had accidentally gone with Zaxis and the others, it was William I was the most worried about. Hopefully *he* had bonded with the corona phoenix, and hadn't been injured during the trial process.

Then, without warning, the pillar of light vanished. The sky returned to normal, the sun halfway to the horizon, heading toward dusk. The world seemed calm.

The corona phoenix—a smaller version of the one I had seen in my dreams—flew into the sky. The flames were just as regal as the first phoenix's, a vibrant red and gold, and the beast's chest was a void of darkness. The dark heart pulsed with power as the phoenix flapped its wings and descended the mountain toward us.

The creature's eyes were shadows.

So was its beak.

And its legs and talons.

They were darkness given physical form, fueled by the god-creature's inky heart. The fire wasn't like a normal phoenix's. There was no soot or physical residue. The creature burned from pure magic alone.

Zaxis and his fenris wolf bounded over the rocks and headed

toward us. Lynus rode his lumbering typhon beast, pulling up the rear. They were massive creatures, capable of moving rather quickly, but they were still bound to the ground. The corona phoenix soared straight to the shore—straight to me—without much difficulty, and well before anyone else.

But then...

I noticed Mesos. She was carrying Devlin.

That meant... he hadn't bonded with the phoenix.

Had William been successful? That was perfect! He hailed from the Isle of Ruma, a place known for phoenixes, and now he was the corona phoenix arcanist? It was so fitting it was poetic.

The majestic phoenix—with a wingspan of twenty feet—landed on the rocks. One shadowy claw was closed, while the other gripped the stone tight enough to dig furrows into the boulder. Then the corona phoenix opened its other foot, revealing Biyu.

The area was warmer with the phoenix nearby, but not hot.

I stared at Biyu for a long moment, confused and frustrated. Why was the phoenix holding her?

Then Mesos landed next to us, and Captain Delvin slid off the back of his bird eldrin.

"Devlin," Biyu said as she slipped from the talons of the phoenix and landed on her feet. "I did it. I told you I would!" Then Biyu glanced over at me, a smile on her face. "Look, Volke!"

She grabbed at her coat and pulled it back to show off her left shoulder.

The lines of a god-arcanist mark were etched into her flesh. The flames of the phoenix's wing were carved into her arm down to her elbow.

I... almost couldn't believe it.

Captain Devlin stepped forward. With shaky hands, he patted her coat and tugged the sleeve back into place. "Are ya doin' okay? Everything fine? By the abyssal hells, lass, I thought you would fall right out of that phoenix's talons."

Biyu rubbed at her face. The eyepatch didn't cover all her scars, and she rubbed her fingers along the length of one as she said, "I'm sorry. *Ovayla* said that, uh, she would keep me safe no matter what."

"What happened?" I demanded.

"*The phoenix wanted none of us,*" Devlin practically barked. "It didn't matter if we were willing to give up our eldrin or not."

Biyu held her coat close to her body. "Um, well, Ovayla said that whoever bonded with her had to have a calm heart. And then she, uh, spoke in my mind, and told me that I was a child of, uh, someone, and that she liked me."

"And you... are the one with the calmest heart?" I asked, confused. "Not William?"

"Well..." Biyu turned to glance up at the red and gold flames. The gargantuan bird was bigger than even Mesos. With a tilt of the phoenix's head, one of her six black eyes stared down at Biyu. "The phoenix said that desire and hate would make her corrupt, so she couldn't bond with someone who had too much of it."

Devlin seemed confused by that. He turned his attention up to the bird. "R-Right..."

The phoenix's fire lit up the area like a bright bonfire. Devlin had to shield his eyes just to glance in her direction.

"You like her, right? You said you like birds." Biyu stepped close to her eldrin and touched the black talon of her eldrin. "I thought you would be proud."

"I... I am. I just didn't think..."

Biyu smiled. "Someone had to bond with her. Because she said if no one did, we'd all likely die."

That was new. I snapped my attention to the corona phoenix, intent on asking it questions, but Biyu continued with her little speech.

"She said, uh, a *Child of Luvi,* I think, was coming to kill them all, and that if I was brave enough to save them, I could bond with her."

A Child of Luvi? Who was the phoenix referring to? The Autarch? Or someone else?

Orwyn bowed to the corona phoenix. Then she offered Biyu a sad smile. "As a god-arcanist, you will one day die to the claws of the apoch dragon."

"Not if I can help it," Devlin said. He stepped close to Biyu and held her shoulder. "And don't go tellin' the lass that right after everythin' happened. Are ya touched in the head?"

"It's just the truth."

"I know," Biyu muttered. She held on to Devlin. "My phoenix said that, too. But that's okay. Because I don't want everyone else to die. So, it's okay. As long as we can cure the plague, it'll be fine."

The phoenix had wanted to bond with someone calm and passionless? Or perhaps just unblinded by deep desires. I wasn't sure which, but Biyu did fit that archetype. Unfortunately, she was no warrior. Perhaps it didn't matter. The corona phoenix in my dreams hadn't seemed like a warrior, either. It seemed like a protector—or a caretaker. Someone who was content to safeguard a select few people they considered near and dear.

I reached into my pocket, wondering which god-creature we would head to next, when one felt warmer than the others. I withdrew it from my pocket, shocked to see the sandstone runestone glowing white and tan.

"What's happening?" Evianna asked, and she leaned in close.

Orwyn lifted an eyebrow and stared as well.

"I don't know." I turned the runestone over. This was for the progenitor behemoth. Why was it glowing? We weren't anywhere near its lair.

"Something isn't right," Orwyn whispered.

Before I could reply, the runestone cracked.

And then it shattered into a hundred tiny pieces.

CHAPTER 30

THE LAST FEW GOD-ARCANISTS

"*Volke*," Evianna said with a gasp. "What did you do?" She knelt and picked up some of the fingernail-sized pieces of the broken runestone.

My mind buzzed. The runestone had just *shattered*.

Orwyn waved her hand, and the wind picked up around my feet. In a matter of seconds, all the pieces of the sandstone runestone were gathered into a whirlwind and carried over to Orwyn's hand.

"You did this?" she whispered.

I frowned. With a shaky hand, I reached into my pocket and withdrew the last two runestones. I had stones for the tempest coatl and the scylla waters. They weren't warm, and they didn't crack, but I kept expecting them to shatter just like the other.

"I don't understand," Evianna stated.

Terrakona lowered his head. His warm breath washed over me, even though the corona phoenix and all her fire were just mere feet from me. Knowing Terrakona was nearby brought me back to the present.

"I didn't break it," I said.

"The runestone broke because the progenitor

behemoth is dead," the corona phoenix said, her voice regal and precise, much like the phoenixes on the Isle of Ruma.

I flinched. I hadn't expected her to say anything. Biyu had been speaking for the phoenix the entire time, and in my mind, the phoenix didn't want to say anything to us.

"It's true," Terrakona muttered. **"I felt it... Just now. The behemoth has perished."**

Orwyn held the shattered runestone close to her chest. After a short sigh, she muttered, "The Keeper of Corpses will be irritated. The first progenitor behemoth was his sire."

It was the same with the Mother of Shapeshifters. She had desperately wanted to meet the new behemoth. Now it had died, and its runestone was no more? I didn't understand.

"How did this happen?" I asked.

Terrakona lifted his head. **"The Children of Balastar would do anything to win in a fight. I suspect our enemies have decided that, if they cannot bond with the progenitor behemoth, no one can."**

"How did they get to it? The lairs are protected with god-creature magic!"

I was shouting, though I didn't know why. Like yelling at the universe for its unfair antics, even if I knew life never played by the rules.

"The Autarch most likely has the power of multiple god-creatures," Terrakona telepathically said, his voice slow and serious. **"And his god-creatures will be enhanced by the magic of his gold kirin. If anyone could break into the lair and kill a newly born god-creature, it would be him."**

That answer enraged me. Was the Autarch that petty? Or did he really just want victory at all costs? Two god-creatures out of the twelve were now dead—the soul forge and the progenitor behemoth. What if we lost too many before we created our salvation aura? We couldn't allow that to happen.

"I suspect this was the Autarch," Orwyn said as she tucked

the runestone pieces into her robe. "Helvetti is a powerful and cunning man. He wants you as weak as possible."

"*Us*," Evianna corrected. "You're with us now, aren't you?"

Orwyn mulled that statement over. Then she slowly nodded. "Yes. You're right. He wants *us* weak. He doesn't want us to have any more god-arcanist allies. And he's willing to kill the unbonded god-creatures to hinder us."

"We have to get to the last two before he does," I muttered.

We couldn't lose. Now that we knew what the Autarch was doing, we had to beat him to the punch. There were only two god-creatures left. If I took a small team of arcanists and went in one direction, and Zaxis took another group and went in the other direction, we could get to both in the shortest time possible.

I glanced down at the runestones. Then I gripped my hand around the lapis lazuli stone. I would head to the scylla waters. The ocean didn't scare me, and Terrakona was an excellent swimmer.

Just as I thought that, Zaxis and his fenris wolf came bounding over the rocks. Vjorn landed on the smoothed shore next to us, his padded wolf feet creating a thin layer of ice wherever he stepped.

"Something has happened," Vjorn growled. **"The progenitor behemoth has fallen."**

Zaxis slid off his eldrin's back and then jogged over to my side. He stared into my eyes and then glared. "You knew already? How?"

"The runestone shattered," I said.

"What happened? Why did he die? Was it the Second Ascension?"

I nodded once. "You need to take this." I handed him the opal runestone. "It's for the tempest coatl. Since there are only two god-creatures left, we need to split up, gather them, and meet back at Fortuna."

Zaxis didn't hesitate. He grabbed the opal runestone and held it firmly in his grasp. "You trust me to handle this?"

"You managed to handle the corona phoenix lair, didn't you?" I patted his shoulder. "You're one of the few people I trust to always get things done, no matter what."

The praise seemed to ease some of Zaxis's doubt. His green eyes locked onto mine as he smiled. "I'm not going to let you down."

A pop of air and glitter alerted everyone of Illia's arrival. She appeared next to me, along with William. She wasn't as upset as Vjorn and Zaxis, and I wondered if she even knew what had happened. Instead, she turned to me, her lips curved down at the corners. She was trying to hold back sadness.

"Biyu did a good job," Illia said. She glanced over at the beautiful phoenix. "I was surprised a creature like that would want to bond with someone so young, but it seemed appropriate."

William said nothing.

And then I understood why Illia was upset. She, too, had wanted William to bond with the phoenix, instead of Biyu. But we didn't have time to quibble about this. We were wasting time just standing around.

"You'll come with me," I said to William. "We're going to take the airship, and we're going to head for the scylla waters."

Again, he said nothing. The man was so stoic he could turn into a glacier.

"Who will *I* take?" Zaxis asked.

I shook my head. "You'll have to find someone." Delegating this task to him would alleviate some of my stress. And I didn't want to leave William.

"Fine." Zaxis waved over his wolf. The massive creature stepped close, allowed him to get on his back. Then he glanced over at Biyu. "I'll take the girl."

"Why?"

"Because she's a phoenix arcanist. Who's going to teach her the ropes?" Zaxis pointed to himself with a jut of his thumb. "*Me*, obviously. I'll talk to her all about phoenixes as we sail for the tempest coatl."

That made sense. I wished Atty were here to help, but since she was off in the Sunset Desert, we only had Zaxis here who knew anything about phoenixes and their magic. Although, I suspected the corona phoenix's shadow abilities would be similar to a knightmare's.

"You will take the *Midnight Thorn*," I said, gesturing to the boat. "Lucian can help in her training as well."

With a curt nod, Zaxis and Vjorn bounded away to the ship. He was eager to go. He didn't even wait for Biyu or Captain Devlin, though he did glance back at Illia. She smiled and teleported onto the back of the fenris wolf, leaving me with a dejected William.

That was fine. I wanted him close, anyway.

Captain Devlin knelt by Biyu and patted her shoulder. He seemed as concerned as any proper father, even though they weren't related by blood. She had just been his cabin girl, but it had obviously grown into something far greater than that.

"Will you two be okay?" I asked, my attention shifting to Biyu and her phoenix.

"There is no comfort to be found in worry," the phoenix said.

Biyu touched the shadowy leg of her phoenix. "This is my eldrin, and I'll take good care of her. You'll see. I've helped Devlin with his roc all the time."

The corona phoenix lowered her black beak, the void of darkness in her chest pulsing a little faster. She was beautiful in an ethereal and mystical way. She was unlike any phoenix I had ever seen before.

Then I turned my attention to Orwyn. "You need to help

Zaxis. If he's taking the sailing ship, you and your sky titan are the only ones to ensure they travel as fast as they possibly can."

She forced a smile. "Of course. And the tempest coatl is known for its storms. I will be there to shield the arcanists from the worst of the gale winds."

"Thank you."

Orwyn, her kirin, and Sytherias took to the skies. They flew with incredible grace to the sailing ship, and I knew the teams had been formed. Zaxis was taking the majority of the individuals, including the sky titan and corona phoenix.

I glanced over my shoulder.

Lynus and the typhon beast were still lumbering over the rocks. Zelfree was with them, along with his mimic, Traces. They would be with me.

Evianna scooted closer, as if to remind me she would always be by my side. I smiled at her, and her cheeks brightened as she returned the gesture. We were the smaller team on the airship, it seemed. Which was fine—I wanted a smaller crew.

"*Volke,*" Adelgis telepathically said.

"Yeah?" I muttered.

"*Fain and I would like to accompany you. That would still make a small crew, don't you think?*"

He was right. That would.

"Don't you want to accompany your sister on the *Midnight Thorn?*" I asked. Cinna was the last unbonded individual in our midst. Although I didn't think she was suited to delve the lairs, perhaps the tempest coatl would find her suitable.

"*Cinna... She will be okay with Orwyn. The two are becoming fast friends.*"

Fast friends? It was likely due to the fact that Cinna stayed in the infirmary of the ship—along with Akiva. Although he was healed, he just never was quite right, and stayed out of sight. If Orwyn visited him frequently, she would run into Cinna more often than not.

"All right," I muttered. "You and Fain can join me. But make sure to tell Zaxis where to go. As soon as you do that, we should take to the skies."

The *Diamond of Dawn* soared through the night sky as silent as a cloud.

Terrakona swam in the ocean below us, his massive serpentine body crashing through the waves with ease. Even at night, he was easy to spot as he moved with a concertina motion through the deep blue waters.

Xor, the mighty typhon beast, sat on the quarterdeck of the airship. Half his ninety-nine heads were asleep. They were coiled around his main head, their eyes shut, their breathing even. Xor stared at the stars above us while we traveled.

Lynus sat next to his eldrin, and Zelfree sat next to him. Traces was curled up into a little loaf, cozy on Zelfree's lap. William stood on the opposite end of the quarterdeck. He spoke with the captain, their conversation quiet and low energy.

Fain and Adelgis had gone to sleep, leaving me and Evianna on the deck of the airship. We were a much smaller team than what we had left with from Fortuna. I hoped—deep in my heart —that we would reach the scylla waters before the Autarch.

At night, when there was no sunlight, knightmare arcanists were their strongest.

Evianna manipulated the darkness, pulling the shadows and forming claws that lifted from the deck. The blade-like hooks she crafted sliced through the air with a *whoosh*.

"I'm going to create an eclipse aura," Evianna stated. She waved a hand and made a claw-like shadow the size of a human adult. It emerged from the deck and grasped at the air—creepy in all regards.

"Right now?" I asked, glancing up at the moon.

Would an eclipse aura block that out?

"Soon," Evianna said with a huff. She waved her arm, and the shadows collapsed onto the deck of the airship. "I'm getting stronger. You've seen."

"I have."

"And if Lucian can create an eclipse aura, so can I."

I stood closer to her, the chill night winds whipping over the airship, and I didn't want her to grow cold. "We'll train together, then. This aura I create... It's important."

"I know." Evianna turned on her heel and faced me. Her white hair was brightest in the moonlight. "But I think you should focus on remaining calm. When you created your aura back on the Rocky Coast... You weren't yourself. I was afraid."

Evianna glanced down at the deck.

"I'm sorry," I muttered. "I didn't mean to, uh..." I rubbed at the back of my neck. "I was just determined to do it."

With half a smile, she stepped closer to me. "I'm sure you'll do it. And I'll help. We can do this together."

I nodded once. "You're right. But maybe in the morning. I want Lynus to train with us. It's important he gets this, too."

A piece of me wondered if Zaxis, Orwyn, and Biyu would master the aura before me. Was I jealous? No. But I was worried. It would be ironic if I were the only one struggling to create the salvation aura.

So I doubled down on my focus.

I would do it.

No matter what.

CHAPTER 31

SWORDPLAY

A week into the trek, and I hadn't yet created another aura.

I feared I would set the airship on fire. If I wasn't careful, my armageddon aura could destroy our vessel, so I only wanted to manifest an aura if I was absolutely certain it would be the salvation version.

The midafternoon sun bathed the *Diamond of Dawn* in a beautiful shower of sunshine. Everything was bright, and it lifted my mood. The ocean sparkled beneath us, Terrakona gliding through the waves. The white clouds, few and far between, couldn't be softer.

Zelfree and Lynus clashed with swords across the center of the main deck. They were practicing swordplay, I supposed, though I didn't understand why they would focus on that. Zelfree was a master swordsman—all the old tales of his swashbuckling exploits said so.

The two men used real swords, as well. Steel blades that shone brightly in the sunlight. When Lynus thrust forward, Zelfree easily parried it aside. Zelfree even kept one hand behind his back, his focus solely on Lynus.

They weren't wearing armor. Lynus was barely wearing any clothes, actually. He had boots and trousers, but that was it, likely to show off his god-arcanist mark. And Zelfree wore a pair of black trousers and a matching tunic. Even his boots were black, like he was a shadow or gradually turning into a knightmare.

Clang. Clink.

The heavy blows echoed across the airship. Lynus was so much stronger than Zelfree—when he swung, Zelfree had to brace himself to keep from falling over. The metal-on-metal screech was enough to disturb the fish far below us.

I leaned on the railing of the airship while I watched their sparring match. Evianna sat next to me, unafraid of falling overboard.

Adelgis and Fain stood next to us, both of them engrossed by the swordplay.

Clang. Clang.

For some reason, Lynus was getting more aggressive with his swings. He moved faster, swung with wild intensity, and seemed like he was aiming to knock Zelfree off balance.

To my surprise, Zelfree ducked under a blow and then moved around Lynus. He was much faster—more skilled. When Lynus swung back around, the whistle of his blade told me he could've carved through the trunk of a thin tree. The man wasn't holding back.

And still, Zelfree avoided the swing. When Lynus tried to strike again, Zelfree chuckled as he blocked the blow with his own blade.

"You never listen to me," Zelfree said, smiling.

Lynus gritted his teeth. When *he* smiled, it seemed feral. It would've unnerved me, but it seemed to amuse Zelfree.

"Master Zelfree is so skilled," Evianna muttered, her eyes wide.

Zelfree leapt away from another wild swing and then lunged

forward. He probably could've stabbed Lynus straight in the gut, but instead, Zelfree just slashed at Lynus's forearm. He broke the skin, drawing a thin line of blood.

Then Zelfree leapt away, chuckling.

Lynus spun his sword around in his hand, his grip on the hilt tightening once he had it at the optimal angle. Although Lynus was bleeding, his smile never left him. That was one of the things I found intimidating about the Dread Pirate Calisto—he reveled in violence. Calisto was never intimidated by a strong opponent, or by deadly tricks and games. He was confident and always rose to the challenge.

Just like right now.

Lynus rushed forward. When he swung this time, it was from above. It was powerful, and fast, and gravity added to the weight of the strike. Zelfree held his sword up, blocking the blow, but staggered backward from the sheer force once the blades collided.

Lynus chortled as he swung again—harder than before.

Zelfree backed away, getting closer and closer to the quarterdeck. He was running out of space, and if he was cornered, he would have to do something drastic.

I leaned forward, tense.

They had agreed not to use any magical abilities. Would Zelfree make it out of this?

Evianna grabbed my arm, her attention on the sparring match. Her grip grew tighter with each swing of the blades.

Just as Zelfree squared his stance, as though he might turn things around, Lynus slashed his sword far to the side—nowhere near Zelfree. The tip of his weapon struck a lantern atop a nearby barrel. The lantern tumbled to the deck and shattered, glass and oil covering a small portion of the deck.

Zelfree flinched and momentarily glanced at the wrecked lantern.

Which was what Lynus had wanted. In that split-second of

distraction, he swung with his blade. He caught Zelfree off-guard, and while Zelfree brought his sword up to block, it wasn't enough. The force of the strike knocked his sword out of his hand.

Lynus slammed Zelfree up against the door to the captain's quarters. With a smooth, and quick, motion, Lynus placed his sword against Zelfree's neck, the blade pressed against the flesh just below his jaw.

"I used your own trick against you," Lynus said with a dark chuckle.

Zelfree half-smiled. "There's no greater ally in a fight than distraction."

It concerned me that Lynus had his sword so close to Zelfree. It was a real blade. And Zelfree was actually pinned. What if Lynus just decided he wanted the man dead? I wouldn't have time to stop them before Lynus sliced the other man's throat.

But that fear was ultimately misplaced.

Lynus kept Zelfree trapped—sword still up—and then brought his lips to bear on Zelfree's. Even in intimacy, Lynus was just aggressive. I was certain Zelfree couldn't breathe, that was how thoroughly they were intertwined.

"Oh, my," Evianna whispered as she turned her attention up to the sky.

"That escalated quickly," Fain quipped, one eyebrow raised.

Rubbing at her pink cheeks, Evianna glanced over. "Is *this* what it was like on a pirate ship? Such intensity and passion?"

"W-What?" Fain shot her a sideways glance. "No. Of course not. If this was how it went most of the time, we *definitely* wouldn't have had time to go pirating."

Adelgis smiled. "It would've added a whole new meaning to the term *plundering booty.*"

I had never seen Fain get so red so very fast. He ran a hand down his face and groaned into his palm. "*Dammit, Moonbeam.*" Then—without warning—Fain vanished.

Shrouded in invisibility, as well as embarrassment, he stomped his way down the deck of the airship, grumbling the entire time.

Evianna giggled into her hand. "Is he okay?"

Adelgis brushed back some of his black hair. It swirled in the winds, but never into his face. "Fain always says he likes that I make him laugh, but anytime I intentionally try to joke, he storms off like this." Adelgis glanced over to me. "I think I should retire from humor."

"I thought it was funny," I said with a shrug.

Evianna slid off the airship railing. "Are you and Fain betrothed? You two are always together."

"Fain believes he isn't suited for such things," Adelgis said matter-of-factly. "His thoughts always revolve around his status as a renegade pirate, and how he has no place in this world once the Second Ascension are gone."

"Oh."

"Additionally, I have had an arranged marriage since I was young. Though, I doubt she would want to go through with it after the disgrace of my father and the Venrover name."

Evianna chuckled nervously. She gave me a quick glance, as if to ask for my help, but I didn't know what to say.

Adelgis smiled, though it seemed wary. Or perhaps woebegone. "I... I worry that once this is all over, Fain will think he needs to leave. So he won't burden me. But if that happens, he truly will have no one, and nothing would make me sadder."

Evianna and I said nothing.

"But Fain doesn't know I have plans. I want to build things. Make the world a better place." Adelgis's gaze lost focus, even if his words grew hopeful. "Of course, my father said the same thing... Maybe I'm not that much different from him, after all."

"You're the complete *opposite* of your father," I said, practically tripping over my words in my haste to say them. "Don't ever think like that. If you want to make the world a better place, I'm sure you will. And I think if you ask Fain to stay by your side through it all, he will."

Fain seemed loyal. Almost to a fault. He was loyal to his dead brother. Loyal to a dread pirate. And now loyal to the Frith Guild, all because person or organization had helped him when he had needed it most.

"I hope so," Adelgis muttered.

Before we could continue the conversation, Lynus and Zelfree stopped their embrace and stepped away from the captain's door. They both were flushed, and breathing deep, and I wondered if they were just going to retire for the day, even though it was still early. They refused to look at each other as they walked back to the middle of the airship deck.

"We should practice manifesting our auras," Lynus announced, his voice aggressively neutral.

"Right," Zelfree said.

"Not you. I meant me and the Warlord over there." Lynus waved me over, though he didn't really look at me, either.

Zelfree crossed his arms and tilted his head. "You worried I'll have a problem with my aura again?"

Lynus scratched at the stubble on his chin. He was dappled in sweat, despite the glorious sunshine. He practically glistened as the wind whipped by.

"I think I know why you're having problems," Lynus finally stated. "Mimics aren't like other mystical creatures. They don't have any real magic all their own."

Zelfree stood a bit straighter. Traces, his mimic, who had been transformed to resemble a coil of rope, sprang into her cat form and then trotted across the deck. Her once long tail, now short, wagged back and forth until she reached Zelfree's legs. She purred as she rubbed against him.

"What do you mean?" Zelfree asked.

"I mean you *draw magic from other sources.*" Lynus pointed to Evianna and then Adelgis. "Your mimic becomes a knightmare or an ethereal whelk before you have magical capabilities. Auras are your magic manifesting outward, but a mimic's are different."

"Yeah..."

"So you need to *pull all the nearby magic inward.*" Lynus made a gathering motion, pantomiming what he meant. "You need to collect it. You're the exact opposite of a normal arcanist. That's why you've been failing all these years. Why you've never mastered it."

That explanation made a lot of sense. I had never pondered Zelfree's dilemma with his aura—he had always been my master, after all—but Lynus knew what he was talking about. He really was an expert on mystical creatures. Lynus just seemed to intuitively understand them.

Zelfree glanced down at Traces. She stared up at him, her cat-like eyes wide.

"Collect it..." he muttered.

Then Lynus waved him away. "But you're not the one I'm concerned about." He pointed at me. "You. Lad. Get over here. Let's do this."

I exhaled as I walked across the deck. There wasn't much for us to test our auras on. No plague-ridden creatures. No corruption. How would we know if we were successful?

"What were you thinkin' about when you made your armageddon aura?" Lynus asked.

I glanced around. What *had* I been thinking about? "Just... that I needed to do it."

"Try to focus on something calming," Lynus said. He flexed his hands, opening and closing them into fists. "Our god-arcanist magic seems to be made up of creation and destruction, and you want to think of things that bring about creative thoughts."

"Like... what?"

Lynus opened his mouth.

No words.

Then he closed his mouth. He rubbed at his chin. "Well, I didn't say I had *all* the damn answers," he growled. "You can think of somethin'."

Zelfree picked up his mimic. He cradled her close and shot Lynus a sideways glance. "You're an expert on this. Why not show the kid how it's done?"

"*Kid?*" I repeated.

Zelfree huffed out a laugh. "You're still young to me, kid. No matter how many positions of authority over me you have, it's always going to be true."

"I'm not ready." Lynus crossed his arms over his bare chest. Then he just sighed. "Perhaps we should all just think about things associated with calming feelings."

Maybe...

Adelgis and Evianna watched from afar. I didn't want to disappoint either of them. Instead of forcing my magic, I just dwelled on the problem.

What could I think about to create my salvation aura?

The scylla waters were farther north than the corona phoenix. The cold winds brought shivering and chills for everyone —except me.

Evianna and I continued to practice our magic at night, but occasionally she stopped so I could warm her with my world serpent magic. She wanted to create an eclipse aura before we reached the lair of the scylla waters, but since I wasn't entirely sure how long it would take us to get there, I wasn't sure if it was possible.

When Evianna attempted to create her eclipse aura, a sliver sheen of shadows shifted in front of the moon.

But that was it.

"Magical auras are difficult," I muttered, staring up at the sky.

"Why?" Evianna huffed. She exhaled, and the shadows slipped away, leaving the night sky as it was before—beautiful and calm.

"They require your magic to spill out of you. If you're too inexperienced, it can be painful and confusing. And if you're not trained enough, it can drain you."

"I think I'm ready. I just don't know what I'm doing."

Evianna walked around the deck of the airship. She wore tight leather trousers, and a giant coat to keep the cold at bay. Since I had no need for a coat, I wore my button-up shirt open to show off my god-arcanist mark, though the wind tugged at my clothes, twisting them with all the zeal of a kitten.

The sailors were in the hold, where it was still semi-warm. Xor remained on the quarterdeck, unable to go anywhere, really. His main dragon head slept, while the ninety-nine snake heads remained alert and watched us with glowing eyes.

"You've almost got it," I said as I motioned to the bright, full moon. "Don't give up on yourself."

When Evianna turned to me, her bluish-purple eyes seemed alight with happiness. She strode over and then removed her coat. She had a thin white shirt that caught the light of the moon and shone like pale ivory. With a casual toss, Evianna dropped her coat on the deck.

"Aren't you worried you'll get cold faster?" I asked.

Evianna half-shrugged. "I have you to keep me warm."

"Yes, but..."

After a short breath, she placed a hand on my chest. "I think *we* should hone our swordsmanship together."

"Oh? Why?"

It seemed silly. My sword wasn't a normal weapon anymore. And most fights wouldn't come down to minute technical detail of parrying and dodging.

"I think we should have a sparring match just like Master Zelfree and Calisto." Evianna threw some of her white hair over her shoulder. "No magic against each other. Just weapons. *Real* weapons."

"Okay. But that didn't answer my question."

"Well, we should do it to maintain our skills. And also..." Evianna wrapped her arms around me as she stared up through her eyelashes and offered a playful smile.

I couldn't stop myself from smiling in response. What was she thinking?

Evianna tugged the collar of my shirt, and I leaned forward so we could kiss. But right as her lips were a feather-touch against mine, she whispered, "Whoever wins our sparring match... they can do whatever they want to the other person."

Chapter 32

Aura Practice

Her one statement put a halt to all my other thoughts.

With a slow turn, I glanced over at Xor on the quarterdeck. The massive typhon beast watched us with one hundred and ninety-eight eyes. When I returned my attention to Evianna, my heart beat faster than before.

"Right here?" I whispered.

Evianna nodded.

"Anything?"

Her face shifted to a bright shade of pink. "You're not supposed to ask for specifics. You're just supposed to… know the line." Evianna ran a hand down my chest. "And you're supposed to lament there is a line, and reluctantly hold yourself back from crossing it."

That seemed more complicated than her game implied, but that didn't stop me from getting excited at the prospect. I suspected, since we weren't wed, this was more a flirtation than an invitation to take things further than we had gone. Still, I liked the idea. Even if Xor was here.

Fortunately, my tremor sense told me Fain was below deck.

And so was Adelgis. Both sleeping. This was probably one of the few times Evianna and I would have without them around.

"All right," I said. "But I need a sword."

Evianna's face never returned to its normal coloration. Instead, she stepped into the shadows and disappeared into the darkness. I was alone on the deck of the airship for only a few moments before she returned. With a graceful stride, Evianna emerged from the shadows, holding two steel swords—one a longsword, the other a short sword.

She handed me the longsword.

"I can't use Retribution?" I asked with a raised eyebrow.

"That wouldn't be fair," she said matter-of-factly.

"It's not fair you have a smaller and lighter weapon."

"Yours is longer, so I think it evens out."

Evianna backed away until she was at least ten feet from me. The night breeze rolled over us, fluttering her white shirt, and tugging at mine. Evianna's beautiful hair flowed with the wind, giving her the appearance of a spirit or specter. She was more beautiful than any other woman I had met.

I supposed I *did* lament there was a line.

The day of our wedding couldn't come fast enough.

"Ready?" she asked.

"How do we determine the winner?" I asked. It wasn't like we could kill each other. This was a sparring match.

"Whoever disarms the other. That's the winner."

"All right."

With a confident stance, I lifted my sword. The clear evening sky, and the twinkling of the stars overhead, set the mood. This was a midnight duel. Not a *magi cross*, but something more akin to what mortals engaged in.

Evianna's shadow shifted around her feet, and her knightmare, Layshl, rose from the darkness and then stepped off to the side. She was a hollow suit of armor, observing the duel. It made me wonder if she would hang around afterward, but I quickly shook that thought away.

Evianna lunged forward.

I braced myself and blocked her first strike with my weapon.

Clang.

The clash of metal was louder than I had anticipated. It had been so quiet moments before. I hoped no one would come up to the deck to investigate.

Evianna slashed with her short sword, aiming for my arm. I dodged, and although my weapon was awkward, I swung it in an arc. Evianna tried to move out of the way, but she wasn't fast enough. My blade caught her shirt, cutting some of the front. The tip of the blade nicked her arm, slicing her a bit. A small bead of blood formed and then dripped off her arm.

The sight caused me to hesitate.

"Evi," I muttered as I held up my other hand. "I'm sorry, I—"

She thrust her sword forward and caught the sleeve of my shirt. When she pulled her sword up, she also removed part of my shirt. Without the buttons in the front, or a sleeve holding it up on one side, it flapped around in the evening wind, held on to me only by one arm.

Still shaken, I stumbled backward.

I held my shoulder for a short moment. She hadn't cut me, just my clothing. I wasn't afraid for myself, but injuring Evianna seemed wrong. Her tiny scratch had healed already, but what if I accidently cut her deep? Perhaps it was best if I just let her win.

Evianna stood a few feet from me. Again, with a playful smile, she said, "You look good without a shirt."

Her confidence, and lack of anger over my mistake, eased some of my worries. With a soft chuckle, I removed the last of my ruined shirt. I tossed it onto her discarded coat. "Maybe I should remove the rest of your shirt as well."

"I'd like to see you try."

Her statement had me red in the face. I hadn't really ever been like this with anyone, and the fear of someone walking up onto the deck had me worried, but excited. It was hard to put into words the feelings. My stomach felt light, my chest twisted in knots, and my head was a buzzing without concrete thoughts.

Other than thoughts about Evianna, of course.

I held up my weapon.

Evianna rushed forward. Our blades clashed, but I was taller and stronger. I pushed her backward, and she stumbled. With her balance thrown off, I tried to follow her lead by slashing at her sleeve. Evianna dodged to the side, however, ruining my aim. I slashed her shirt more across the chest.

Fortunately, I managed to pull back before actually cutting her flesh.

It just... left most of her shirt open. She wore bindings over her chest, like most women who took up combat. The bindings helped to... keep things in place.

I stepped away, uncertain how Evianna felt. If she wanted to stop, and call this off, I would understand, even if I was ultimately disappointed.

To my surprise, Evianna tugged at her ruined shirt. She unbuttoned the last of the buttons and also tossed it aside. Her chest bindings weren't tight enough to restrict her breathing, but they were tight enough to cover her perfectly. If she had started the battle like this, I probably would've been too distracted to land a blow.

"Volke..."

Evianna's voice was both soft and husky.

I half-lowered my weapon. "Y-Yes?"

Before Evianna said anything else, the airship grew dark. I caught my breath as I turned my attention to the sky overhead.

The moon...

A shadowy circle moved in front of it, creating a total lunar eclipse. It was Evianna's eclipse aura! She had formed it while we were sparring. I hadn't even been paying attention.

The darkness that fell over everything was nearly absolute. A normal person wouldn't be able to see a thing. Even the stars were no help. The void we found ourselves in had no light.

That was when Evianna lunged forward. I heard the laugh on the edge of her breath as she moved in to strike. Clearly, she thought she had me defeated—she thought I couldn't see. And she was right. I couldn't see with my eyes, but my tremor sense still worked, even on the deck of the airship.

But I didn't let her know that.

I pretended to fumble as Evianna got close. She slashed, and I "surprise" gasped as I backed away, though I knew where she was at every moment.

Evianna pressed forward. As a knightmare arcanist, she could see in the darkest of settings. When she reached for my wrist, in an attempt to disarm me, I switched it around on her. I brought my blade up, caught her hand, and then pulled back.

She shouted, likely both from surprise and the sudden flare of pain. Then I stepped forward, into her stance, and slashed upward. Evianna leaned away before I cut her flesh, but I did catch the bottom of her bindings. I sliced them half open, and Evianna's eyes went wide in shock.

She knew now that I could see her just fine.

"Cheater," Evianna whispered with a smirk.

She stumbled backward and held an arm over her chest, protecting the last of her clothes there.

"You're the cheater," I said with a chuckle. "You said *no magic.*"

"I said we wouldn't use magic on each other. The eclipse isn't hurting you."

"What a fine bit of wordplay. I don't think that's how it works."

Evianna lunged forward.

I held up my weapon, ready to parry or counterattack, but then she dove into the darkness. When she shadow-stepped, it was impossible for me to track her. I figured she'd appear behind me, since that was the classic tactic, so I half turned, prepared to strike.

Evianna emerged from the darkness right in front of me. She slashed upward with her sword, about to cut me, but instead, I leaned away. While her sword arm was up, I grabbed her wrist and twisted. Evianna grimaced and dropped her weapon. It clattered to the deck of the airship.

Then she placed her foot between my legs, caught my ankle, and grabbed my shoulders. I was surprised enough, and a little distracted, to the point that when she leaned backward, and knocked me off balance, I didn't even mind that much. She rolled onto her back, took me with her, and then kicked up with her feet, throwing me over her.

I hit the deck on my back, winded.

The eclipse aura—a perfect use of her magic—disappeared from the sky. The *Diamond of Dawn* was once again bathed in the light of a full moon. It was a shame, because Evianna's aura hadn't been up for long.

Evianna moved over and then straddled me, her white hair blowing in the evening breeze. She stared down at me with a smile, but she didn't have her weapon.

"I win," I said, my longsword still in hand.

Evianna took ragged breaths. Then she wiped some sweat from her brow. "I suppose."

"Your aura... it was amazing."

That was when her face grew red. She glanced away from me, as though she couldn't look me directly in the eye. "I..."

And while she was distracted, I grabbed her arm and rolled her over. Once her back was on the deck, I got on top of her, pinning her. Evianna stared up at me with wide eyes, her face redder than I had ever seen it before.

For a long moment, we just stared at each other, both taking heavy breaths.

"I think I'm owed a prize," I finally muttered.

Layshl, whom I had almost forgotten about, disappeared into the shadows. She practically melted into the deck of the airship, vanishing from sight. Xor didn't go anywhere, though. Nor did he make a sound.

"As long as you keep me warm," Evianna whispered. She slowly brought both her hands up to my chest and gently grazed her fingers over my skin.

"Of course."

I leaned down, pressing my lips to hers. Then I released my weapon, and allowed my hands to explore her sides, from her taut stomach to the curve of her rib cage, to everything soft.

I'd never let her get cold.

Poetry didn't do *love* justice.

Even though I was racing against a clock to beat the Second Ascension to the last of the god-creatures, everything felt good. Better than good. The sun was bright, the sky a vibrant blue. When I thought about my future—or the apoch dragon—I was filled with hope.

Everything would work out. That was how I felt.

So, while I stood on the deck of the *Diamond of Dawn,* with Lynus and his god-creature, I decided I would create another aura. Today would be the day.

Lynus waited in the middle of the deck, trying to focus. He was quiet, he had been since this morning, and he shared my distant gaze. Lynus and Zelfree had been spending a lot of time together this trek, just like me and Evianna.

"Do you think you'll be able to create a salvation aura?" I asked him. He was only a few feet from me, but he didn't react to my question. Had he heard me? Or was he ignoring me? "I ask because—"

"I'll do it," Lynus stated, cutting me off.

"Oh? What makes you so sure?"

Lynus narrowed his eyes and gave me a sideways glance. "Ya know what I've learned over the course of my long, and painful life?"

I didn't like the start to this conversation. But I decided to humor him. "What?"

"No one throws away a useful tool."

The statement seemed like a non sequitur to me. I mulled it over before asking, "You think you're a tool?"

Lynus snorted a laugh and then glanced away. "Oh, I'm a tool, all right. And I've got one last role to play." He slid his hands into his pockets. "You don't have to worry about me. I'll make your *salvation aura*." He said the last two words like they tasted bad.

"I don't think—"

But I stopped myself before I finished my thought. I wanted to say *no one thinks you're a tool*, but that wasn't right. *I* thought of him as a tool. I didn't care for the man. I wanted him dead. But the only reason we hadn't "thrown him away" was because he was a god-arcanist and we needed him.

No.

There was one more reason...

"Zelfree doesn't think you're a tool," I finally said. It was as accurate as I could get.

"He has before," Lynus muttered under his breath.

I stepped around until I was in front of the man. Lynus was one of the few people who just stood around with an intimidating demeanor, even when he seemed dejected. His coppery-red hair fluttered in the wind.

"Zelfree did everything he could to save you." I remembered it well, because I had thought he was so foolish. "I think he genuinely regrets what happened between you two. And even before you bonded with the typhon beast, he was willing to do whatever it took to make sure you were okay."

Lynus didn't respond. He just stared at me, his eyes half-lidded, like I was mildly irritating, but he couldn't say anything about it.

I remained quiet for a moment, wondering if Lynus believed me.

The silence between us lasted a few awkward seconds.

"Was that a pep talk?" Lynus drawled.

I stood a little straighter. "Er, well, it was... something."

"I don't need motivation. I have plenty. Focus on your own magic—you're the one who everyone will be looking to. If *you* can't get the salvation aura correct, it'll shake the others."

With a slow nod, I said, "I know."

"No matter how difficult it is, never let it show. That's all you need to worry about, lad. Not me. Not anything else."

Lynus was probably right. I didn't like ignoring others, though. But if I could create my aura without problem, it would be for the best.

I turned away from him and crossed my arms. I just had to focus. With a smile, I glanced over my shoulder. "Thank you."

He didn't reply. He just rolled his eyes.

Still, this was a good day. Everything would work out.

I just knew.

Chapter 33

The Lair Of The Scylla Waters

I had another strange dream.

Another memory that wasn't my own, brought to me by the master dreamweaver, Adelgis Venrover.

This time, it was underwater. Light filtered into the depths, broken and sparkling. It reminded me of the Isle of Ruma. Beautiful and pristine. I wasn't sure whose memory this was, since I was under the water for such a long time, but there was never any fear of drowning.

When I finally swam upward and brought my head above the waves, there were stars shooting across the sky. Actually... not stars. They were *star shards*. The corrupted kind. The blight of the sky.

Then there were ships. Dozens of them. And they weren't anything I recognized. None of the ships had masts or giant sails, or even flags. They were wide and flat and mostly manned by people with oars. They headed toward a distant shore, sailing by me. But before the strange ships could reach their destination, whirlpools appeared in the waters.

One by one, the ships were dragged beneath the surface of the water.

Somehow, I knew this was my doing.

The ships couldn't do anything about my magic. They were helpless, and most broke to the fury of the ocean.

Until ice shot across the waves. A powerful form of winter blanketed the area. I recognized the abilities of the fenris wolf long before I saw the beast. It appeared on one of the boats—it had been using illusions to hide its gargantuan wolf form.

Balastar, the first fenris wolf arcanist, rode on the back of his god-creature. In this memory, he seemed blurry, just as Luvi had been in the previous dream. Why couldn't I see his details?

He pointed a spear at me, and the wolf howled. Winter mists spread out from the boats. Balastar had come for me. That was what I felt in the dream.

"Come, *Equinox*," Balastar shouted, his voice filled with dark laughter. "You can't hide forever. You can't hide from the Hunter."

Equinox...

That was the title of the god-arcanist who bonded with the scylla waters. Unlike a solstice, where the day was long or short, the equinox was a day where the sunlight and the darkness were exactly equal. They were rare and mysterious phenomena, and Schoolmaster Tyms used to claim that some mystical creatures could only be born on those days.

When I slipped back into the water, far beneath the surface, the fenris wolf couldn't seem to see me.

Balastar and his wolf tried using their magic on the water. Yet nothing happened.

When I waved my hands, they were scaled and fish-like.

This was...

A memory of the scylla waters. From the actual god-creature.

It was just as mysterious as a normal equinox. I wasn't sure why it would hide, or why there would be conflict, but here it was.

The scylla waters lurked beneath the depths, avoiding Balastar's attacks. I wondered why. But then I realized something amusing. The scylla waters was invisible when in the ocean. Just as the sky titan was invisible while flying through the air.

All the god-creatures seemed to have powerful abilities that made them impressive, even when just standing around.

But why was Balastar attacking? Had the scylla waters created an armageddon aura? And now it was slated to die? It made me wonder.

I never managed to figure it out, though. The dream ended before anything came of the conflict. When I woke, I did so with a gulp of air. My chest hurt, as though I hadn't been breathing. It was night, and my cot was just as uncomfortable as ever.

But it was warm.

When I glanced over, I spotted Evianna curled up next to me. This wasn't a cot built for two, but we made it work. Her body was half on top of mine, and my arm was tightly wrapped around her waist.

What was Adelgis trying to tell me?

Or perhaps he just wanted to let me know the scylla waters worked in mysterious ways.

Whatever the reason, I closed my eyes and allowed myself to fall back asleep.

Six more weeks of travel, and I hadn't quite created the perfect salvation aura.

I had managed to allow my magic to pour from me, and Terrakona, down in the ocean, telepathically whispered words of support, but it wasn't perfect. They were halfway auras—slow and small steps toward my goal.

I never again created an armageddon aura, which I was thankful for.

However, without something to really test my aura on, it was difficult to know what my magic was doing. It felt as though I had created it properly a few times, but what was happening? Was I curing the arcane plague of the creatures dwelling deep beneath the waves?

Was I doing *anything?*

I stood near the railing of the *Diamond of Dawn*. The blue waves below were beautiful.

"Volke?"

The question caught me a little off guard. I had been alone, and my tremor sense told me that Adelgis, Fain, and Evianna were a deck below, enjoying a meal. Lynus and Zelfree... they were busy. That left only William.

When I turned, it was him, certainly, but his voice had sounded different.

"Are you okay?" I asked him.

The weeks hadn't been the kindest to William. He had lost a little weight, and his normally short hair had gotten longer. Despite all that, he had not a speck of stubble. And he kept his clothes crisp and clean. Everything had a place, and William kept them in their place.

"Do you know when we'll reach our destination?" William asked.

I shook my head. "Adelgis said we're close. He said the scylla waters is located in a strait—a narrow corridor of water between cliffs."

William took a deep breath, and then exhaled. When he shifted his weight from one foot to the other, I felt the hesitation. He was nervous. He had failed to become an arcanist in his youth, he hadn't bonded to the typhon beast, and he hadn't bonded with the corona phoenix. I knew what he wanted to say. He wanted to say he wasn't worthy.

He wanted to say rejection was painful, and that one man could only take so much of it.

"Everything will be fine," I said, cutting to the chase of the conversation I knew we would have.

William forced himself to smile, but it was tired and wary. "You don't know that, my boy."

"*Persistence. Without it, we fail to achieve our greatest feats.*"

He snorted once. "The forty-first step of the Pillar."

"You remember?" I asked, honestly surprised he could recall the number.

"Of course." William tapped the side of his head. "I might not remember everything, but I'll never forget your obsession. You read those steps forever. Dreamt of becoming an arcanist. Now look at you." He motioned to my whole body. "It all comes easy."

"No," I said, thinking back on everything.

"Don't be modest."

"It never gets easy, but it does get easier."

William thought on that for a moment before nodding. "That's a good way to put it."

"It'll get easier for you, too." Then I motioned to his body. "I wouldn't be here if it weren't for you. Please—I need your help. Don't give up on us."

William ran a hand through his longer hair. The wind played with it while we sailed through the sky. After a long exhale, he said, "You have so much faith in me. It may be misplaced."

Self-doubt plagued me like a second shadow, so I understood his fear. But no one allowed me to give up, and for that, I was thankful. So I wouldn't allow William to give up either.

"Illia and I agreed that whichever one of us has a boy first, we'll name him William." I chuckled as I added, "It seems a fitting tribute to the man who gave us a home when he didn't have to."

I told him because I wanted to distract him from the task at hand. Perhaps if he didn't think about it, the doubt wouldn't sink its cruel claws into his thoughts. Unfortunately, my statement didn't have the effect I desired.

William stared at me, his eyes glazed with water. He sniffed deeply before rubbing his face.

I held my breath, my chest tight. I hadn't been expecting that.

Once William collected himself, he exhaled, smiled, and even laughed. With a solid pat to my shoulder, he said, "I'm the lucky one. You and Illia feel like the prizes of a life well lived."

I placed one of my hands on top of his. "No matter what happens, we'll be a family. You don't have to worry about this. About the god-creatures."

"Well..."

"I know what kind of man you are. If none of the god-creatures bond with you, it's their loss."

William playfully pushed my shoulder. "All right, boy. No more saccharine. My heart can't handle it." He laughed, his gut practically shaking. "I should've known that you would be so encouraging. That's just who ya are."

I crossed my arms and half-shrugged. "I learned from the best."

Our laughter felt right, and as we continued sailing through the sky, I knew William would do whatever it took to impress one of the god-creatures.

"*Volke. We're here.*"

The *Diamond of Dawn* soared through the sky, heading toward two large cliffs. A narrow channel of water went between them. A strait. Just as Adelgis had described. And unlike the Lightning Straits, which were populated by thunderbirds, this strait was devoid of life.

Gray rocks, tall enough to scratch the sky, and waves crashing against cliffs were a grave reminder of nature's power. A normal ship wouldn't dare sail through such a narrow channel of water. It would be dashed against the cliffs and the stones, and then tossed into the icy waves. Those who survived would be dragged away by the powerful currents.

Snow filled the winds and landed on all the rocks jutting from the waves, crusting everything in rime. Climbing this would be impossible for a normal mortal.

Each breath I exhaled was visible and lingered as a mist.

Fortunately, I felt none of the chill. I was warm and cozy and protected, even when I wore a shirt that was half-open to expose my chest. Lynus must've been the same way because that man never wore a shirt, not even when it was frigid outside.

We weren't mortals, and nothing about the environment would stop us. This was a place untouched by human hands, and the scylla waters was lurking somewhere below.

"Adelgis," I asked aloud as I hurried up the stairs to the quarterdeck. "Are there any creatures nearby?"

"*What do you mean?*" he telepathically replied.

"Every time I went to a god-creature's lair, there was always something nearby. Either the Second Ascension or plague-ridden creatures... Is there anything here? I need to know."

For a long moment, Adelgis didn't respond.

I hurried to the tallest deck on the airship and then leaned against the railing. Xor was nearby, and his many heads also glanced over the side of the ship to get a better look.

We were above the strait. If the airship flew down, we'd be able to disembark onto one of the cliffs. I would have to tell the captain.

"*It's difficult to tell,*" Adelgis finally replied to me. "*But I think we can make it to the lair without getting harassed, if that's what you want.*"

"I do," I said as I tightened my grip on the railing. "Tell everyone to prepare to disembark. I want us to find that lair before sunset."

"*Of course. I'll make sure everyone knows what to do.*"

Chapter 34

Troubled Waters

Apparently, according to Captain Wiley, the man piloting our airship, this was the *Quietus Strait*. Which was rather ominous. The captain claimed this was a shortcut into the *Blue Rose Sea*, but that was far beyond any place I had ever traveled. The sailors said any ships that attempted to navigate the Quietus Strait were all never heard from ever again.

None of that was comforting, but I didn't care.

Terrakona waited at the entrance of the strait, the ice floating in the water attempting to batter him. But his scales were hard and his blood filled with the heat of molten rock. Steam wafted up from him, just as he sat around waiting for us.

The *Diamond of Dawn* landed on a flat stretch of rocks. Xor managed to disembark without much trouble, but Lynus insisted he wait by the airship. Taking his typhon beast into the strait was a terrible idea, I agreed with him. That was how the first typhon beast had been killed—getting trapped in a canyon he couldn't escape. If Xor fell into the water, he would never return.

Evianna slipped through the darkness and then emerged on

the rocks. After a deep breath, and a shiver, she walked to the edge of the cliff and glanced down to the narrow waterway below. The crash of waves and ice along the rocks echoed upward, creating a haunting melody.

"What're those lights?" she asked.

My tremor sense felt nothing. Did glowstones appear here naturally?

I walked to the edge of the cliff and glanced over as well. Sure enough, a dozen or so lights danced through the air, just above the chilly waters. They moved with a familiar twirl, neither controlled by the winds or bound by gravity.

They weren't will-o-wisps. I would've recognized them.

"They're ethereal whelks," Adelgis said, his voice half-carried by the wind.

I turned around. He was standing next to the airship, his robes pulled tight around his body. Then he pointed to the edge of the cliff. "There are several sunken ships down there. Many of them were carrying children."

Both my eyebrows lifted as I returned my attention to the dancing lights. They *were* ethereal whelks. Their little shells and tentacles were difficult to see from so high up, but now that Adelgis had mentioned it, there could be no mistaking their forms.

"Should we gather them up?" Evianna asked. "Leaving mystical creatures out in the middle of nowhere seems like a shame."

"Ethereal whelks don't like to abandon the area they're born in until they're bonded," Adelgis replied matter-of-factly. "I think we should let them be. Someday, someone will come seek them out."

I had forgotten for a moment—ethereal whelks were fable born when a child drowned. Not all children, just some. If there were a dozen whelks down there, more than a hundred or so kids had to have perished in the rough waters.

My chest hurt for a moment as I thought about the fear they must've experienced before finally passing. I pushed the thoughts away, though. Now wasn't the time to mourn the dead.

"Do you know where the lair is?" I asked Adelgis.

He nodded once. "It should be just where the water meets the rocks, right down there, near the entrance of the strait."

"Why here?" Evianna asked.

"Something about these waters seems to call to it. The creature likes the dead." Adelgis held his long, black hair down as wind came rushing by. "Volke... I think I'm sensing the thoughts of the undead. It's difficult, though. They're... harder to understand."

In that moment, I wished we had taken the Keeper of Corpses with us. *He* would've known what to do with a bunch of creepy creatures.

We couldn't lament that now. And mystical creatures that were unbonded would be young and weak. They wouldn't be able to bother us. We just had to press forward and search the area.

"Terrakona, please search the waters," I muttered.

"As you wish, Warlord."

"We're close."

"Yes. Soon, the Equinox will be named."

While Terrakona swam through the narrow waterway, Evianna, William, Lynus, Zelfree, and I searched down the side of the cliff. With my manipulation, I made us a path toward the icy waters below. The rocks shifted out of the face of the cliff, one at a time, each step rough enough that we wouldn't slide off them. Evianna shadow-stepped down faster than us, emerging on rocky outcroppings to scout ahead. I told her it wasn't necessary, but she seemed to enjoy it, so I didn't fight her.

Xor insisted on following us at least halfway. There were several caves here, both above the water and below it. While Terrakona searched some of the caves below the waves, Xor wanted to explore the caves above. My tremor sense mapped out a complex maze, but it didn't tell me where the lair door was—and I couldn't sense the interior of the lair. Which meant we needed to physically find it.

So, I made a pathway halfway down for Xor. The typhon beast was mighty, and large, so I suspected he wouldn't get far, but he also wouldn't be harassed by anything.

I pitied the poor soul who stumbled upon him and wanted a fight.

The caves near the water were coated in a thick sheet of ice, but were deeper than the rest. They caught my interest. Some were much too narrow for either Terrakona or Xor.

When I shifted the rocks on the cliff face around, ice shattered off the surface and fell to the waters below. The splashes scared some of the baby ethereal whelks. They disappeared in a flash of light, leaving the Quietus Strait a dark and gloomy place.

As we reached the cave entrance, there was a rush of air that howled as it exited into the strait. With a wave of my hand, I crafted us one last set of stairs to the cave entrance. Terrakona emerged from the chill waters, his eyes on me as he lifted his head. I carefully walked down the steps until I was close enough to pat his snout.

"Find anything?" I asked.

"The sunken ships are riddled with corpses."

His morbid statement had me frowning.

"What did he say?" Zelfree asked as he stepped close to me. Traces hung on his shoulder, her gray fur practically standing on end as she glared at the waves.

"Terrakona hasn't found anything," I replied.

"Hm."

Evianna shifted through the darkness and entered the cave long before I did. As I reached the entrance, surprised by the sharp edges of the rocks around this area, she called out, "It's here!" Her voice echoed throughout the entire cave, and then through the strait itself. The rumble of noise caused some of the ice to shift.

"You might want to keep it down," I mumbled.

Evianna stepped through the shadows and emerged by my side. "I apologize." She pointed to the cave. "But there's a stone door in there. Circular, like all the others. I'm sure the runestone will open it."

"What's the plan?" Lynus asked, a few steps above us.

I glanced up. "We'll go through the lair, clear it out, and then see if William can bond with the scylla waters. If he can't we'll have to find someone else."

William shifted his weight from one foot to the other with nervous energy. He doubted himself. I hoped it wouldn't last long.

Without waiting for the others, I shifted the stones so the rocks themselves brought me to the entrance of the cave. Once situated, I stepped off the stone step and headed into the cave. The ceiling was a good twelve feet above me, and the walls were smooth, as though they had been created by human hands, rather than nature.

The place was gray and white, the perfect coloration to match the chill.

But somehow...

It seemed tranquil. Unlike the other god-creatures and their lairs, this was more relaxing. Although I didn't know much about the scylla waters, I somehow found the creature comforting. Like... I knew the creature would side with us once we managed to find it.

And fortunately, Evianna was correct. A gigantic circular door was at the back of the cave. It had a half-fish monster carved into the face—a monster with a tail that seemingly dissolved into water. When I removed the lapis lazuli runestone from my pocket, it glowed with an intense inner light.

The others reached the entrance of the cave as I placed the runestone against the door.

The cave rumbled, but I used my magic to make sure the quaking didn't disturb too much of the cliff face. The stone door cracked down the middle and then opened wide, swinging inward like a normal door.

I held my breath until the rumbling and the movement all stopped.

My heart pounded, but I shook away the anxiety. This was good. We were here first.

"This way," I said, waving the others to the inner room. Before I went any further, I evoked molten rock from the creases of my palm. The bright, fiery display was enough to light the way. With confident steps, I went deeper into the icy cave.

I had thought this lair would be similar to the fenris wolf's—giant, mystical, and filled with wonder. But it was the exact opposite. I stepped into a room with stone walls, a flat, even floor, and a single pedestal in the center. With a furrowed brow, I glanced around.

Nothing.

This was an empty room. I didn't even see another door. I stepped inside, and my tremor sense narrowed. I could no longer feel the world outside the lair. It was as if the walls themselves dampened my magic. All I felt was the room I stood in.

When I approached the pedestal, it was in confusion. The others joined me in the cavernous room, their steps hesitant and their glances just as bewildered as mine. The area was at least forty feet across, and the walls slick with ice.

"This reminds me of the soul forge lair," Lynus muttered, his tone grim.

The pedestal...

There were words written across the surface. I stepped close and gently brushed my fingers over the etchings. It read:

There's a somber day,
That always draws near,
A promise no one can escape.
What do you most fear?

Some say *death*,
But they'd be wrong.
What's the price,
For love's great song?

A riddle?

I didn't like this at all.

Lynus stomped over and glanced at the pedestal. With a sneer he stepped away. "The soul forge had *puzzles* as well. I didn't like it." He glanced at the ceiling, like something would attack us at any moment.

"What happened in the lair of the soul forge?" Zelfree asked as he examined the riddle himself.

"Theasin had to sacrifice an arm."

Traces wrinkled her nose. "Hm. Well, it couldn't have happened to a nicer man," she quipped.

"It was entertaining," Lynus said with a huffed laugh.

What was the answer to the riddle? I mulled it over a few times, trying to think of a clever solution. What was the price of love? And it was somehow a day that no one could escape? I folded my arms over my chest as I tried to think.

"It really *isn't* death?" Evianna shook her head. Then she paced around the pedestal. "It seems like the answer."

William walked over and narrowed his eyes. When he brushed his fingers over the pedestal, his melancholic expression worried me. "The thing most people fear… The eventual reality that the people you love will die… The answer is *loss.*"

The moment William spoke the word, the cave rumbled. A portion of the floor sank, revealing a tunnel that angled deep into the earth. The sloshing of water echoed up into our cavern. It seemed the scylla waters had more rooms and trials for us.

I took a deep breath. If there had been monsters here, I would've happily fought them, but riddles were more difficult. What if we ran across one we couldn't solve? What would we do then?

I rubbed the back of my neck, mulling over the possibility.

Evianna straightened her posture and then turned her attention to the exit. Her shadows darted away from her feet as her knightmare went to the entrance and then returned a moment later. Layshl emerged from the depths, her shadowy body coalescing into something substantial.

"There's commotion outside," she said.

I glanced at the entrance. "In the strait?"

"That's correct."

Lynus, William, and Zelfree turned to me. I motioned them to the tunnel. "You three continue. Evianna and I will investigate the cause of the commotion." It was probably the undead. They were in the area. And I could handle them myself, without the aid of anyone else.

Zelfree nodded. "All right. But let us know if you need us."

"I will."

Evianna leapt to my side and walked with me.

The moment I stepped out of the cave, and my tremor sense snaked through the cliff face and up to the airship, I knew something was wrong. There were more footfalls than before. More people. And they were hurried and frantic.

Terrakona was deep beneath the waves, with the wrecked ships. Did he not feel it? Or was it because he was swimming? The water never felt the same as land.

And Xor was deep in the caves, his stomping loud, but not capable of causing quakes. Did he not feel it, either?

"Adelgis?" I asked aloud.

But he didn't answer.

Shaken, I ran for the stairs I had made in the rocks. What was going on?

Chapter 35

Magic Manipulation

Evianna stepped into the darkness and darted up the side of the cliff. Her shadow slipped from stone step to stone step, traveling faster than me, even though I could manipulate the terrain.

I raced up the rocks, my breathing hard, my heart hammering. While I was fast, and had a walkway that appeared for my every step, getting up the side of the cliff took longer than I wanted. Every second that ticked by added to my anger and panic.

Something was happening. A fight.

There were creatures at the airship. Creatures I couldn't identify.

But I didn't need to. They weren't supposed to be there. So, I slammed my hand onto the side of the cliff and then flooded the terrain with my magic. Every stone and mineral answered my command. With my eyes closed to better visualize the environment, I warped the cliff. The ground cracked and split apart, rumbling and quaking. The people above, near the airship, stopped their movements, likely confused.

Now that they were distracted, I caused the rocks to lift me up the face of the cliff. Evianna reached the top at about the same time I did. She wore her knightmare, and even created a sword of darkness, preparing herself for conflict.

"We should stay close," Evianna and Layshl said together, their voices intertwined.

I pulled Retribution from its sheath and turned my attention to the airship. To my surprise, there were *two* airships —the *Diamond of Dawn* and another ship I didn't recognize. Something smaller, with no identifying flags.

It was an airship belonging to the Second Ascension, there was no doubt in my mind.

The creatures around the second airship were the beasts I had sensed. They were misshapen and disgusting, malformed and corrupted.

Plague-ridden. But not the normal kind, laughing and manic. The more advanced plague—the one meant to destroy even gods.

There was a griffin, and it was unlike anything I had ever seen. Its fur was an unnatural yellowish-green, and it was matted with sticky goo and grime, as though it had been half-digested and then vomited out. The griffin's body was practically a skeleton, and it had no eyes.

The wings were freakishly long, with an extra joint. The feathers were diseased and rotted, and they fell off at a frightening rate. The beast didn't speak, it just acted as a vessel for its fell illness.

And there was a pegasus, but it was just as rotted and disgusting as the griffin. Its coat had completely fallen off, revealing its muscles and the ridges of its spine. The beast's hooves were rotted away, like yellowed teeth, and its neck was broken. The head of the pegasus swung back and forth, its mouth agape and leaking tainted blood.

The wings of the creature practically worked independently, flapping and carrying the limp body. Blasts of wind whipped over the rocks, knocking over the airship crew, and somehow preventing the airship from lifting off.

Dread form mystical creatures were stronger than their normal counterparts, but I hadn't realized they were *that* powerful.

And the two creatures were specifically targeting the *Diamond of Dawn*. The airship was just fifty feet from us, still on the rocks, and there was extensive damage to the hull. The sailors used flintlock pistols and crossbows to attack from the deck of the ship, but it obviously wasn't enough.

Their bullets and bolts tore through the bodies of the plague-ridden creatures, but it didn't stop their mad assault. Captain Wiley and his griffin were unconscious—or dead—on the deck of the airship. Had they been victim to a surprise attack? Their injuries told me that, if they weren't dead, they would become plague-ridden.

When the enemy griffin attacked the airship, it did so with single-minded intensity. The beast raked its claws into the wood, and it rotted from the touch, the exact opposite of what normal griffins could do with their reinforcement magic.

Evianna stepped forward, but I held out my hand.

"*No*," I snapped. "Stand back."

My shout caught the attention of the plague-ridden griffin and pegasus, but that was fine. I had been practicing my aura, and now I had targets. After a deep breath, and putting Retribution back in its sheath, I inhaled. Hopefully I could end this fight in one swift action.

"Warlord!"

Who had called me?

A man stood on the side of the second airship, his black hair tied in a tight bun, his eyes beady and filled with condescension. Despite that, he was thin, and frail, and somehow both the least threatening arcanist I had seen, and the most disturbing. His cheeks were sunken in, his eyes bloodshot, and his fingers were longer than those of anyone else I had ever met.

Almost like he had three joints to each finger, rather than two.

His robes gave him away, though. It was like the man had raided the wardrobe of his late father.

This was Theasin's son. Yevin Venrover.

His airship lowered slightly, the wind threatening to sting my eyes. I held up an arm as the man waved his hand, and the airship stopped its descent. The vessel floated above the cliff, at least fifteen feet up.

"The Autarch thought you would rush to these lairs," Yevin yelled, his voice carried by the violent winds. "And here you are."

"You're too late," I shouted back.

That was when I focused inward on my magic, trying to flood my body. Once it filled every pore and vessel, the magic would spill outward, creating my salvation aura—so long as I remained calm and focused. It was easier now, whenever I glanced over at Evianna.

My aura would help the griffin and the pegasus.

In theory.

I just had to trust it, not fall to anger.

"You won't be doing anything," Yevin said, his voice lancing into my thoughts.

Something twisted in my gut. I almost vomited, but I swallowed it back. When I glanced up, I noticed Yevin was waving his hand. There was now a tether between us—something invisible. It was pure magic, and he was using it to *change* something in me.

I grabbed at my chest, my teeth gritted. What was Yevin doing? It felt like... he was manipulating my magic.

Then it struck me.

Yevin was the abyssal leech arcanist. The reason people had hunted abyssal leeches to extinction was because of their damaging abilities. They manipulated magic and caused arcanists great suffering. The leeches also needed magical hosts to reproduce, which was disgusting and harmful to whomever they inhabited. The leech was the whole reason Adelgis's magic didn't function properly. It had lived in him so long...

"Warlord?" Terrakona's telepathy entered my thoughts.

"Volke?" Evianna and Layshl asked together. She placed a hand on my shoulder. "Are you okay?"

I motioned to Yevin. "Kill him."

Unlike his sister, Adelgis had never asked me to spare Yevin's life. I knew Adelgis didn't want me to harm his siblings, but Yevin felt different. He felt... more like Theasin than any of Adelgis's other family members.

And if he had some sort of magical manipulation, and that was how this plague was getting out of control, we needed to end this. I was almost secretly glad Yevin had shown up here. It saved me the time of hunting him down.

Evianna stepped into the shadows and darted forward as pure darkness, snaking across the rocks and heading closer to the airship. It was still in the air, though. She wouldn't be able to shadow-step to the deck, so I manipulated the rocks beneath the ship, trying to hit it, but unable to focus all my magic. Instead, I created a long stone pillar so she could get close.

The plague-ridden griffin screamed and lunged for Evianna's shadow. It vomited blood from its disgustingly thin body, but Evianna wasn't something solid for it to strike.

Despite my pain, I focused on creating my aura. If I could just...

"I'll be there soon, Warlord. Just focus."

His words were comforting.

The plague-ridden pegasus flew toward me. The winds whipped up around my feet, flaring like a screeching tornado. It made it difficult to hear, but I kept my eyes closed and my mind focused. The creature wanted me trapped so I wouldn't move—

it was rushing toward me with a bloody mouth and hooves so rotted, they looked like diseased slivers of wood.

Surely, its one goal was to stab me.

But my magic… I wanted to create my aura.

Something Yevin did stung. Every second I focused on my aura was another moment of pure agony. What was happening? And if I just ignored it, could I still create my salvation aura?

Right as the pegasus entered its own tornado, my heart beat harder than before. I kept my thoughts on Evianna, on my happiness, on tranquility. And it helped me. I relaxed.

My magic flooded outward, permeating the area.

The tornado around me died. The pegasus's evocation… It just faded in an instant.

And the pegasus itself…

The beast landed on the rocks in front of me. It twitched and spasmed, its decrepit body jerking around. At first, I thought it would die, just like the fire giant, but then I realized it wasn't shriveling or shrinking. The pegasus actually started to grew new coat. White patches appeared across the muscles of its body, sprouting like beautiful grass.

The feathers of its wings became full and bright.

Its wings cracked and set back into place, becoming normal again.

The eyes…

The pegasus's face plumped and filled, and the holes in its head brightened with magic as its eyes started to reform.

It was working! This had to be the power of the *salvation aura*. It was changing the corruption! It was making the pegasus right again. The relief I felt was like a warm summer breeze filling my heart.

"A wise judgment," Terrakona telepathically said. It felt as though he were closer, but I knew the ascent up the cliff face would be difficult for him, even though he could manipulate terrain. The ice, and the potential to damage the strait, meant he would have to go slower. **"Keep going, Warlord."**

But then the pain from Yevin's magic manipulation snapped me out of elation. What was going on? My aura... the magic in the air... it all shifted when Yevin waved his hand.

It felt like Yevin was strangling my magic. Causing me to fail. I couldn't allow that. I stumbled backward, my heart beating harder and faster than before. Abyssal leech magic had a disgusting slime to it that lingered on the edge of my thoughts.

I fought against Yevin's manipulation, my own frustrations boiling over. It was difficult to imagine *tranquility* when stabbing pain rushed through my body. And it felt like... Yevin was *trying* to mess with my magic. Change it to something I didn't want.

Then it happened.

The pegasus screamed out.

And then it exploded.

The creature popped as my aura shifted from *salvation* to *armageddon*. The guts and blood splattered across the stones, creating a pool of crimson so vile and filled with writhing maggots, my stomach flipped.

The ground quaked, and the temperature in the air went higher and higher.

"*What's happening?*" Yevin shouted, obviously confused by the devastation he had created.

With a clenched jaw, I tried to refocus on my magic and shut out Yevin's attack. I had to take control—or I had to stop my aura altogether. I was trying to save these plague-ridden creatures, and I couldn't do that if my aura was destroying them.

But then the griffin screeched.

It, too, exploded like a ripe pimple. Blood and pus shot across the damaged hull of the *Diamond of Dawn*, painting the airship in a foul shade of scarlet.

The shock of it rocked me. In that moment of panic, I

managed to end my aura before the whole cliff crumbled in on itself and sent us all falling into the strait.

Evianna created a rope ladder made of shadow and managed to connect it to the enemy airship. She slipped up her own creation and landed on the deck of the airship, her cape fluttering in the chill winds.

"I'm capable of manipulating the magic of god-arcanists," Yevin said with a chuckle. "You think *you're* going to harm me?"

When Yevin turned his attention to her, I panicked. He waved his hand, and the shadows in the area warped and wiggled. One even lashed out at Evianna, like Yevin was manipulating anything that had been infused with magic.

When Evianna tried to take back control, it was obviously a struggle.

I ran forward, around the pool of pegasus blood, and headed for the underside of the airship. Although I couldn't fly, I could still evoke molten rock, and the hull of the ship wouldn't stand a chance. I'd destroy that whole vessel and bring it crashing down.

When I drew close, Evianna lunged for Yevin. I thought she would cut him with her shadowy blade, but something worse happened.

The darkness in the area—the whole cliffside—intensified. It was as if the shadows were suddenly absorbing the light. A shadow lifted off the deck of the airship and slammed into Evianna, sending her tumbling off the side.

I managed to catch her in both arms, but then I stumbled and almost hit the rocks myself. Fortunately, I manipulated the terrain to help keep my balance.

What was creating the intense darkness? Was it Yevin? It seemed far worse than anything he could do.

"Kill the world serpent arcanist," Yevin commanded. He pointed over the edge of his airship. "The Autarch doesn't want him alive! He doesn't want *any* of the other god-arcanists alive. Infect them! Shred them!"

I set Evianna on her feet.

"I'm sorry," she and Layshl said together. "I wasn't expecting that."

"Next time, try less magic. Yevin's powers might be useless if—"

But I caught my breath mid-sentence. A creature emerged from the depths of the airship and then leapt off the deck. It wasn't like the griffin or the pegasus—it wasn't a nameless creature I hadn't met before.

This was a knightmare.

It was...

It was Luthair.

Chapter 36

Darkness Made Flesh

I almost hadn't recognized him.

He was a twisted version of his former self. Something disgusting, yet familiar, like an infected limb.

Luthair's black shadow armor was covered in protruding spikes. Thorns. Jagged, sharp pieces. One large spike jutted straight out from his chest, just over where the heart should be. His helmet was closed, and the visor was nothing but long, thin bars reminiscent of a jail cell.

Normally, knightmares were hollow, but Luthair's helmet had red eyes that moved around inside, almost with no rhyme or reason. They weren't fixed in place by a skull, but rather floating in a void of darkness, peering out through the slits of the helmet.

The inner lining of his cape had once shown the stars, like a brilliant night sky.

Now the stars twinkled red, and the darkness around them was far thicker than any terror in a dream.

Luthair was skeletal and thin in places, every inch of him jagged and sharp. His cape was tattered at the edges and practically unraveling. When he fell from the airship, the cape ripped down the middle to become bat-like wings. He flew through the sky, his wings contorting and changing until they were four wings, each sparkling with the sinister stars.

And then Luthair drew a sword from the darkness of his own body, yanking it out of his chest piece. It was a wicked blade, at least four feet in length, thin and jagged near the hilt.

This was a plague-ridden knightmare.

But not even a normal one—a plague-ridden true form knightmare, a creature no one had ever seen before.

"Is that…?" Evianna and Layshl asked.

Luthair swooped down. When he drew near the darkness, it all sprang to life, fueled by his mere corrupted presence. The shadows lashed out at everything. Dark tendrils bashed the *Diamond of Dawn*. Inky voids lunged for the sailors. Knives crafted from solid darkness slashed at everyone and everything.

The whole world had turned against us.

Although there wasn't an eclipse, the intensity of the darkness seemed to sap the light, creating a twilight atmosphere —dim and haunting.

Luthair came for us. His feet were clawed and spiked with thorns. He grabbed for Evianna, but she shadow-shifted away.

Then Luthair flapped his many wings and kicked one of his clawed feet at me. I pulled Retribution out on instinct, and it crackled with power. With a quick sidestep, and a slash of my sword, I caught Luthair in the leg. My blade passed through him as though he weren't even there.

And then black blood gushed from his injured calf. I had almost removed the leg entirely, but he wasn't normal. The arcane plague had formed into some sort of grotesque body inside his armor, wearing him just as knightmares should be worn.

Luthair didn't even grunt, his madness on full display.

"Luthair," I said, my voice shaky. I took a step backward, my heart hammering so hard, I almost couldn't hear myself think.

The plague-ridden knightmare flew up a few feet and then

swung his fell sword. The blade was made of nothing but coalesced shadows, so it could move with the desire of the wielder. The sword extended outward, like a whip, twisting and forming into something sinister. Thorns sprouted from the dark tendril whip, and the barbed weapon cracked through the air.

When Luthair swung it a second time, the tip of the whip caught me across the face. The barbs slashed up my chin, cheek, and eyebrow, gouging me in a single instant. I barked and stumbled backward, fearing for my eye. Hot blood wept down my face.

But I wasn't blinded.

Luthair dove for me.

I slashed with Retribution again, catching him in the gut. It was a shallow blow, but enough that Luthair took to the sky again, bleeding worse than before.

Evianna rose from the shadows and threw dart-like blades at him. Had she learned that from watching Lucian? Her aim was impressive.

When the darkness struck Luthair, it was absorbed straight into his hellish armor. No injury.

"Luthair," I called out. "*Luthair, just hang on!*"

My salvation aura would save him. I tried focusing on it again—tried thinking of something tranquil—but Yevin's manipulation stabbed at my chest. It was like he was *waiting* for me to use this ability.

The intense void in the area swelled and then lashed out again, stabbing and slashing at everything. All the shadows around the airships, all the darkness in the crevasses between rocks—they all shot outward. The sailors on the *Diamond of Dawn* shouted. When I turned to help, the darkness attempted to grab me. The tendrils tethered themselves to my legs and arms, making it difficult to focus on my aura.

Luthair lashed out with his whip again, striking me across the top of my right leg. He gouged out another chunk of my flesh. I barely felt it. Not because I wasn't injured—but because my mind buzzed with discordant thoughts.

"Volke!" Evianna and Layshl shouted.

If I created my armageddon aura...

I wouldn't be able to save Luthair.

And all the distractions were making it difficult. Especially Yevin's presence.

The shadows reached for Evianna as well. They were the darkest I had ever seen, and when she attempted to manipulate them, it was a real struggle. She was fighting against Luthair's corrupted magic. Shadow tendrils grabbed her legs and started pulling her into the darkness, similar to quicksand.

I didn't want to kill Luthair, but I couldn't allow myself to lose. And I wouldn't allow him to harm Evianna.

"Luthair!" I barked, my anger replacing some of my concern.

That got his attention.

He flapped his wings and then dove for me. When he got close, my attention was on the eyes behind the visor. They moved around, focusing on me with slit pupils. Then Luthair reached out with his clawed feet.

If I hadn't been distracted, I would've used Forfend. But instead, I lifted my arm, and Luthair's claws dug straight into my flesh. I raised Retribution, thankful he had made the mistake of getting close.

But then he spoke.

"Foolish," Luthair said, his voice darker than before, almost an echo. "I'm not Luthair. *I'm darkness made flesh.* Your nightmares given life."

Then his visor opened like a maw of teeth.

Luthair's claws encircled my left arm, tearing the flesh.

I managed to grit my teeth and slash with Retribution. The blade sliced through one wing and his arm, but that didn't stop him. Luthair vomited blood across my body, coating my injuries in his scarlet corruption.

If this had been any other creature, I would've been upset, even angry. But two thoughts raged in me. The anger for whoever did this to Luthair, and the regret I had for failing him.

But...

Now I was infected with the arcane plague.

And Yevin was still here. And our airship was in trouble.

Luthair chuckled. He let go of my arm and took to the sky with three uninjured wings, the red stars glittering inside the lining of his cape.

But before I could act, a blast of light shone over the entire cliff.

The light...

It dispelled the twilight.

Adelgis stood next to the *Diamond of Dawn*, his feet firmly planted on the rocks. His ethereal whelk, Felicity, floated around his head. Her brilliant snail body, spiral and mystical, was glowing with inner light, helping her arcanist combat the gloom. Her rainbow coloration was iridescent and wondrous.

Adelgis evoked even more light. I squinted, half-blinded by his magic.

The light broke apart the dark tendrils in the area—shattering the restraints on me and Evianna, freeing us both. The sailors on the *Diamond of Dawn* quickly began prepping the ship for departure.

I evoked molten rock in the palm of my hand. I threw it at Luthair as he dove close. My magma burned straight through his arm with devastating destruction, creating a crater in his shadowy flesh. Whoever was inside bled as Luthair flapped his wings and went higher into the sky.

When Adelgis focused his light on Luthair, the person inside chuckled. The twisted double voice was hideous.

Then Luthair dove for Adelgis.

Felicity evoked more rainbow light, and the brightness reminded me of staring at the sun. The intense shadows, fueled by corrupted magic, lifted from the ground and attempted to block out the light. The darkness went for Adelgis, the airship, his ethereal whelk—anything near him.

A wave of ice shot across the ship and the rocks.

Although I couldn't see though the blinding light and impenetrable darkness, I knew Fain and Wraith's magic like it was my own. They were helping Adelgis.

Evianna appeared on the deck of the *Diamond of Dawn*. She attacked Luthair, though she danced away from him, likely trying to avoid his blood.

I stopped focusing on manifesting an aura. Instead, I manipulated the terrain and shot a sharp and jagged rock up at the enemy airship. It smashed into the hull, breaking apart the wood. The rocking of the airship knocked Yevin over.

I lifted the rocks and sent myself over to the ship. Evoking more magma, which seemed to ooze from every pore, I flung the molten rock at the enemy airship. It burned through the wood, caught fire, and even melted through some of the metal reinforcements to the vessel's structure.

I slammed into the side of the ship and continued to set everything on fire.

My goal was to kill Yevin.

He must've known, but lancing pain swept through my body again. The magma I created began to harden and turn to stone—even the magma in my hands or around my body. It made it difficult to move, but I grabbed the railing of his half-ruined ship and pulled myself up.

The light shining over the area vanished.

I glanced over my shoulder and spotted Luthair fighting Adelgis. The knightmare had raked its claws over his body, and cracked parts of Felicity's shell.

If I stopped my attack on Yevin, I could rush to Adelgis, but it was more important that the abyssal leech and his arcanist be removed from the battlefield. If I didn't deal with this, Yevin could continue to manipulate my magic.

With a deep breath, I leapt onto the deck of the enemy airship.

Yevin held out a hand, and his manipulation caused more agony to flare in my chest. My body had become sluggish, weighted down by my own basalt bones and the hardened magma that crusted over some of my joints.

But I didn't care.

I stopped using my evocation and manipulation, and stomped toward him. I still had Retribution in hand, and there wasn't anything he could do about that.

Two airship sailors rushed me with longswords. I slashed at the first, power crackling off my weapon, my blade piercing his gut. Retribution cut through anything magical like it wasn't there, but non-magical objects were still solid. I had to thrust with some strength to puncture his armor and stab straight into the soft part of his gut.

The second sailor hit me with his blade—I was too slow to spin around and deal with him, even if my mind knew he was there and wanted me to respond. The enemy's attack cut me, but the weapon hit my basalt bones and didn't go any further.

I turned and swung my blade upward, catching the man in the chin and slicing through the right side of his face.

He stumbled backward, his hand on the injury, and then—thankfully—ran.

When I turned to face Yevin, the man threw something at me.

At first, I thought it was a rope. It was thin, long, and wiggling, but as soon as it landed on my body, I realized it was the abyssal leech. The mystical creature dug its leech-like mouth straight into the flesh of my chest. I grabbed at its long body, but the abyssal leech clearly had some ability to melt into magical creatures.

The abyssal leech became an ooze that was absorbed into my skin.

And while that was concerning, I knew what I needed to do. Nothing would deter me.

I stomped toward Yevin, my sword held so tightly in my hand it almost hurt.

His eyes went wide as he stumbled backward, heading straight for the quarterdeck. "Y-You should be immobilized!"

The leech... It burned in my chest. But I had felt worse.

And it seemed Yevin had no other options. He didn't have a sword or a pistol, though I saw he carried pouches of decay dust, a weapon used by the Second Ascension to break trinkets and other minor magical objects.

I wasn't wearing any of those, so that didn't matter.

Yevin slammed his back into the stairs that led up to the quarterdeck. He held up a hand. "This isn't right. I've trained with this magic! You shouldn't be able to move. You should be wrecked!"

His abyssal leech desperately wanted to immobilize me, but it just couldn't. I suspected, in the fleeting moment my thoughts weren't consumed with Yevin's death, that Terrakona had grown too old, and my powers too advanced, for the abyssal leech to do anything about it. God-creatures and their arcanists were on a whole new level when it came to magic, and while the abyssal leech had become a menace to normal arcanists long ago, its powers just weren't up to snuff to deal with me.

I gripped Retribution.

Yevin shook his head. "You're already corrupted! You can't win against the Autarch now. You need him to—"

I stabbed with my blade, effortlessly piercing his heart. I tried not to do it in anger—not to revel in his death—and I made sure it was as painless as possible. But I also couldn't help but feel some satisfaction when his words died in his throat and he slumped to the deck.

The abyssal leech squirmed, no doubt in grief.

"Volke!"

Evianna.

I turned, ready to keep fighting. I didn't care how many things tried to ravage me. I wasn't going to stop fighting until all these threats were dealt with.

Chapter 37

Magiborne Runes

Evianna, Fain, and his wendigo, Wraith, fought aboard the *Diamond of Dawn*.

Ice covered everything. Intense darkness crawled from every corner of the airship, attempting to grab and cut the feet of everyone aboard.

With as much magical control as she could muster, Evianna fought back the shadows. She kept them from hurting the sailors—from slicing Wraith's padded feet—and even from damaging the airship itself. When Luthair came for her, Evianna blocked his wicked sword with a parry of her own, but it was clear she was being pulled in too many directions.

Despite that, she kept fighting.

It reminded me of the Grandmaster Inquisitor, and how he had done everything in his power to protect as many people as possible.

I leapt off the side of the enemy airship and manipulated the rocks to lift higher so my fall wasn't far. Then I jutted the stones upward, some of them lancing toward Luthair. The knightmare flew around them, his cape-wings flapping powerfully.

If I could focus on my aura...

Evianna lashed out with darkness, but again, Luthair just absorbed the attack. When ice came his way, he flew higher and higher.

I ran to the *Diamond of Dawn*. To my anger, Luthair just kept going. Was he fleeing? The darkness settled and stopped attacking everyone and everything. But once I got onto the deck of the airship, I realized Luthair had done a substantial amount of damage.

Like me, Evianna was wounded and bleeding. She and her knightmare stayed together, but the suit of shadowy armor couldn't hide all their injuries.

Fain and Wraith didn't look too hurt, but they refused to move from their spot near the far side of the deck. They both stood protectively around Adelgis, who was on the deck, as though he had fallen over and hadn't the energy to get back up. Adelgis took deep breaths, his inky hair soaked in sweat and matted with blood.

I first went to Evianna. "Are you okay?"

She shook her head, her hands unsteady. "The plague-ridden monster," she whispered. Then she showed me her hands. "His blood is everywhere."

I took her arm and held her close. Luthair and his arcanist had one goal, and they seemed to have accomplished it. Was that why they had left?

Would they return?

Luthair...

I wanted to help him—to save him—but I had to focus.

I headed over to Fain, Wraith, and Adelgis. The twilight atmosphere faded, leaving us bathed in an afternoon sun. Despite the warmth, I still felt cold with anger and frustration. Where was Felicity? Had she disappeared back into a beam of light? Or...

Fain knelt next to Adelgis. "Everything will be okay," he whispered.

"I... can't hear anyone else's thoughts," Adelgis replied, his voice barely audible.

Wraith's ears drooped. With a whine, he sat next to Adelgis, his wolf-like tail curled around his feet. Although they hadn't told me what had happened, I already knew. Felicity had been killed.

When Adelgis glanced over to me, I saw it in his arcanist mark. It was faded, and he rubbed at the etching in his flesh as though it burned. Although he had been injured during the fighting, the arcane plague only affected those with magic. And since Adelgis was no longer an arcanist...

Evianna hugged herself.

The sailors ran from one part of the airship to the other, hastily making repairs. A few of them stopped and thanked me, but all I could do was nod in reply.

"What're we going to do?" Evianna and Layshl asked as one.

I glanced down at my mangled arm. Then I stared at my chest. The leech writhed beneath my skin. If I tried to make my salvation aura, I knew the beast would hinder me.

So it had to go.

"Everything will be okay," I stated, my heart hammering, but my conviction true.

I lifted Retribution and turned the point to my own flesh. This would hurt, but not as much as failing Evianna. With no real effort, I slid the point of the blade into my flesh, placing it just over the right side of my ribcage. Then I pushed the weapon into me, aiming for the leech. Retribution cut through my skin and muscle as though it weren't there, the blood pouring from the small incision I had made.

"*What're you doing?*" Fain shouted. He leapt to my side and grabbed my wrist, his panic apparent.

"The abyssal leech is inside me," I said through gritted teeth.

Fain pulled my wrist, removing the tip of the sword from my chest. Then Fain grabbed my shoulder and held me close. "I can do this," he said. "Wendigo arcanists manipulate flesh." He placed his other hand on my injury, his fingers bent like claws.

I took a deep breath and then nodded.

Fain pressed his nails into me, and his magic made the process less painful. He grabbed the leech in my body, practically pinching it with three of his fingers, and then yanked. Without warning, or bedside manner, he pulled the leech from my chest like a stray string being removed from a blanket.

With a grunt of disgust, Fain threw it to the deck of the airship. The creature was several feet long and as thin as an eel. It hit the deck, and a splat of blood went everywhere. My blood. The leech was coated in my vital fluids.

Then Wraith evoked ice, trapping the creature in place.

And Fain stomped it with his boot.

The leech exploded, almost like the plague-ridden pegasus had.

I grabbed at my chest, the agony of everything slowly creeping into my perceptions. During the fight, my body had shunted the pain aside, my adrenaline numbing everything. Now that the threats were gone, it all came crashing back. My injuries weighed me down, like walking around with water-soaked clothing.

Fain placed his hand back on my chest and attempted to "patch me up." His magic wasn't meant for healing, though. While he manipulated my flesh, and managed to stop some of the bleeding, the pain still lingered, my chest still throbbed in agony, and I was certain I needed actual medical attention.

The rocks around us slowly shifted and moved. Terrakona came up the side of the cliff, his massive body requiring much of the terrain to move around him. The climb must have been difficult, but the moment he was here, I felt better.

His scales were flared, his black crystal mane glittering...

Terrakona came straight to me. He lowered his serpentine

head until his snout touched my shoulder, his warm breath filled with the scent of sulfur.

He flicked his tongue out—a tongue covered in small, glowing runes—and snaked it over my body. I placed a hand on his nose.

"Don't," I said. "You shouldn't touch me."

"Our fates are intertwined." Terrakona bopped my shoulder a second time. **"A salvation aura would undo this."**

"I don't think I can—"

"The Children of Luvi are clever and devoted—but the Children of Balastar never relent."

Evianna stared at me, her knightmare armor covering her whole body except for her face. Layshl's cowl hung over her like a shadowy hood, but Evianna's purplish-blue eyes met mine with hopeful anticipation.

I could never let her down.

So I closed my eyes.

Without Yevin and his magic, perhaps I could focus? Perhaps I could keep my tranquility.

Although, scary visions flashed in my mind. What if I messed up? What if Evianna died just like the plague-ridden pegasus and griffin? What if *I* killed her?

"Doubt will kill all great things," Terrakona telepathically said. **"But only if you let it."**

Nothing had left me so frightened before. Not the twisted visages of monsters, not even my own death. What if I were responsible for the destruction of the people I loved? What a terrible fate.

But I couldn't allow that to stop me. Terrakona was right. If I didn't act now, Evianna and I wouldn't make it. We would lose ourselves to a slow descent into madness.

So I had no room in my heart for fear and doubt.

After a long exhale, where I focused on the tranquil memories—and where I imagined life *after* the plague was dealt with—I filled my being with magic. My injuries felt like holes, but they were small, and I could push past them.

The longer I went, the more I thought this would be impossible, but I didn't quit. Just like when I first evoked terrors with Luthair, and I had thought I was failing... I refused to stop until I achieved my goal.

That determination fueled me, even when things felt grave.

And once my magic flooded out into the world as an aura, I held my breath. This was the moment of truth. Had I done what I had set out to do, or had I done the unthinkable?

The injury to my arm...

It felt warm. Almost inviting. I slowly opened my eyes and stared down at my left forearm. The wounds were gone. My skin and muscles had stitched themselves together. But now there were markings across my arm. Sparkling silver lines that reminded me of tattoos.

What was this?

I ran my hand over my arm.

The sparkling silver tattoos glittered in the sunlight, but I couldn't feel them, just like any other tattoo. Some lines were straight, others were jagged, like lightning.

"Your salvation aura," Terrakona said. **"You successfully manifested it."**

When I glanced up at Evianna, I noticed she had unmerged with her knightmare. Her arms, neck, and part of her shoulders were covered in the same lines I was. They glittered, just as beautiful, practically matching her hair.

"What is this?" I asked.

Terrakona shook his head. **"The opposite of corruption. Just as the *blight of the sky* once ruined everything it touched, it became star shards with the help of the previous god-arcanists. The *arcane plague...* has transformed."**

The plague had transformed? But into what? Were these

tattoo markings harmful? They didn't feel like it. And if the *blight of the sky* had become star shards—which allowed us to imbue our magic to create permanent items—what would *this* allow us to do?

"Are we saved?" Evianna asked.

Her knightmare stepped forward. Unlike Evianna, who was covered in sparkling tattoos, Layshl didn't seem to have them. The hollow suit of armor turned over her bracers and even checked her boots. Nothing. No tattoos.

"Yeah," I said, a slight chuckle on my breath. "No more plague... Not for us."

"Will these tattoos ever go away?"

I stared at my arm and frowned. "I don't know."

"What are we going to call this?" Evianna whispered, her attention on the tattoos. She rubbed at her skin, as if to wipe them away. But they wouldn't go. They were permanent.

What would I tell the others? How would I explain this to other arcanists? To the world? I would have to let them know it was safe—it was the opposite of the arcane plague.

Borne was the word used to describe something *carried by* something else. *Bloodborne disease* meant: *a disease carried by blood*. And since these marks were made by the arcane plague, a bloodborne disease, I figured it was only fitting to give it a similar name.

"Until we write this down and send the information to all nations, I'm going to call this *magiborne runes*," I said. Markings carried by magic. Basically. The term *rune* was a little abstract, but I had always known them as marks of magic, so it fit in my mind.

The sparkling tattoos reminded me of the runes on all the god-creatures. Terrakona's tongue glowed with his rune marks. Adelgis didn't have them—only those with magic did.

Magiborne runes.

That was what we got from the arcane plague.

But what would they do for us? How had the first god-arcanists figured out how to use star shards?

I pushed the thought from my mind and turned to Adelgis.

Fain and Wraith had helped him up and were swaddling him in blankets brought by the sailors.

"Are you okay?" I asked.

Adelgis stared at the deck of the airship, but he managed to nod once. "I am," he muttered. Then with a weary smile, he glanced up. "Felicity saved me from the worst of it."

"There are other ethereal whelks," Fain said, motioning to the strait. "Remember? We saw them earlier. We can take you down there, and—"

"No." Adelgis shook his head and refused to even glance at the narrow passage between cliffs. "Never. Felicity... She was one of a kind. I wouldn't exchange her with another. I don't want... I don't want to bond with a second ethereal whelk, just replacing her."

Fain said nothing else. He just held Adelgis close, his expression distant and cold.

And then the sky went black. The sun disappeared, and a pillar of blue light shot up out of the strait.

The scylla waters had bonded.

Chapter 38

Enchantment

I stayed with Adelgis on the *Diamond of Dawn* while we waited for Lynus and the others to return to us. Evianna and Fain stayed with me, their eldrin being just as supportive. I almost wished the Second Ascension had attacked us before we went into the lair. If Adelgis was going to lose Felicity, I wished he could've submitted himself to one of the god-creatures for judgment.

But perhaps he wouldn't have taken it.

Thankfully, Captain Wiley regained consciousness while we waited. He, too, had magiborne runes. He thanked me for rescuing him, and he and his sailors fixed the airship just as Lynus, Zelfree, Xor, and William returned.

Xor was likely the reason they had taken so long. The lumbering typhon beast was far worse than any hydra I had ever seen when it came to mobility. Xor wasn't fast, but what he lacked in agility, he made up for in power.

With his main dragon head, he carried a bloodied corpse. It used to be a wyvern, but now it was just a bloody mess. His ninety-nine snake heads hissed and bit at the body, but it was pointless.

Had the wyvern once been plague ridden? Probably. But after my aura, it reverted to its normal state.

The scylla waters wasn't with them, and I knew why. The waves in the strait weren't acting right. Our newest god-creature was down below, at home in the ocean. It would likely swim with Terrakona back to the mainland.

I didn't want to speak with the others.

I was thankful we had the scylla waters, but I didn't want to explain what had happened. The rage I felt was different than normal. It was a slow, simmering anger that wouldn't be quelled until this was all over. If I had to recount what had happened—explain it all and relive the individual moments—I feared I would lose composure.

Perhaps Evianna sensed my hesitation.

She shadow-shifted to the others before they reached the deck of the airship. She spoke to them, and with my tremor sense, I probably could've spied on the conversation, but I didn't care to. When they boarded the vessel, Zelfree went straight for me.

"Are you okay?" he asked.

I nodded once. But before I could say anything, Zelfree grabbed my left arm and held it up to the light.

The sparkling tattoos made a distinct impression. Every time I saw them, I was in awe.

"*You* did this?" Zelfree asked.

Again, I nodded.

"And it used to be the plague?"

"Yes." I bit my tongue, half wanting to apologize for failing and half wanting to destroy the Quietus Strait as a monument to my anger.

Zelfree patted my forearm. "This is amazing. You did it, kid. I can't believe it. You have a real solution to all our problems."

"Well, yes, but—"

"The princess told us everything." Zelfree placed his hand on my shoulder. "About the mess you found yourself in when you got to the ship. Listen." He ran a hand through his dark hair, slicking it back. "I'm sorry. We continued with the lair, thinking you had it handled… I should've been here for you."

But that wasn't necessary. He didn't understand how I felt. It wasn't that the others hadn't been here—it was that some people thought they could get away with everything. The Autarch, the Second Ascension—they answered to no one for their vile crimes. How was that not frustrating?

"Don't worry about it," I stated as firmly as I could. "As long as we have the scylla waters, you did what you should've."

Prolonged silence stretched between us. Then Zelfree met my gaze and said, "We'll face the Autarch soon. You can't be dragging extra weight when you enter that fight. It'll slow you down—it'll cause you to make the wrong choices."

Extra weight?

For a brief moment, I thought he meant physical weight, but I quickly understood that wasn't the case. And I couldn't even argue with the man.

He was right. I didn't need extra weight.

"Can you speak to Adelgis?" I asked.

Zelfree must've thought it an odd request because he took a moment to think it over. Then he nodded. "I will."

"My father…"

I hadn't seen William yet. If he hadn't bonded, I would be confused and disappointed. He must've, though. Of course he had. Right?

"He bonded with the waters," Zelfree muttered.

"What's wrong?"

With a shrug, Zelfree said, "Nothing is wrong, per se. The scylla waters is just a darker creature than I thought it would be. Just as hydras seem to be some sort of off-shoot of the typhon beast, kappas seem to be related to the scylla waters. The beast required that William sacrifice his future children to the depths, if he ever had any."

That startled me. The scylla waters wanted the blood of babes? "Why?"

"I don't know. William told us nothing of his time in the deepest part of the lair. He was the only one who made it there. The walls trapped me and Lynus."

Strange.

It made me wonder what had happened.

"I'll go see him." I nodded to Zelfree, hoping he would help Adelgis in some way.

When I went to see William, he wasn't on the airship. He wasn't just around it, either. I had to use my tremor sense to locate the man, but fortunately, he wasn't too far. He stood near the edge of the cliff, staring down into the straits. The crash of the waves hitting the rocks echoed upward.

I leapt off the airship, landed on the stones with a grunt, and then made my way to him.

Terrakona watched me go, his eyes round and filled with worry. I waved to him, and he coiled himself up like a sleeping snake. But still, he watched me over his scales.

When I reached William's side, I gently placed a hand on his shoulder. He didn't flinch, but he didn't say anything, either. Then I waited, half expecting him to explain everything.

Instead, William pointed to the waters far below us. "There she is."

She?

I glanced over the edge of the cliff. In the strait below us, rising out of the waves, was an interesting creature. She was part humanoid, part fish. When the scylla waters lifted out of the waves, I could see her, but the parts of her body that remained in the depths were invisible.

Just as the sky titan was made of air, so the scylla waters was made of the ocean.

She was blue, with scales that glistened. Not just in the light, but with inner magical power. Her face was more fish and serpentine than human, but her torso was a mix of human and aquatic creature. She had gills, arms, and even claws, but fins that covered more portions of her body. Her tail, when it lifted out of the waves, reminded me of a shark's fin.

She was both monstrous and fascinating. The scylla waters glanced up at us, her inky black eyes like the night sky.

"Her name is *Leclair*," he said.

"She demanded your children?" I asked, unable to wait through pleasant conversation.

William nodded as he folded his arms over his barrel chest. "Aye. That she did."

"Why?"

"She said the *waters are the provider of life* and that I should devote my magic to the waves, so she can watch over the nymphs."

I stared at the scylla waters, her piercing gaze never leaving us. When she opened her mouth, a sinister hiss echoed through the strait. She was... scarier than I had thought she would be.

"Nymphs?" I asked.

"Hm. Something about the water elementals, too. And kappas, and all the creatures of the waters. She says we need to *seed the world with magic.* Sounded inappropriate to me, but..." He scratched at his smooth chin. "I couldn't say no. I couldn't let you all down."

That kind of weight was what Zelfree was talking about. I couldn't allow the weight of things to affect my judgments. "You didn't have to do this," I said. "If you didn't want to accept the terms of the agreement."

"I'm a grown-ass man," William said with a chuckle. He turned, a genuine smile on his face. "I know how to balance such decisions, my boy. You don't need to fret. I am here for you, and

I already have two wonderful children. If the waters needs me to seed things, I'll do so, however reluctantly."

"I-I don't think it's like what you're implying. It's more like, the more powerful your god-creature grows, the more mystical creatures will come into existence. You don't have to do anything other than survive."

"Ah. Yes. Well..." He grunted as he scratched his neck. "That makes more sense than what I was thinkin'."

We shared a chuckle, but then I pointed back to the airship. William must've understood, because he glanced down at his eldrin and seemed to communicate via telepathy, like Terrakona and I could. Then the scylla waters melted into the waves, disappearing from sight.

"Let's go, my boy," William said as he patted my back.

The first evening, we flew south, beyond the icy waves and toward the islands.

Terrakona and Leclair swam below us, and Xor stayed on the quarterdeck. I kept track of them at all times, my thoughts preoccupied with their growth. Lynus, William, and Zelfree were on the deck of the *Diamond of Dawn*, practicing their magic and auras, but I remained below deck, with Evianna, Fain, and Adelgis.

There was a single cabin we shared, complete with six cots. None of us slept, though. The lanterns remained on, even as the sun died outside the porthole. Evianna sat on her cot in the far corner. She had rolled up her sleeves to get a better look at her new mystical tattoos.

Evianna didn't like them. I could tell by her slight frown, and how she tried to roll the sleeves down her wrists in an attempt to hide them.

My one arm was bizarre, but I didn't want to think about it.

"There are dryads outside Regal Heights," Fain said.

He and Adelgis sat on a single cot, each at opposite ends. They had their backs to each other, as though fighting, but neither raised their voices.

Adelgis kept his attention on the porthole. "I'd rather not think about it at the moment."

"You should. This is your future." Fain petted the air, but in reality, he was just stroking his invisible wendigo. The icy dog panted slightly, even though we couldn't see him. "What about grifter crows? I see them all over the place."

"They only bond with tricksters and con men," Adelgis replied absent-mindedly.

"We could do that. I could help you pass the Trial of Worth."

Adelgis slowly shook his head.

He didn't look right. He wore the same robes he had during the fight. They were once pristine white, but now they were smudged with mud and dark blood. His black hair hadn't been combed, and he wore as much exhaustion as he did clothing.

"Maybe you should get some sleep," I said.

I stood against the bulkhead opposite them. The creaks of an airship didn't compare to the noises of a normal sailing ship. Despite that, I still appreciated the familiar space and sounds. I used it to help me stay focused on the current moment, rather than dwell on the future.

"I've been thinking about your marks," Adelgis said, not really answering my statement. "I have a theory."

I lifted an eyebrow. "You do? What is it?"

Adelgis stood from his cot. He rubbed at his old arcanist mark as he ambled over to the door. "One moment, please. I'll be right back." He opened the door and then shut it behind him as he exited. The soft click of the latch was as quiet as Adelgis could make it.

Fain immediately stood. "Why aren't you two helping?" He

motioned to me and Evianna. "You want Adelgis to be an arcanist, too, don't you?"

"I think you should give it a day or two before you talk to him about it," I stated.

Evianna nodded. She kept her attention on her sparkling tattoos as she said, "I wouldn't want to think about another eldrin so quickly after losing my first."

Fain paced around our tiny cabin. He shoved his frostbitten fingers into his pockets and huffed. "I just... I just don't want to wait. There has to be something I can do to help him." He snapped his black fingers. "I'll just find more creatures. That's what mystic seekers do, right? Gather them up and sell them to people? I'll just... I'll just become a mystic seeker."

Evianna finally tore her focus away from her new markings. "Most mystic seekers are in guilds, and they don't just train anybody. You have to join them."

"Then I'll join one."

"And then what? They don't let you take whatever creatures you want for your friends. It's a business—they follow guild rules. They typically only sell to nations or nobles."

Fain slowly turned to her, his eyes narrowed. "I'll do whatever it takes to help Adelgis."

She placed her hands on her hips. "You'll steal them?"

"If that's what it takes," Fain snapped, his voice louder, his tone heated.

Evianna shook her head. "You need to relax. This won't help Adelgis. It'll just—"

The door opened, and Evianna swallowed the remainder of her tirade. When Adelgis stepped into the cabin, he wasn't holding anything. He kept his gaze on the floor, but briefly lifted it to Evianna and then Fain.

"It's strange," he muttered. "Even though I have no magic, I swear I know what the two of you are thinking." When he glanced in my direction, he added, "And I'll always know your thoughts, Volke. They are always straightforward. Not that I mean offense by that."

"I understand," I said.

Adelgis walked over to me, his movements shaky, his complexion wan. He reached into his robes and withdrew a single thumb-sized star shard. The brilliance surprised me. The inside glittered with magical power, and I stared at the crystal for a moment, remembering how beautiful they were.

"Where did you get that?"

"The captain allowed me to borrow it." Adelgis held up the star shard. Everyone else paid careful attention, never glancing away. "See? The insides here? It reminds me of your new *magiborne runes.*"

He slowly lowered the star shard to my skin. The glitter inside matched the glitter of my new tattoos. The star shard was pinkish in coloration, though. My tattoos were silver.

With a frown, I said, "I don't know what this means."

"I think the markings on your skin are like the star shards. If I'm correct, someone would, in theory, permanently adhere their magic to you. Like *imbuing a magical item*, but just... on your body."

I stared at the tattoos on my arm for a long moment. "What does that mean?" I asked again, unable to fully grasp a permanent change on my body.

Adelgis tucked the star shard away in his robes. Then he motioned Evianna over. She hurried to my side, her eyes wide. "You want me?" she asked.

"Why don't you try imbuing your knightmare magic into his arm?" Adelgis held up my forearm and pointed to the markings. "Imagine these lines as star shards."

"Well, but, I'm not a talented artificer."

"This is just for a test."

Evianna's frown deepened. "But if you're correct, this is a

permanent change. I can't just use my imbuing. What if I don't do it correctly? Or what if my magic is too weak?"

She was right. Then again, talented artificers could improve trinkets and artifacts after they were made, so long as they had more star shards.

"There's no other person I'd want to try this with more than you," I said as I took Evianna's hand. "I say we try this."

While I understood this was a lot of pressure, there wasn't much I could do about that. These were new waters for all of us. If we tripped, and made a mistake, I'd rather do that with my betrothed than with someone else.

I offered my arm. "Go ahead. I want to see if Adelgis is correct."

Evianna hesitantly grabbed my wrist. She waited for a long moment, staring at my silvery markings. Even if this was permanent, the knowledge of the process was probably far greater than a single lost opportunity for power.

She closed her eyes.

In response, I held my breath.

I thought the process might sting or burn. It was the opposite, actually. The cold sensation reminded me of drinking water after a long hike through a desert. Calming—refreshing. Was Evianna doing it?

The runes on my arms...

They *moved*.

The silver lines, once straight or jagged slowly swirled across my skin. They shifted position until stopping as tight little coils. They were no longer silver, but black. They reminded me of Luthair's armor—a deep void-like black that couldn't be ignored.

When Evianna pulled her hand away from my arm, I touched the new marks.

They were tattoos, just like before, but different in coloration and style.

"Did I do it?" Evianna asked. She glanced at my arm and frowned. "Is that... what it *should* look like?"

"I don't know," I muttered. "This is the first time it's ever happened. We're writing the first instructional tome as we speak."

Adelgis grazed his fingers along my new runes as well. "Do you feel different, Volke?"

I half-shrugged. "It felt empowering. I suppose."

"Perhaps you have a tiny fragment of knightmare magic now. The ability to wield shadows, or perhaps see in the dark."

"On my body?" I lifted my arm closer to the lantern light. The tattoos still sparkled, just with a different shade. "You think that's what happened?" With a tilt of my head, I motioned to the nearby lanterns.

Evianna nodded in understanding, and then manipulated the shadow around the small cabin. Darkness from under the cots lifted and snuffed all our small lanterns, instantly blanketing the room in the void of night.

It took me a moment as I focused on the surroundings, but eventually it happened.

The darkness...

It didn't prevent me from seeing. Evianna really *had* given me a small sliver of knightmare magic. I glanced down at my arm, surprised by the ability. It was the standard knightmare augmentation, but with the rune on my arm... it was permanent?

"Well?" Evianna demanded. "Anything?"

"It worked," I whispered.

"It did?" she practically shouted.

Fain stepped forward. "Really?"

"Yes." I walked over to the nearest lamp and used some of my evocation to light it. Then I had to snuff the molten rock and turn it into sandstone. Once it was a tiny bit lighter in our cabin, I turned to Adelgis. "How did you know?"

Adelgis smoothed some of his matted black hair. After a long moment of contemplation, he muttered, "It just seemed logical. That's what my father would've said. The link between the star shards and your marks, the fact that the plague was a magical alteration to the body… That's what your magiborne runes are. Magical alterations."

Fain stared at my arm. "Do you think he could get *physical* alterations with those runes? Like… mystical creatures sometimes have wings? Maybe *he* could have wings?"

"I don't know, but I wouldn't rule it out." Adelgis pointed to Evianna. She had more silvery markings than I did. "If I were going to test it, she would be the perfect subject."

Evianna held a hand up to her collarbone and then stepped closer to me. "Volke. Tell them *no*."

"You can do that yourself," I said with a chuckle.

"You're the Warlord of Magic. You have all the authority. Tell them I'm no one's *subject*."

I glanced over at Fain and Adelgis. "She's no one's subject, all right?"

Fain held up a hand. "Just imagine it. You have wings. *You can fly*."

Evianna hugged my arm and glared at the man. "Don't. Even. Think about it."

"What will you call this phenomenon?" Adelgis asked. "I know you named the transformation of the arcane plague into the magiborne runes, but just like star shards can allow us to *imbue*, these runes allow us to… what?"

"You should name it," I said. "My naming wasn't very good." And this was a difficult question. I didn't want to write instructional tomes—I wanted to focus on my many other problems. Adelgis was more knowledgeable, anyway.

Fain nodded. "You name it, Moonbeam."

Adelgis fidgeted with his fingers. Then he brushed back some of his long hair. "Very well. The magiborne runes allow us to *enchant* ourselves," he muttered. "This is an enchantment. A knightmare enchantment."

I didn't know if it was the best name it could be, but I liked it.

Adelgis nodded once, though he never smiled. "If I still had my abilities, I would telepathically tell everyone. As it stands, I'll have to go to them in person." He turned on his heel. "Plus, I need to return this star shard."

"I'll go with you," Fain said as he jumped to Adelgis's side.

"All right."

The two of them left the cabin, but all I could think about was the new markings on my arms. A knightmare enchantment. And I wondered if Fain was right. Maybe someday, in the future, we *would* be able to magically alter people in new physical ways.

Chapter 39

The Turning Of An Age

Five more weeks of travel.

The *Diamond of Dawn* flew to warmer waters faster than I had thought it would.

Island waters were just a little bluer and more inviting than other parts of the vast ocean. Seeing the shining waves lifted my spirits.

Our airship flew closer to the water, allowing William to practice his sorcery. He evoked waters, both fresh and salt. That didn't seem useful, until I noticed how powerful his blasts were. They could launch a man off the airship if they weren't paying attention.

Fresh water was his creation evocation, and salt water seemed to be his destructive one. Although salt water was the heart of the ocean, it *did* kill most plants and life that walked the land. The scylla waters seemed to care little about that.

And William could manipulate all waters, but especially the currents and tides. He created whirlpools as we flew.

Every moment of spare time I had went to manipulating rocks and other materials. I wanted to master this aspect of my magic before I faced the Autarch. I needed to. I needed to be as strong as I possibly could.

But while I stood on the deck of the airship, Terrakona's telepathy broke me out of my concentration.

"Warlord. The nearby island is infested with corruption."

I stiffened and then walked to the railing of the ship. Off in the distance, not too far from our location, was an island in the middle of a shimmering sea of blue. It wasn't an island with a city—it was too small for that. It was the type of island with only a few trees, a long beach, and enough life to accommodate a lone sailor who washed ashore.

"What's there?" I asked aloud.

"Leviathans."

Sea-dwelling creatures had been the target of the Second Ascension for a long time. They carried the plague to all corners of civilization by traveling through the veins of civilization.

"I'll handle it."

I went to the captain, told him we needed to stop, and then headed to inform the others. As the airship began its gradual descent, Lynus approached me with Zelfree at his side. "Why are we stopping?" he asked, his voice a growl.

"I have my salvation aura now," I stated. "We need to change the leviathans back." I patted my blade, which hung at my side. "We're not in any danger."

"We shouldn't slow our travels to handle creatures out in the middle of nowhere. We should be runnin' down the Second Ascension."

"This is important." I pointed to the island as we drew closer. "This is the whole reason we're god-arcanists. We have to be able to change them."

Although, Lynus was somewhat correct. We didn't have time to just flit from one location to another, helping all the plague-ridden creatures. There was so much to be done, but...

"Once all of us have mastered the salvation aura, our power will cover the whole planet," Lynus stated. He crossed his arms. "That includes every pathetic island out in the ocean. Which means we don't have to stop."

"Have *you* manifested your aura yet?"

Lynus opened his mouth and then hesitated for a long moment. "Not yet," he finally said.

"Then we should take this moment for you to try." As the airship drew closer to the pristine shores, I ran over to the railing. "C'mon. It's just as important that you manifest an aura as well."

Zelfree held up a finger. "Actually, I was hoping to test something while we are here. Before anyone manifests their salvation aura, I want to interact with the plague-ridden creatures."

"Why?" I asked.

"Because he wants his own runes," Lynus said with a growl in his voice. He glared at Zelfree, his whole body tense. "*What did I say about this?* Using yourself to test a few theories is pathetic. Get one of the others to do this."

Zelfree joined me near the railing. His mimic was in the shape of bangles around his wrists—perfectly disguised. He gave Lynus a sideways glance. "What did I tell *you?* As a mentor—as a master who instructs others—I'm not going to endanger my wards."

"Feh." Lynus rolled his eyes.

Fain, William, and Evianna joined us on the deck of the airship as it carefully touched down on the shore of the deserted island. Adelgis remained below, in his cabin, away from everyone else.

Grief was the price everyone paid when they lost somebody important. We couldn't rush him through it, and I wouldn't want to force the issue. So I said nothing. I just gave Adelgis his space.

I leapt over the railing and landed hard in the white sand. Evianna slipped through the shadows and joined me. My instinct was to head to the water. I went right up to the lines of the waves and glanced out over the ocean.

Terrakona lifted from the depths, his crystal mane drenched. With a snort that sprayed a mist of ocean through the air, he slithered up onto the beach.

The scylla waters was next. When she emerged from the waves, she didn't disturb the water at all. Her humanoid body, blue and cold with scales, was a frightening sight. She turned her eyes to me—black eyes that practically saw into my soul—and then slowly went back into the ocean, disappearing from view once again.

"She says the leviathans are over on the opposite shore," William said as he trudged through the sand. "She says there are three in total, all plague-ridden."

I glanced over my shoulder. Lynus and Zelfree stood near the airship, both arguing in whispered voices. Finally, they came to some kind of agreement.

Zelfree waved. "Let's head over there, and once one of the creatures has bitten me, Lynus will manifest his salvation aura."

Now I understood why Lynus didn't like this plan. Zelfree could still die from normal injuries. And if Lynus failed to manifest an aura—or made the wrong one—Zelfree would melt or explode, just like the previous creatures.

I stepped forward, my hand out. "Wait. I think... we shouldn't do this. I think Lynus should just practice his aura right here."

The island winds were calm and pleasant. Everything smelled of salt and palm trees, and I wanted to enjoy the midafternoon sun as it cascaded through the frilled leaves. I didn't want to have to think of Zelfree dying—I really never wanted to think of anyone passing on ever again.

"Even the boy thinks this is foolish," Lynus growled.

Zelfree glanced at the markings on my arm. I kept my sleeve up to see if anything happened to them. What if they moved? They never did, but just in case. Either way, they sparkled in the daylight, and even I stared at them for a moment.

Lynus grabbed Zelfree by the upper arm and held him close. "It's not worth risking your life over."

"Very well," Zelfree said as he jerked his arm from the other man's grip. With a sardonic grin, he said, "It's ironic that you're the one advocating for *safety first.*"

"Is it? Because all I'm doin' is askin' myself, *what would all these fools do?*" Lynus motioned to our surroundings. "And here we are."

Fain snorted a half-laugh. William just shook his head.

With a sigh, Zelfree held out his hand and allowed his bangle to transform into his mimic, Traces. She leapt from his wrist and hit the sand, her gray fur glistening in the island sun. After she licked her paw, she trotted over to the water and then transformed into a blue, serpentine creature.

A little leviathan. A hatchling, at most.

The shimmering sapphire scales caught the light just right as Traces slid into the waves.

"What's she doing?" Evianna asked.

Zelfree motioned to the far beach. As a group, we headed in that direction, and while we walked, he said, "I have a second theory, and it has to do with mystical creatures that have transformed. Traces is going to confirm a few things for me."

We headed around the picturesque island, practically on a vacation from the awful in the world. When we made it to the beach, William pointed to a series of waves. "There. The leviathans are there."

I didn't ask how he knew. His scylla waters magic was likely at play.

We all turned to Lynus.

As long as we remained on land, I suspected the plague-ridden leviathans wouldn't touch us. Leviathans were creatures of the ocean—some of the largest around, even bigger than most dragons.

When I glanced at the waves, I caught a glimpse of one. The blue scales were rotted green at the edges. The body was sickly thin and oozing pus from small scrapes down the side. And a series of eyes, nowhere near the skull, blinked back the sunlight.

It reminded me of the legendary Gregory Ruma and his plague-ridden leviathan, Decimus.

But I pushed the thought aside.

"Any time," Zelfree said, slapping Lynus's shoulder.

Again, we all turned to the man. In the island sunlight, without a shirt and with his god-arcanist mark clear, he looked like a legend himself. Not like a real person—someone larger than life. I straightened my posture, and I wondered if I had the same kind of demeanor.

Lynus closed his eyes.

Everyone waited, tense and anxious.

I felt their hearts beat faster and faster through the vibration underfoot. Even through the slipping sands, their worry was apparent.

I kept my attention on the far-off creatures. Once Lynus had mastered his salvation aura, we would have *two* who could do it. A part of me wondered if Zaxis and Orwyn had been practicing. I hoped they had. We needed all the help we could get.

Then I felt it.

Lynus's aura.

It blanketed the area like the shadow of a cloud over the sunny beaches. I couldn't look away from the leviathans. I had to know if his magic had worked.

And to my delight, the scales of the creatures shifted and changed. The rot faded. Their bodies filled out. The mysterious eyes that dotted their bodies sparkled and then disappeared. The corruption left them.

They were whole again.

Although... they were different. Stranger than before. They had serpentine bodies, but some of their scales were spotted, and a few had fins that were shaped like claws. Still leviathans, just more menacing in appearance.

"You did it," Fain whispered.

Zelfree crossed his arms and smirked. "I knew it. If I had just gone out there and gotten bitten, I would have had some runes as well."

"You cheeky dastard," Lynus said as he snapped his eyes open. With a sneer, he faced Zelfree. "If you're not going to let *me* die, I'm not going to let you die either, understand?"

"Oh, is *that* what's happening?" Zelfree huffed a laugh. "Revenge? We both have to live?"

"Damn straight."

I would've been content to laugh and listen to them argue, but I knew we didn't have time for frivolities. If Lynus had his salvation aura mastered, we needed to head out.

But that was when I noticed Traces. As a leviathan, she swam out to the others in the waves. After a short talk, Traces and one of the creatures swam to the shore. Zelfree noticed her as well and hurried to the waves in order to meet them.

The rest of us followed, but at a distance. I didn't know what Zelfree was trying to accomplish, though I was curious to see if the once plague-ridden leviathan remembered anything about its past life.

To my surprise, when Traces and the leviathan slithered onto the beach, the creature wasn't normal. It looked like a leviathan, but it had silver sparkles on its scales, beautiful and transfixing.

Zelfree went straight for the beast. He waved, said a few words, and then slowly placed his hands on the silvery sheen of the scales. The hatchling leviathan didn't protest or fight back. It just watched with reptilian eyes.

The sparkles...

After a few minutes, they diminished, like the water rushing off the creature's scales.

But the silver sheen didn't disappear. It went to Zelfree's hand. He lifted his arm to the light and showed everyone. The same magiborne runes that Evianna and I had were now on his arm. And the leviathan was no longer sparkling.

"What happened?" Fain whispered.

"The corrupted magic transformed..." I shook my head. "And now it lingers, like a beneficial disease. Just like a cold can pass from one person to another, the leviathan passed its magiborne runes to Zelfree."

"Why doesn't the leviathan have them, though?"

"I don't know."

But did it matter? We were in a new age now. One where the arcane plague was a thing of the past. Now that we had multiple salvation auras... We could finally put an end to this dark chapter.

Chapter 40

Return To Fortuna

The *Diamond of Dawn* took us the rest of the way to Fortuna.

That required another fortnight, meaning our entire trek to retrieve the scylla waters had taken us four months. That seemed like an impossibly long time, but also shockingly short. It had passed in the blink of an eye.

Thankfully, as we flew close to the beautiful coastal city, I spotted the *Midnight Thorn* in port. That meant the other arcanists of the Frith Guild were here. And while I wanted to meet up with them immediately, I noticed something else in port.

An atlas turtle.

Gentel.

She hadn't been here when we left, but now she was in port. Was she feeling okay? Did it matter? Even if the arcane plague had affected her before Liet, I could cure them both now. And I knew I would. As soon as I concluded some of my business here, I would fly to New Norra and help her.

No delays.

The airship touched down, and before I could even make a

plan, Illia teleported right next to me. I leapt back, a puff of glitter and a pop of air the only heralds of her arrival.

"Volke," she said as she brushed some of her wavy hair to the side. Her eyepatch was bright and crisp, as though she had just cleaned it. "What's going on? Adelgis said he would inform us when you were heading back, but he never reached out. Everyone is worried."

Nicholin teleported onto her shoulder, his white fur puffy and clean. "Volke! You're never going to believe what happened. I was there, and *I* still don't even believe it." He stood on his hind legs and pressed a paw onto Illia's cheek for support. "We found the lair of the tempest coatl, and also, Illia and I weren't eaten by anything!"

I wanted to answer him, but before I could, Illia turned her attention to the airship. Evianna was on the deck, along with Lynus and Zelfree.

"Did our father make it?" she whispered.

I nodded once. "He's the scylla waters arcanist." I rubbed at the back of my neck. "And Adelgis... We ended up fighting a plague-ridden knightmare, and he lost Felicity."

Nicholin straightened himself. Then his ears fell back and his blue eyes glazed over with water. "Y-You're joking, right? Because that's the worst joke ever, if you are. The worst."

Illia stared at me with her one eye, and she didn't need me to confirm or deny anything. She saw for herself that I was telling the truth. "Oh," she whispered. "I'm so sorry."

"Wait." Nicholin frowned. "A plague-ridden knightmare? It wasn't someone we know... Right?"

I didn't want to talk about that, so I didn't say anything. Instead, William disembarked from the airship, and Illia immediately turned her attention to him. After a quiet and thoughtful pat on my shoulder, she teleported to William's side, no doubt wanting to hear his story.

Evianna shifted through the darkness until she was at my

side. With a forced smile, she took hold of my hand. "You should head back to your estate," she whispered. "I can tell this is taking a lot out of you. I'll explain everything to everyone, okay?"

She was looking out for me. Making everything easier. I was lucky to have her by my side.

"Are you sure?" I asked.

"I can handle this. And you need to rest. Trust me. It'll be fine."

When I dreamt, it wasn't the structured narrative I had become used to.

No, these were abstract thoughts and images, sewn together through imagination. Scenes of battles I had gone through, people I had met, and desires unfulfilled all mixed together. In my dream, Luthair was there, plague-ridden, and I was doing everything I could to help him.

But in the end, the apoch dragon sprang from a pool of blood and consumed the world itself.

It was a bizarre dream, and when I awoke, the sun was setting. The dying sunlight streamed into my bedroom through the far window. I reminded myself this was my estate because it was so foreign and strange. I was more familiar on the back of Gentel, in the Frith Guild.

Exhaustion seeped through every muscle in my body.

For so long, I had been training my magic and straining my will to remain ever optimistic.

Just a little longer. That was what I told myself whenever things felt too grim. Just a little more. It would all be over. We had all the god-creatures, even if I hadn't yet seen the tempest coatl.

That fact filled me with relief.

I sat up and rotated my shoulders. It was almost night, but

there was so much to do. I needed to meet the new tempest coatl arcanist, I needed to make sure everyone was training their aura, I needed to speak with the council of Fortuna, I needed to know the soldiers were ready, I needed to find the Second Ascension, and I also needed to—

"Oh, Volke!"

I snapped my attention to the opposite end of the room. Evianna sat in a chair near the fireplace, her long white hair down and spilling around her shoulders. She wore a white nightgown, something between alluring and comfortable. It shimmered when she stood from her chair and walked over to me. The gown was an opaque that pretended at transparency.

Evianna took a seat on the edge of my mattress, just inches from me. Then she scooted closer, until she could easily take my hand into her own. "Are you okay, Volke? Why are you so stiff?"

"That's a well-worded question," I said with a chuckle, my face hot. "But nothing is wrong, I'm just... not used to waking up to someone so beautiful."

She glanced away, unable to hide a slight smile. "Volke..."

"Is something wrong?"

"No. Everything is fine. Um. I told everyone you needed your rest, so they said they would leave you alone until morning."

"You sound uneasy." I rubbed at my eyes, dispelling the sleep.

"I didn't want to bother you until the morning..." Evianna brushed some of her white hair aside. Then she scooted even closer, until we were practically cuddling.

But she didn't say anything else.

"What is it?" I asked, harder-edged than before.

"Queen Ladislava sent word to the arcanists of Fortuna, but because you weren't here, they didn't know how to respond."

Queen Ladislava?

She was the new ruler of the Argo Empire. The woman I

had helped ascend to the throne. She was rather aggressive, and every interaction I ever had with her ended in a metaphorical pissing match.

Curse the abyssal hells...

I was tired just thinking about her.

"What does Queen Ladislava want?" I asked.

Evianna nuzzled her head against my bare chest. "Well, Fortuna requested troops under your name, but Queen Ladislava said that the march through the mountains, and through the city of Ellios, would be too treacherous and time consuming. She requested you alter the terrain of the Clawdam Mountain pass to accommodate her troops."

"So, she hasn't sent anyone?"

I felt Evianna cringe, and I knew the answer. Why was Queen Ladislava so difficult? The Argo Empire had marched soldiers through Ellios many times in the past. Additionally, the capital city, Thronehold, had the option of sending boats down the river and into the sea—where they could then sail around to Fortuna. There were multiple routes to send a minor army, why demand I make a new one?

The sun set, blanketing my room in darkness.

Evianna's runes glittered with dim illumination. My own arm sparkled black. I could still see in the darkness, lending to the theory that this change was permanent.

"I think Ladislava wants you to demonstrate you have the capacity to alter a mountain," Evianna whispered. "I think she wants to test you."

"For the fifth time," I quipped.

"Hm?"

I shook my head. "Never mind. I just mean to say the queen is never satisfied."

"Do you think you can do it?" Evianna glanced up at me through her eyelashes. "Alter the Clawdam Mountains, I mean. All by yourself."

"Yeah. And I wouldn't be by myself. Terrakona would be there. We could do it together."

That seemed to perk her up. Evianna's eyes went even wider. "Really?"

"Yeah. Why? You seem... concerned."

The shadows in the corner of the room shifted and moved. Then they shot for the door, and slipped underneath. Evianna's knightmare took off, for some reason. I briefly wondered why.

"Well, because I have more news," Evianna stated. "The arcanists of Fortuna received messengers from several nations across the western sea asking Fortuna to join their alliance."

"An alliance with the Autarch at the center?" Much like *my* alliance with the Argo Empire and the smaller nations around it.

"That's right. They claim the Autarch has three god-creatures, and the ability to control souls." Evianna let the last bit sink in for a moment. "And since no one really understands the capacities of the god-creatures, some arcanists are panicking."

"I see..."

Evianna frowned. "You'll speak to them, won't you, Volke? Tell them everything will be okay?"

"Right now?" I asked, half tempted to leap out of bed. Should I address the city? Or just the council itself?

She shook her head. "In the near future. They said the Autarch also has alliances with a few guilds that control some of the trade routes, and that's causing trouble as well, but nothing they can't handle in the short run. However..."

"His alliance is forming an army." I already knew the punch line to this whole interaction. The Autarch wasn't messing around. It was to his benefit to kill us off earlier rather than later. The older our creatures got, the more powerful we became.

Evianna nodded once.

"Fortuna is a major port," I said, more to myself than anyone else. “And the council is worried he’ll want to secure this area if the Autarch plans to invade the Argo Empire to the south.”

That was a lot to handle. I didn’t have time for sleep.

I threw off the blankets and slid to the edge of the mattress. Evianna went with me, but I barely noticed. I had my trousers, but I glanced around, looking for the rest of my clothing.

“We don’t have any time to waste,” I said, still a bit groggy. “I need to get things done. I’ll head to Ellios, change the landscape, go to Thronehold, speak to Queen Ladislava, and then head to New Norra. After that, I’ll travel with the soldiers and knights of the Argo Empire up to Fortuna so we can defend the ports and face off against the Autarch.”

I felt like I had to do a million things.

Sleep was in the way. Rest was slowing me down. Relaxation was just a myth.

Evianna jumped off the bed at the same time I did. She tapped the tips of her fingers, her shoulders bunched near the base of her neck. “I thought you said you needed to stay here to help all the god-arcanists with their aura.”

“Lynus can help them.”

I grabbed Retribution and Forfend. Then I shoved my feet into my boots. When I went for the door, Evianna actually jumped in my way.

“Do you really think you’ll face the Autarch?” Evianna whispered. “Here in Fortuna?”

“Perhaps. If he comes here himself, I won’t let him get away.”

“But...”

She waited, the air thick with unspoken words. Did she want me to run from this fight? Why? That was counter to everything we needed to do.

“I’m afraid,” she said, her voice softer than before. When she looked up at me, her eyes were glazed. “What if you don’t make it?”

"Evi..."

I ran a hand down my face. There were many times in my life where doubt had held me back. But today wasn't one of them. How could I help Evianna dispel it herself?

"I'm not going to let the Autarch win," I stated.

"Yeah, but, I know you, Volke. You're the type of guy who would trade his own life for the peace of the world, and I'm afraid I'm going to lose you." She placed her hands on her hips. "I don't want that."

"I'll try not to sacrifice my life." It sounded silly to say aloud. I didn't *want* to die. I just knew that sometimes it was the only decision. But if I could, I would avoid it. I had dreams beyond this fight. "I want to begin a whole new life with you afterward," I whispered.

Then I pulled Evianna close and kissed her. Her soft lips reminded me that life could be equally amazing and wonderful.

Once we separated, Evianna's face was pink. "I want that, too." She playfully glared at me. "So you better remember that promise. If I have to go all the way to the abyssal hells to bring you back, I will."

I chuckled as I reached for the door handle. "I don't doubt it."

Chapter 41

An Army

I stood before the council of Fortuna, inside the Astral Tower. The clang of the massive clock created mechanized music that filled the halls beyond the conference room door.

Although I still hadn't recovered from my trip across the seas, I kept my exhaustion to myself. Now wasn't the time to falter. The five councilors of Fortuna sat around a U-shaped table, while Evianna and Zaxis stood on either side of me. I had wanted *all* the god-arcanists here, but waiting for them to assemble wasn't really an option.

I needed information.

The five councilors of Fortuna all had their mongwu owls perched on the back of their tall wooden chairs. The owls practically glared at me the entire time. It was the middle of the night, and their arcanists were groggy. I suspected none of the owls liked that their routine had been broken. I glanced between their arcanists.

Walter Gonni, Master of Coin.

Penelope Gonni, the Grand Justice.

Marx Ten, Head of Law Enforcement.

Veena Yaani, Commissioner of Public Works.

Mayor Halladay Lanes.

They all wore the same style of outfit. Blue doublets, gold sashes, laces on their sleeves. Most of them had medals arranged on their shoulders, though it was hastily done, without much thought. It made me think they had all gotten dressed in a hurry.

They sat in their chairs with a slump, and they stared at me with slight frowns.

Veena, a tall woman with graying hair—but few wrinkles—leaned forward onto the desk. "Warlord, the council has met your demands as best we could. We called for soldiers, both here and in the surrounding territories that have sworn fealty to you. We're pleased to say we have three hundred infantry and two hundred longbowmen."

Penelope, the Grand Justice, nodded once. "The nation of Javin provided the longbowmen. Emperor Barnett sent soldiers from Sellix. King Kalasardo ordered his finest knights to fight for you as well."

"And several guilds have offered arcanists to the cause," Veena added. "The Southern Flier Guild, the Shikara Guild, and the Trapper Guild."

Veena's owl eldrin hooted and then lowered its head so its neck feathers flared outward like a collar on a coat. "Maintaining a standing army is difficult, world serpent arcanist. We have tents and barracks, but not for so many. And the cost of food alone will mean we can't keep the soldiers too long."

"It's wartime," Zaxis said, interjecting with a loud and confident statement. "Fortuna, the islands—everyone—should be contributing war time taxes."

Walter, the Master of Coin, straightened his posture. Even before he spoke, I heard his *matter-of-fact* tone as clear as the clang of the clockwork machinery.

"The Argo Empire has agreed to dedicate half a legion of men to your efforts, as well as cover the upkeep for two years' time, but only if you change the Clawdam Mountains by Ellios," Walter stated, his words just as crisp and *authoritative* as I had imagined them in my head.

How many soldiers were in a legion? I had read it in William's books a while back... It was five thousand men. So half would be two thousand five hundred. In total, that would bring us to three thousand, which was substantial, but not enormous.

"What about the knights?" Evianna asked. She threw back some of her white hair, almost in a haughty fashion. "The *Knights Draconic* and the *New Order of Sky Legionnaires* should be joining in this combat."

The new order... after the old one had been disbanded. I wondered what had changed in Thronehold. But I shoved the thought aside.

Walter nodded once. "Queen Ladislava has agreed to send arcanists as well. They will lead the battalions of her soldiers."

Zaxis stepped forward, his voice louder than before. "But the queen isn't coming?"

I held up a hand. "It's fine. Sovereign dragons aren't known for their combat prowess. Queen Ladislava needs to stay in Thronehold and maintain her aura." The sovereign dragon aura helped the people of her nation grow and prosper—having her fight on the front lines with god-arcanists wasn't necessary.

"There are arcanists around the islands who have agreed to help," Mayor Lanes stated. "And the navies of various nations have offered to send arcanists with control of the tides. The new Marshall of the Southern Seas has agreed to sail his ships in this direction, though it will be a month before he arrives in port."

"But won't navies require even more food and supplies?" I asked.

How much could we possibly tax the people to pay for all this? From what I had read, though it was a long time ago, some wars were lost because their soldiers had no support or supplies. We couldn't allow that to happen.

"The Marshall of the Southern Seas will support his ships," the Master of Coin said. He smiled, his wrinkled face fighting gravity and losing badly. "But you needn't concern yourself with that. We're more concerned about the mountain pass. If the queen of the Argo Empire doesn't provide us the half legion she promised, our standing army will be considered quite weak."

It was important to know the strength of the enemy. I couldn't gauge our capabilities otherwise.

"Do we have any numbers or information about the enemy forces?" I asked.

The five mongwu arcanists exchanged quick glances. Even their owls shared in the gesture, a few of them hooting.

The mayor leaned forward. "We have arcanists spying on the enemy. We hope to have a better number soon, but what we do know is the Autarch has the support of five maritime nations."

"Which ones?" Zaxis barked. "Because any nation that supports the Second Ascension should be burned and their land salted."

I held up a hand again, trying to calm Zaxis's unbridled anger. When he was quiet, I asked, "Why only maritime nations?"

"The Autarch had made arrangements with several nations, according to the rumors—but the nations would only agree to help if he bonded with the world serpent. They wanted the ability to change their terrains. When it turned out *you* became the world serpent arcanist, the Autarch couldn't fulfill his promises."

Evianna furrowed her brow. "So what is he offering these other nations?"

"He is bonded with the abyssal kraken." The mayor frowned. "He claims he can rearrange the waters, and even control people's souls."

That claim again.

It made him sound much more intimidating than he really was.

"He wears a suit of armor immune to magic," the mayor's owl stated. "Or so the rumors claim."

A suit of armor...

I had seen the Autarch's armor. It was made from the same black bones as my sword. The bones of the previous apoch dragon. Which meant his armor probably *was* immune to magic, just like nullstone.

"However," the mayor cut in. "The nations he's aligned with —the Kingdom of Tarraco and Lugdim, specifically—are known for their shipwrights. The Autarch will have about fifty galleon ships at his disposal, by our estimates."

Fifty ships...

That was significant. Better yet, that number gave me a better understanding of the Autarch's forces. I knew galleons well, and thus, I knew those ships could only really move a hundred soldiers at a time, maximum. Which meant the Autarch had a moving legion of soldiers—five thousand—that could land and attack at a moment's notice.

Five thousand enemy soldiers...

That wasn't counting whatever arcanists the Autarch had at his command. Most of them would likely be plague-ridden, which meant that once we used our salvation aura, they would be less dangerous, but still quite capable.

And the Autarch likely had three god-creatures—the garuda bird, the endless undead, and the abyssal kraken, since those were the ones the Second Ascension had access to. Plus, the Autarch had his gold kirin. He was the one we needed to defeat first. Once he fell, the other threats would be easy pickings.

"Which other nations are helping the Autarch?" Zaxis asked again, this time calmer than before.

The mayor replied, "The Isles of Rorrith, the Kingdom of Tarraco, Lugdim, the Suirm Kingdom, and the Castle Rocks of

Lorn. All of them are smaller, more specialized, and across the shortest length of ocean."

"Far beyond Port Crown," I muttered.

I only recognized one of those nations, and it was the Castle Rocks of Lorn. They had sent several ships to Port Crown—and created several famous dread pirates, from what I could remember. They were a people who loved sailing the coasts and establishing small settlements. Some described their people as a plague, but since I had never met any myself, I couldn't say.

"Can we send messages to the rulers of those nations?" I tried to think of a way to take some of the Autarch's allies away from him. "We can offer them a place in our alliance, and we now have a real cure for the arcane plague."

The councilors squinted their eyes or lifted eyebrows. Their owls turned their heads—one even turned all the way around in a circle.

I held up my arm. The glittering tattoos were a sight to behold. "This is the result of curing the plague. These magiborne runes. Please. Send them a message as soon as possible."

"We will," the mayor muttered. "But I doubt they will take kindly to the offer. The Autarch has claimed he will handle the plague for them. It's less of an incentive."

Curse the abyssal hells. But the Autarch wouldn't make the runes—he would just destroy all the creatures with an armageddon aura. Was there a way to prove that, though? Probably not.

"So, the Autarch will likely have double our numbers?" I asked. "Do we know where he'll be landing?"

A two-to-one ratio wasn't the best. If he was landing in Fortuna, we would at least have a strong defendable location.

"We have reason to believe he plans to attack Fortuna," Walter said. He steepled his fingers, revealing a ring that signified his position as the master of coin. It glittered a bright and polished gold. "But we aren't certain when."

The five mongwu owls hooted as they shifted on their perches.

Evianna and Zaxis both turned to me.

If the Autarch had gathered himself a legion of soldiers, he would have the same problems we had. He couldn't keep a standing army forever. He had to feed them. And the ships used for transport wouldn't wait around forever. If these numbers were accurate, it meant the Autarch had already done most of the work, and he didn't want to wait any longer.

He was going to attack soon.

That made sense. The weaker our god-creatures were, the more he had an advantage. His gold kirin empowered his creatures, so even though they were still young, they would be much stronger than ours. Well, maybe not stronger than Terrakona, but for things like the scylla waters and the corona phoenix, yes.

The Autarch wanted to take advantage of that.

We hadn't mastered our abilities. Some of us were still learning. Now was the perfect time to attack.

"I'll head to Ellios," I said to the room, breaking the silence that lingered. "And I'll return with the soldiers from the Argo Empire."

The council members all nodded.

"In the meantime, I want the defenses around Fortuna improved. We can place cannons on the docks, and reinforce the walls." After a short sigh, I added, "And send scouts along the coast, just to make sure we're not missing something. There was a war I read about where the enemy general attacked a city through the port, but then also sent ships to land on nearby shores so he could have his soldiers sneak-attack the city from land as well, effectively blocking off their supplies."

The siege of the city had left the people inside starving. They hadn't been able to access their ports or the land routes for trade...

We couldn't allow that to happen.

"We will do as you ask, Warlord," the mayor replied.

"Thank you."

I turned to go, and both Evianna and Zaxis shadowed my steps. When we exited the conference room, and shut the door tightly behind us, Zaxis grabbed my upper arm.

"Are you sure about this?" he asked. "The Autarch will outnumber us two to one."

I met his gaze. "We'll have the superior position. We'll be on land, and defended. And we have more god-creatures than the Autarch, including the scylla waters, who can help defend the ports."

The scylla waters in the sea...

The sky titan in the air...

Terrakona and I controlling the terrain...

We had everything covered.

"You know what Orwyn would say," Evianna said as she held up a single finger. "She would remind you the Autarch has a gold kirin. We need to be careful."

"Once I return with the soldiers, we can discuss all this," I stated. "But I have to head out if I'm going to rearrange a whole mountain and march a bunch of troops all the way to Fortuna."

Zaxis didn't let go of my arm.

"Aren't you going to meet the tempest coatl arcanist?" he asked. Zaxis practically shook my shoulder. "You're the one in charge. You should be giving orders to all the other god-arcanists before you leave."

He was right.

I hadn't even met the tempest coatl arcanist yet.

I just... I had so much to do.

I took a deep breath, and allowed my worries to leave with my exhale.

"Who bonded with the tempest coatl?" I asked. "Was it Adelgis's sister, Cinna?" I hoped it was.

Zaxis released my arm. He frowned and hesitated a long moment, like he didn't want to tell me. The clang of the machinery around us was unsettling. Worse than silence.

"Just tell me," I stated.

"Fine. *Lucian* bonded with the coatl. That crazy knightmare arcanist bonded with the tempest coatl, and now he thinks he's the star of the show."

Chapter 42

The Dauntless

"What do you mean?" I asked. "It can't be Lucian."

I walked with Evianna and Zaxis through the halls of the Astral Tower. I thought I was going at a normal pace, but Evianna was hopping to keep up with me, and Zaxis was practically storming along. I couldn't help it. I needed to speak with Lucian.

He would never kill his knightmare. Never.

"It's Lucian," Evianna said as she quickened her steps to keep up with me. "I met him while you were sleeping. He's bonded with *Amoxtil*, the tempest coatl, and she's beautiful."

"What happened to Azir, his knightmare?" I pushed open the main doors of the Astral Tower, the darkness of night nothing now that I had Evianna's runes and my own tremor sense. "He killed his eldrin? *Lucian?* I can't believe it. He would never do that just to bond with a god-creature."

Zaxis hurried along with me, his breathing coming out as icy frost. "Do you hear yourself? Not everyone *kills* their eldrin."

He jumped in front of me and then stopped. I halted before I ran into him, but I was a little shocked by his attitude. Zaxis stared me in the eyes, his irritation as clear as day.

So was his height. I sometimes forgot he was a few inches shorter than I was.

"I never would've given up Forsythe," Zaxis said, practically shouting. "And Lucian didn't give up Azir! He and his knightmare were caught in a trap."

I took a deep breath. "What kind of trap?"

Evianna walked up to the side of us. Her shadow moved around her feet. She was the only knightmare arcanist I knew, now. All the other knightmare arcanists had either died or lost their knightmare.

There was a knightmare I had found in Regal Heights—Thurin—but he hadn't bonded. I wondered if he would ever bond, but the thought was fleeting.

"According to Lucian, there was a dungeon," Zaxis said. He slicked back his red hair. With a huff, he added, "Lucian and Orwyn went in to the tempest coatl, but the deeper they went, the worse it became."

"And?" I whispered.

"You should just ask him. He was the one who was there." Zaxis scoffed as he stepped away from me.

Guilt ate at me. I hadn't meant to imply everyone wanted power so much that they would kill their eldrin to get it. I hadn't killed Luthair. Zaxis never would've abandoned Forsythe. I supposed it was the same with Lucian.

But that was why I had wanted Cinna to bond. She had no eldrin. Why hadn't she been picked?

Perhaps Orwyn was right. Maybe the god-creatures were designed for kirin arcanists. They were the ones who didn't have to give up their previous eldrin in order to bond.

"I'll go speak with Lucian," I said. "And then I'll head to Ellios. Can I count on you to handle things here in Fortuna?"

Zaxis lifted an eyebrow. "Handle what?"

"Helping the other god-arcanists with their magic. Well...

maybe you *and* Lynus should do that. But also, with combat. We should be prepared."

He was one of the few people I knew who could always muster the courage to face death itself. He probably wasn't the most skilled, but there were others here. And once I brought back Liet, we would have our best mentors in one place.

"I'll handle it," Zaxis said. He opened his mouth as though he wanted to say something more, but he was cut off by a low rumble of thunder.

We all turned our attention to the distant horizon across the waters. There were only a few clouds, but all of them crackled with inner power. Lightning flashed, striking the waves and lighting up the docks of Fortuna.

"Curse the abyssal hells," Zaxis muttered. "I told him not to do anything that could damage the ships, but look what he's doing." He threw a hand up in the air and rolled his eyes. "Well, there he is. Lucian—*the Dauntless*—the tempest coatl arcanist."

Was that his title?

The god-creatures and their names for everything fascinated me. It was like they carried lingo over from their ancient past, where everything was legendary, even their titles.

The world serpent arcanist. His title? *Warlord.*

The soul forge. *Scholar.*

The fenris wolf. *Hunter.*

The sky titan. *Falcon.*

The garuda bird… I hadn't yet met the garuda bird. He was with the Autarch.

"Lancer," Terrakona telepathically said. **"The garuda bird arcanist is known as the Lancer."**

"Interesting…"

Evianna grabbed my arm, drawing me back to the present. She pointed as another flash of lightning brightened Fortuna. The rumble of thunder that followed sent a shiver up my spine.

"We should go meet him," Evianna said.

"And tell him to stop his evocation," Zaxis growled. "Maybe he'll listen to you—since you were both knightmare arcanists and he can never let me forget that."

I nodded once. "I'll tell him."

As a pair, Evianna and I hurried down the streets of Fortuna. If we had taken a horse, or if Evianna had just shadow-stepped, one of us would have reached Lucian sooner, but we stuck together. The streets were empty, the chilly night air adding extra incentive for the denizens of Fortuna to stay in their homes.

As we made our way down the hilly roads toward the dock, my mind drifted to the last of the god-creatures and their titles. For some reason, I wanted to know them all. I wanted to know everything about them.

The abyssal kraken... What was its arcanist's title?

"The Warden."

That sent a second shiver down my spine.

"Why?" I asked as I reached the gates to the docks themselves. A salty breeze swept over me and Evianna. I felt wet afterward, the mists of the ocean soaking my trousers and loose shirt. "Is it because the abyssal hells are a prison?"

Evianna glanced over at me, her eyebrow raised. "Hm? Are you mumbling about the abyssal hells? They're locked away. Everyone knows that."

"That is correct," Terrakona said. **"The gates to the abyssal hells are locked. Very few things or arcanists can open them. The abyssal kraken is one—that was how its arcanist gained the title. It was the keeper of prisoners. The Warden of Souls."**

That was more ominous than I had been anticipating.

Evianna and I walked onto the docks. I glanced around, a little confused. My tremor sense picked up the dockhands and a few sailors busy moving supplies off their boats. Where was Lucian? Was he on a boat? I couldn't really feel anything on the decks of the ships.

Or was he in the water?

"This way," I said, motioning to the far dock. The lightning seemed to flash closer there.

Evianna followed me, her dark-sight giving her confidence, even though there weren't many lanterns. Again, my thoughts drifted to the god-arcanists.

The typhon beast arcanist was known as the *Monster*.

The scylla waters arcanist was known as the *Equinox*.

The tempest coatl? The *Dauntless*, at least according to Zaxis.

"He's correct, Warlord. The dauntless storm heeds nothing and no one."

That was interesting. Even as I ran to the last dock, I took note of how powerful the thunder sounded, and how bright the flashes of lightning were. Nature was often scary, because it didn't act with intent or malice. It could come for anyone or anything, and it couldn't be convinced or reasoned with.

Dauntless. Unyielding. Unstoppable.

"Are you okay, Volke?" Evianna asked me. She glanced over several times, her eyebrows knitted.

"Yeah," I muttered.

I stopped at the last dock and stood on the first few planks. My heart hammered as the waters beyond the pier swirled and moved. It wasn't the scylla waters. William and his god-creature were near Gentel and the other boats.

Evianna and I waited.

Another flash of lightning. It was zigzag and beautiful. The brilliant white reminded me of the runestone that shattered. The progenitor behemoth...

What was its title?

"The Shepherd."

Which made sense. I didn't know anything about the behemoth other than the children who had sprung from it.

"The progenitor behemoth strived to take care of all

the creatures it could. It protected them. A Shepherd of Magic."

The waters near the docks exploded upward into the sky. The tempest coatl screeched as it shot for the clouds, leaving the water at such a blinding speed, I was surprised I even caught sight of it.

The scales...

They glowed.

I hadn't been expecting that.

The tempest coatl—a snake with wings—glowed with the brilliance of lightning. Her scales were a gold that crackled black from time to time, flicking like a storm cloud filled with thunder.

The beast had a mane of feathers, and a set of feathery wings that matched her scales. She had two more sets of tinier wings, both of which were further along her long body. The coatl shot into the sky, flying with the same bizarre, jagged path as the lightning she represented.

The tempest coatl disappeared into the clouds.

The air tasted... sharp. And like static. It was hard to describe. Even my eyes hurt, like the water in the air had disappeared.

"Wow," Evianna muttered, her eyes wide.

I took a breath and waited a moment. The coatl stayed in the clouds. How interesting.

I glanced over my shoulder and turned my attention to the Astral Tower. It was a massive clock that watched over the city, perched on the highest hill. The corona phoenix sat atop the tower, its bright wings and shadowy claws a sight to behold.

The corona phoenix... the Solstice.

And the last god-creature, another one bonded to the Autarch... The endless undead. What was title did it confer?

"The Gravemaster."

I didn't need an explanation for that one. It was perfect. Self-explanatory.

Lucian stepped out of the water. He just *walked* straight out of the waters around the pier, his black clothing drenched, seaweed clinging to one of his ears. His skin was pale, but not blue, and his eyes carried dark rings, but otherwise, he was fine.

Evianna gasped once she noticed him. Then she hardened her expression as Lucian dragged himself up onto the dock, fully escaping the grasp of the tide.

"You look like a zombie," she stated.

Lucian's shirt was half-open, much like mine. The mark on his chest carried the zigzag patterning of the tempest coatl. It covered his chest, his shoulder, his arm… It was beautiful and mythic.

"What're you two doing here?" he asked as he picked away the seaweed and threw it back into the waters.

"Zaxis said you shouldn't use your abilities so close to the city," I said. Then I pointed to the clouds. "He might be right. What if something happens?"

"I'm in control."

Lucian always had a cold, confident demeanor. It was borderline callous, though. One mistake could cost the city the life of a dockhand or sailor. Wasn't he concerned about that?

"I'd prefer if you practiced your magic farther away from mortals." I gestured to the rocks halfway to the horizon. "If you can breathe underwater, you could swim over there."

Lucian ran a hand over his head. His hair was cut so short, it wasn't affected by the water. He just sprayed a fine mist from the short strands off into the night sky.

"What happened?" Evianna asked.

She didn't say *what happened to your knightmare*, but I knew that was what she meant. Her own knightmare, Layshl, shifted around her feet as though agitated.

"We entered the lair of the tempest coatl," Lucian said. "And there was a pit. We all descended, but there were thorns, brambles, and barbs. They were electric to the touch, and we were caught within. Even Orwyn and her wind couldn't seem to power her way through. But..."

"You could shadow-step," I stated.

Lucian curtly nodded. "I slipped through the bizarre brambles and made my way deeper. But then I was attacked by some sort of... beast. Azir and I fought it, but during the conflict, it was clear we wouldn't survive."

"What kind of beast?" I asked, my voice low.

"A panther. Some sort of large cat. It was made of... something. Not flesh. Just magic. And it wanted me dead. But Azir wouldn't allow that."

Just like Luthair.

The memory hurt. Even now. After so long. And now, when I thought of Luthair, all I could think of was the plague-ridden version of him that had attacked my arm.

Lucian went to open his mouth, to tell us the rest, but I held up my hand.

"I understand," I said, cutting him off. "You don't need to say any more." I turned my attention to the clouds so I wouldn't have to look at the others. I feared they might see the pain in my eyes if I met their gazes. "Your coatl... She's beautiful."

Lucian must've appreciated the fact that I cut him off. His heart slowed, and he exhaled. Only my tremor sense picked it up, though. The man was adept at hiding his emotions.

"Amoxtil knows why we're fighting," Lucian stated. "And she shares my lust for revenge. We won't be the weak link that fails."

His statements reassured me. I had half feared he would fly off on his own crusade, but he was a man who had been loyal to a guild before. Perhaps he yearned for a team to stand with.

"I'm heading to Ellios," I said. "I'll be returning with soldiers from the Argo Empire. I need you and the other god-arcanists to hold the city."

Lucian bowed his head slightly, but otherwise said nothing.

"When I return, I fear the Autarch might attack."

"Fear?" Lucian straightened his posture. "Unless you're afraid for the Autarch's life, there's no need for you to fret. We're ready, Warlord. Nothing is going to stop this war from happening. And nothing will stop me from making sure we win in the name of the Grandmaster Inquisitor."

Chapter 43

The Clawdam Mountains

In the morning, I left Fortuna.

Flying with the sky titan probably would've been the fastest way to get to Ellios, but I wanted to ride Terrakona into Ellios. Part of being the Warlord of Magic meant I had to present myself as such. The soldiers, and the knights, would expect me to ride along the land, altering as I went. And Terrakona was fast enough for this mission. I reasoned we would reach Ellios within a fortnight.

Orwyn still traveled with us, high in the sky. She and Akiva would take me to New Norra after I altered the Clawdam Mountains. We could reach the city within a few days, and then return to Ellios to ride Terrakona back to Fortuna.

Evianna traveled with me. It was easy. Her knightmare resided in her shadow, and she was eager to go wherever was needed to make sure this war came to an end.

I thought it would just be the two of us, but Adelgis had requested to come along as well. Ellios was his old home, after all. I couldn't deny him. He and Fain rode on the back of Terrakona, who grew larger each day.

The Clawdam Mountains were mostly gray, with occasional pine trees dotting the scenery. The closer we got to Ellios, however, the denser the forests became. Adelgis pointed to the surroundings, motioning to the narrow roads into the mountains.

Before we even reached Ellios, I had Terrakona slow down so we could rearrange the area. We needed enough room for the soldiers to march comfortably, and we had to remove any potential obstacles.

With a wave of my hand, I made the dirt pathways wide and smooth, and packed with dirt. I moved the trees away from the side of the road, and allowed grass to grow there instead, so that nothing could hide in the groves.

As we climbed the mountain pass, I widened everything and lessened the steep incline. It reminded me of when I had created those steps into Hydra's Gorge, and I almost wanted to add the lessons of the Pillars to the grooves in the stones. But that would take too much time.

For hours as we traveled, I just focused on making sure the path could support soldiers. I made no artistic decisions other than the practicality of the trek.

I stood at the tallest point of the Clawdam Mountain pass. The great city of Ellios was below, sparkling white like ivory. I remembered when I had first visited. It was just as beautiful now as it had been then—one of the few places untouched by the corruption of the Second Ascension and their plague.

But just beyond the southern wall was an interesting sight.

Half a legion of soldiers from the Argo Empire. Their red and black armor, uniform across the men, created a wall of power no one could deny. They carried short swords, crossbows, and spears, and each man had their own shield. I suspected there was a division of riflemen, given the smell of gunpowder on the air. They were prepared.

Their tents dotted the mountain pass leading to Ellios, and I wondered how long they had been waiting for me. I doubted it was too long since the area surrounding their encampment still seemed intact.

Adelgis, Evianna, and Terrakona were by my side, observing the masses below. The citizens of Ellios had noticed me, and they pointed and cheered, though I couldn't hear them from our vantage point.

They hadn't spotted Orwyn and Akiva, who were on one of the tallest peaks on the mountain. She had told me she would meet me in the city, once I descended to the streets, but I wondered if she would just avoid people altogether. Both she and Akiva didn't seem very sociable.

"Volke," Adelgis whispered, startling me.

I flinched and turned to face him. "Yes?"

"Will it upset you if I change my mind? I want to stay here in the city, rather than traveling to New Norra. Or even returning to Fortuna."

That was fine by me. "You can stay in your old family home."

"I could. But I won't. I'd rather stay at Ellios University, away from most of the town."

I was about to say something, but Evianna stepped close and frowned. "Why?" she asked.

"When I was younger, my father wanted me to bond with a relickeeper, but I... didn't. Most people thought I would amount to nothing, but after I bonded with an ethereal whelk, they all said I should follow in my father's steps. I... wanted to join the Frith Guild, and I did, but that was another disappointment, in their eyes."

Adelgis recounted the story with the interest of a

schoolmaster reading from a dictionary. I wondered if he was doing that to hide his feelings on the matter.

"If I show up with this faded arcanist mark..." Adelgis touched the mark on his forehead. "They'll assume I failed yet again."

"You have nothing to be ashamed of," I stated. "If anything, Felicity's death was my—"

Adelgis held up his hand, cutting me off. With a neutral expression, he stared at the city below. "It doesn't matter how logical you are. They don't care. *I'm* not powerful, therefore, *I* have failed. That is all they will see. And the frustration of explaining to them what happened isn't worth the effort."

"You don't have to stay here," Evianna said matter-of-factly. "Travel south with us and stay in Thronehold."

"No, but thank you. Ellios is... still a comforting place. Even if I'd rather not mingle with the citizens."

The grass rustled, and twigs snapped. I glanced over my shoulder and spotted Fain stomping out of a grove of *evergrow trees*. The pine-like appearance, and vibrant green needles, made the whole side of the mountain beautiful.

Fain held his hands closed together in front of his chest. He was holding something, and rather proud of it, apparently. He couldn't stop smiling.

"I found one, Moonbeam," Fain said as he walked to us. He stopped next to Adelgis and held up both his hands. "Your mother is a minerva owl arcanist, right? That's what you told me?"

Adelgis frowned. "Please, tell me you didn't."

With slow movements, Fain carefully opened his hands. His black fingers stayed together, creating a little cage. An owlet fluttered around in his palm, its tiny wings beating a mile a minute.

"Help!" the little minerva owl cried. Its giant golden eyes

were glancing around from person to person, its panic on full display. "I'm not supposed to be here!"

"Where did you find him?" Adelgis asked. He stepped forward and held his hand out. "The owls around here are cared for by the arcanists of Ellios University. You shouldn't have had access to them."

"The hatchery isn't far from here," Fain said with a huff. His icy breath came out as mist. "And they didn't account for my invisibility. Or Wraith's smaller form."

"This is a *kidnapping*," the little owl said. Then he hooted. "It's a criminal offense! *A felony* as described by the codex of laws!"

Minerva owls were known for their knowledge and intelligence. I wasn't surprised the little one knew what a codex of laws was.

Fain handed Adelgis the owl. "You could pass its Trial of Worth."

"Not with your ever-growing criminal record," the owl said, fluffing his feathers.

Adelgis immediately lifted his hand, allowing the owl to go. It took the owl a few moments before he realized he was free. Then he flapped his wings, but he was too little to fly. "Take him back to the hatchery," Adelgis said. He returned the owl to Fain. "Please. I don't wish to bond with a minerva owl. I don't wish to bond at all."

"Moonbeam, don't be—"

Adelgis immediately turned away. Fain swallowed his own words. Then he just cursed under his breath and vanished from sight. My tremor sense picked up on his footfalls as he flounced away from us, heading back into the trees.

The owl's cries were easy to hear for quite some time.

"*Intentional infliction of emotional distress* is a serious crime, too, ya know!"

But the owl was mostly ignored. Hopefully the little mystical creature wouldn't be too traumatized by the abduction.

"Will you ever bond with another mystical creature again?" Evianna asked.

Adelgis didn't seem interested in the conversation. He waited a long moment, his gaze downcast. "I don't want to think about it at the moment. Every thought of something else feels like a betrayal to Felicity. Perhaps, if it didn't feel that way, I would search for another eldrin, but not now."

That made sense.

And unlike Fain, I wasn't going to push the matter.

I had a lot of other problems to deal with.

The citizens of Ellios came out in droves to watch me alter the mountains. Terrakona slithered into the side of town, his emerald scales glistening as much as the pristine windows that dotted the walls of the university.

With a wave of my hand, the rocks sank into the earth, lessening the drastic topography. I widened the pass, but that was harder. Every inch of stone that shifted also somehow affected the trees and their roots. Then the mudslides happened, and Terrakona had to slam some of his serpentine body down to catch the cascade of dirt that threatened to flood the streets of Ellios.

The soldiers were watching.

So were the university scholars.

Part of me felt... the harsh weight of their judgment.

But I pushed it away from my thoughts. This was the first time I was changing *this* much of the terrain, and I really didn't need any more anxiety. I had a war to win, the Autarch to defeat, and an aura to manifest. Everything else was childish and insignificant.

I closed my eyes and imagined *all* of the mountain.

The deep parts, with the caves, that only my tremor sense could detect. The forests that grew along the sides. The large boulders that gathered at the base.

Everything.

This time, when I moved part of the pass—the gap between two large slabs of stone—I also shifted the dirt, and lifted the trees, and crushed the caves. I had to do it all together, or else everything would collapse or create some sort of disaster.

And in that moment...

Something in my chest grew warm and comforting. I gritted my teeth as power flooded me.

Then everything felt right. I opened my eyes, used both my hands, and manipulated the *entire* terrain around Ellios, even shifting the stones of the street to make them a little wider and easier to walk on.

I had done it. I had mastered my *creation* manipulation. Which meant I had lost the ability to manipulate the waters... But that was fine. I had rarely used it. Now my terrain manipulation would be stronger, and easier to use.

I exhaled as the Clawdam Mountains settled into place. The road through Ellios—that led to Fortuna—was wide, safe, and easy to traverse. The mountains were less of a problem, and trade would become more prevalent, I was sure of it.

"Warlord, you've done it," Terrakona telepathically said. **"Our magic... It has changed."**

"I know," I replied, breathless.

"The world is your canvas. Paint it well."

I glanced down at my palms. My left arm... the tattooed lines of black... I felt as though my whole body was becoming soaked in magics I had never even thought possible. Terrakona always spoke of "seeding the world" with magic, and maybe now I knew more what he was saying.

Everything was different.

The march of the soldiers drew my attention.

I turned on my heel and watched as the people of Ellios opened the southern gates to accommodate the Argo Empire soldiers. Led by unicorn arcanists—members of the Knights Draconic—the two thousand five hundred soldiers picked up their encampments and headed north, toward Fortuna.

And while I suspected they wanted to march with me, I knew it wasn't to be. I still had to head to New Norra.

To see Liet.

Chapter 44

The Salvation Aura

Orwyn and her sky titan flew me, Evianna, and Akiva south through the Argo Empire. Terrakona waited in Ellios, standing guard as the soldiers marched through the Clawdam Mountain pass. He wanted to wait for me there, to welcome me when I returned.

And a dryad appeared in Ellios, so of course, Terrakona had to make the dryad its own little grove of trees to live.

However, a dryad wasn't the only strange mystical creature who had appeared. A *sylph* had appeared as well. A creature of air—normally described as "spirits of air." Although it was odd, because they weren't native to the mountains, everyone knew why. Just as Terrakona was causing dryads to appear, the sky titan was causing sylphs to form.

I tried not to think about it too long, though. The presence of more mystical creatures was a good thing—nothing to worry about.

Right?

The Argo Empire stretched out below us. Whenever the clouds parted, I was able to take in a glorious view of the largest nation I had ever visited. Thronehold was at the heart of it all, the city where several rivers connected. The walls were tall and sturdy, and the streets ran in every direction. The rivers glittered with sapphire brilliance—blue blood for the land.

The fields of agriculture to the south, the beautiful forests to the east, and the iron mines to the west gave the Argo Empire everything it could ever need. Not only that, but the auras of the sovereign dragons made sure the citizens were prosperous and productive.

I glanced over at Evianna.

Did she regret bonding with a knightmare? Only sovereign dragon arcanists were allowed to rule in the Argo Empire. Perhaps she missed her homeland. Perhaps she lamented the fact she wouldn't rule over it as a queen.

When she glanced over and caught me staring, she smiled. Her white hair rippled across her back as we flew through the sky, and her magiborne runes still glittered with a silvery power. Evianna looked like she had been born from magic.

We continued to stare at each other, and her face grew red.

Although we said nothing, I knew what she was thinking.

And for a long while, while we sailed across the blue sky, we just stared at each other.

The mountains to the north of New Norra were red.

We flew over them faster than the Clawdam Mountains because it was a smaller formation. The mountains were just tall enough to separate the Argo Empire from the Amber Dunes. Seeing it from the sky made everything clearer to me.

The borders of nations relied on terrain.

Mountains and rivers formed irrefutable boundaries.

That was why every ruler wanted the world serpent arcanist —wanted *me*—to change their landscape. They wanted a land like the Argo Empire, where nature itself was set up in a pleasant way.

Orwyn brought us to the Amber Dunes, but she didn't command her god-creature to fly close to the ground. That was a good call. If Sytherias flew too low, she'd kick up sand and perhaps create a storm.

The oppressive sun was worse here, however. Even though heat didn't affect me like it did the others, I wasn't immune to the harsh glare and the dry atmosphere. To make things easier, Sytherias seemingly evoked clouds. We flew into them and traveled with cover from the sunlight. It obstructed my vision, though. Which was disappointing. I had enjoyed seeing everything from high up.

The city of New Norra...

I remembered it well.

And when Sytherias eventually took us down, and dispelled the clouds, I caught sight of the never-ending sands of the desert and the single river that provided life for the city. The Lion's Tail River. Surrounding New Norra was a wall unlike any other. Giant crystals were positioned all throughout the wall, glittering with a myriad of colors. When light filtered through the twenty-foot-high crystals, it cast rainbows across the sand, watchtowers, and walkways.

The crystals protected the city from sandstorms.

I loved everything about them.

And they slightly reminded me of the magiborne runes. I wondered if magic itself was somehow all related.

Orwyn and her kirin touched down onto the stone walkway that led to the gates of the massive city. The cloven hooves of her glorious eldrin hit the stones with a clatter of clacking.

"Here we are," Orwyn stated.

Akiva landed next to her, but stumbled as he tried to find his footing. He said nothing, and avoided looking at any of us. When Evianna landed, she went straight to me through the shadows. With a squint, she emerged from the darkness, glaring at the sun.

New Norra had its own city guard and golem arcanists who defended it from trouble, but I was surprised to see the gates open and a short woman in long yellow robes come hurrying out. The sun was starting to set, and the scarlet in the sky made her outfit seem like molten gold.

The woman had a cowl drawn over her head, protecting her from the desert sun. Her black hair spilled out on either side of her face, however, too unruly to be contained by the garment.

She had no mark on her forehead, which meant she wasn't an arcanist.

"Oh, Warlord!" the woman said as she hurried over. "I am Baha Nippe, a scribe." The woman, Baha, stopped once she reached my side. With a smile, and a couple gulped breaths, she continued, "Are you here for the pair of all-seeing sphinxes? You've come just in time."

I caught my breath and held it. All-seeing sphinxes were extinct. Everyone knew that. Why did this woman think she had two?

Orwyn tilted her head, her short hair clinging to her face with sweat. "Those sphinxes were hunted until they were no more. Perhaps you are mistaken?"

"Oh, no," Baha said as she held a hand to her chest. "These are all-seeing sphinxes. They came from Thronehold! After all those mystical creatures had been resurrected."

It all came together then. So many creatures were resurrected in Thronehold, it was hard to keep track. King basilisks? All-seeing sphinxes? The charybdis? So many that were once thought gone had returned to the world.

"There are *two* here?" I asked.

The scribe frowned. "Aren't you here for them? I... I thought the god-arcanists would want to have them. They're so rare. And powerful."

I shook my head. "No. I apologize. I'm here for Liet Eventide. She came here with members of the Frith Guild, and I've come to collect them."

Baha's eyebrows went for her hairline. "B-But... the sphinxes..." With a frown, she took a moment to compose herself. "They want to bond. They say their Trial of Worth is complete. Should we allow *anyone* to bond with them? The arcanists of New Norra have kept the sister sphinxes away from everyone, debating on when you'd arrive."

The legends around all-seeing sphinxes were quite interesting. They could find nearly anything, and were said to be rather wise. But I didn't have time to solve every problem. Surely, the arcanists of New Norra could handle this themselves.

"I'm sorry," I said. "I'm just here for the members of the Frith Guild. If you want me to handle this, I'll have to do it when I return."

Orwyn nodded once. "We are in quite a hurry, scribe."

She said it with a dreamy far-off tone that almost made the whole statement sarcastic. I knew she was genuine—she just spoke oddly—but Baha seemed distressed.

"Nubia and Maye say they don't want to wait too long," the scribe stated. "They say their arcanists are waiting for them. I think they might be confused. They need guidance, as their magics could bring change to the world."

"Afterward," I said as I stepped around Baha. "Take care of them until I return, but I can't delay my trip any longer than necessary." War was brewing, and every moment I spent with this woman, out in the middle of the desert, was a moment I wasn't preparing.

"Nubia and Maye—"

"Will have to learn patience," I said.

And then I headed into New Norra, the city in the middle of the Amber Dunes. Evianna, Orwyn, and Akiva shadowed me inside.

Liet had been staying in a research lab.

That wasn't where I had thought I would find her, but I wasn't going to complain, either. Hexa and Vethica were there as well, making sure Liet was safe. Apparently, after Vethica's khepera was reformed in the great maze under the city, she had used her magic to delay the effects of the arcane plague. The new, more powerful version would've likely taken hold of Liet if it weren't for Vethica.

I was glad she was on our side.

I found Liet in one of the back rooms. The lab had no windows, which I found strange, but rimestones were built into the walls, cooling the whole building. Just like glowstones, the rimestones were palm-sized, and radiated magic. The blue rocks were always cold—always.

When I entered Liet's room, I found her sitting on a cot and reading a book. Her gray hair was down, and she had the appearance of someone who had been locked in an infirmary for several years. She wore a white robe, her hands were shaking, and when she glanced up, the bags under her eyes were rather blatant.

"Volke?" she asked, her voice raspy.

The room was only five feet by five feet. Simple. Plain. No decorations. No personal belongings.

Liet's glowing arcanist mark was the brightest thing in the room.

And perhaps her personality.

She smiled when she spotted me, her posture straightening. "You've come with a cure?" she asked.

I strode over to her cot, matching her smile. "How did you know?"

"I saw it in your eyes. No one is as hopeful as you are if they have bad news to deliver."

With a chuckle, I held out my hand. Liet took it and then stood. Although she was clearly weak from the ill effects of the plague, she never gave up. That was what I liked about her.

"I've managed to create my salvation aura." Unable to stop smiling, I added, "And it completely removes the arcane plague and bestows the arcanist with something new. Something magical."

"Let's see it, lad."

I wanted to explain everything—even the first time I had used my aura—but I knew now wasn't the time. I could explain while we flew back to Fortuna.

What Liet needed now was my aura. So I closed my eyes, took a deep breath, and then relaxed. My thoughts immediately went to Evianna, and then they drifted to the Isle of Ruma. I liked to imagine a life there. Or maybe a life on the open ocean, exploring places I had never seen before. The adventure—the happiness—all filled my thoughts and body until it spilled outward with my magic.

My salvation aura.

When I opened my eyes again, Liet was staring at her arms. The magiborne runes had appeared across her skin as fine, silvery lines. They disappeared into her sleeves, but I suspected they didn't go beyond her shoulders.

She glanced at the marks on my arm. "This is what the plague becomes?" Liet whispered.

I nodded once.

"Who else has had this happen to them?"

"Just me, Evianna, and Zelfree." I couldn't remember anyone else.

Liet hesitantly smiled. "And your aura... Did you maintain it all the way here?"

I slowly shook my head and silently cursed at myself. I should've been doing that! What if there were plague-ridden creatures hiding in the desert? Or in the mountains? Or in forests? I should've maintained my aura through the entire trek.

"I'll do so on the way back," I said.

Liet gently placed a hand on my shoulder. "Then let's hurry." She still seemed frail, and tired, but her eyes flared with determination. "The more god-arcanists who develop this, the more territory it'll cover, correct? We haven't a moment to lose."

I turned toward the door. "That's what I thought. We should leave as soon as possible."

As I headed for the door, Liet asked, "What about the others?"

"The sky titan can only take so many of us," I muttered as I grabbed the door handle. "So we can take a few."

"What about Atty?"

I glanced over my shoulder. "Is she here? I thought she went to the Sunset Desert."

Liet walked to the door. She tied her long hair back into a ponytail. "Yes. She did, but that was over six months ago. I've been in contact with her since she left. Writing letters, I should say. Once a month."

"And she wants to fight with us?"

"Well..." Liet shook her head. "I don't know. I told her to head to Fortuna, but I haven't yet heard back from her. She said she was ready to fight, but whether she'll actually arrive in Fortuna, I'm unsure."

"Did she... manage to get Titania to achieve true form?"

"I don't know. She didn't mention it."

Curse the abyssal hells. Why was Atty like this? Even now, at the eleventh hour, she was playing as though she would help us. I wished she would just make up her mind. It was fine if she left, but I couldn't rely on her. If she showed, great. If not, I wouldn't waste another thought on it.

"Hopefully she has her own method of making it to Fortuna," I said as I exited the room.

Half the Frith Guild was here, but most of them weren't suited for war. Hexa was, fortunately, and Orwyn could easily carry Raisen on the wind, even if he was a huge hydra.

Before we left, I wanted to see my brother.

Ryker and Karna were in one of the local inns, a place called the *Desert Tuna*. A strange name, but I didn't question it. I thought I'd have something to eat and speak with him, but I actually spotted Ryker outside the building. The three stories of the inn cast a long shadow, and my brother lingered in it.

Ryker's eldrin, the Mother of Shapeshifters, waited on his shoulder. She was shaped as a white mouse, her red eyes watching me as I approached.

Night would soon be upon the city, and the temperature would go from oppressively hot to icy cold.

Ryker glanced over, his eyes going wide. "Brother? What're you doing here?"

I gave him a slight nod, but then I turned my attention to MOS. The little mouse wiggled her nose. "I'm sorry," I muttered.

MOS just stared at me, her red eyes alight with intelligence.

"What's happening?" Ryker rubbed his hands together. "Are you here to speak with me about Karna? Because, well, I think we're perfect for each other."

My face heated as I shook my head. "No. I mean, congratulations. But I wanted to speak with you, and MOS, about what happened." I reached into my pocket and withdrew the shards of the broken runestone.

The sandstone fragments were all that remained of the progenitor behemoth.

"I know you wanted to meet your father," I said as I stared into the mouse's eyes.

"The behemoth was both male and female." MOS wiggled

her nose again. "But *father* is a fine title." The mouse stared at the sandstone pieces. "Bring it closer."

That was a bizarre command, but everything about MOS was bizarre. I took a deep breath and then held up the fragments. MOS's cute mouse form bubbled and shifted, and then fleshy tendrils reached out toward the broken runestone.

The flesh was pale and shiny, like the skin had been scarred or burned.

Once MOS grabbed the runestone, the mouse absorbed the pieces into her body. The fragments just *disappeared*. Straight into MOS's body. I held back a gag.

"Yeeessss, thank you, Warlord," she said with a cute little squeak. Her body melted back into the shape of a normal mouse. "I will use this when the next behemoth comes to this world again. I will be ready. Stronger. Better."

That sounded ominous. But MOS had never been sinister, and the longer she was bonded to Ryker, the calmer she would become, I suspected.

Ryker gently patted his eldrin. Then he turned to me, his black hair getting tossed around by the evening wind. "Brother? We... we don't have one of the god-creatures?"

"We have enough. The world serpent, the fenris wolf, the sky titan, the typhon beast, the scylla waters, corona phoenix, and tempest coatl. It should be enough. We have more than half of all of them, and the Autarch only has three."

My brother slowly nodded along with my words. "So... after all this is over, do you think we could visit Mother? Together?"

"Of course. I'd like that."

That got my brother smiling. He patted MOS a second time, and the little mouse hissed. Or purred. I wasn't entirely sure which.

"Wait here," I said to Ryker. "I'll be back once this is all over. But right now, I have to return to Fortuna."

Chapter 45

The Defense Of Fortuna

Flying back to Ellios felt like a dream—something Adelgis would weave together as a form of entertainment. We sailed through the brilliant blue of a clear day, flightless eldrin twirling in the breeze beside us.

This was probably the first time a hydra had ever flown.

Raisen kept all his mouths open as wind rushed across his prickly scales. His alligator-style body wasn't made to be aerodynamic. It was a hilarious sight to see such a fat and stout creature hurtle through the air, smiling wide, not a care in the world.

Orwyn rode her kirin, Akiva never leaving her side, not even during these aerial travels. Occasionally, they glanced over to each other, and it reminded me of how I looked at Evianna.

But I pushed that from my mind.

I kept my thoughts on pleasant things as I maintained my aura through the trek. I hoped my magic would reach the lands below, but I wasn't certain the exact extent of my powers. Did my salvation aura cover a mile? Two miles? Maybe it only went two hundred feet from my body. I wasn't certain. I hadn't yet tested it enough to find out.

It didn't matter. As soon as the others had mastered theirs, we would cover the entire world.

I hoped.

We arrived back at Ellios only two weeks after we had departed.

It felt like a lifetime, though. Travel took too much time. It ate at my sanity. However, that meant the soldiers from the Argo Empire had likely reached Fortuna by this point.

When Orwyn brought us down to the ground, Terrakona slithered out to meet us, his colossal body big enough to wreck the whole city. Fortunately, his magic caused everything to part away—the trees, the roads, the fences—and then sewed it back together once Terrakona had passed by.

The university town was mostly quiet and undisturbed, but the massive road down the center was a clear deviation from the previous iteration of the city's design.

"Warlord," Terrakona said as my feet touched the ground. He bowed his head so his snout was close to my face. **"You have returned. And your aura... it's stronger than ever before."**

"I need to master it," I muttered. Then I patted his nose. His warm breath made me think of rain on a hot summer day.

"You will. Have confidence in your convictions. It gives them strength."

But would I do it all in time? I shook my head, trying to focus on the positive. I would do it. We would do it. Everything would be fine.

The glimmering university stood on the far side of the city. Part of me wanted to visit Adelgis and Fain, but we didn't have time for frivolities. Adelgis needed time to rest and renew himself, and the only person who consistently stayed by his side was Fain.

And while Fain had sworn himself to me and my cause, he

had done everything I had asked of him. Now all I needed to do was deal with the Autarch, so Fain could take a moment to rest with his beloved.

Liet's braided hair was puffed as much as a squirrel's tail from all the flying. Unlike her time in New Norra, she seemed more alive and vibrant. Liet strode over with a spring in her step.

"Are you okay?" I asked.

"The closer I get to Gentel, the more my magic returns to me." She smoothed her braid and smiled. "I'm sure my eldrin feels the same. The more we were apart, the more the grass on her shell yellowed and wilted."

The farther apart an arcanist was from their eldrin, the weaker their magic became, which was probably why Liet's age had caught up with her a bit in New Norra.

"These runes," Liet said, touching her arm. "Will they make me immune to the arcane plague from here on out?"

I didn't know the answer to the question. Perhaps that showed on my face, because Liet nodded once in response.

"Just keep it in mind when we engage with the Second Ascension. They may have plague-ridden arcanists in their ranks. And dread form creatures are far more deadly than normal creatures without the sinister alterations."

She was right. She was always right.

But if my salvation aura was active… Perhaps our enemies wouldn't have as much of an advantage.

And perhaps Luthair would be with them. If he entered my salvation aura, I would be able to save him.

Hopefully.

I rode Terrakona from Ellios to Fortuna.

The road we had created held up well, even after the soldiers had gone through. Travel north would be so much easier, and as we neared Fortuna, I was pleased with our efforts. I couldn't wait to tell the others about what we had done, how quickly it had all happened, and how I mastered my terrain manipulation.

But as the sun slid downward, toward the horizon, I noticed pillars of smoke in the distance.

The sight disturbed me. It was enough that my aura ended as my heart pounded in dread anticipation.

Something was wrong.

Terrakona lifted his head high, and I clung to his crystal mane, wondering if my tremor sense could detect something so far away. It couldn't, but fortunately, I had the ability to see in the dark.

It was the city of Fortuna, only a mile away.

Fires lit up the streets. Smoke gushed toward the sky. The Astral Tower, aglow in orange from the flames, continued ticking on, keeping the time even amid the chaos.

Out beyond the walls and the port, sailing on the distant waves, were many ships. They shot cannons that rumbled the area as badly as thunder.

Enemy ships. So many.

"Volke!"

I glanced up. Orwyn and her sky titan flew past me, heading straight for Fortuna.

"Orwyn?" I shouted.

"We must help!" she yelled back, her voice dying as she hurried forward. "The Keeper of Corpse and Ezril might be in danger!"

The whole damn city was in trouble, not just a few individuals. But Orwyn had made it clear that perhaps she didn't care about much—just those important to her.And we had left Ezril in the city.

Evianna stood on Terrakona's back. She pointed to the ocean beyond the port. "Look! What's happening? Is that... is that the scylla waters?"

With urgency in his movements, Terrakona shot forward. We rushed toward the southern walls of the city, the terrain moving out of Terrakona's way as he crossed the fields of grass and agriculture. Fortuna had been built upon a great hill, which made seeing the ocean an easy task. It was below us at almost all points.

When we reached the city, I managed to catch a glimpse of the waters.

A whirlpool of epic proportions swirled in front of the docks.

Evianna was right. It *was* the scylla waters. The fish creature half-emerged from the depths, becoming visible for a few movements while she rearranged the very tides. Waves kicked up all around the gigantic god-creature, crashing against the scylla waters's sapphire scales.

The nearby ships were caught in the downward spiral.

There were fifty ships in total, but most of them were man-o-war ships, not galleons, like I had been led to believe. These were heavy vessels capable of carrying hundreds of cannons each. They were the ships of combat. No other compared.

And the ships flew a strange flag I had never seen. They didn't fly flags of nations, just one flag with a gold kirin on it. I had to assume it was the mark of the Autarch. They had sworn allegiance to him, and him alone.

To my horror, the scylla waters wasn't the only thing in the water.

Tentacles lifted out of the whirlpool. Two latched onto the massive scylla waters, grabbing the fishwoman by her arms.

The tentacles were blood red and black in coloration, like a rotted corpse. Gold hooks stuck out of the tentacles, acting as disgusting claws. The vile monster dug its fishhooks into the scylla waters, trapping the god-creature in place.

Then the tentacled monster lifted out of the water.

The abyssal kraken.

This was it. The Autarch was here. He had come to claim the lives of the other god-creatures.

The abyssal kraken was a disturbing octopus with a gargantuan body made of pure muscle and slime. Its head lifted out of the waves to reveal the bulbous shape of a colossal octopus, but also a skull mask. The abyssal kraken wore bone over most of its octopus face—the skull face of a human being. Obviously, it wasn't the skull of a real person, because it was far too large for that.

Perhaps the skull of a giant. Or perhaps it was just part of the abyssal kraken itself. Either way, the white bone mask had sharp teeth and spines along the forehead. The abyssal kraken hissed and screamed as it wrapped two more tentacles around the arms of the scylla waters.

The two god-creatures were fighting over control of the ocean, and the scylla waters was clearly losing.

Terrakona slithered over the walls of Fortuna and made his way through the narrow streets.

Our soldiers had set up defensive measures near the walls before the ports. They were ready for combat, the Argo Empire knights giving orders while their soldiers rushed to fulfill the commands.

Terrakona traveled slower than I would've liked, but he moved in such a way as to avoid most people and fortifications. The city blocks moved around Terrakona, as his ambient magic altered the terrain as he traveled, but it was still disturbing some crucial barriers.

We couldn't manipulate water anymore. Could we even help the scylla waters?

Clouds swiftly gathered over the ocean like a firework exploding in the sky.

Lightning formed in the clouds, angry and crackling. Then the tempest coatl shot toward the waves, her glowing scales lighting up the entirety of the docks as she slammed into the abyssal kraken.

Lightning lanced from her body, striking the kraken and a few of the ships as though the coatl had total control over where it went. With powerful beats of her wings, the tempest coatl attempted to lift the abyssal kraken from the waters.

The two roared, their fight disturbing the waters and creating a massive storm that rocked the piers.

Both the scylla waters and the tempest coatl were young god-creatures. They were slightly smaller than the gargantuan abyssal kraken, which was at least the size of four man-o-war ships all by its lonesome.

The abyssal kraken used its fishhook claws and skewered one of the tempest coatl's wings, attempting to remove her ability to fly. Blood gushed out into the waters. The tempest coatl exploded lightning in all directions from her body, shocking anything and everything nearby.

The scylla waters and the tempest coatl, even with their magic combined, were struggling against the abyssal kraken.

I wished Adelgis were here, and with his telepathy. I could've coordinated tactics. Instead, I had to rely on the others to make decisions. Fortunately, William was a navy man, and Lucian had been one of the Steel Thorn Inquisitors. They had training. They knew how to handle themselves in a fight.

Then the air grew thick with untold pressure.

I blinked back tears as my eyes burned. Was this the power of the sky titan?

I glanced upward and caught sight of the most intimidating bird I had ever seen in my life. It wasn't even really a *bird*. It had wings. It had feathers. It had a head with a beak. But it also had the body of a muscular man—and chains around his neck and arms that the creature wore as armor. His arms were lean with muscle, and his fingers were tipped with sharp talons.

And he was two stories tall, with talon feet that reminded me of a gargoyle.

The bird creature screamed as he slammed down into Fortuna, his black and coal feathers similar to a raven's. He had a golden beak, two gold horns, and taloned feet that matched—a beautiful monster that had all the presence of a war god.

It was the garuda bird.

A legendary warrior of a mystical creature.

The garuda bird attempted to flap his inky wings, but the winds kept him down. With unbridled anger in his screech, the garuda bird clawed at the nearby buildings. He tried to climb up, but the wind continued its relentless howl, swirling around the bird.

Orwyn and her sky titan were trying to subdue the garuda bird.

And then came the flames.

The corona phoenix entered the city from the western border. Had Biyu and Captain Devlin been away? The massive phoenix soared into the sky and went straight for the garuda bird. Fire and shadows mixed in perfect combination, washing over a section of Fortuna.

I thought the citizens would be burned, but the shadows—immune to fire—rose up like shields. Buildings and people were protected from the heat of the phoenix's might. Instead, the garuda bird was slammed with a wall of fire.

Between the fight with the abyssal kraken and the fight with the garuda bird, I knew I would be more help with the creature on land.

But before I could make my way to the phoenix, the sky titan, and the garuda bird, a bell rang out from the port. It rang with furious energy, clanging in rapid succession.

The boats of the enemy...

They drew closer.

More cannons fired. The iron balls hit buildings and

shattered the walls. Some cannonballs were nothing more than oil-soaked bombs that exploded into flame the moment they hit. More ships positioned themselves to fire, but a shimmering barrier of magic lifted out of the water.

Gentel, the true form atlas turtle, moved to the edge of the whirlpool, the Frith Guild manor house on her back. Her powerful shielding magic blocked the cannons from striking Fortuna, but now that Gentel was close to the fighting, the abyssal kraken turned its skull-mask in her direction.

And through it all, I sensed a powerful magic approaching us. It was unlike anything I had felt before.

It was the Autarch.

Chapter 46

The Autarch

Although I couldn't see him, I knew his ship was approaching Fortuna.

With my jaw clenched, I turned to Evianna. "Go! Help Orwyn and the others! I have to protect the city."

Evianna nodded once. She was hardened and ready, no hesitation in her actions. With a few swift shadow-steps, she entered the city and dashed down the streets.

I waved my hand and lifted stones from the bay. Fortuna already had a wall, but I created a second one—a sheer cliff made of gray stone. As the rocks emerged from the depths, people in the city pointed and gasped. Waves crashed against the new barrier, sending mist into the air.

I couldn't allow the Autarch to touch shore.

Terrakona's scales flared. He turned his head as the garuda bird screeched. The warrior bird couldn't sink his claws into either the sky titan or the corona phoenix—both were made of either incorporeal or semi-incorporeal material. The bird slashed with his taloned hands, but when nothing happened, the bird opened his mouth, and light gathered in his beak.

The garuda bird blasted a beam of light the same golden color as his armor.

The light cut through the flames of the corona phoenix, slicing through her shadowy legs. The void heart at the center of the phoenix pulsed faster than before, even as the majestic creature crashed to the streets of Fortuna.

The garuda bird kicked a nearby building, raining stones across a portion of the city.

Riflemen and archers let loose with a volley of attacks. The arrows were tiny, and the bullets even smaller. They peppered the garuda bird. The monster gathered more light in his beak, preparing for another attack.

To my surprise, Liet hurried through the streets and held up a hand. She evoked a barrier across the longbowmen just before the garuda bird blasted them with a beam of raw magic. The bird's attack struck the shield and almost broke through, but Liet's true form magic held firm.

Terrakona moved to join the fight, but I held up a hand. "Wait!"

"Warlord?"

The Autarch's ships continued their course.

The abyssal kraken skewered the scylla waters, interrupting the whirlpool. Then the tide shifted, helping the ships move closer and closer to port. But the piers were ruined, and my new secondary wall was in place. What was the Autarch thinking?

Cannon fire echoed across the land.

Magical barriers sprang to life, stopping some of the shots. Gentel stood guard by the land, her magic protecting the people of Fortuna.

The abyssal kraken lashed out at Gentel. Its hook tentacles raked her shell and then her head, cutting into her flesh. The kraken smashed the guild manor house in one swift blow.

Bleeding, Gentel moved away, but not entirely out of the fight.

More cannon fire. This time the enemy wrecked our piers.

Without a port, how would the Autarch land his soldiers? There was no way. He should've retreated and found another place to land, but instead, his many ships continued forward, as though blind to the rocks and turbulent waves.

The corona phoenix managed to pull herself from the ground and unleash another wave of fire. Liet and her barriers attempted to shield the nearby soldiers. The sky titan wrapped itself around the garuda bird, preventing him from flying.

And while I wanted to help them, I watched in horror as the enemy ships increased their speed. They headed for the barrier of rocks, not one altering course.

The abyssal kraken lifted a tentacle from the waves and smashed open a small hole.

I waved my hand, attempting to repair it.

One ship managed to sail over the jagged rocks before my magic could patch everything together. The hull of the ship was torn open as it slid over the rock in an attempt to reach shore. Then the man-o-war *collided* with the port and kept going, ripping up wooden boards until it finally crashed onto land, losing its ability to sail ever again.

If there were any sailors or soldiers aboard, they had surely been injured during the crash.

What was the Autarch thinking? That was insanity!

The abyssal kraken broke another hole, and another ship did the same thing. It sailed through, damaging itself in the process, and then slammed into land. The second ship actually made it deeper into the port, ripping up more of the wood planking, and even crashing into the wall of the city.

What was going on?

Again, any sailors or soldiers aboard would've been injured in that maneuver. It wasn't worth it.

"Warlord! The warrior of the skies!"

I turned just as the garuda bird broke free of the sky titan.

The giant eagle-man leapt into the air, flapped his black wings once, and then fell in my direction, his clawed hands outstretched.

"Die, Warlord," the garuda bird growled, his eyes gold and fiery. **"You're a weakness that must be *purged*."**

I pulled Retribution and just barely managed to stumble away before the bird slammed his talons into the road, shattering the bricks and disrupting the city.

Terrakona lunged forward, his fangs ready. He bit the bird on the shoulder, and then wrapped his serpentine body around him.

The garuda bird tried to pierce Terrakona's scales, but they held solid—the world serpent's hide was almost impenetrable now that Terrakona had grown just a little older. Despite that, Terrakona's *eyes* weren't as tough. The garuda bird clawed at Terrakona's red eye, slashing it in one brutal swipe.

"You'll never win," the garuda bird said with a chuckle. **"I have the rightful ruler on my side. His magic *empowers* me."**

The warrior bird grabbed Terrakona and yanked, as though to rip the serpent off his body. Normally, Terrakona was much stronger than his opponents, but the garuda bird was proving that wrong. Terrakona released his bite and screamed.

I empathetically felt his pain. His muscles were being torn as the garuda bird attempted to rend him in half.

I ran forward, and although the two creatures were gigantic, I slashed at the garuda bird's legs with my sword. The blade went right through the flesh of the god-creature as though it wasn't even there. With a quick swing, I removed one of the garuda bird's feet, his taloned claw hitting the street, his blood gushing into the gutters.

Terrakona released the garuda bird from his serpentine hold, and the beast took to the sky, its missing foot splattering blood across the roofs of Fortuna.

Another crash rang out across the city. It was difficult to see the port through the many pillars of smoke, but most of the larger buildings had fallen, and we were still on the incline of the hill. A third ship had crashed into the piers.

And into the other two ships.

My skin crawled when I realized what was happening.

The large sailing vessels practically split open. Hundreds of corpses—no, *thousands*—spilled into Fortuna. The man-o-war ships had been floating crypts, each carrying enormous piles of decaying human bodies. Now the land, the port and the main street were covered in vile cadavers.

Then the bodies began to stir.

They wore armor, held shields, and carried weapons, and when they stood, they shuffled into formation, taking up positions, side by side. Some of the corpses linked shields before marching forward, their rotted flesh and bones empowered by threads of magic.

When I had calculated the enemy forces, I had assumed the Autarch wouldn't be able to carry more than one hundred human soldiers per boat. But with corpses... he could pile them into a boat five high, from bow to stern. He probably had close to *twenty thousand* undead soldiers on all his boats. If they all landed, we would be overwhelmed.

A dragon emerged from the third ship.

Not a normal dragon, made of muscles, scales, and spikes. This was a corpse dragon. And not just a single corpse. It was the skeleton of a dragon draped in hundreds of bodies. Human bodies. Mystical creature bodies. They were twisted together over the skeleton, acting as flesh and skin, including wings, though I doubted the beast could fly.

And tombstones spotted its head, like horns.

This was the *endless undead*. The last god-creature.

It was a walking graveyard.

The soldiers of the Argo Empire met the corpse army in the

streets of Fortuna. The trained troops had already erected barricades and defenses. They had prepared for the worst. So when the corpses came, they were ready—they held back the first wave of bodies, even though the undead men were using their weapons with skill beyond the average man.

Terrakona slithered to me, and I grabbed on to his mane. We headed for the dock, ready to rid Fortuna of this blight.

I manipulated the terrain, and tried to trap the corpses, but moving the stone streets around to engulf hundreds of individuals—without getting my own soldiers—proved difficult. I had the ground swallow dozens of undead by the time I joined the fight.

The endless undead, in all its dragon glory, reared back and then unleashed its breath weapon. It wasn't fire, like a classic sovereign dragon, or even magma, like a pyroclastic dragon—it was blood.

Just blood.

The scarlet river of vital fluid spewed over the soldiers of the Argo Empire, painting their armor crimson with gore. The Knights Draconic were splashed the most, and when the Sky Legionnaires tore through the storm-soaked skies in order to help in the fight, the endless undead vomited blood on them, too.

A howl pierced the night.

Zaxis and Vjorn, the two lying in wait to surprise the enemy, raced down the streets of Fortuna. They ran past Terrakona, charging forward. Zaxis rode his eldrin, holding onto the fenris wolf's black fur, leaning forward, smiling wide.

Vjorn *leapt* into the undead army.

Ice blasted from the wolf's body, freezing the fleshy soldiers. Then the wolf proceeded to crunch his fangs down on the corpses, breaking their rotted bodies with a few snaps of his jaw.

Lynus and Xor stormed down another street, the multi-headed typhon beast roaring as it went. When the god-creature drew close to the corpses, the ninety-nine snake heads chattered their mouths, creating a song of madness. The undead were unaffected, but the corpse dragon screamed in defiance, obviously disturbed by the sounds of insanity.

More ships approached the docks.

I wanted to create another wall of stone, but the garuda bird had other plans.

The massive warrior bird slammed into the street next to me, shattering the road, toppling buildings, and screeching loud enough to burst one of my eardrums.

The sky titan and corona phoenix both swooped in. The titan's wind fueled the flames of the phoenix, creating a pyre that rose to the sky. The fires circled the garuda bird, but the creature reached a taloned hand out through the inferno and grabbed me.

Which was a mistake.

Molten rock erupted from almost every pore of my body. My bones hardened into basalt. I burned the garuda bird's hand with my powerful evocation, and the beast released me with another screech.

I hit the ground, my head spinning.

Terrakona slammed the bird with his tail, sending it stumbling backward and crashing into a building. Then my world serpent moved to coil around me, protecting me from any random attacks.

The yelling and chaos of war...

Two more ships hit land. I felt it with my tremor sense. One had live soldiers. The other was filled with powerful magic.

It had to be the Autarch. He had reached land. He was here.

Arcanists from around the city must've known it, too. Cannons fired from Fortuna, slamming into the ships that neared. Several arcanists with the ability to fly went straight for the Autarch's vessel. Arcanists on the ground fought with the corpses, pushing the undead army away from the streets.

Through the confusion, I sensed Illia and Nicholin. They teleported in and out of the battle, the silvery sparkles appearing throughout the battlefield. Her white flames broke apart the undead. She aimed for their legs, and once their feet were disintegrated, the soldiers fell, breaking the formation. Before the undead could counterattack, Illia teleported away.

And just like Illia, I sensed Evianna, too.

She used the shadows to her advantage, manipulating them to hold down enemy soldiers so our troops could decimate them. She held down dozens at a time, stopping their advancement with her magic alone.

Hexa's poison gas didn't do much against the undead. Devlin's wind knocked over the corpses, sending some hurtling into the waters. I was certain Zelfree was here, but his magics were always varying.

Akiva fought, but his king basilisk venom didn't do anything against corpses. Instead, he targeted the living enemy soldiers. Despite his mangled body, he was a deadly combatant. Every person he touched died instantly.

The Keeper of Corpses and his arcanist, Ezril, had merged to become a humanoid monster that stood fifteen feet tall. Clothed in dead bodies, the beast charged forward into the enemy ranks. The undead were weaker around the Keeper of Corpses, like *his* magic was competing with the endless undead's. When the enemy soldiers attacked with swords or spears, they skewered Keeper's dead bodies, basically dealing no real damage. And Keeper was so large, he towered over the enemy. With a swing of his rotting arm, he bashed the front line, bowling over soldiers.

When the enemy undead attempted to march down a narrow street, a barrier shimmered into place. Liet had created a wall of magic to keep them away, and force them down the main central road.

Even Gillie, the Grand Apothecary, and the legendary fighter, Yesna, the Ace of Cutlasses, were here in the battle. Gillie healed anyone and everyone who came to her, her white caladrius a beacon of hope amid the din of war. With her two swords, both powerful artifacts, Yesna slashed her way through the undead.

There were arcanists I didn't recognize fighting for our side as well. Many from the guilds that had all sworn loyalty to me—and even a few arcanists who hadn't. The arcanists of the Finders Guild were here to lend their support.

I got to my feet, gripping Retribution firmly in my sword hand. Then I hefted Forfend off my back and attached it to my shield arm. My shirt had been burned away by my molten rock, and one leg of my trousers was nothing more than a smoking mess.

I looked like I had been through a war and back, but I had never felt better.

Terrakona uncoiled, his scales flaring.

The endless undead vomited more blood across the masses. That confused me. It wasn't damaging—it didn't burn flesh or melt stone or drain someone of strength. It was just disgusting. Why bother doing it? Why was the corpse dragon just coating our side in crimson?

Then I felt it.

A powerful presence of magic. It swept over Fortuna like an invisible wave.

An aura.

One of the Knights Draconic, a unicorn arcanist on the front lines, fighting the undead, exploded. His body burst outward, his armor torn asunder. His unicorn popped as well, its white fur tearing as it gushed its insides across Fortuna.

And then a pegasus and its arcanist became a bloody firework, bursting overhead.

The ground rumbled. More clouds gathered in the sky. It was like a natural disaster was swelling all around us.

This was the result of the *armageddon aura*. But why? Were

those arcanists plague-ridden? They hadn't been when they joined the fight.

But the blood...

The endless undead vomited plague-tainted blood onto the battlefield. And then the Autarch created his armageddon aura. Everyone infected instantly died while his aura was in effect. They just *exploded* from the might of god-arcanist magic.

Why wasn't the endless undead dying? Was it because it was immune to blood plagues because it was undead? Why was its tainted vomit allowed to remain even when the aura surrounded us all? I didn't know. All I knew was that it needed to die.

And I needed to counteract the Autarch.

Although we were in the middle of a war zone, in the thick of combat, I held my breath and thought of everything pleasant. I thought about the Isle of Ruma, the lessons of the Pillar, my love for Evianna, the good days when I was traveling with the Frith Guild...

And Luthair. How we had met. How we had grown together.

All those memories fueled my salvation aura. And when my magic flooded out of me, it filled the streets of Fortuna, clashing with the Autarch's will.

Arcanists stopped dying. Those covered in blood didn't explode. They weren't cured, but they weren't about to rupture, either. My aura was negating the Autarch's.

But ground continued to quake, and the sky remained agitated.

The Autarch must've known what I was doing, because a man emerged from the main ship, wearing black full plate armor from head to toe. His helmet had horns that curved backward, and his gauntlets ended with clawed fingers. He wielded a sword, similar to mine, but without the stars and emerald constellation. A blade made from the bones of the apoch dragon.

The Autarch.

Behind him stood his gold kirin. Unlike Orwyn's silver kirin, this beast was much more magical. The gold kirin glowed with a soft amber power. The scales across its body resembled a dragon's. Its cloven hooves glittered with each step, as though made of diamonds. Its eyes appeared as molten amber, liquid and swirling.

Instead of a single twisted horn, the gold kirin had a set of antlers, both of which shone like they were made of star shards.

The Autarch had three god-creature eldrin, and it was all because of *this* beast.

He wore a helmet, so I couldn't see the Autarch's face, but the way he lifted his sword and slashed it through the air told me he wasn't pleased.

Then a second wave of magic permeated the area.

Another aura.

Not the Autarch's armageddon aura. Something different.

And then it occurred to me... kirins had auras, too.

Chapter 47

The Preeminence Aura

The abyssal kraken glowed gold. The waters around its body swirled and filled with ghostly visions of people. The scylla waters attempted to take control of the tides, but the abyssal kraken's hook claws elongated and sharpened. The beast slammed more hooks into the scylla waters, carving out some of her scaly hide.

When the tempest coatl attempted to blast the kraken with lightning, the kraken grabbed the coatl's serpentine body and yanked her into the ocean. The kraken was clearly more powerful than ever before. The ghost-filled waves swarmed around the scylla waters, dragging the god-creature under. It looked like the ghosts were feasting on the scales of the scylla waters, clawing at her body, attempting to rip it apart.

The tempest coatl and scylla waters were losing.

Gentel stayed away. The atlas turtle didn't have much in the way of offensive abilities.

The garuda bird, clothed in a golden glow, screeched. The warrior bird leapt into the air, and then slammed down on his one foot. It blasted into a building, shattering it completely, sending bricks and chunks of stone careening through the air. The bird had broken open a path for the undead army.

The soldiers from the Argo Empire scrambled to close the opening.

The abyssal kraken destroyed my stone barrier out in the bay.

Three more ships crashed onto the shore, some of them away from the docks and just on a beach. More corpses slid out of the broken vessels.

The corona phoenix and sky titan tried to battle the garuda bird again, but even with a missing foot, and a bloody hand, the warrior was too much. The garuda bird was somehow empowered by the Autarch's second aura. The bird smashed the nearby buildings, and then took to the air, despite the sky titan's attempts to keep him grounded.

The garuda bird smashed into the Astral Tower, shattering the clock and sending parts of the broken building rolling down the hill Fortuna was built upon. With another screech, the bird continued his rampage, unhindered by the other two god-creatures.

"Volke!" a woman shouted.

I glanced upward and spotted Orwyn on her silver kirin. She pointed to the Autarch's ship, her expression pained. She was bleeding from the side, a river of crimson spilled across the beautiful scales of her eldrin mount.

"This aura—it's the gold kirin's *preeminence aura*. You must stop it!"

I motioned to Terrakona. My eldrin lowered his head, and I climbed onto his crystal mane. Orwyn didn't wait around. She flew off with her kirin, her attention clearly on the garuda bird, who was smashing our back lines.

That warrior bird could easily destroy the walls of the city, and even our supply line. If we left him unchecked, he'd attack our army from behind, while the endless undead attacked from the front with an army of corpses. We wouldn't be able to handle it.

Orwyn, the sky titan, and the corona phoenix had to hold the beast off for just a bit longer.

Terrakona and I rode straight into the docks. Our soldiers had parted, giving us a path, and then they leapt straight back into place, attempting to keep the enemy from swarming into the city.

The endless undead...

It, too, was wrapped in a golden glow.

Vjorn and Xor leapt at the corpse dragon, one on either side. The fenris wolf sank his fangs into the forearm of the dragon and then shook his head. He ripped flesh from the endless undead, but the dragon didn't even acknowledge the damage.

Xor breathed flames from his one hundred heads.

The explosion of fire lit up half of Fortuna. The endless undead cooked under the inferno blast.

Zaxis was there, evoking his ice at the stray flames, keeping them from our soldiers. He frosted over the roads, the nearby buildings, and even covered most of the docks in thick rime. Some of the undead soldiers got stuck in the ice, and others slipped and fell.

Lynus ran forward, through the flames of his eldrin, and then slammed his hand on the flesh of the corpse dragon. He unleashed his own flame evocation, blasting a charred hole into the beast's undead gut.

Despite their efforts, the endless undead *sprouted another head*. The bones *burst* out of the dragon's body, and then fleshy pieces of other creatures sewed themselves together, creating skin and muscle for the second dragon head. The golden glow seemed to make everything go faster...

The endless undead attacked both the fenris wolf and typhon beast at the same time. One head crunched down on

Vjorn, catching his back leg, and the other head sank its fangs into Xor, straight into his chest.

The typhon beast stopped evoking its torrent of flame.

Although the Autarch's army didn't have as many god-creatures as we did, his kirin's aura was giving all his eldrin untold strength. It was like each of the Autarch's god-creatures were worth *three* of ours.

Instead of helping with the endless undead, Terrakona and I charged for the Autarch's vessel. He stood on the bow, his gold kirin just behind him, with his weapon in hand.

Terrakona didn't need me to command him to kill the man —we both knew what we needed to do. Terrakona lunged forward, mouth open, fangs out.

The waters near the Autarch's beached ship rose up to greet us. They were waves filled with ghostly shapes. Whole people with tortured faces reached from the water and grabbed at anything and everything.

When Terrakona attempted to crunch his fangs down on the Autarch, the ghostly waters slammed him on both sides of the head. The specters couldn't tear through Terrakona's scales, but they did dig at his injured eye. Some even slipped into Terrakona's injury like only liquid could.

Rocked back and forth by the haunted waves, Terrakona missed his mark. He crashed into the ship's deck, cracking through the wooden hull. When he attempted to lift his head and go again, the Autarch slashed with his sword.

The blade caught part of Terrakona's mouth.

Just like Retribution, the blade slid through Terrakona with little effort, slicing off his tongue. The rune-covered appendage slammed onto a portion of the ruined ship.

Terrakona screeched and whipped his head back and forth.

"Watch for his strikes," I said as I held on to him. "Manipulate the terrain! Help the others if you can!"

Then I leapt off and landed on the very tip of the ship. The wood was half-shattered, and I almost tumbled onto the beach, but I managed to keep my balance.

The Autarch came rushing forward—he barely gave me a moment to catch my breath.

He swung with his sword, and I had nowhere to back up. I lifted Retribution, my heart hammering. What if the Autarch's blade went through mine? One strike could end me.

But when the Autarch's sword struck Retribution, a loud *clang* echoed into the night. The glowing green stars on my blade shone brighter than before, as though reacting to the presence of the apoch dragon.

I lifted my hand. A part of the beach became stone, and then it shot up through the hull of the ship and smashed the deck from underneath. I had been aiming for the gold kirin, but the majestic beast dodged long before the stone jutted out of the deck. And when it moved, it was like it weighed nothing—the diamond hooves glittered, and I swear the kirin walked on air and air alone.

But...

If I killed the gold kirin—a creature with no offensive magic for itself—the Autarch would lose the ability to bond with multiple creatures. When that happened, he would die. That was the outcome for arcanists who bonded with more than one creature—their soul was drained from them, and they swiftly withered to death.

And without the kirin, the Autarch couldn't empower his god-creatures. They would become weak, and we would win.

It was the easiest option to win the whole fight.

I evoked molten rock in the palm of my hand and then gushed it out across the ruined ship. There were barely any places to stand properly, and I figured we would tumble into the hold at any moment, but the deck remained partially intact.

Not anymore.

As soon as my magma hit the wood, flames and smoke sprouted up.

The Autarch manipulated the ghost waters again. They washed over the wrecked ship, snuffing out my magma and then rushing over me. The icy embrace of the ocean felt like death itself.

I gritted my teeth as the waves threatened to take me into the depths.

The ghosts...

They wailed in the water. Crying. Sobbing. Clinging to me as though they wanted to steal my life for their own. Their little hands gouged injuries into my flesh, cutting my arms, and my chest.

I evoked more magma. It exploded from me, dispelling the water in a haze of hot steam.

But then another wave hit, and it knocked me from the shattered ship. I landed on the sand of the beach, shoulder-first. With all the wind knocked out of me, I struggled to stand.

My aura slipped.

A pegasus arcanist overhead screamed and ruptured.

I closed my eyes and focused, my aura flickering back into place as I gulped down a panic-fueled breath. Despite the madness, I had to protect everyone from the plague. What if the endless undead vomited blood onto Illia? Or Evianna? Or any of the others in the Frith Guild?

If I failed to maintain my salvation aura, they would all instantly die.

Would the god-creatures die, too?

The new and improved plague—the one enhanced with the abyssal leech magic—was capable of infecting the god-creatures. It was possible that if they were in the armageddon aura too long, they would suffer the same fate as all the others.

Which meant I had to maintain it no matter what.

"Warlord."

I stood straight, Retribution in hand, Forfend still on my other arm. I had no other armor, though. No knightmare—no Luthair.

The Autarch strode toward me, his matte black armor unable to reflect the night sky or the glow of the fires all around us. I saw not an inch of skin. Just the imposing full suit of apoch dragon armor.

"You have stalled my plans and ambitions for some time, *Volke Savan*." The Autarch held his weapon close.

His gold kirin walked off the broken ship, but stayed in the air. It didn't fly, per se, but it walked on the breeze as though it were solid ground. The beast pranced around and then "landed" on the beach a good twenty feet behind its arcanist.

The Autarch was a fool for challenging me on the ground. I readied myself.

"This ends tonight," the Autarch said. "Cower before me."

"I'm not afraid of *you*."

"Words people have said to me many times," he replied, his tone cold and distorted through his helmet. "Often their last."

I manipulated the sands of the beach, hoping to catch the Autarch and pull him under. The ground beneath his feet shifted, and just as he was sinking, he yanked his leg up and then stepped onto the air as well. He just... walked, as though on an invisible staircase, off the ground.

It wasn't a kirin ability. It was the garuda bird's.

That wouldn't matter. I hardened the ground and stabbed upward with a slab of rock—targeting both the Autarch and his kirin.

The kirin leapt away, dodging it. Like it knew the attack had been coming.

The Autarch wasn't as lucky. The rock slammed into him, but once it did, I couldn't manipulate the rock any longer. It was his *armor*. Once the rock had touched his armor, it was like all the magic had been sucked right out of it.

With a flick of his wrist, the Autarch called forth more ghostly waters. A wave crashed across the beach, washing over me.

I lifted a wall of stone, cutting off the water. Although the ghosts clawed at me, I shook them off as I stumbled farther up the beach. Their wails and sobs lingered on my thoughts. For a brief moment, I thought I would switch from a salvation aura to an armageddon one, but I managed to maintain my magic.

Blood wept from several small injuries across my body. Were they from the ghosts? I barely felt anything.

"Warlord? I can come to your side."

Terrakona roared. I glanced up, and spotted him fighting with the endless undead. He and Vjorn had the god-creature pinned while the typhon beast was unleashing more fire. The wolf was burning under the heat, but Terrakona wasn't.

"Keep helping them," I said as I straightened myself.

The Autarch held out his hand, and light gathered in the palm of it. Just like with the garuda bird. Then he pointed his hand in my direction, and a beam of raw magic shot through the air, sailing straight for me.

I held up Forfend. The force of the blast caused me to stagger backward, but my shield absorbed the magic used. Then my shield glowed from within.

With gritted teeth, I aimed Forfend at the Autarch. The beam shot back at him. But when it hit his armor, it, too, stopped. The beam broke apart and disappeared. None of the Autarch was harmed.

He and his gold kirin stood in the air, just fifteen feet above the sandy beach.

"*Volke Savan*," the Autarch drawled, speaking my name as though it were venom on his tongue. "You're young. Confused. Brainwashed into fighting against me when you know nothing."

I tightened my grip on my sword. "You're wrong, Helvetti. I know more than you think. I know what you did. I know the suffering you've caused in the name of change. Your plague. Your plan to bring the god-creatures back. No one needed to *brainwash* me to fight against you."

"I once served the world as a healer," the Autarch said. "But I've seen the corruption lurking in the shadows—and I'm not talking about the plague."

"I don't care," I stated.

With as much magic as I could muster, I lifted a boulder under my feet and then leapt into the air. I went for the kirin, Retribution ready. But the Autarch moved into the way. When my sword struck his chest piece, the blade collided, and it didn't slice through.

Again, the stars on my weapon glowed.

I fell to the beach and tumbled. Once on my feet, I evoked molten rock and lobbed it at the kirin, hoping to burn a heart-sized hole through its chest.

The creature evaded the attack as though it knew the strike was coming. It danced to the side, its hooves glittering.

"I toiled away under the name of another," the Autarch stated. "A man who knew of hidden villages where rare creatures are kept secret. But once I found these villages, and learned of their ways, I realized that the most powerful magics were being squandered and kept from the world."

The gold kirin lifted its head, its mystical antlers sparkling, even at night.

Then I noticed the kirin wore an odd necklace made of pink flesh.

What was that?

The Autarch held out his hand again. "But no one changes anything in this world without power. And healers are considered some of the most powerless of them all. Well, I showed them, didn't I? Theasin and I crafted an arcane plague no one could *punch their way out of*. No one could *stab it* or *burn it* or *drown it in their magic*. I changed the world—I took away their power. And now I will make it right, and rule under no name but my own."

I really didn't know what he was talking about.

There were people in this world hoarding mystical creatures? Perhaps. And perhaps those people deserved the pain and anguish of the arcane plague, but everyone else didn't. Most didn't.

What about the hundreds of arcanists and their eldrin who were twisted and killed through insanity? Like Gregory Ruma? Or the ones who took their own life to avoid becoming a monster, like Forsythe? They didn't deserve that.

"*You'll answer for your crimes, Helvetti*. You had no right to harm the people you did!"

The Autarch's helmet revealed none of his emotions. His kirin snorted and shook its head.

"I had to tear it all down to start anew," the Autarch said, his voice lower, more confident. "Everything was corrupt. But now I've completed the many tasks I set out to do. The only step left is to rule the world, and change the unjust. Those *crimes* you speak of will be nothing more than tragedies if you kill me. But if I rule, and make everything grand, those *sacrifices* will be remembered in monuments and song as the building blocks to a better future."

I mulled over his statements, thinking back to the times I had no power to change what I thought unfair.

I had thought the Autarch would be a lot like Theasin, who saw everyone as an inferior that needed to stay quiet and do what he told them to do. Helvetti was different. He thought he was making everything better for everyone.

"The winner of this conflict writes the history books, Volke Savan. And when I write the next one, you will be portrayed as the villain you are. Brainwashed. Lazy. Arrogant to think you know what's best. You allow corruption to dwell in the darkness.

You're a champion of apathy—a steward for the least amount of change."

As soon as he said the last of his words, I knew how I felt about them.

"It's so much easier to destroy than it is to create," I said as I widened my stance. "Villainous people—stupid people—care only about what they want, and wreck everything they touch. Great people—*real* leaders—build things so amazing, they elevate us all. You say there's corruption in the darkness? You should've built a light so bright it casts it all away. Instead, you brought nothing but darkness with you."

"My rulership—my magic—will cast all the darkness away."

"Are you serious? *I've seen how you handle things!* You think someone who murdered hundreds, destroyed the lives of thousands, and indirectly harmed millions has the capacity to dispel darkness? If you can justify these heinous actions now, you'll justify them again whenever you need! You have no remorse!"

"Heh. Worthless words spoken by someone who has never attempted change on a grand level. I'm old enough to know you must destroy your opposition before you can create something new—lest they become termites that eat away at your efforts. You, Warlord, are one such termite."

"I can't wait to see your tombstone," I said with a smirk. "*Here lies a man killed by a single termite.*"

A little graveyard humor. William would've appreciated it.

But the Autarch didn't.

He kept his hand out. "I apologize, Warlord. But I'll be taking your soul now."

Chapter 48

The Grand Finale

The Autarch dragged his fingers through the air.

Something tugged at my insides. I knew the Autarch had some ability he had been saving. And when my chest twisted and hurt, I remembered the terrible sensations of the abyssal leech. What was this? Could the Autarch really take my soul?

I manipulated the terrain.

All of it.

Stones flew upward, some jagged, some so large, they could wreck whole buildings. I cut off line of sight with the Autarch, and the pain in my chest subsided.

A crash of broken stone drew my attention. I whirled around to find the abyssal kraken had destroyed some of my barriers out in the bay. More ghost waters rushed up to greet me. The specters attempted to drag me out to sea, like a violent undertow that wanted my life.

"Terrakona!" I shouted.

The world serpent, with all his might, slammed through a portion of Fortuna—the fastest route to me, a straight line—and crashed onto the beach. Terrakona roared, his scales flaring.

Then he snaked his tail into the ghost waters, offering me a way out. I grabbed on to him, and Terrakona lifted me onto his back.

The endless undead tossed the fenris wolf away, and then clawed the typhon beast hard enough to send it tumbling into a nearby bakery. The corpse dragon turned and also crashed onto the beach. Its roar was an answer to Terrakona's, though it was a ghastly sound akin to a wail.

When the endless undead vomited blood from its two heads, a shimmering barrier snapped up around Terrakona. Another one specifically shielded me. The blood splashed away.

I glanced around.

Liet was near the beach—and so was Zelfree.

With a smirk, Zelfree waved his hand. A blast of air went straight for the Autarch and his gold kirin. The gale-force winds almost sent the two of them tumbling.

Then I saw it. Zelfree's eldrin. Traces, the mimic, was actually three mystical creatures fused together. This was the mimic's aura—*the chimera aura*.

The bizarre creature had the wings of a roc, the body of a pyroclastic dragon, and the fins of a sea turtle. Traces's three heads represented each creature she was borrowing magic from. A dragon, a turtle, and a bird. It was a freakish monstrosity, but when she was combined like this, Zelfree had access to the magic of all three creatures at once.

The Autarch shot a beam of magic at him.

Zelfree blocked with a shimmering barrier. Then he shot molten rock all across the beach. He had been aiming for the Autarch, but missed and instead splashed the endless undead.

"Your aura is stable?" I shouted down to him.

"Of course it is," Zelfree replied, smiling wide.

He had never successfully manifested his aura before...

But now wasn't the time for that.

Lynus and Xor smashed their way onto the beach. A blast of

flame cooked more of the endless undead. Then Zaxis arrived. His ice swept over the corpse dragon, slowing the beast down.

Using the winds of roc magic, Zelfree took to the air. He flew for the Autarch and evoked more magma. When the molten rock touched the Autarch's armor, it hardened into stone and then fell harmlessly to the beach.

No magic would pierce the Autarch's armor.

Zelfree must have come to the same conclusion as I had. He aimed the magma at the gold kirin. The majestic horse moved out of the way of the attack, though, allowing magma to spill onto the sands below it.

Terrakona hissed and then lunged for the kirin. He crunched his fangs down, but didn't catch the beast.

Why?

Could it just predict our actions?

Just as I was about to order Terrakona to bring me closer, Orwyn shot through the air on her kirin. They flew to the beach, the sparkling silver scales of her mount a welcome sight. Out of all the god-arcanists, she could allow *everyone* to fly.

"Warlord!" she cried. "I'm here. I... I can help."

She touched her hand to the neck of her kirin. The horse-like creature reared back, even while in the sky, and lifted its front legs. A silvery glow wrapped itself around Orwyn—and also around a portion of the sky.

The four-winged colossal bird...

With the silvery glow, I was able to make out its shape and size. The sky titan was otherworldly.

The god-creature was being empowered by Orwyn's kirin.

Winds rushed over all of Fortuna. The pegasus arcanists flew higher and faster than ever before. Devlin's roc evoked winds with no equal. The roar of a hurricane surrounded us all. The sky titan's abilities allowed it to keep the garuda bird grounded, even from its position on the beach.

And it even did the same for the Autarch and his gold kirin.

Both were forced to the ground as the winds picked up speed.

Zelfree blasted them with wind. Lynus evoked fire that mixed with the gale. The Autarch shielded his kirin with his body, but that wasn't entirely enough. His gold kirin was burned.

If we were relentless, the beast *couldn't* dodge.

When the ghost waters came, Zelfree and Liet used their barriers to keep them away from us.

Zaxis used more of his ice on the endless undead. His winter, combined with the winds, held the beast down. The pressure and the frigid cold were too much. Xor turned his many heads on the corpse dragon. They wanted it dead.

I pointed Terrakona forward. We rushed to meet the Autarch and challenge him on the beach, but just as we moved a few feet toward our target, a tentacle lifted out of the ocean. With hook claws, and a golden glow, the creature lashed out at Orwyn and her kirin.

In one brutal blow, the kraken sliced through most of the fragile kirin, and even through some of Orwyn's body.

They were thrown onto the streets of Fortuna. They hit the cracked stone walkways, bones shattering.

As quickly as it had started, the howling hurricane came to an end.

While everyone turned to see her fall, the Autarch blasted both Zelfree and Lynus with a beam of raw magic, sending them to the sands. The fire ceased. The powerful winds stopped.

"*Kill the traitor*," the Autarch shouted.

The endless undead turned both its dragon heads toward Orwyn and her downed kirin.

Even the garuda bird smashed his way closer to us.

Through the quaking of the city, the rumble of war, the crash of the waves, the shouts of commands, I never saw Akiva arrive on the battlefield until he was right behind the Autarch and his gold kirin. Perhaps if I hadn't been distracted, I would've sensed his movements, but there were thousands of people here, and I had long ago stopped tracking.

Akiva grabbed the gold kirin, his palm laced with deadly venom.

"You won't lay another finger on Orwyn," he said, his voice barely loud enough for me to hear.

And he used his king basilisk venom…

The gold kirin instantly died. It slumped forward and collapsed onto the beach, its beautiful scales and antlers still sparkling, even as a corpse.

The Autarch wouldn't die right away. His soul would be sapped by the hunger of his god-creatures. He would wither and fade, but it was only a matter of time. If he wasn't bonded to his kirin, there was no saving him now.

Our victory was an inevitability.

The preeminence aura faded. The golden glow around the god-creatures was wiped away.

The Autarch dropped his sword and grabbed at his head. He shook it as violently as a madman. I thought he might break and turn to lunacy.

"*What are you doing?*" he shouted. "*The gall!* I… I can't believe it's come to this!"

The next few moments caught me by surprise.

With the rage of the fallen, the ocean rushed onto land. It wasn't a wave or a tsunami, it was as if someone had tilted the whole world sideways, and the water was simply being pulled by gravity along its new route.

The ghosts lingered in the waters…

They clawed at Terrakona.

"Warlord… they're parasites sapping my strength."

The world serpent thrashed and attempted to rid himself of the poltergeists, but nothing worked. The ghosts were incorporeal. Terrakona evoked magma, and it splashed into the waters, but they were endless, fed by the ocean itself. And they were rising.

Terrakona struggled to move.

I tried to lift more stone—to create a wall to protect us—but each boulder and rock wall I created, the water just rushed over. The ocean itself was spilling onto land. How could I stop it?

When Akiva tried to attack the Autarch, the endless undead intervened.

The corpse dragon sloshed through the haunted waters and swung a rotted claw. It struck Akiva, piercing him through the gut. The dragon slammed him into a broken section of pier and then moved closer to his arcanist.

The water…

It didn't touch the Autarch. It flowed around him in a circle. His dead kirin was also unaffected.

The ghosts floated from the ocean, creating a hazy mist that now swirled over every inch of Fortuna.

It had all happened so quickly, I wasn't even sure it was the Autarch who was solely making it happen. Was this a power of the abyssal kraken?

Was this… the abyssal hells?

"You're all fools!" the Autarch shouted, his voice threatening to crack. "*I can't believe what you're making me do.*"

The pink necklace around the gold kirin's neck giggled and writhed. Was it alive?

A second later, it popped.

The slug-like slime that burst outward on the kirin reminded me of the soul forge. The Second Ascension had taken the body of the soul forge right after it died. I had always figured it was to make trinkets and artifacts with, but I hadn't seen anything crafted from the beast's flesh.

Until right now.

What was it doing?

"I didn't want to kill everyone here!" the Autarch yelled. He sounded more unstable the longer he spoke. With unsteady hands, he picked his weapon back up. "You all... don't understand. I'm the only one who can kill the apoch dragon. If you kill *me*, you'll all suffer! That dragon will tear you all apart!"

I slid off Terrakona, but the mist in the air was sapping my strength just as much as it was sapping Terrakona.

Weakened by the hellish environment, Zelfree collapsed to his knees, the waters already to his chest. His mimic... she broke apart. He lost his chimera aura to the ghastly wails of the ghosts' leeching abilities.

Traces plummeted from the sky in her cat form.

And that was when the Autarch's gold kirin stood back up. The odd necklace had been a piece of the soul forge—crafted to help the Autarch make sure his kirin wasn't killed. But now the necklace was broken.

Our inevitable victory was slipping from our fingers.

The kirin glanced around as though in a daze.

The Autarch stomped forward. The water parted for him, never slowing his steps. He swung his blade at Liet. She evoked a barrier, but it did nothing. The weapon cut right through her magic, and then right through her chest.

Liet shouted and then fell into the waters.

And she never emerged.

I evoked magma, heating the waves around me. My molten rock sizzled as steam rose into the air, but my magic wasn't enough to evaporate the whole ocean.

When the Autarch lifted his hand, he aimed at Zelfree.

Lynus, even while weakened by the abyssal waters, lunged. He slammed into Zelfree, protecting him from the raw blast of magic. The two of them tumbled into the waters. They, too, disappeared beneath the ghostly waves.

The endless undead, unaffected by the waters, slammed into Zaxis, and with its other head, crunched its fangs onto the fenris wolf.

Xor tried to fight it, and they were caught in a tangle of undead flesh, but it wasn't enough.

The garuda bird was near…

But it was just me and Terrakona left to face the Autarch.

I held Retribution close. The Autarch turned to me.

"I had it all planned," he said with a rasp. "Theasin helped. The Second Ascension made it *real*. All I need… is to kill you all… and take my place as the one final god-arcanist."

I couldn't find the strength to speak. Instead, I focused on maintaining my aura, and on maintaining my ability to stand.

"The apoch dragon… I can kill it. But not *you*. You're just doomed to repeat the same *idiotic cycle*. You're a simpleton. This is all your doing. All of this. Everyone's demise—it's on your head."

With my teeth gritted, I exhaled. Then a plan struck me.

I waved my hand, manipulating the ground. I didn't elevate the ground—I opened it up.

A quake hit all of Fortuna. Buildings crumbled. The water stirred, becoming violent waves. But then my mini canyon opened through the middle of the city. The ghost-infested waters spilled into it.

The little canyon cracked outward to the beach, sucking up the water like a dehydrated man in the desert. It rushed away from me and Terrakona, and the moment the ghastly specters weren't clawing at my body, I felt better.

Terrakona, too, shook off the fatigue.

The quaking stopped.

My magic…

I was at my limits.

The Autarch stomped forward, his fell blade in hand. He swung for Terrakona, but I stepped in the way and answered his swing with my own blade. Our weapons clashed.

I opened another small hole around the Autarch's feet. I couldn't hit him with rocks, because his armor would drain the magic, but he wasn't immune to holes. He stumbled, but only for a second. Then he stepped onto the air. Without Orwyn keeping him grounded, he could fly, but that wasn't what I was trying to do.

I yelled, "Terrakona!"

My eldrin knew me well.

The Autarch had been distracted and fumbled.

Terrakona slithered around me and went straight for the confused kirin.

The Autarch shot a beam of magic. It crashed against Terrakona's scales, but it didn't damage him much.

And Terrakona bit down on the gold kirin, crunching it completely in one deadly strike. Twice in one battle, the creature had died.

"Once again, our victory is inevitable," I said.

The mists swirled around us, the ghostly faces enraged.

The Autarch was so angry, he couldn't seem to speak. He charged at me. Our blades clashed, but mine... Mine was different. The glow of the green stars across the blade of Retribution grew brighter whenever the Autarch was close.

And Retribution cracked the Autarch's armor.

When we clashed a third time, I looked for even a small opening in the armor. It was made of bone, not metal, and pieced together to fit a human. These weren't whole bones, they were fragments taken from the previous apoch dragon.

One more clash, and I realized the helmet was separate from the rest, not as secure.

I realized... that if I swung as hard as I could... and managed to connect with my desired location... it might break away.

With Retribution glowing bright, I stepped away from the Autarch.

"You'll never rule anything, not even the abyssal hells," I taunted.

With anger that bordered on the deranged, the Autarch charged.

And then I swung. It was a large arc, too heavy to correct. If I missed—or if I was incorrect in my assessment—the Autarch would surely stab me once I was off balance.

My aim was true.

I hit the Autarch right at the base of his neck, where his armor seemed the weakest. My sword glowed, empowered by knightmare and world serpent magic.

And then the blade broke through.

I decapitated the Autarch.

I stumbled forward, my heart beating fast.

The Autarch had swung his blade, too. And it had gone through me as easily as I thought it would.

Chapter 49

Architect

Forfend had been buckled to my left arm, but it hadn't been strong enough to resist a blade made from the bones of the apoch dragon.

The Autarch had sliced through my left arm, and then through my chest. My arm dangled by my side, not completely severed. But I didn't really care. I hit my knees on the sand as I gulped down air.

The Autarch's armageddon aura ended.

The mists cleared.

The ocean rushed back to its rightful place.

The army of undead soldiers became nothing more than cadavers once again.

It was hard to concentrate. Thankfully, Terrakona returned to my side. A kirin limb hung from his mouth, like Terrakona was a child who hadn't fully slurped up all their noodles.

"Warlord?" Terrakona leaned his snout down and touched my head. **"Fret not. I will take you to a healer."**

Where were the others? What were they doing? Was everyone okay? I couldn't go to a healer yet. I couldn't sleep. I had to maintain my salvation aura, lest they die.

"The threats have gone, Warlord. We won."

It was hard to take in. Especially since I was losing so much blood. I wobbled back and forth, my vision tunneling.

"Make sure Evianna is okay," was the last thing I said before I fell back onto the beach.

When I woke, I was in an infirmary. A single room with a bed all to myself. I recognized the place. It belonged to Gillie, the Grand Apothecary. But the windows were cracked—some shattered completely—and the walls looked ready to collapse. If someone sneezed, the roof might crush us all.

A short woman dressed in a crisp yellow, blue, and white robe stood next to my bed.

Gillie.

Her short golden hair had been pulled back in a tight ponytail, and her eyes had laugh lines at the edges. With one bright smile, she erased my worries. Why would she be this happy, unless we had won?

Her arcanist star had the image of a caladrius woven throughout it, and I knew I was in good hands. No other creature had healing abilities quite like the caladrius.

"Volke," she said with a cheery disposition. "Don't worry. You'll be able to use the arm."

I held my breath for a moment as her words sank in. Then I tried to move my arms, fearful I would find nothing when I did so. Fortunately, I was able to lift the blankets and toss them aside. After a long exhale, I rested back on the pillow.

My left arm was slightly more discolored compared to the other, and it felt numb, but it was still there. And it worked, if just a little slower than the other. I smiled to myself, thankful the fight with the Autarch hadn't cost me my life.

But thinking of lives sent a lance of pain through my chest.

"Is Evianna okay?" I asked.

Gillie walked over to a heavy desk that had been toppled over. A stack of paperwork sat on the side of the leg, like someone had just started using the deck without fixing it. The desk itself appeared to be carved from a single piece of oak wood, so I understood. It probably weighed hundreds of pounds.

"I have a report sent from the field medics here," Gillie said. She straightened the paperwork. "Evianna, you say? The knightmare arcanist registered with the Frith Guild?" Gillie slid her finger down the parchment.

Then she reached the end.

My heart sank. I couldn't breathe.

"She's alive," Gillie suddenly said with a wide smile. With a wave of her hand, she added, "*I'm* here, dear boy. Her injuries were minor."

I exhaled so loudly that chips of the ceiling sprinkled around us. A crack grew larger on the far wall.

"I can't believe you did that," I breathed.

"I apologize. In my line of work, I like to revel in the good news." Gillie hurried back over to my bed, the report still clutched in her hand.

"And Illia?"

"She's fine, of course."

"The members of the Frith Guild?"

"All accounted for. Liet had some major wounds, but she pulled through."

"The other god-arcanists?"

"Some of them were more injured than others… But they're all okay." Gillie frowned. "Well, except one…"

I turned to her. "Orwyn?" I whispered.

"Ah, yes. The sky titan arcanist. I'm afraid… her kirin didn't make it through the battle."

The news hurt, but not as much as Orwyn's death would've.

When Gillie didn't say anything else, I exhaled and rested on the pillow once again.

"What about the soldiers?" I asked.

"Ah. Well. There I have some bad news." Gillie walked around to the other side of my bed. She riffled through some of the papers, reading more of the reports. "Mortals don't heal like arcanists do, I'm afraid. Many died out in the streets—both those on our side, and those of the enemy. Many Fortuna citizens perished as well."

"How many soldiers did we lose?"

"Nearly all of them. This report says two thousand."

That was... devastating. I stared at the ceiling of the infirmary, worried for the families of the soldiers. I would need to write to Queen Ladislava.

"And the people of Fortuna?" I asked.

"We don't know the exact number yet." Gillie took a seat and scooted close to the edge of the bed. "Liet told me to watch over you until your strength returned."

"I have orders to give," I said as I forced myself to sit up. "I can rest here, but you need to send a messenger."

"For what purpose?"

"The corpses of the Autarch's god-creatures... I want them collected. As fast as possible. I don't want the enemy to have them, and scavengers shouldn't be allowed near the remains."

Gillie stood. "Oh. Of course."

"And... about the city..." I turned to her, my brow furrowed. "How bad is the destruction?"

"Very bad." Gillie crinkled the papers a bit a she fidgeted with them. "I apologize, but most of it came from the destruction of the center square. A fissure opened, and the hill the city is built on couldn't handle it. Several homes and businesses sank into the ground."

"R-Right. Well... please send word that I'll rebuild Fortuna. Maybe not here. In a new location. Better than before."

"Of course. I'll let everyone know."

It didn't take me long to recover. And while I had a new city to build, and an army to help recover, I needed to speak with someone first.

Evianna and I rode on Terrakona. We went south from the ruins of Fortuna and straight for the Clawdam Mountains. I wanted to say that once the Autarch had died, every nation surrendered to me and the other god-arcanists, but that wasn't the case.

Which meant we'd have more warring to do, but it wouldn't be anywhere near as bad as with the Autarch. And if I was diplomatic enough, perhaps we could avoid any more bloodshed altogether.

From what I understood, many nations feared my power, which was understandable. I would just have to convince them I wanted to make the world a better place. Which was why I needed to speak with Adelgis.

Ellios was a beautiful city. As soon as Terrakona, Evianna, Layshl, and I arrived, I breathed in the deep and luscious smell of the evergrow forests. Terrakona brought us closer to the city, where we were met with cheers. I waved to the citizens, but we ultimately went straight for the university.

Terrakona lowered his head at the edge of the massive garden that surrounded the building of learning. I slid off, and then Evianna joined me on the ground. Fortunately, I didn't have to go searching anywhere. The students and professors all pointed and shouted at my arrival.

Adelgis and Fain exited the building moments later, both surprised to see me.

No doubt, news of the battle in Fortuna had reached them. Everyone here knew—the Second Ascension was no more.

"Volke!" Adelgis hurried across the garden. He wore university robes and a cap worn by past graduates. They were ivory white and laced with frills. When he neared, Adelgis smiled wide. "Thank the good stars you're okay."

Fain walked up behind Adelgis. "The Autarch perished? You're certain?"

I nodded once. "Why wouldn't he have died?"

"I don't know... I just worried. I had nightmares about the abyssal kraken protecting him. About them being together in the abyssal hells."

"It was your fears painting themselves out in your mind," Adelgis said matter-of-factly. He held up a finger. "You should let go of your fear of the Autarch. Now that his organization is gone, what does it matter if the man is in the abyssal hells or not? He's just one man."

I stepped forward. "Adelgis?"

He glanced over. "Hm? Yes?"

"Speaking of being *just one man*..." I rubbed at the back of my neck with my right arm, mulling over my fight with the Autarch. "I was thinking that I want to build more things. I want to, uh... make the world better. But I need your help."

"My help?" Adelgis pointed to himself. "Why me?"

"I want to know where to start. And maybe... help me design things to build. Forests. Rivers. Schools. Cities. Ports. I want... to be a light. To lift everyone up."

I had scolded the Autarch because his solution to the problem had been to burn everything down. What had I built to help the world? Only a few things. I needed to do more. I *wanted* to do more. I wanted to be a light that chased away the darkness, even long after I was gone.

Rivers brought life.

Schools brought knowledge.

Markets brought wealth.

I could make these things with my world serpent magic. I *would* make them.

"Will you help me?" I asked.

Adelgis nodded once. "Well, I'm glad you spoke with me, because I have many ideas for the future, if you'll listen."

"Of course. Now that the Second Ascension has been dealt with, I feel like... I have more time for everything."

Chapter 50

Birthday Ghosts

A lot happened in ten years.

Time sailed on, even when I didn't want it to.

Ten whole years… I tried to build as much as possible. To make good on my words.

At least it was mostly a peaceful time, outside the few battles we fought to subdue enemy nations. Probably why it vanished so quickly.

I wanted to say my children woke me in the morning—when they entered my bedroom giggling like madmen—but that would've been a lie. I had been awake for several minutes, an odd anxious sensation clawing around my gut.

I kept my eyes closed as a little one approached the side of my bed. She couldn't stifle her mirth. With tiny giggles, she tiptoed to me and then gently patted my cheek.

"Dad," she whispered. "*Dad.* Wake up." Another giggle. "*Daaad*. Look what I am!"

I slowly opened my eyes, pretending to wake for the first

time. Standing next to my bed was my middle child, Rylee. For some reason, she wore a blue sheet over her body. Two eyeholes had been cut into it, but they were so far apart, only one of Rylee's eyes could glance out of the costume at a time.

Rylee laughed as she lifted her arms.

"Boo!" she said.

Her eyes were purplish-blue, just like her mother's. Rylee's hair—as black as mine—was tangled underneath the sheet. Some of her locks poked through the other eye hole.

"What is this?" I said as I feigned surprise. I sat up in my bed. "A *ghost*? Am I being haunted? Or are you a mystical creature?"

Rylee giggled as she twirled around. She was only five years old, but already she loved life more than anything else. "I'm a *birthday ghost!* Because it's your birthday."

My oldest child huffed as he walked over. He, too, wore a blue sheet. His eyeholes matched, but he kept his arms crossed and his shoulders slightly slumped. William—we just called him *Will*—never really liked dressing up.

"I'm sorry, Dad," Will muttered. "I tried to tell her to do something else, but you know Rylee."

Will was seven and already so much bigger than his sister. He stood a foot taller, but he had all the stockiness of a lamppost. He rolled his eyes when Rylee spun around a second time.

"I don't know," I playfully said. "I kinda like birthday ghosts."

Will narrowed his eyes at me. "C'mon. Really? What even is a *birthday ghost*? That's just silly."

I rubbed my chin. "Perhaps they're the ghost of birthdays past?"

"So, the birthdays *died*? It's just not very realistic." Will glanced down at his sister. "I told her we should dress up like knightmares, because you would like that, but she just insisted on this birthday ghost idea..."

Rylee stopped spinning. Although I couldn't see much of

her face, it was obvious she was smiling from ear to ear. "Birthday ghosts are here to celebrate, too!"

"She's very creative," I said to Will. I leaned forward, my blankets and bed warm, but my anxiety grew with each passing moment. Nothing was wrong, but something wasn't right, either.

"She doesn't have to be *this* creative," Will mumbled. He motioned to Rylee.

His sister grabbed her costume and spun it around her body. "See? I'm transforming!"

I held up a finger. "Creativity. Without it, we cannot express our heart's deepest wonders." I smiled as I added, "Life is too sorrow-filled to chase away imagination. You'll understand when you're older."

Will pulled off his ghost sheet. His eyes matched Evianna's—purple and blue in even amounts—but his hair was even stranger than his mother's. Black, but with a single streak of white along the side. His sisters sometimes teased him by calling him *Old Man Will*, but I liked it. I once told him it reminded me of a scar, and from that day out, that was the story Will told others. It was his *hair scar*.

"Well, we were supposed to surprise you with a present, but Lyvia is taking forever." Will sighed. His skin was darker tanned, like mine. The girls had a complexion that was a mix of mine and Evianna's.

"Four-year-olds work at their own speed," I said.

As if summoned by our conversation about her, my third child—my youngest—slowly made her way into my bedroom. It was a large space, with a sitting area, a fireplace, a bed, and a series of drawers. Lyvia carried a small glass vase with pink roses poking out the top. Water sloshed inside with each step she took.

She wore a birthday ghost costume like the others, but hers was a little too long. She half-stepped on her blue sheet each little bit of the trek.

Lyvia made it past the drawers, and then toward my bed. Will became tenser and tenser with each of her steps, like he wanted to rush over and take the vase from Lyvia before she dropped it. But he didn't. He waited, giving her all the time she needed for this task, which I appreciated.

Rylee giggled and twirled again. When she finally noticed her sister, she stopped and waved. "Oh, Lyvia! Hi. You brought the flowers! Yay!"

Although Lyvia also wore a sheet that covered most of her face, I practically heard her smiling. She loved to do things like *all the grownups*.

"Dad!" Lyvia shouted—way too loud for my bedroom. "Look! I brought your present!"

But just as she was about to walk around the corner of my bed and give it to me, she stepped on her ghost sheet and tripped.

The vase flew forward and smashed on the stone floor, the pink flowers scattering everywhere. Lyvia was on her stomach, her arms stretched out.

Rylee and Will froze in place, their eyes wide, their breath held.

I tossed off my blankets, but at the same moment, Lyvia leapt from the floor. She tore off her birthday ghost sheet and ran out the door, her sobbing muffled by her strangled breathing.

Unlike my other children, Lyvia had white hair as beautiful as Evianna's. It fluttered behind her when she ran, twigs and leaves all throughout. She must've picked the flowers from the garden herself.

"I'm s-sorry, Dad." Will knelt and gathered up the broken pieces of the vase. "I should've just done it."

"There's no need to apologize," I said as I stood from the bed. I scratched at my trousers and glanced around for my clothes. The feeling of anxiety never left me. It wasn't related to the vase or the flowers. It was something else.

Rylee pulled off her ghost sheet and knelt next to her brother. She reached for some of the stray pieces of the vase.

"D-Don't," Will said. He pushed her hand away before Rylee grabbed anything. "You'll cut yourself. See? The edges of the vase are sharp." He gently picked one up to show her. "I've got this."

"But I want to help," Rylee whispered. She placed her hands on her knees and stared at her brother with big eyes.

"You can get the flowers. But be careful because they might have thorns, okay?"

Rylee smiled and nodded. Then she carefully—and gently—picked up the flower petals and stems. With delicate motions, she gathered them in a little pile, and even whispered reassuring things to them, as if telling the flowers it wasn't their fault they had made a mess.

"I'm going to go speak with your sister," I said as I grabbed a tunic from the top of my drawer and pulled it over my head. My pendant and betrothal shell *clinked* as I moved them around. "I'll be right back."

"Okay," Will said.

Rylee offered me a smile as I headed for the door. "We'll have a better present for you later!"

With a chuckle, I headed out the door and into the hallway. My home wasn't as large as the estate I used to have in Fortuna. It was a modest manse overlooking a small forest on the eastern tip of the mainland. When I walked by the windows, I caught sight of the glorious ocean—and of islands far off in the distance.

I appreciated my home. I had built it with Evianna, and filled it with love when we had our children. It was just close enough to a city and port that we could see people from all over the world, but just far enough away from everything that it was quiet.

Despite how much I enjoyed staring out the windows, and walking the halls, or listening to my children giggle, my anxiety had blossomed into dread.

This was a wonderful day.

But I knew I had somewhere I needed to be, and that knowledge frightened me.

With my tremor sense, I knew exactly where Lyvia was hiding. She had run into the kitchen, and crawled into a cupboard. Her sobbing pained me, even if it was silly. There was no need to cry over the broken vase. I could always make another.

I entered the kitchen and slowly made my way over to the cupboard. No one was here—I suspected Evianna had gathered our friends and family in the local port town to surprise me—and the quiet atmosphere only made it possible to hear Lyvia's muffled sobs.

I sat down in front of the cupboard, but I didn't open it.

"I wonder if there are any birthday ghosts in here," I said, probably too loud.

"Go away," Lyvia whispered. Then she sniffled. "I just mess up everything."

"Hm? Is that a ghost I hear?"

The cupboard door opened with a creak. Lyvia peeked out the tiny sliver of an opening. Her eyes matched the others. Purplish-blue and beautiful.

"I'm not a birthday ghost, Dad," she said.

I leaned against the other cupboard door and shook my head. "Why's that?"

"Because... I'm bad at it."

"Oh, really? That's not how I see it." I smiled as I said, "I think you're one step closer to becoming a *master* birthday ghost."

Lyvia half-giggled. Then she wiped some of the tears from her eyes. "How?"

"Well, because now you know that birthday ghost sheets can't be too long. If they touch the floor, you'll trip."

Lyvia gently pushed open the cupboard door. She poked her head out and smiled, even if her lip still quavered. "Y-Yeah."

"Now that you know that, you can improve the design. You can make an even better birthday ghost costume. And *if* you make another mistake, you'll learn another *new* way to improve things. Until one day, you're a master birthday ghost, because you've learned so much."

"Really?"

Lyvia slid out of the cupboard and then sat on the kitchen floor next to me. Again, she rubbed at her eyes—and the rest of her face—until all the tears were dispelled.

"Yes, really." I scooped her up and hugged her close. "That's the essence of progression. Learning and improving, one step at a time."

"Happy birthday, Dad," Lyvia whispered into my shoulder. She tried to give me a big strong hug, but four-year-olds weren't built like a bear trap.

I chuckled as I hugged her back. "Well, if you're feeling better, I think we should meet up with your mother." I stood, keeping her in my arms. "I think a trio of birthday ghosts needs to visit me during breakfast."

Lyvia giggled and wrapped her arms around my neck. "Okay! But I need to make my ghost costume better first."

"Of course."

The feeling of dread never left me. Not while I ate breakfast, not during my magic practice during the day, nor with Evianna. It only grew worse. And more urgent.

I needed to go.

"So, I was thinking we could go into town later tonight," Evianna said.

I sat on the end of our bed, my feet on the floor, my attention on the far window. Sunshine streamed in through the glass, illuminating everything with cheer and warmth.

Evianna slipped into a long black dress. It was fluid and seemed like it was made of the shadows themselves. She smoothed the stray creases and then fluffed her wavy white hair. She was so athletic, so strong, so gorgeous, and so loving when she turned her attention to me. Why wasn't there a single word that captured all of that? Or perhaps there was, and it was *Evianna*.

The runes on her arms and neck sparkled green and red. She wore no sleeves, likely to show them off.

"Have you finished helping Adelgis build the Astra Academy?" she asked as she took a seat next to me.

I nodded once. "I have, but there's still more to be done. He wants instructors—really skilled individuals—and a way to get people to the academy who might not otherwise have an opportunity to get there."

"Really?" Evianna's eyebrows lifted. "That's admirable."

"I like all his plans. I told him I wanted to build things—to create—and he really came through on his end. Can you imagine all the arcanists who will go through there?"

"Are you going to teach them all the steps of the Pillar?" She lifted an eyebrow. "Let me guess. It's a requirement to graduate."

I rubbed at the back of my neck and chuckled. "No, sadly. I mean, I *did* build the lessons into the school at odd places. But they're hidden. I mean, a clever kid will find them."

Evianna leaned in close to me and kissed my shoulder. "What about the nations near the Sunset Desert and the Amber Dunes? Did you finish making them rivers?"

"I did, yeah. Months ago."

"And what about the islands? Didn't you say you wanted to make them bigger, and expand them further east?"

I had been meaning to do that, but I hadn't yet. There were so many other things that took priority. The rivers to the desert brought life where there had previously been none. I had split forests, to allow for travel, but also to keep the trees. I had rearranged mountains, and created tunnels, and even dams or lakes when there hadn't been any previously.

So much to do...

And still, the dread lingered.

Someone was waiting for me.

"Volke?"

"Yes, love?" I answered absentmindedly.

"Is something wrong?"

Her words sent ice down my spine. But how was I supposed to respond? *I've had a really bad feeling all day.* Some part of me didn't want to say, though. Like telling her would only cause distress.

"I think I need to do something before we go into town tonight," I muttered.

Evianna tilted her head. "Oh? What do you need to do on your birthday? Surely it can wait."

"I don't think it can."

I stood and headed for the wardrobe. Evianna watched me as I grabbed my coat, my shield, and my sword. Then I pulled on my boots and turned around.

"I'll try to make it back in time," I said with a smile.

She must've known I was feeling odd, because she didn't say anything. Instead, Evianna just nodded, her attention on my weapon.

I didn't normally take Retribution with me when I did *pleasant* activities.

"The kids will miss you if you go," Evianna finally said, as if trying to persuade me to stay. "*I'll* miss you."

"I'll miss you all, too. But I'm sure everyone will live if I sneak away for a bit."

"Just for a bit, though, right?"

I didn't answer.

For some reason, the words wouldn't come to me. Would I be back in a bit? Shaken by my own thoughts, I walked over to Evianna, kissed her goodbye, and smiled. She stared up at me, her confusion evident, but it didn't mar her beauty. Nothing ever would.

Then I left, drawn by the dread that tugged me toward a single destination.

Chapter 51

Eternal Stars

Terrakona waited for me in the bay near our mountain home.

He was humongous. The length of a large city, perhaps more. His crystal mane was practically a forest that grew around his head, and even halfway down his back. Crystals hung from his chin, reminding me of a beard—or perhaps stalactites.

Each breath Terrakona exhaled warmed the area around him. The ocean was calmed when he waded through it, though. His emerald scales were brilliant underwater, sparkling brighter than ever before.

A thousand people could easily ride on his back, if they wanted to. Most people were too afraid, however. Terrakona was quite imposing.

I walked to the beach, and Terrakona waited for me in the water.

"Warlord," he telepathically said, his tone melancholy. **"It's time."**

I didn't ask what he meant. In my heart, I already knew.

Terrakona craned his neck, and then lowered his head. I could fit in one of his nostrils, no problem. Instead, I grabbed the tip of his snout and allowed him to lift me into the air. Then I climbed onto his nose and walked back to his mane.

"Take us there," I said.

"Have you said your farewells?"

"I... don't think it's necessary." I patted the crystals of his mane. "Just take us there. Please."

With a low growl that rumbled the waters and even the beach, Terrakona slid away from the shore and headed west. I didn't have to give him instructions. Terrakona knew where to go. The feeling of dread—and the tug toward a location—was shared by him as well.

"You once told me that you wanted to find Luthair."

"Maybe he's happy with another arcanist somewhere," I muttered as the ocean winds whipped through my hair. "Biyu was the last to master her salvation aura, and once she did, our magic reached every corner of the world. If he's still alive, he's been cured of the plague."

"You're not bothered that you never found him? That you can't wish him farewell?"

"Adelgis said he would look for him... But I..."

My throat tightened. Luthair wouldn't want me to have regrets, but I didn't know what to do about this. Luthair could be anywhere, and I suspected I didn't have the time left to find him. He had been cured of the plague, though. He would be fine. Adelgis or his sister would locate him.

I hoped.

"Everything will be okay," I said aloud.

Terrakona picked up speed, swimming through the clear waters I knew so well. A flock of birds sailed out of the trees on shore and flew with us for a little while. I lifted a hand to shield my eyes from the afternoon sunshine, admiring their flight.

Off in the distance, away from the coastal cities and the ports, were forests that were growing disturbingly thick. I hadn't mentioned my concerns to anyone other than Terrakona, but we both knew it was a problem. Ghostwood was sprouting more often, as well as *redstone trees*—a new kind of magical vegetation that grew ten stories tall, and whose bark was as red and hard as garnet.

A war had almost been fought because of them. The trees were nearly impossible to cut down, and when they grew, they did so at such a rapid rate that it harmed agriculture across multiple nations.

I had to fix it before fighting broke out—no one wanted the land with the redstone trees.

And Terrakona's dryads...

They were so numerous now, but not just them. Larger creatures had started appearing. Tree golems, bunyips, and otways panthers were appearing in random places, with no explanation for how they arrived.

I tried to keep the forests down, to make sure they weren't overgrowing, but it was becoming harder and harder.

I shook the thought from my head as the birds abandoned us and returned to the trees. Terrakona picked up his speed, heading farther and farther west.

We weren't far from Old Fortuna. From the war zone of the battle that started the God-Arcanists' War.

Several reapers had appeared near the memorials I had built, and some people thought the mystical creatures were cursed. It wasn't the fault of the reapers, though. Reapers were creatures with fable births. They appeared in areas where at least one thousand people had died—their blood spilled across the land. And since so many had died in Fortuna, of course they would arrive.

"Do you think my dryads will be cared for?"

"I do," I said as I held on to his mane.

"Do you think they'll be happy?"

"Without a doubt."

The elation I felt from Terrakona was a relief.

As the sun began its fall, we reached the waters around Old Fortuna. Terrakona slowed his speed and made his way to the monuments near the largest beach. When he neared, he lowered his head so I could dismount.

I jumped onto the white sand and walked toward the ruined city. Although it was more of a memorial and graveyard, I felt the tremors of people nearby. That was odd, but I wasn't afraid. Perhaps they were just wayward souls who needed a place to stay. Old Fortuna still had several buildings, and there were parks and shacks around the cemetery.

But then I felt something else...

Large creatures heading this way.

I braced myself. With my hand on the hilt of Retribution, I kept my gaze on the road through Old Fortuna. Then I saw it. The people arriving.

Zaxis and Vjorn. They raced down the roads, straight to my location. I removed my hand from my blade and smiled. Zaxis's red hair—cut short, but still fluttering wildly in the wind—was a welcome sight. The man smiled when he spotted me. He pointed, and Vjorn bounded to my side.

The fenris wolf...

He was monstrous in size. At least twenty-five feet at the shoulder.

His chains rattled as he lowered his head and allowed Zaxis to slide off. **"Greetings, Warlord,"** Vjorn growled. **"It's time."**

He said it the same way Terrakona had.

Before I could ask him about it, Zaxis held out his arms.

He was massive. He had grown nearly as much as his eldrin.

With muscles to spare, Zaxis pulled me into a tight embrace. He had a beard that fell to his collarbone. Something I never thought I would ever see. It was as red as the hair on his head, like he was turning into a phoenix himself.

Still wasn't as tall as me, but he probably had twice the muscle mass. I groaned as he squeezed the hug.

I patted his bare shoulder.

He wore no shirt, just armored pants made from salamander scale. Some called him the *Red Wolf*, but I would never call him that. He was always *Zaxis* to me, no matter his many titles and accomplishments.

"You've grown soft," Zaxis said with a huff the moment he released me. "That's what kids do to you."

I rubbed at the back of my neck. "Says the man with two kids of his own."

"Yeah. And if I didn't have them, I would be massive right now." Zaxis flexed a bit. Then he hesitated and glanced over at me. "But I wouldn't trade that for my son and daughter. Robbin and Roark are everything to me. Well, and Illia." Zaxis pointed at me. "Don't you ever tell Nicholin I didn't immediately include her, got it?"

I hadn't seen Robbin and Roark in some time, but they had been some of the cutest little babes right after their births.

"My son could probably take yours in a fight," Zaxis said as he crossed his arms. "I started the boy on martial training."

"Isn't he only five years old?" I asked, lifting an eyebrow. "I think Will is a little bigger."

"Feh. Roark has all the bulk."

I laughed, because I couldn't help it. Will had never expressed interest in competing with Roark—or vice versa—but Zaxis couldn't help himself.

The winds picked up. I closed my eyes as a powerful gust washed over the beach, taking sand with it into the air. Zaxis growled something I didn't hear, but in my heart, I knew he was simply irritated.

Orwyn's sky titan was difficult to deal with, even on a personal level.

Once the winds died down a bit, I opened my eyes and spotted her descending onto the beach. She landed with the grace of a fallen leaf, her strawberry-blonde hair long enough to reach her waist. Orwyn tossed some of it back as she strode forward, her eyes wide and thoughtful.

"Warlord, Hunter," she said as she half-bowed her head to us. "A pleasure to see you both again."

She wore a long white dress with several kirin stitched into the hem. Her skin was clean, and she wore no shoes.

"Falcon," Zaxis said with a grunt. "Took you long enough. I thought you were fast?"

Orwyn half-smiled. "My apologies. I wanted to say goodbye to Akiva and Elias before I came."

"*Elias?* Not Ezril?"

"Elias is my son," Orwyn stated with a tilt of her head. "Ezril didn't want to say goodbye. He was... upset... that I was leaving. So I didn't say it to him."

Everyone had children, apparently.

Zaxis elbowed me in the ribs. "Did you hear that? A son? *Everyone* has been having children, apparently."

I shot him a sideways glance. At least we were on the same page. That rarely happened. We should've cherished the moment.

Another rumble of footfalls caught my attention. I turned toward the city. Orwyn and Zaxis did the same. The fenris wolf trotted down the beach to the water. He stared out at Terrakona, and the two of them had a silent conversation.

Another god-creature made its way through Old Fortuna, this one almost as big as the world serpent.

It was the typhon beast. His one hundred heads were almost a burden as he dragged his massive body down the road. The beast's heads kept their attention on the water, though occasionally one of the snakes would glance left and right, as if searching for something.

Lynus walked alongside his eldrin. He, like Zaxis, wore no shirt. Lynus kept his hands in the pockets of his trousers as he made his way to the beach. He was in no hurry. He even stopped at one point to smooth over his coppery hair.

I was surprised Zelfree wasn't with him.

When Xor stepped onto the beach, his body shook the whole city. The multi-headed monster slid across the sand until he was close enough to feel the waves on his scales.

"Well, well, well," Lynus said as he sauntered over to us. "If it isn't a trio of troublemakers."

"What're you talking about?" Zaxis barked.

Lynus scratched at his chin and lifted an eyebrow. He maintained his calm—almost intimidating—demeanor after all these years. "I've heard all about your exploits. Rearranging continents? Making academies? Starting merchant businesses? Expanding a kirin village? All anyone can ever talk about is you three. Well, you and the moon-ray kid."

"Moonbeam," I muttered.

"Yeah, yeah. That's what I said."

"My kirin village is still hidden," Orwyn said in a singsong tone. "I want to protect the kirins as much as possible. How is anyone talking about us?"

"It's the doppelgänger girl and her husband." Lynus shook his head. "Those two visit, tell us everything that's been happening—including your ridiculous hidden village—and then they fly off on the wind to some other bizarre location."

Ryker and Karna? Traveling the world? That seemed unusual. My brother had always been so fearful, but perhaps Karna had shaken that fear out of him. She loved traveling, and helping others. I wondered if that was what they were doing.

"Wait, did you say *us*?" Zaxis rotated a shoulder. "You and Zelfree still together? I heard you both lived on a ship or something."

Lynus nodded once. He ran a hand down his face, and for probably the first time since I had ever known him, his cheeks seemed red. "We go around helping orphan children. But don't think too hard about it."

"Where *is* Zelfree? I figured he would've joined you."

"I didn't tell him. He'd never want me to come." Lynus gestured to the beach. "And since I don't see your lady, I figure you're the same way."

Zaxis swallowed all his words after that. He glanced at the sand, almost sheepish.

The winds warmed with another presence. I glanced over my shoulder and actually caught sight of *two* individuals joining us. The corona phoenix and the tempest coatl.

The corona phoenix flew in and landed on the beach, barely making a sound. Her void heart pulsed with life, and she was so large, the void was practically the size of a horse. Biyu clung to the shadowy legs of her eldrin, her short hair swirling around her head.

Biyu leapt onto the white sands. She had glowing runes across her arms, and a smile far brighter than even her mystical markings. She wore an eyepatch, similar to Illia's, that matched the rest of her outfit. Today, Biyu had the coat of a swashbuckler, as well as the knee-high boots of a sailor.

She reminded me of Captain Devlin.

"You're all here," Biyu said as she walked over. "I didn't know if... we would all feel the same thing. Ovayla said it was time, and I just knew..."

The tempest coatl shone as bright as lightning as she landed on the beach. She was so long, she coiled herself several times before calming down. Lucian, who had been clinging to her back, leapt off. He landed on the beach, kicking up sand that sticking to his black trousers. He wiped all of it off before heading our way.

"Where's William?" was the first question out of Lucian's mouth. "He said he would meet me here."

"How're things?" I asked.

Supposedly, from what William had told me in his letters, he and Lucian had been hunting down the many pirates who sailed the waters. They had personally apprehended five dread pirates, and were even the ones who'd had managed to shut down most of Port Crown. It was Lucian's calling in life, and William was more than happy to help.

"They're fine," Lucian said. Then he motioned to the beach. "Well, as fine as *this* can allow."

I didn't reply to that.

Fortunately, the waters near the beach swelled. Everyone glanced over and watched the bizarre shift in the tide. William then *walked* out of the water, as though the waves didn't even affect him. He wore a sturdy suit of armor, and kept a sword at his hip that I had crafted for him. With a giant smile, William headed for me.

"Ah, there's my boy!" Once he neared, he pulled me in for a tight hug. "Happy birthday." He patted my back several times, and I returned the favor.

"It's your birthday?" Lynus asked. He snorted out a laugh. "What a terrible day for this, eh?"

The others remained silent. I didn't blame them. No one seemed to know what to say. The feeling of dread never left me, but at least the persistent *tug* had faded the moment I arrived at the beach.

William released the hug and looked me up and down. "How're the little ones?"

"Good," I said, smiling as soon as I thought about them. "You should've seen their birthday ghosts this morning."

"Birthday... *ghosts?*" William laughed so hard his belly shook a little. "Let me guess. It was Rylee's idea."

"Of course it was."

"She'll be an artist, that one." William smiled wider than I had seen in a long time. "An amazing artist. Or perhaps an excellent teacher. I have a knack for calling these things, ya know."

"Did you know I was going to become a god-arcanist?" I asked with a playful pat on his shoulder.

"No... But I knew you were destined for greatness."

I didn't know how to reply to that.

Then the sun began to set.

The winds picked up, carrying an icy chill like no other.

The god-creatures turned their attention to the horizon beyond the waters. It was quiet. Although I still felt people inside Old Fortuna, none of them stirred. None of them headed our way. We were alone on the beach of our fiercest battle.

About to meet the apoch dragon.

And then it happened.

At first, it was a swirl in the water. Then it grew larger and deeper, becoming a full-blown whirlpool that stretched from one side of the bay to the other. Somehow defying the laws of nature, the center of the whirl went deeper and deeper, until it became a dark void that seemingly went to the depths of the abyssal hells themselves.

And while that was eerie, it didn't compare to the silence.

I figured the waves crashing around in a circle would make plenty of noise, but it was barely anything. It was as though the world were mute. The beat of my heart, and the raggedness of my breath, were all I heard.

The arrival of the apoch dragon...

It was the exact opposite of the arrival of the god-creatures.

The dragon emerged from the hole in the waters, slowly ascending from the whirlpool, one clawed hand at a time.

Its scales were bluish-black, like nullstone. Its claws were black diamonds. When its wings emerged from the hole in the water, I noticed they were dotted with hooked spines.

The apoch dragon emerged just as silently as the whirlpool was created.

When I finally got a good look at the dragon, I realized it was much like a phoenix. Its inner body glowed with fire. Whenever the scales parted *just slightly*, I spotted the flare of fire from within.

Over the beast's chest, just like us god-arcanists, the dragon had a twelve-pointed star. It was emblazoned on its scales, and radiated light far brighter than any true form mark I had ever seen.

Once the apoch dragon was in the air, the whirlpool closed, and the sky shimmered and shifted. The sunset disappeared. A night sky filled with twinkling stars took its place. Some stars streaked overhead, painting the night with mystic wonder.

I couldn't breathe.

The clouds overhead swirled around us, giving us a clear view to the sky, while circling tightly.

The apoch dragon landed in shallow water.

It was a high dragon—the type that stood on two legs, and had forearms like hands. Its long tail had many spines, and its head was adorned with half a dozen horns that curved toward its back.

When the apoch dragon opened its mouth, all I saw was the blaze of bright fire.

And the majestic dragon stood over four stories tall. When it flapped its leathery wings, the icy winds of destiny once again swirled around us.

But it said and did nothing. The feeling of dread I had all day was more intense now. Somewhere in the distance, I heard the faint clang of bells. The apoch dragon didn't move to attack us, or prepare to receive an attack.

It just stood there.

Waiting.

"I think it's finally time," Lynus said, the cold winds leaving goosebumps across most of his skin.

He walked over to the typhon beast. Xor's many heads

glanced at Lynus, and then returned their attention to the apoch dragon.

Biyu rubbed at her one eye. For some reason, she couldn't stop crying. When she noticed me staring, she smiled. "I'm fine. I'm ready. It's just... I hope Devlin forgives me for not telling him I left to fight the apoch dragon."

She hurried over to the corona phoenix and held on to her black taloned foot.

I glanced out to the water. Terrakona was just beyond the apoch dragon, waiting in the deeper portion of the bay. He didn't move, but he locked eyes with me. If I asked, he would attack, but it was clear he wasn't certain how we should begin.

Would we attempt to stop this?

As I desperately tried to think of a strategy to defeat a creature as large as the apoch dragon, a new voice entered my thoughts. A telepathic voice both regal and forceful. Something powerful, but benevolent.

"Don't be afraid."

I took a hesitant step backward as I glanced upward.

The apoch dragon met my gaze, its eyes as fiery red as the inside of its body.

"Oh, I'm not *afraid*," Lucian shouted at the dragon, breaking me from my thoughts. Everyone turned their attention to him.

His tempest coatl flared her scales and flashed her fangs.

Lucian held up a hand and evoked enough lightning bolts to electrify an entire nation. For a moment, the world consisted of nothing but light and the roar of thunder as Lucian blasted his full power into the apoch dragon.

And did nothing.

Just like with the Autarch's armor, the apoch dragon was immune to magic. All the tempest coatl's mighty thunder and lightning would do *nothing* to the dragon.

I grabbed Retribution, certain the apoch dragon would attack us now.

But it didn't.

"Lucian Nellit," the regal voice said, almost a kind whisper. ***"You have fought long and hard for the side of justice. Truly, you are the Dauntless they will speak of in legend."***

Lucian slowly lowered his hand. His coatl wrapped her body around a portion of his.

"I'm not ready to die," Lucian shouted. "I refuse to go just because you say so. I've only been an arcanist for a short while. *I won't go.*"

"The world needs an equal balance of land and water, light and darkness, calm days and rainy ones. Your god magic threatens that balance."

"No, it doesn't!" Lucian yelled. He swung his arm, a bolt of raw magic crackling over the sands of the beach. "We can control it! You'll see."

But the apoch dragon didn't reply.

Despite that, I knew it was correct. I had been fearful of that fact for quite some time. While I could prune the new magical forests near me, and care for the mystical creatures I found, I couldn't be everywhere at once. Many parts of the world were a mystery to me. What of them?

I had always known this day would come.

"Warlord," Terrakona telepathically said. **"We can fight it."**

The bells sounded louder than before.

"I don't think we should," I whispered.

Lucian snapped his attention to me. "What was that?"

"We went through the abyssal hells and back to cure the arcane plague," I said to him. The winds seemed colder than ever. "We made the world a better place. Are we really going to stay, and make it worse, just because we don't want our reign to end?"

"This isn't about a reign. This is about..." Lucian cursed under his breath and shook his head. He ran a hand over his short, black hair. "All the things I haven't finished." Lucian glared at me. "Do you really want to leave your children fatherless? *Do you?*"

Will...

Rylee...

Lyvia...

And Evianna...

The thought of leaving them hurt so much I almost invited death.

But could I hurt the world for my own selfish desires? That went against everything I had ever stood for. If I stayed, I'd be no better than the Autarch. *He'd* had wanted to kill the apoch dragon to rule forever, no matter how twisted the world became.

"Warlord..."

Terrakona met my gaze across the waters. More stars streaked across the sky in a dazzling display of natural beauty. Why was it so quiet?

"If I could free you from my magic, I would. I apologize. It is my existence that the apoch dragon wants to end. Not necessarily you."

"I understand," I said.

But as soon as Terrakona died, I would join him. I had known that from the beginning, even if I lamented that fact now.

"Does it have to be *now*?" I asked as I glanced up at the dragon. I didn't know when tears had filled my eyes, but they were making it hard to see. "Can't we stay... perhaps a little bit longer?"

"Warlord—no one has fought as long, or as hard, for the world as you have. You can stop fighting now. You can rest."

I wiped a hot tear off my face and swallowed the last of my words.

This was it, then.

The bells wouldn't stop ringing.

"That's it?" Lucian barked. He waved a hand in my direction. "You're going to give up? You're going to leave your family? Your children?"

"Maybe I'm just going to leave them a world in better shape than I found it," I said with a forced smile.

"But..." Lucian cursed the abyssal hells and turned away from me.

Zaxis stepped forward, his fenris wolf at his back. "And what about you, dragon? You're going to fly the skies and rule once we're gone?"

The apoch dragon touched the star on its chest. The diamond claws scraped across its scales. I hadn't realized until that moment, but the twelve points of the star weren't all the same level of brightness. Some were faded.

Five of them were faded, in fact.

For the five god-creatures who had already died.

"Once the magic of the gods has faded, I will join them."

Zaxis rubbed his bicep.

"Hunter—you have taken care of your pack well. Never has there been someone so loyal, or someone so dedicated to proving themselves."

"I tried," Zaxis whispered. He shook his head and glared at the sand. Even though he was an arcanist of winter, the strange, icy winds around us caused even him to shiver.

Despite the circumstance, Orwyn stepped forward. She held her hands together and breathed her hot breath into them. She glanced over and nodded once.

"If my kirin were here, she would tell me to trust the magic,"

Orwyn muttered. "That was one of the reasons I sided with you, Volke. My kirin was never wrong."

"You think everything will be okay?" I whispered.

"I think it already is."

"Falcon—you've shifted in as many directions as the wind, but always you've given your all. There is no longer a need to doubt."

While everyone else hesitated, Lynus snapped his fingers. He motioned to Xor to move forward, and then he walked down the beach to the very edge of the water, to where the waves lapped up to the line in the sand.

"I'm ready," he said, his arms out. "As far as I'm concerned, you took your sweet time gettin' here. Where's my death, huh? When do I get to see the abyssal hells? It's the only place I belong."

"Savior—you have dedicated your new life to helping others. Few can change their life's course, and fewer still do so without ever looking back. You did both."

Lynus hesitated, as did his typhon beast.

"Savior?" Xor's main head asked.

Lynus huffed. "Aren't I known as *the Monster?*"

"I see no monsters here."

"I..."

The bells rang in my ears and in my thoughts. While I didn't want everything to end, I also didn't want it to drag on. If this was our fate, I was ready.

Lynus held out his hand.

"I don't care what they call me," he said, his voice raw. "But I told Everett I wouldn't harm any more innocents, and I'm not gonna break my word. If my magic is gonna hurt people, get rid of it. *C'mon*. Do this, dragon. I'm done waiting."

The apoch dragon lowered its head and claws.

I thought the beast was going to eat Lynus and Xor. I tensed as I imagined it, the fangs crunching down on them, and their blood soaking into the sands.

But that didn't happen.

The apoch dragon gently touched Xor on the head. A single claw, a single touch. There was no hate or malice, or even any violent action.

Then Xor's many eyes fluttered closed. The typhon beast slumped, his six legs giving out underneath him as he collapsed onto the sand. It was so peaceful—like Xor was just lying down to sleep.

No pain. No suffering.

Parts of Xor flaked off his body. His magic unraveled. Like sparkles. Or perhaps like stars. More than half his body became a glitter that lifted into the sky. The rest remained on the beach—a still corpse with no blood or flesh. Just bones and scales. A monument to the god-creature's death.

A lot like the corpse of the first typhon beast I had found in Hydra's Gorge.

I watched the glittering sparkles of magic ascend into the sky. Was that the part of Xor that would be reborn into the next typhon beast? The part that would remember Lynus and all of us?

Then Lynus slowly sat on the sand. With a sigh, he leaned back, and rested on the sand. It only took a moment, and his breath left him. The mark on his chest... it faded.

And they were gone.

It was as tranquil and kind as a death could be.

"I should go next," William said, almost startling me.

He stood by the water already, his hands behind his back, like he was in the navy all over again.

"Equinox—even-handed and well meaning. You are a symbol of balance and stability."

"Father?" I asked.

William offered me a smile. "No parent should watch their

child go before them. Let me have this, my boy. I want it as peaceful as it was for the typhon beast."

I didn't object. I supposed I understood.

When the apoch dragon reached for William, I turned my attention to the sky. It only took a few moments before I saw the blue sparkles of the scylla waters lifting up to join the rest of the stars. When I heard William sit, I gulped down my breath.

"I don't think anyone can ever be ready," Orwyn muttered. "But I suppose now is my turn."

I just...

I kept staring at the sky.

And when the sparkling stars of the sky titan joined the rest, I tried not to think about everything I would leave behind. I tried not to think about Will, and Rylee, and Lyvia, and how much I would miss them.

I tried.

I promise you, I tried.

But being a parent means you never stop thinking about your children.

"I'll go," Biyu said, her voice betraying her sadness.

"Solstice—you have brought warmth and happiness to all you encounter. A peaceful presence, you know the importance of balance more than most."

When the phoenix's glittering stars joined the others, my chest tightened with the worst of dread. Time was almost up.

"I..." Zaxis took a deep breath. "I don't want to go. But I'll do it. Like Forsythe. I'll... not make a fuss about it."

I couldn't bring myself to watch Zaxis's passing, either. I gulped back my sorrow and watched the fenris wolf's stars join the rest. It was as though a part of Zaxis would live on forever. His soul had added to the fenris wolf, and whoever found the next would know the great tales of one of my closest friends.

It seemed colder when he was gone.

It was just me and Lucian now.

"I hate that everyone just went along with this," Lucian practically shouted.

Despite his yelling, I kept my attention on the fenris wolf's sparkling stars in the sky.

The apoch dragon never forced him. It never attacked or shouted back. It simply waited.

"The Grandmaster Inquisitor did this, too," Lucian whispered. "He died... for the good of everyone else. To save those he had the capacity to save." He must've stomped around the sand, because I sensed his movement. It grew slower, though. And after a moment, he exhaled. "I would've preferred if the apoch dragon had attacked us. If we had a battle."

Yeah. Maybe that would've been better.

"I don't want to accept death. I want to fight against it until the very end."

"Some problems can't be punched through," I muttered.

"It would've been... easier to accept if I had died in combat."

"I understand."

Lucian stopped next to his tempest coatl. "You're not afraid?"

With a nervous chuckle, I said, "I'm definitely afraid." I wiped another tear that spilled silently from my eyes. "But like I tell my children... *Bravery. Without it, we cannot act in the face of fear.* I'd be a terrible father if I didn't take my own advice."

The silence that stretched between us only lasted a moment.

"All right," Lucian whispered. "Then let's get this over with. *Quickly.* Before I change my mind."

I was glad I kept my attention on the sky. The tempest coatl's stars were so golden and vibrant. They were beautiful. So were all the others. I wished... everyone else had been here to see them, too.

"I wish it were possible to send you back to your family, Warlord."

I shook my head. "Don't apologize, Terrakona. I'm really thankful for all the time I've had."

"I enjoyed my time with the dryads. And with the forests. And the many places we've seen. The people we've met."

"Yeah. We had a lot of great times." I rubbed at my face, unable to stop the tears. "Okay. I'm ready."

Although it was difficult to see through the tears welling in my eyes, I did manage to spot the glittering green stars that represented Terrakona. They were my favorite. None of the others even compared.

Then...

Fatigue came over me.

I sat down on the beach, my heart hammering less than before.

Finally, the sense of dread was gone. A terrible weight had been lifted from my shoulders.

A smile came to me. I was finally a hero, just as I had set out to become all those years ago, when I had stood at the base of the Pillar, waiting to take the phoenix's Trial of Worth.

I lay back. Closed my eyes.

Maybe one day the legends about my life would inspire others as well. I thought about that, and my family, until I couldn't any longer.

Chapter 52

Forgiveness

When I opened my eyes, I felt nothing but warmth, and saw only light.

After a deep inhale, I contemplated my last few moments. Was this the abyssal hells? Or some other place souls went once they left the body? Perhaps a new place? A new adventure?

I exhaled.

And felt very much… alive.

The squawking of seagulls confused me. I didn't think gulls would be in the abyssal hells. Or perhaps, since they were so vexing, they were the perfect creatures to dwell there. But as I took another breath, the scents of sea salt and flotsam filled my nose.

My vision gradually cleared, until I saw the blue sky overhead.

A seagull poked its head directly into my line of sight, its beak inches from my face. Was this a dream? The gull tilted its head as though it was baffled to see me, too. Then it mewed and took to the sky, flapping its white wings as fast as it could.

I grabbed my chest. Then I clenched my other fist. After a panicked moment, I sat up and coughed.

This was...

The beach around the docks of Old Fortuna.

I glanced around, my heart racing all over again. It was morning. The sun sparkled off the waves. A crab scuttled across the white sand. With a shaky hand, I rubbed my face, trying to piece together what had happened.

The remains of the typhon beast, tempest coatl, corona phoenix, scylla waters, and fenris wolf were all here. The bones of the creatures, and perhaps a few other body parts. I didn't see the sky titan. Then again, I had never really seen her.

They were all dead.

Terrakona...

His bones filled the bay, serpentine and mighty.

Never had there been a better world serpent. Luvi probably wouldn't agree, but I didn't care. Just seeing the bones made my chest hurt all over again. Terrakona deserved a proper place to rest—with his dryads, in a grove of tranquil beauty.

But...

What was going on?

To my shock, the bones and body of the apoch dragon filled the bay as well. Its black carcass jutted from the water, its purpose completed. True to its word, the beast had died once all the god-creatures had perished.

What a sad existence.

A dragon born to bring about its own demise.

I shook my head. How could I feel sorry for the apoch dragon? It had just killed me.

Hadn't it?

Unlike all the other bodies, the apoch dragon slowly sank beneath the waves, its fell magic—or anti-magic, rather—seemingly rotting away part of the seabed. It was burying itself, as though it knew it should never be left out in the light of the glorious day.

Why was I here? Why did I feel so warm? Like fire had washed over my body and vanished?

"Volke... There you are."

The feminine voice was familiar. When I turned around, I spotted two individuals I had thought I would never see again.

Atty.

And Luthair.

This had to be a dream. My eyes couldn't get any wider.

And the sound of bells rang in my ears again. Only softer, cheerier.

Flying in the sky, high above us, dropping golden dust upon Old Fortuna and the beach, was a glorious phoenix. It had feathers that shone like polished gold, flames that matched the hue, and a peacock tail laced with silvers, whites, blues, and reds —every color of fire.

I almost couldn't take it all in.

With each flap of its wings, it dropped more golden dust, like soot.

That was a true form phoenix.

Luthair stood next to Atty, his black shadow armor just as imposing as I remembered, even in broad daylight. Maybe more so. There were spikes on his armor—one over his heart—like when he had been plague-ridden. But his cape had returned to normal. The inner lining was dotted with stars that twinkled brightly.

"My arcanist," Luthair said, his voice filling me with shock and joy. "I'm glad to see you're awake."

"I'm so sorry I'm late," Atty said. She laced her fingers together and then lifted her hands to her collarbone. "I hope you'll forgive me, Volke. It took me a long time... too long... to realize you were right."

"What's going on?" was all I managed to ask.

My mind buzzed as though filled with a million confused bees.

"I did it." Atty smiled as she stepped across the sands of the beach. "I finally did it." Her blonde hair was tied back in a ponytail, and she wore white robes with the Isle of Ruma's symbol, a phoenix, stitched into the collar. "I'm sorry. I..." She shook her head and stopped once she was next to me. "I should've told you."

Her arcanist mark glowed brightly, indicating she had a true form eldrin.

"But... what happened?"

"True form phoenixes can bring people back to life. But they can only do it so many times. I didn't know that until Titania transformed."

The phoenix overhead spiraled downward. She landed on the beach, her glory on full display. But then seven of her peacock tail feathers fell off. They burst into flames, and became ash, right in front of my eyes.

She only had one left.

Atty had struggled for years to achieve a true form with her phoenix, and she had used the phoenix's most powerful magic on me and the other god-arcanists?

I... almost couldn't believe it.

She hadn't gone straight to her family?

I said nothing, my mind slowly absorbing the information.

"I went back to my family. I told them everything. My mother—she demanded I use the phoenix magic on all our family members who had passed. When I told her I wanted to wait, because I thought the Frith Guild might need my magic, she..."

Atty shook her head, her eyes clenched shut. It took a moment for her to regain her composure.

I rubbed the side of my face.

"I learned a valuable lesson. I wanted to help the Frith Guild because you all had helped me for years. My family… was just using me. They didn't care."

"Atty?" I asked.

"You all helped me, even when I was being selfish. So, when Guildmaster Eventide told me you would one day face the apoch dragon, I told my family I wouldn't help them until I repaid that kindness to the guild."

I nodded once, both elated and confused. When had this happened? Over the many years we had been apart? Why had she never told me?

"My family disowned me," Atty said with a pained chuckle.

"You waited… to help me?" I asked, wanting to make absolutely certain I had heard everything correctly. Was this really happening?

"You all waited for me. You all were so patient." Atty smoothed her blonde hair, her lip quavering. "People sent word that the god-arcanists had died in Old Fortuna. I came here as fast as I could. I didn't realize… all seven of you would be here."

Titania let out a piercing cry that echoed throughout the monument of a city. Then she fluffed her golden feathers. "You need not fear," she said. "My arcanist and I refused to abandon you."

"We did it," Atty said again as she knelt beside me. "We saved you all. Finally. Even though… you've all saved me so many times before."

I glanced around.

Sure enough…

Lynus, Zaxis, Lucian, Orwyn, Biyu, and William were stirring. They woke up as confused and groggy as me. None of them were injured, and everyone's god-arcanist mark was faded, but they were alive.

I glanced back to the bay, half-hoping to see Terrakona stirring as well. That was foolish, but I still stared for a moment, observing his bones. He didn't wake.

"Are you kiddin' me?" Lynus half-shouted. He shot me a glare, then he glowered at the phoenix overhead. "You all even *cheat me* out of death? Curse the abyssal hells and all the ships at sea."

Then Lynus rested back on the beach and sighed.

A smile crept across his face as he relaxed.

I rubbed my eyes. Fueled by sheer delight, I stood up and dusted the sand off my trousers.

"You saved us?" I asked, louder than I wanted. I had to make certain this was real.

Atty stood. "If I had used this ability on my family, I might not have been able to help all the god-arcanists. So... I've been waiting." She closed her eyes and shook her head. "I'm so sorry, Volke. I'm sorry it took this long for me to realize."

With a giddy laugh, I pulled her into a tight hug. "I don't care. Forget all that. Thank you, Atty. *Thank you*."

She awkwardly patted my shoulder. "You're not upset?"

"No. How could I be upset?" I grabbed her shoulders and held her at arm's length. "*You did it.* You got your true form phoenix! And you saved me. I can see my family again."

I didn't care how it had happened or why. Atty could've ventured into the abyssal hells, punched a Death Lord in the face, and single-handedly dragged all our souls to the surface. She could've permanently opened the gates to the abyssal hells, and I still probably would've just shaken her hand. Well, probably not, but that was how I felt in the moment.

It didn't really matter. All that *did* matter was that this was a new day, and it was a day I could see my family again.

Atty wiped at the corners of her eyes. "I'm sorry I've been such a fool."

"Don't worry about it." I hugged her a second time, I couldn't stop myself. "You did amazingly."

I released her and turned to Luthair. I wanted to hug him, too, but I stopped myself short.

All my mirth drained in an instant.

I stared into his hollow suit of armor—into the helmet that had no arcanist. "I'm sorry," I said.

"Why, my arcanist?" he asked, his voice dark and regal.

"For not saving you sooner."

"You are forgiven. I didn't save Mathis in time, and I wish I could've told him about my regret... But I know he would've forgiven me. Just as I'm forgiving you."

"You were plague-ridden..."

Luthair motioned to himself with a shadowy gauntlet. "Not anymore." He touched one of the spikes. "Perhaps I am one of the few true-form-dread-form mystical creatures in the world. A rarity indeed."

"I... almost can't believe you're here. I wish Terrakona could see this."

"The world serpent?" Luthair turned his empty helmet to the bay. "Was he a worthy eldrin while I was away?"

With a smile, I nodded. "Better than worthy. He was... amazing. Both compassionate and fearsome—a creature perfect for the Warlord of Magic."

"I'm pleased to hear it. And I'm sad I never managed to meet him."

That was a shame. I wished they had, even for a moment. "Where have you been?" I asked. "How did you get here now?"

"That would be my doing," someone called out from the ruins of the city.

I would recognize Adelgis's voice anywhere. He stood at the very end of the beach, right where it transformed into Old Fortuna. He was so much more confident. He stood tall, his black hair waving in the wind. With a smile, he conveyed everything he needed to.

"I wanted to bring Luthair to your home as a birthday gift," he said. "But I suppose this is probably better."

Adelgis's eldrin—his second eldrin—stood by his side. A sphinx. Nubia.

She had a lioness's body, the wings of an eagle, and the head of a woman. Her golden fur had the hue of honey, and the feathers on her wings glistened in the beautiful morning sunlight. Her hair was brown, like a lion's mane, and her eyes...

She had two human eyes, and a third eye on her forehead that remained closed.

Not just any sphinx, but an *all-seeing* sphinx. Adelgis must've used her magic to help find Luthair.

"Wait," I said as I glanced between Adelgis and Luthair. "You remember me, Luthair? Through everything?"

"The salvation aura." Adelgis smiled. "It has purged all corruption, even that brought about by the soul forge."

"Is this real?" Zaxis shouted.

I turned around, my heart hammering.

Zaxis stormed across the beach, straight for Atty. He constantly glanced around, from me to the water, to the sky, to Old Fortuna—he couldn't settle on a single thing of interest. When he drew close, he pointed at Atty.

"Was this you?" he demanded.

Atty nodded once. "Zaxis, I'm so sorry it took me so long to—"

He grabbed her and yanked her so fast into a hug that all she could do was gasp. Zaxis squeezed tight. Then he lifted her off the ground and spun around once.

"Are you serious?" he asked, a laugh at the end of his words. "This was *you?*"

Atty, trapped in his embrace, nodded against his chest. "I trained in the Sunset Desert, where the masters of martial arts said—"

"I don't care," Zaxis said, cutting her off. "This took you *how long?* Twenty years to finally achieve? I get it. It was difficult." He set her down, kissed her on the cheek and then laughed so hard it disturbed all the nearby seagulls. They flew off squawking.

"But I'm trying to tell you that I'm sorry, and—"

"It doesn't matter. You know what matters? How good sand smells." Zaxis laughed again. He patted Atty's shoulder, smacked my chest, and then pointed to the beach. "I was lying there, facedown on the beach, when suddenly I could smell the sand. Do you know how amazing that is? I don't care how it happened. This is incredible."

Atty tapped the tips of her fingers together. "You're not upset? About the fenris wolf?"

"I came to terms with that." Zaxis waited a moment, hesitating as he glanced back at Vjorn. "We both did." Then he chuckled as he stroked his red beard as he returned his attention to Atty. "But you know what I didn't come to terms with? Never seeing my kids again."

"*Zaxis Ren!*"

I knew Illia's voice the instant I heard it. With a smile, I turned to see her standing near Adelgis, her arms crossed. Nicholin was on her shoulders, long enough that he was practically a scarf. He looked like a mongoose—a white mongoose with silver stripes that sparkled. He crossed his little forearms and glared at Zaxis as well.

"You came here to die?" Illia shouted. "And you said *nothing to me?*"

Zaxis let out a loud sigh of relief. That reaction seemed to momentarily confuse Illia. She rubbed at her eyepatch, and glared with her eye.

"I'm so happy to hear you yelling, starfish," Zaxis said.

"Oh..." Illia's face reddened.

Nicholin clicked his tongue. "You're not going to be happy about what I left in your shoes, though. *That's* for running off without us!"

I wanted to laugh and hug them all for the entire rest of the day, even if that was childish and unrealistic. I didn't care. But then I remembered Evianna, and my children, and my desire to see them trumped all others.

With a heart filled with hope, I held my hand out to Luthair.

"I have a lot more to build," I said. "Will you help me do it?"

Luthair placed his cold gauntlet on my hand. "Indeed."

THE END

A Note From The Author

Thank you so much for reading the Frith Chronicles. I hope you enjoyed reading it just as much as I did writing it! The entire series is a love letter to all my favorite things. Talking familiars. Epic magic. Heroes and villains. Can you believe I watched Pokémon and Digimon as a child? Who would've guessed, right? Haha!

If you enjoyed the world of arcanists, and want to see more adventures, please check out Academy Arcanist (the direct sequel series to this one) or check out Crown Tournament (a side story involving a huge tournament involving arcanists who also practice martial arts). I will also be creating a bestiary for all the many creatures that appeared in these novels! Please join my newsletter if you'd like more information on release dates and fun giveaways.

Also! Please remember to leave a review. Every little bit helps.
Thank you so much for reading.
Shami Stovall

To find out more about Shami Stovall and the Frith Chronicles, take a look at her website:
https://sastovallauthor.com/newsletter/

To help Shami Stovall (and see advanced chapters ahead of time) take a look at her Patreon:
https://www.patreon.com/shamistovall

Want more arcanist novels? Good news! Academy Arcanist, the spin-off series, is already on the shelves! Join a whole new cast of arcanists on a fun adventure (set in the future of the Frith Chronicles).

See you at Astra Academy!

Or check out Crown Tournament if you love competitions and martial arts!

The Crown Tournament
Stovall · Tang

About the Author

Shami Stovall is a multi-award-winning author of fantasy and science fiction, with several best-selling novels under her belt. Before that, she taught history and criminal law at the college level, and loved every second. When she's not reading fascinating articles and books about ancient China or the Byzantine Empire, Stovall can be found playing way too many video games, especially RPGs and tactics simulators.

If you want to contact her, you can do so at the following locations:

Website: https://sastovallauthor.com
Email: s.adelle.s@gmail.com